ABYSS

The Abyss line of cutting-edge psychological horror is committed to publishing the best, most innovative works of dark fiction available. Abyss is horror unlike anything you've ever read before. It's not about haunted houses or evil children or ancient Indian burial grounds. We've all read those books and we all know their plots by heart.

Abyss is for the seeker of truth, no matter how disturbing or twisted it may be. It's about people, and the darkness we all carry within us. Abyss is the new horror from the dark frontier. And in that place, where we come face-to-face with terror, what we find is ourselves.

"Thank you for introducing me to the remarkable line of novels currently being issued under Dell's Abyss imprint. I have given a great many blurbs over the last twelve years or so, but this one marks two firsts: first *unsolicited* blurb (*I* called *you*) and the first time I have blurbed a whole *line* of books. In terms of quality, production, and plain old storytelling reliability (that's the bottom line, isn't it?), Dell's new line is amazingly satisfying . . . a rare and wonderful bargain for readers. I hope to be looking into the Abyss for a long time to come."

—Stephen King

Please turn the page for more extraordinary acclaim . . .

PRAISE FOR *ABYSS*

"What *The Twilight Zone* was to TV in 1959, what *Night of the Living Dead* was to horror films in 1968, what Stephen King was to dark fiction in the mid-70s—Abyss books will be to horror in the 1990s."
—Mark Hurst, editor of *The Golden Man*

"Gorgeously macabre eye-catching packages . . . I don't think Abyss could have picked a weirder, more accomplished novel [than *The Cipher*] to demonstrate by example what the tone and level of ambition of the new line might be."
—*Locus*

"A splendid debut."
—*Rave Reviews*

"Dell is leading the way."
—*Writer's Digest*

"They are exploring new themes and dimensions in the horror field. My hat's off to Koja, Hodge, Dee and Dillard, and the others forthcoming! And hats off to Dell Abyss!"
—Gary S. Potter, author of *The Point Beyond*

RAPID GROWTH

MARY L. HANNER

A DELL BOOK

Published by
Dell Publishing
a division of
Bantam Doubleday Dell Publishing Group, Inc.
666 Fifth Avenue
New York, New York 10103

Copyright © 1993 by Mary L. Hanner

The trademark Dell® is registered in the U.S. Patent and Trademark Office.

ISBN: 0-440-21337-1

Printed in the United States of America

Published simultaneously in Canada

April 1993

10 9 8 7 6 5 4 3 2 1

OPM

*This book is for
Agnes Birnbaum
who still believes
after all this time.*

ACKNOWLEDGMENTS

I owe a great debt of thanks to the medical staff at the University of California, San Francisco, especially Dr. Ken Drasner, Dr. Nicholas Barbaro, and Dr. Alan Gruber. And Dr. Richard Bobis, Dr. Nick Zirpolo, and Dr. William Hopkins in the South Bay Area. All of these people turned my own personal horror story into a mere incident and made it possible for me to write again. I am deeply grateful. If there is anything good or worthy in this book it is because of them.

My family has put up with me for the last year. Dave, Nate, and Karen have eaten strange meals at odd hours, worn wrinkled shirts, put gas in my car, and turned down their stereos so I could think. My son, Nate, organizes my files and keeps my computer running. Without him this book would never have happened on a word processor.

I want to thank Sue and Burr Nissen for the gentle encouragement, the staff at the hospital for their unflagging interest in my writing, Pipe Major Douglas Snodgrass and the Stewart Tartan Bagpipe Band who have managed to keep me inspired through the entire process, Sean Castner who is kind to me despite the fact that I don't practice enough because I'm busy writing, and Dr. Sherry Bendall who has answered my desperate questions at all times of the day and night. And then there's Catherine and Joan and Donna who have luckily remained my friends. And Mariam Rowan who taught me another way to look at dreams.

Mary L. Hanner

1

Dr. J. Alan Campbell slept beside his wife, Katie, in their home in the Serenity Hills development of Los Altos, California. They slept between eggshell-white one hundred percent cotton sheets that rasped against Alan Campbell's skin. He sweated like most people cry, a salty icing coating his freckled shoulders.

He clenched his teeth and trembled. He was dreaming again. He could not wake up. His hair, faintly red, was darkened with perspiration. A fist clutched the pillow. The knuckles of that fist were bone-white.

As long as he lived he would hear the sound in his dreams. He had heard it before, this half moan, half cry that came out of a terrible, lovely stillness like the moments before a summer storm when not a blade of grass stirred, or a leaf quivered on the trees, and the world was as silent as the day before it was created. From that deeply quiet place the cry shattered his sleep. The sound was human and not human. He had heard it before, and not in dreams.

He groaned softly. But the sound rose, ripped at his backbone, tearing bone from sinew as if he were wet sheets of tissue paper. It hurt him again and again, sinking its conjured teeth deep, over and over.

A blur of colored circus lights caught hold of his breath, circled around him and pulled him dizzily down into a black well so fast his lungs nearly burst. And the teeth hung on, rending skin and muscle into tattered shreds that descended with him like the hides of small slaughtered animals.

"Ahhh," he gasped.

It was not enough to wake him. Sweat rolled down his narrow cheekbone, across one eyelid, and welled in the small pocket at the bridge of his nose.

"Don't cry, Alan," he heard someone whisper, someone close to the dream, close to the dreamer.

And he heard the sound again. Louder this time, nearer, and mingled with the pungent odor of hot candle wax and wet black loam and dead grass putrefied by a spring thaw.

Perhaps it was the sound of a rabbit caught in a trap. Alan Campbell could not trap animals out in the dusky fields of Illinois where he grew up. He couldn't stand the thought of the creature's ferocious struggle against the claw teeth. Or the remembrance of the mangled remains of a fox that, once snared, became sport for the dogs that knew the trap lines as well as Gordon Campbell, Alan's father.

"It's nature's way," Gordon Campbell used to say in the softened Highland brogue of a man displaced from his homeland. But it was not the way of Alan Campbell. Only in dreams now did he have to endure that sound.

Or, perhaps, the cry came from the collie, Lady, Alan had had as a boy. The dog was hit by a car out on the highway that ran past the farm, and she'd pulled herself back to the house to lie on the back porch in freezing weather for three days until Gordon Campbell dragged her, screaming, out in the snow.

"Don't shoot her," the boy had begged. "Please, Daddy, don't shoot Lady."

Now he waited in his dreams for the sound of that shot. But there were no gunshots in Dr. J. Alan Campbell's dreams. Only the terror of that cry. And teeth. And hair.

With a sharp snap of his neck he woke up. "Ahhh," he groaned again. His breath was hot and stale.

The sound was gone, but he was sure it would return. He covered his face with the long, pale fingers and tasted the salty slick of sweat. Or was it tears?

He glanced at Katie, sleeping undisturbed beside him, and he listened for his two sons asleep in the bedrooms down the hall. The house was quiet. He heard only Katie's soft, shallow breathing, and a mockingbird, he guessed, rehearsing under the noonday brilliance of a streetlight. But that reality was no consolation. The dream would wait. The sound would crouch in the caverns of his sleep, poised for his return. If he stayed awake forever the dream would wait, because he was certain this was no dream. This time it was real.

Katie Campbell did not dream, or if she did she rarely remembered. Within moments of waking her day crowded in on her, prodded and poked her wide awake. In the dim bedroom with windows facing east, she watched the few strands of light filter through white blinds. She closed her eyes.

The room smelled damp. She didn't like the smell. Given a choice she would have slept with the windows wide open to the softness of a spring night in California. One of her most pleasant childhood memories was of waking on a bright summer morning to see white lace curtains billowing in the breeze.

But Alan insisted on battening down the house at night. He locked the front door, tightened metal bolts on their sliding glass patio doors, secured the windows, checked the alarm system, and pulled the vertical blinds tight against the world. Even the bedroom door had to be closed tight. Katie sometimes left it ajar, keeping her connection with her comfortable house and her sons, Doug and Robbie. In sleep Katie did not feel severed from life, while Alan seemed in danger of losing the protection of his home and family.

He had had the dream again. She could tell by the wisps of dark, wet hair clinging to his forehead. He slept now as if he were exhausted, his delicate, almost child-like face furrowed. There was a certain darkness under his eyes. And from the musky odor in the room Katie was sure he'd been dreaming again, dreaming that torturous dream that smelled like fear.

She used to wake to his cries, but more often than not, now, she didn't. Even when she did awaken, Alan refused her comforting.

"Alan, wake up!" she'd plead. "It's only a dream."

And at those times he would turn away from her, or disentangle himself from the sticky sheets and stagger to the bathroom. So she no longer woke to his nightly horrors, only aware of the telltale signs in the morning.

By squinting her eyes she read the alarm clock on the maple nightstand. It was almost six o'clock. In fifteen minutes the alarm would ring and Alan would rise like a zombie to shower and dress in twelve minutes flat. He had to be at the hospital by seven fifteen. Surgery began at seven thirty.

Kate slid into her pink chenille robe and slippers. May mornings tended to be cool. In the kitchen of the

Campbell house that peculiar gray morning light blurred the details of the large room, distilling its essence of warmth and coziness. Kate measured coffee into the paper filter and started a pot of water boiling. For herself she would make tea. Alan survived on strong, black coffee.

She plucked the dewy morning newspaper from the front steps, and while she waited for the water to boil, Kate surveyed her kitchen. It was clearly the most cheerful room in the Campbell house, a concession to her when they had searched and searched for a home both of them liked and could afford. Finally, narrowing the search to the Serenity Hills development, Katie had rejected one house after another—houses with long galley kitchens, sunless kitchens, or chilly and elegant kitchens, until they found this one. The house was larger than they needed at the time. None of the landscaping or fencing was finished, and there were rather exotic problems with the septic tank. But she loved the kitchen that was to be the center of her family's life, as it had been when she was a child.

The first long yellow fingers of sunlight streaked the breakfast nook, tiled in red quarry stones. Katie checked the teapot. She smiled, remembering that her kitchen alone was larger than the apartment she and Alan rented during his residency at Lorimar Medical Center.

She'd learned a great deal from this house. She'd learned it was better to let experts deal with fencing, landscaping, and septic tanks, for one thing. After several brave but useless attempts at sinking fence posts into soggy cement, she and Alan had hired four men to finish the job. The azaleas and liquidambar trees she planted died instantly, and so she'd settled for the recommendations of the local nursery—low-maintenance junipers, a showy flowering plum, and several weeping birch. And several large boulders for texture and interest. It wasn't exactly what she'd wanted, but at least those plants and trees survived, and no one in history had been known to kill a boulder.

Unfortunately, there were other problems the experts couldn't manage. More serious problems than fences or junipers.

For one thing, a brown-yellow blanket of air hung over the area like soap scum. And there were large paint companies in the Santa Clara Valley that vented volatile liquids directly into the air, semiconductor industries dumping organic chemicals that seemed to end up in the Los Altos water supply, spray cans with fluorocarbons, wood fires, car exhaust . . . and an obvious menace, the Lawrence Livermore Lab, where radiation leaks could prove to be more than just a threat. Especially in an earthquake.

No wonder the azaleas died, Katie considered. The water in the blue enamel teapot began to bubble and hiss, and at the same moment she heard the alarm clock buzz insistently in the bedroom.

Katie poured water through the coffee in the filter and saved the last bit of hot water for herself, plopping a tea bag in a mug and submerging it in the still-boiling liquid. The burst of cinnamon and horehound–tinged steam rising from the cup made her shiver. She loved cooking the old-fashioned way even though Alan had had the kitchen remodeled last winter, a kitchen complete with bird's-eye maple cupboards; a refrigerator that froze, defrosted, crisped, cooled, and produced perfectly round ice cubes with holes in the center; the newest model of microwave oven, the Dettler Liberty 5000; a gas range that braised, grilled, and broiled, and exhausted the fumes at the touch of a button; a convection oven, that she'd never used, and a message center that connected the kitchen to the rest of the house by intercoms. Katie, however, liked the old ways of brewing coffee and shirring eggs. She saw no reason to give up her teapot.

Twelve minutes after the alarm rang, Alan walked through the kitchen door. He looked like he hadn't slept since January. Purplish-gray circles ringed his eyes. His eyelids were red and putty. Showered, and dressed in a white shirt with tiny navy stripes and a navy-blue suit, he looked like a small boy who'd put on his father's clothes. He'd lost weight recently, and his hands were thin and white.

"Do you feel okay?" she asked him.

Alan squinted at her in the morning sun. He picked up the *San Jose Mercury News* lying next to his plate. "Sure, I feel fine."

At six twenty-eight A.M. Alan Campbell did not look fine.

"Things going okay at the hospital?" She broke one egg in the cast-iron skillet and stirred it three times. Twice a week Alan ate an egg cooked precisely this way. To Katie it looked like a process of dehydration rather than frying. Alan insisted on frying fat-free and Katie refused to use Teflon-coated utensils. After all, she argued with clerks and advocates of nonstick cooking, just where do all those little dark brown chips go when they invariably scratch off the bottom on the pan? No answer had ever satisfied her.

"Things are fine at the hospital," Alan answered about the time Katie forgot the question.

"You had the dream again last night." She hadn't mentioned the dream for a week, although this bout with his night demon had gone on for a month.

He fumbled with his fork. "Did I wake you?" His blue eyes were darkly flecked with gray. His voice was husky.

"No, you didn't wake me." Katie set his plate of un-buttered egg, dry toast, and warm applesauce in front of him. She would have liked to take him in her arms and soothe away the bad dreams the way she used to do for Doug and Rob when they were very small. Instead, she tenderly stroked the few curls of Alan's hair that strayed down over his shirt collar. "You look so tired, that's all."

"I'm all right."

Kate retrieved her cup of tea and joined Alan at the table. He ate his breakfast one bite at a time, never mixing the egg, toast, or sauce. He seemed to have some methodology about eating that was a curiosity to Kate.

"What are you up to today?" he asked.

She considered lying, but he'd probably know it. Her nose would grow a foot, or something. "We're out at the Livermore Lab today. I have to be there at nine." She heard the irritable scrape of his fork against the china plate. "I'm sorry, Alan. I know how you feel about the demonstrations, but this is important to me."

His blue eyes darkened even more. "I never said it wasn't important." His voice faltered. The last syllables were, evidently, an enormous drain of energy. "You *aren't* taking the boys . . ."

Katie's hand tightened on the cup. "Of course not. They still have school." Most of the mothers brought their preschool children to the demonstrations. MANA, Mothers Against Nuclear Activity, knew that children were a powerful force on a picket line. Maybe it was *using* the kids, but MANA had discussed the issue at length. Weren't the demonstrations *for* the children, af-ter all?

"I don't want Doug and Rob at those stupid, *danger-*

ous protests," Alan told her. "It's bad enough that you feel compelled to go."

"I already told you I'm not taking them. And it's *not* stupid." She said it softly. Alan was exhausted. He was talking out of his own frustration.

She made a second cup of tea for herself, and then she returned to the breakfast table, determined not to argue.

"I'm sorry, Katie," he said. He hadn't touched his coffee yet. He sat staring into the cup. "I know what you're doing is important to you."

"It scares me that the government and intelligent people are willing to tolerate higher and higher levels of radiation pollution without doing anything about it. It's more serious than car exhaust—at least we can *see* that in the air. But the radiation is there. You, of all people, see the effects."

Alan shook his head, warding off another ecology lecture. "We don't know what's causing this increase in tumors . . ."

Katie felt the flush of anger creep up her neck. He refused to see what was right under his nose. Or under his scalpel. "Then what do you suggest we do, Alan? Sit back and wait until everyone has colon cancer or a brain tumor, or *every* baby that's born—if there are any born —has some genetic defect? Is that what *you* experts advise? Wait for things to get worse?"

She had promised herself she wouldn't argue with him. It was too much like having a political debate with a beloved puppy. "Oh—never mind. I'm sorry. I hate to start out the day with an argument, Alan."

Alan dabbed at his wide mouth with the napkin. The flicker of a weary smile creased the corners of his eyes. "We were having a discussion, not an argument."

Katie grinned. "Of course." Even when they disagreed, Alan never forbid her to do what she needed to do.

It was six forty-two. Alan carefully stacked his cup, saucer, and juice glass on top of the plate. He bent and kissed the top of her head on his way to the sink with the dishes. "Go to your demonstration," he said. "Keep the atmosphere pure and I'll see you tonight." And Kate knew he was smiling, too.

By six forty-five he was on his way to the hospital, and she reheated her tea in the microwave oven. Katie watched the ceramic cup illuminated like a fine museum piece of pottery inside the microwave. Wouldn't Grandmother have had a fit if she saw tea heated in ten seconds? Grandmother never drank coffee, but kept an old blackened teapot on the back burner of the gas range twenty-four hours a day. By midafternoon the tea had been the color of iodine and as thick as apple butter, its heady vapors clinging to the upholstery and drapes.

Kate'd grown up in the small, backwater town of Medicine Falls, Idaho, with her mother and grandmother. Grandmother believed a woman's place was in the kitchen with an apron around her waist, but Katie grew up loving everything noisy and strenuous. She could run faster than any boy at school, eat more and shout louder than almost anyone else she knew, but that was well before those years at the University of California at Berkeley getting a master's degree in microbiology, and the job at Lorimar Medical Center where she'd met Alan. By that time her interests tended slightly more toward ruffles and French perfume, along with recombinant DNA and the ponderous silence of the research department at Lorimar. After Doug was born she quit her research job and hadn't been involved in anything more risky than washing windows since then. The boisterous demonstrations at the University of Berkeley were only a memory until Kate joined MANA and its campaign to protect the environment.

Kate removed her cup of tea from the microwave oven. Robbie Campbell, her younger son, interrupted her quiet reflection. "Mom, can we get the hamster today?" Shocks of sandy hair stood askew on his small head. He was barely awake.

The purchase of a hamster had been the big question at the Campbell household for nearly a week now. Rob wanted a hamster. Doug wanted a hamster. Alan thought a hamster might teach the boys responsibility. Katie didn't want a rodent of any sort in the house. She didn't even want to *think* about a hamster this early in the morning. And why couldn't the boys learn about responsibility by doing their homework?

"I don't know, sweetie," she said. "We'll see."

"Please, Mom. I'll feed him. I promise. Really, I will."

"I know, Rob." Katie was determined to be firm, but patient, about the matter. "But feeding a hamster is not the problem. There's the job of keeping the cage clean. And not letting it out." She shivered.

"I can do that. And Doug will, too." Long, dark eyelashes partially hid his marble-blue eyes. "Amanda will clean the cage if I ask her real nice."

Amanda was the housekeeper who came twice a week. She was fastidious about the house, and without her Kate knew she'd be hopelessly behind in everything.

"Amanda will *not* clean the cage, Rob." Katie felt herself being backed into a premature decision. "We'll decide today. I just need a little more time to think it over. Okay?"

His eyes, so like Alan's, brightened. "Really? You promise? We can get the hamster today?"

"I said we'd *decide* today." Sometimes she wondered if the communication difficulties with an eight-year-old were inherent in the language or a peculiarity of her son. "Right now I suggest you wake up Doug and get dressed. I'll get your breakfast ready and pack your lunches."

"Just don't put in any of those old granola bars," he grumbled on his way out of the kitchen. "Everybody else gets Oreos."

Robbie had already eaten and was ready for school by the time Doug Campbell, a stocky, handsome boy of ten, dragged himself to the table. He was dressed for school if Kate was willing to ignore the more formal connotations of the word. His green and black polo shirt was inside out, and he'd pulled on brown corduroy jeans. She would have to get him into something coordinated, if possible, before the school bus arrived. And she'd have to do it tactfully. Doug was sultry, darker in temperament than Rob. Doug hid his feelings in a camouflage of small rebellions. Whenever there was cauliflower for dinner, Doug developed a stomachache. Rob, on the other hand, simply announced he hated cauliflower and didn't intend to eat any of it. Katie understood Doug because she'd had plenty of stomachaches herself, as a child, whenever there was something she didn't want to eat. Or do. Robbie had the high energy level of his father, along with Alan's sheer doggedness.

"Can I just drink my juice?" Doug asked softly. "I'm not very hungry."

Katie touched the boy's cool forehead beneath the swirl of dark hair. "Are you feeling okay?"

"Sure, I feel okay. I'm just not hungry."

"You'll be starving by lunch if you don't eat anything now," Katie told him.

"I'll be fine, Mom. I want a peanut butter sandwich for lunch." He finished his juice.

"You know there's aflatoxin in peanut butter," she said. "It's just not good for you."

"The other kids have peanut butter sandwiches," he grumbled.

"I don't care what the other kids eat. I'd be a terrible mother if I knowingly made you sandwiches that weren't good for you."

It was nearly ten minutes to eight. Time to collect books, homework, and lunches and walk to the corner to catch the bus.

"Dougy," she said, "your shirt's inside out." She used his baby nickname.

He threw her a stern look. "It is not." He scowled down at the front of his polo. His shoulders were wide and straight, but, as yet, he hadn't tapered down to the narrow waist that was promised in his build. He still carried some of the preteen bulk of ten-year-old boys.

Kate wondered if she should have his eyes checked. The shirt was obviously inside out. She spotted the bus rumbling along toward the corner of Portola and Serenity Road.

"Better hurry," she called to the boys, who were scrambling toward the yellow school bus. "I'll see you at three."

"And we'll get the hamster!" Robbie shouted back to her.

2

Interstate 580 led out of Castro Valley, through the green, rolling hills toward the city of Livermore, California, and the Livermore Valley with its vineyards, cattle lands, and sycamore groves. Katie enjoyed the morning ride. The air was soft and misty that morning, but she knew it was an illusion. Livermore had some of the worst air pollution in the Bay Area, and the temperatures would soar into the nineties by midafternoon.

Greenville Road exit led the MANA caravan south nearly three miles. The broad, paved road shimmered in the late spring heat. The first security post was located two hundred feet from the road, and beyond lay the long, low buildings that housed the Lawrence Livermore Lab. A thick wire fence was well disguised by immaculately trimmed cedars.

Benny Halvorson knew they were in for trouble that morning when the cars crept up the road and stopped well short of his security post. The Lab had been expecting trouble ever since the rumors of possible radiation leaks in April. They could handle demonstrators. What Benny Halvorson didn't want to see was the white Ford with *San Jose Mercury News* emblazoned on the car door. The media was more of a problem than a bunch of women and a dozen kids.

He straightened his cap and strolled out to meet the demonstrators clambering out of their parked cars. "Sorry, ladies," he said amiably, "you can't park your cars along this road."

Phyllis Latimer, the president of the local MANA organization, glanced up and down the road. She was a small blond woman with slate-blue eyes that functioned like two ice picks. "I don't see any No Parking signs."

"They just paved the road," he informed her. "The new signs ain't up yet. But you have got to move them cars or they'll be towed."

Katie stood at Phyllis's shoulder. "They'll have to run over us to do it," she said nicely. She turned to Bill Kane from the newspaper. "Do you have film in that camera, Bill? They are threatening to mow us down with tow trucks."

Bill Kane smiled and touched the exquisite Minolta around his neck as if it were the Hope diamond hanging there.

Phyllis Latimer leaned toward Benny. "You better tell the tow trucks to bring chains when they come. Traction on new asphalt is terrible when there's blood all over it."

Benny blinked steadily at her. Bunch of goddamned rich bitches, he swore silently. He thought about Celia, his own wife, who spent her days working in a truck-stop cafe. Celia didn't have an ounce of energy when she got home at night. Not like these women who spent their time protesting—and probably fed their kids junk, he thought bitterly. He watched the MANA group haul picnic baskets, insulated coolers, and blankets out of the parked cars. Benny's boss had instructed him to deal firmly, but politely, with demonstrators, but that was getting more and more difficult at the moment. Especially the polite part. "We got deliveries coming through here this morning," he boomed, his voice crackly and harsh. "Now, you move them cars!"

"Deliveries?" Phyllis Latimer looked up at him with wide, calm blue eyes. "Really?"

Although the group looked like a Sunday school outing there was a rigid methodology in the way they sauntered along the road with the children and finally settled themselves between the line of cars. The surface of the road was warm, almost spongy, in the heat.

Katie picked up little Megan Carter, who was having a difficult time with the long weeds that flourished along the roadside. Megan, with her dark hair in ringlets and serious gray eyes, settled trustingly in Katie's arms.

"We're going to have a picnic," Katie said to the little girl. "Won't that be fun?"

Megan nodded and slung her arm across Kate's shoulder. "I like picnics," she said.

Elaine Calder caught up with Kate. Elaine was six months pregnant and already huffing loudly.

"Elaine," Kate said happily. "I didn't see you! I thought you weren't coming today."

Perspiration stood out in translucent pearls on Elaine's forehead and upper lip. "I was late, so I drove up alone. Had to take the day off work for this. I parked right behind you."

Katie hefted Megan to her other arm. The child was heavier than she looked. "When are you going to quit working? I thought you said this month."

"Sometime this month. Maybe. We need the money."

Katie sighed. Elaine worked at an appliance store in

Mountain View. Her hands showed the evidence of cleaning ovens that came in on trade-ins. The skin was red and itchy-looking.

"Besides, Mr. Amans is letting me do some of the cooking demonstrations. They're a lot easier."

"Still . . ." Kate protested silently. Elaine hadn't looked well for at least six weeks. Her eyes had a wild look about them, and the color had been wrung from her tightly drawn face.

They found a spot at the edge of the road with a bit of shade provided by a blue Subaru parked there. Katie had brought an umbrella, too. And about a gallon of sunblock lotion. Radiation was radiation, after all, whatever the source. Megan Carter inspected Kate's picnic lunch and decided to stay there instead of eating with her mother.

"Mama made peanut butter sandwiches," she announced. "Ugh. I hate peanut butter. I like yours a lot better."

"Good." Katie laughed. "You help yourself whenever you're hungry." She glanced at Elaine, who had paled at the mention of food.

Phyllis Latimer and Benny Halvorson continued their discussions while Benny hovered near his air-conditioned kiosk.

"You know radiation can affect the climate," Phyllis told him doggedly. "You know we're losing our ozone protection."

"Aw, that's a bunch of horse—crap," he grumbled. "We had weather just like this back in '88. I remember. Now you gotta get this crowd outta here, lady. Otherwise I'm calling the cops."

Phyllis grinned wickedly. "You just do that, sir. Won't that look terrific in tomorrow's newspaper! Lawrence Lab arrests women and babies!"

The sun stood well overhead, promising uncomfortably warm temperatures again that day. Most of May had been unseasonably hot, and they'd had a dry, smoggy winter. So far it had not been the idyllic California year, and many people blamed it on worsening air-quality conditions in the Bay Area. Others thought it was the delayed effect of erupting volcanoes in Asia and Hawaii, but MANA clearly suspected low-level radiation leaks at the Lawrence Livermore Lab.

Katie kept an eye on Elaine, who was wilting in front of her eyes. Phyllis Latimer had the group organized and seated quickly. The women in the center of the road, and those at either end, were the most likely to encounter difficulties with police or tow trucks. They had all been thoroughly trained in the art of passive protest. There would be no violence. The women and children would sit there in silent protest, blockading the road to deliveries. It had proved to be a very effective method. Especially when the media showed up.

Bill Kane was snapping pictures and interviewing women. "What do you expect to prove?" he asked Katie.

"We're protesting the nuclear activity at the Lab. Nuclear experimentation is endangering the health of everyone in the Bay Area. All you have to do is look at the cancer rate in our valley to know that something's poisoning all of us."

"What about the cancer rate?" Kane scribbled in his notebook.

"Certain kinds of tumors are increasing at more than five times the national rate!"

"What kinds of tumors?" he asked.

"Teratomas, for one."

"What the hell's a teratoma, lady? And isn't it dangerous—I mean, if radiation and nuclear testing is such a menace to life, aren't you endangering yourself and these children just by being here?" Bill Kane was writing and talking furiously.

"It's worth it," Elaine responded. "It's worth it *because* of our children." She laid a long, pale hand over her belly.

Benny Halvorson, his hands on his thick hips, was purple with rage. "You ladies have *got* to move right this minute. This is ridiculous. I never saw nothing like it. You're acting like a bunch of teenagers."

Phyllis Latimer had stationed herself between the group and Halvorson. "Really?"

By eleven thirty everyone had been interviewed, even some of the children. Bill Kane had taken his pictures and he was obviously bored. The asphalt was sticky and uncomfortably hard. Women sweated. Children whined. There was talk that any deliveries to the Lab had probably been rerouted to the north entrance, even though that road was gravel.

But at eleven thirty-five the first delivery truck growled up Greenville Road. It was a white, squarish truck that said Dick's Deli, Pleasanton, California. The lunch truck, providing a respite from the Lab's cafeteria or brown bag lunches for hungry employees, stopped abruptly.

Phyllis Latimer ruffled her short blond hair in frustration. They'd hoped to stop the delivery of something important, like heavy water. But sandwiches and dill pickles?

"What's going on?" The driver of the deli truck leaned far out of the window of the cab.

"We're MANA," Phyllis bellowed. "We're protesting the use of nuclear material here—nuclear material that is *killing our children*!"

"Oh, yeah?" The driver didn't smile. "Well, lady, I got

to get in there and sell sandwiches so's my own kids don't starve. So if you don't mind—"

In unison, the women turned their backs on the truck and stared straight ahead. Even Bill Kane gaped in surprise at the quick, even movement of the group. Loud slogans printed on placards would never have had the effect of one silent, mass shift in position. Kane aimed his camera at the fragile back of Phyllis Latimer against a sky so blue it almost hurt his eyes, contrasted by the belligerent, ruddy face of Benny Halvorson.

Katie didn't look back at the driver. She had Megan Carter tucked between her knees. The child ate a warm pear, and the juice spilled down Megan's mouth to Katie's navy slacks, leaving dark, wet splotches like small tears.

Benny Halvorson strode through the weeds to the deli truck. "Bunch of damn women," he muttered loudly.

In the motionless, blazing air, the driver's voice carried well. "If you ask me it ain't nothing like nuclear stuff that'll get us," he said. "It'll be the watch on your wrist, or the lamp beside your bed. You're looking at this all wrong, I'm telling you. I've seen it happen lots of times before. A bunch of do-gooders who can't see the poison growing on their own windowsills."

Katie glanced quickly over her shoulder. The driver was a man in his thirties with brown hair slicked back alongside his small, angular head. He seemed more indignant than angry. Benny Halvorson glowered enough for both of them.

"You'd better wake up before it's too late," the driver added, addressing only the backs of the women.

Katie rocked the child nestled in her lap.

"I don't like it when that man yells," Megan whispered. She rummaged in the cooler and brought out a cold sandwich. The faintest aroma of egg salad, baby shampoo, and the hint of the sweetly salted sweat of children enveloped Megan.

"The man's not mad at you, honey," Kate reassured her.

"Who's he mad at then?"

"Maybe he's just mad because we have to be here today." Kate rested her cheek on the top of Megan's tousled hair. The truck driver's words stung like small rocks flung at Kate's back and shoulders. Because in a place separated from the rhetoric of protests and idealistic philosophy about a clean earth for the children, that driver was probably right.

They heard the truck engine start and grind noisily backward down the road to a place where it could turn around. Kate imagined a hungry animal, frustrated by its prey's failure to fight. Finally, it roared off in the distance.

The minutes wore on. There were sunburns to tend, cool water was handed around, and the older children began to find diversion in the long grass beside the road. Megan wandered back to her mother, and Kate and Elaine sat in silence.

By noon, Elaine lay down with a pillow, and Katie adjusted the blue and red umbrella to shade the woman. "Why don't you go home, Elaine? We can manage this one without you."

Elaine shook her head. Her body looked rigid on the mat. She didn't sleep.

"Have you told your obstetrician how you feel?" Katie asked. "It doesn't seem like you should be so tired all the time."

"I haven't been to an obstetrician," the woman said softly. "My health plan has a five-hundred-dollar deductible for outpatient visits."

"Elaine—you have to find an obstetrician. Soon."

"I will. I'm taking vitamins. You don't know what it's like with Dick unemployed . . ." She closed her eyes. "I pray a lot. It's the best I can do."

At twelve thirty Kate insisted Elaine leave. "Are you all right? Can you drive home?"

"I'm fine. Just tired."

Katie watched her make her way slowly to her car. Was she all right? It was difficult to remember what it was like to be six months pregnant. Kate hadn't experienced the condition for nearly nine years, and her pregnancies had somehow energized her. Or perhaps she'd forgotten. She clamped her browned arms around her knees.

During the long afternoon they managed to halt two more trucks, one from Young Scientific Products in Palo Alto, and a second unmarked vehicle that made a swift retreat down the road.

At two thirty Phyllis Latimer stood up and stretched. The group followed her cue, packed up blankets and picnic baskets and trudged to their cars. There wasn't much to say. They'd done what they came to do, and now their legs hurt from too much sitting and they carried their sleeping children like corpses dangling from their arms.

Benny Halvorson watched in relief from his air-conditioned post. If the protesters hadn't moved by three o'clock, when the early shift ended at the Lab, they would have had to use the north exit. That would have been a mess.

Kate folded the straw mat she brought to place under the cotton throw. She leaned down for the red and white cooler. Several dark spots on the new asphalt caught her eyes. They were flaking, rusty-looking droplets in the sun.

Katie bent closer. It was blood. A few drops of blood. Her heart seemed to stutter and then recovered. Elaine? Kate shaded her eyes and studied the western horizon. It had been hours since Elaine left, and there was no sign of the woman or her car as far down Greenville Road as Kate could see.

3

At Lorimar Medical Center Dr. Alan Campbell finished the cholecystectomy in Operating Room number six earlier than expected. It had already been a very long day for him, but it had not affected his surgical technique.

In the operating room Alan Campbell was at his best. He knew it, and everyone around him knew it. He could tell jokes, get the punch line straight, and close a peritoneum with the best of them. Perhaps better.

Other men jogged or played golf to relax. Alan Campbell repaired aneurysms. He made a thoracotomy into an art form. Each mastectomy became a theater of muscles and secretive tissue, the craniotomy a symphony of blood vessels, axons, and tissue, and when he closed he considered the cloth whole once more.

The operating rooms at Lorimar Medical Center were kept at a crisp fifty-five degrees, which had a bacteriostatic effect, decreased electrostatic problems, slowed the respiration and cardiac function of patients, and, mercifully, kept Alan Campbell from sweating. But once out in the hall adjoining the operating amphitheaters, the faint pall of perspiration began again on the back of his neck and spread quickly down his back.

Several gowned nurses had gathered at the door of Operating Room number one. One of them, a nurse Alan recognized vaguely, hurried toward him. Her mask, tied only at her neck, joggled loosely down over ample breasts shrouded under the surgical greens.

"Dr. Campbell!" She grasped his arm. "We've been paging you. Didn't you hear it?"

It was well known that Dr. Alan Campbell liked to play classical music during surgery. Strains of Mozart had been detected that morning.

"No," he said. "We were closing the gallbladder in number six. What's going on?"

"I'm not sure, but Dr. Greer's been yelling for you for fifteen minutes."

It took Alan several minutes to scrub in again, and he smiled the whole time. Dr. Lawrence Greer was one of an increasing number of surgeons who were specializing in just one kind of surgery. They chose among gynecological, thoracic, cardiac, neurological . . . Greer's choice was gynecology. Alan believed a surgeon should be versed in more than one specialty. And now, Dr. Greer, who'd argued for specialization vociferously on numerous occasions, had gotten himself into some difficulty. And needed Alan, a surgical generalist. The latex gloves snapped smartly over his hands, and he brushed past the scrub nurse into OR number one.

Lawrence Greer's eyes, above the white mask, were dark and angry. "Jesus, Alan," he half whistled through the mask.

The OR team was drenched. It was only partially blood. The smell was unmistakable. Bowel contents. For a moment Alan was unsure *whose* bowel contents were in question.

"What's going on?" he asked.

"Ruptured uterus. Uteroparietal lacerations, ruptured bowel . . . you name it, we've got it with this one —and she's still bleeding like a stuck pig."

Alan, while disagreeing with Lawrence Greer's imagery, took the hemostat collections out of the man's wet, gloved hands, and peered deep into the abdominal lumen. The uterus lay collapsed on the floor of the peritoneal cavity. Behind it the colon coiled. "How the hell did *this* happen?" Alan closed off a bleeder and sopped up blood with more sponges, dropping them into a green plastic bucket at Greer's feet.

"She came into ER hemorrhaging. Primipara. Six months."

While examining the thick, muscular cecum, a strong peristaltic movement almost wriggled the organ out of Alan's hands. "Ice her down," he told the nurse.

Lowering the temperature had a remarkable effect on body functions. Blood, previously spurting from the uterus, slowed to a gelatinous red gleam oozing throughout the woman's opened belly. And Alan got a much better look at the small tears in the uterus.

"What does she do? Swallow razor blades for a hobby?" he quipped. Each tear was approximately five millimeters long and occurred in parallel rows.

"She's a clerk in an appliance store," Greer said. He did not look up. He extracted the shredded uterus from the abdominal cavity. It was white and shattered. "Those are teeth marks."

"What?"

"Those may be teeth marks," Lawrence Greer repeated softly.

"She delivered a twelve-year-old?" Alan had begun

the resection of the bowel while Greer sutured the cervix. "An orthodontist's dream . . ."

No one laughed. The nurse kept her attention focused on the hemostats and sponges she handed to both Alan and Dr. Greer. The anesthesiologist, Dr. Roger Adams, tended to the oxygen level of his patient. Alan didn't press his humor further.

They swabbed out the abdominal cavity with antibiotic, and meticulously cleansed it of every bit of blood and bowel debris. The cervical opening was lapped closed and the sponges counted when Alan began the elaborate process of closure, muscle over muscle, skin over skin, with rows of absorbable suture. Often the task of closing was turned over to a resident, but Alan preferred to do his own closure.

Finally he looked up. "You can warm her up now," he said to Dr. Adams, who was still looking grim. The process of restoring the body temperature from thirty-two degrees to thirty-seven degrees Celsius again would take fifteen or twenty minutes. It took careful monitoring of the blood pressure to make sure no bleeders had been missed. If the blood pressure dropped they'd have to open her up again.

"Is anyone going to tell me what in God's name happened in here?" Alan asked.

Lawrence Greer looked miserable and very weary. "The thing chewed its way out, Alan. I've never seen anything like it."

Alan reached out and caught the well-muscled arm of Dr. Greer. "What thing? The baby? You mean the baby? A six-month fetus?"

Dr. Greer nodded toward the corner of the operating room where a gowned nurse stood over an incubator. Alan hadn't even noticed it before. She turned and stared at him with liquid blue eyes.

"What shall I do with this, Doctor?" she asked.

The words sent a sharp chill down Alan's spinal column. He instructed his feet to carry him over to that incubator, but they refused, and he was afraid he'd fall over. The sweat started again. He walked to the incubator.

"It's alive?" he asked.

Lawrence Greer lifted the plastic cover of the incubator and carefully moved aside the flannel scrap of blanket. What lay on the pale blue sheet was not a baby. It was the parts of a baby, or most of the parts, but without any order that could be called human.

Sweat slid down Alan's top lip. He tasted salt. This was no dream. He saw the teeth, and the clumps of black hair, and the pinkish-gray shimmer of brain tissue. The room grayed around him. From that jangle of tissue a low gurgle began.

"Dear God," Greer murmured. "What in the world am I going to tell Elaine Calder about *this* when she wakes up?"

"How could you!" Elaine Calder wept through her words. She did not sob. She let the tears rush unaided from her reddened, swollen eyes. Both hands were clutched in tight fists. "You let our baby die?"

Dick Calder, her husband, and Dr. Lawrence Greer exchanged quick glances. They knew this wouldn't be easy, but Dick had insisted they tell Elaine immediately.

"It *wasn't* a baby, Elaine." Lawrence Greer spoke softly. "It was like a tumor we removed. You must not think about it as a baby. Your body—well, it tricked you into believing you were pregnant."

"I felt it move," she whispered.

Dick Calder cradled his wife's balled fist in his hands.

Gently he massaged the taut, ivory skin with his thumb. "I know how hard this is for you—"

Her stricken eyes brimmed with fresh tears. "Hard for me?" Her voice was throaty and thick. "I felt it move. Tumors don't move."

Dr. Greer stepped closer to the bed. "Elaine, don't talk now. I just want you to listen to me." His voice was kind. "The, uh, tissue was severely deformed. It didn't look like a baby. We call them teratomas—they're like the parts of a baby all arranged wrong—much like a tumor. Your body rebelled against itself, in a way. Do you understand what I'm saying?"

Her chin quivered violently. Large, brilliant tears glistened in her husband's eyes, too.

"Did it die?" she asked.

"Yes," he said, "it died. There was no chance for it to survive. Not like that."

"And it very nearly killed you," Dick Calder added.

Elaine Calder bit down on her bottom lip. "Can we have more children?"

"I'm sorry. I'm afraid not."

Her eyes squeezed shut. The wall of pain, a grinding monument to abdominal surgery, toppled down over her. Dr. Greer had seen it all so many times before. He nodded to the nurse, who plunged a syringe of barbiturates into the IV tubing. Within a minute Elaine was in its merciful clutches.

"Was it baptized?" she asked. Unconsciousness followed swiftly.

Dick Calder rested his wife's hand once more on the yellow blanket. He brushed away the tears in his eyes. "I'm sorry."

Greer motioned toward the door. "Come on. There's a lounge down here. We can get a cup of coffee. It'll probably be instant, though."

The lounge on the gynecology wing of Lorimar was never as crowded as the maternity lounge. When the two men entered, a woman who'd been idly paging through an old copy of *Good Housekeeping* stood up and left.

Greer emptied two packets of instant coffee into two foam cups and filled them with hot water. He handed one cup to Dick Calder. "That was pretty rough," he said.

Dick Calder only nodded. He accepted the coffee but did not take a sip. "She wanted a baby so badly—you have no idea." The rims of his eyes were very red. "I told her it wasn't a good idea to go on working with all those chemicals. But she wouldn't quit that job. And now—"

"What chemicals?" Lawrence Greer sank into the low sofa.

"She worked at Amans Appliance. She was a clerk there, but she had to clean all those old ovens—I told her it wasn't safe. Not for a pregnant woman. All that sodium hydroxide and borosilicate and—"

"We don't know what causes a teratoma," Greer told him. "The best theory is that a woman is exposed to a teratogenic agent during the second to the tenth day after conception. But what those agents are exactly is pure speculation . . . X rays, perhaps, or drugs . . . Several years ago we found out that the tranquilizer thalidomide caused severe birth defects. But in the teratoma, there is generally a chromosomal dysfunction."

"If you ask me," Calder said softly, "it was all those chemicals. And who knows what else they used at that store. Fred Amans—" Dick Calder shook his head. "He uses employees like personal slaves. Elaine told him she was pregnant and didn't want to clean those ovens anymore. And you know what he did? He laughed. Fred Amans laughed. Can you imagine that?"

Lawrence Greer sipped his coffee. "Had she been seen by a doctor about the pregnancy? When she came in she didn't know the name of her obstetrician."

Dick Calder squirmed uncomfortably. "She went to a clinic a couple of times that I know of. She got some vitamins . . ." A bright flush, like a stain, appeared on his neck and crept up toward his jaw "I was laid off in January—we didn't have health insurance then. And her policy doesn't cover much—you know how those insurance companies are . . ." Calder's hands fussed uneasily with the buttons on his jacket. "Besides, I think it was all those chemicals."

"Why didn't she find another job when she knew she was pregnant?" Lawrence Greer was increasingly surprised at the risks intelligent women took with their unborn children. When malathion spraying began in the Santa Clara Valley to get rid of the Mediterranean fruit fly, any number of Dr. Greer's pregnant patients risked their lives on the freeway day after day, fleeing a chemical that was proven safe. Two of those patients were involved in car accidents. Only one infant survived.

"She did look for another job. But things are tight." Dick Calder did not look up at the doctor. "And who wants to hire a pregnant woman?"

Lawrence Greer stood up. His large frame was definitely not built for rising from low sofas. "Well, if it's any consolation, by the time she knew she was pregnant, it was probably too late." It was nearly seven o'clock, and Greer was exhausted. "I'm sure Elaine is going to be fine."

"Dr. Greer?" Far from being tearful, Dick Calder's eyes were narrowed. "Is it possible that those chemicals caused this—this teratoma?"

Dr. Lawrence Greer knew that question. When a genetic accident occurred in a child the parents searched for a reason, any reason other than themselves. "I don't know," he answered. "It's impossible to say for sure that they caused it. There are many suspected teratogenic agents, as I mentioned. My recommendation, Mr. Calder, is that you forget about all this. Perhaps you and your wife can adopt children. It's the best advice I can offer."

Lawrence Greer wanted out of that room. He wanted time to think about what was happening. Hadn't he seen more than his share of teratomas lately? And the growth he'd removed from the Carlson woman just two weeks ago? Hadn't that been teratomaceous? He wanted to check the records.

"But is it *possible* that the chemicals did this—this monstrosity?"

Greer sighed. "Yes, it's possible." He turned to leave the lounge, hoping to escape before that final, inevitable question.

"Did it die?"

Lawrence Greer turned slowly to face the man. "I can't always tell you when life begins. How can I tell you when it ends?"

"Then it didn't." Dick Calder's voice sounded constricted.

"As of four o'clock this afternoon the *tissue*—and I emphasize the word 'tissue'—remained responsive to a stimulus—that doesn't mean it was necessarily alive." Within reason Dick Calder had the right to know what had happened. "I ordered no life support be given."

"But you said it wasn't really a baby."

"It wasn't. A teratoma is a neoplasm."

Dick Calder stood up and edged toward the doctor. "Was it baptized? My wife wants it baptized."

Dr. Greer wondered if his small groan was audible. "We don't baptize neoplasms, Mr. Calder." He escaped any further questions by departing the lounge. That kind of encounter with parents was certainly the least favorite part of his job. Especially when he could smell a lawsuit clinging to every word. He'd be glad when this case was over. He'd spend the week caring for Elaine Calder. But how could he look at her without seeing those rows of shining teeth and that jumble of human tissue he'd delivered from her body?

Not that it was the first time he'd been half-sickened by the monstrosity of a fetus. There'd been others. He thought he was safe in obstetrics and gynecological surgeries. But now there were infants born with parasitic neoplasms bulging from their necks. Or exuding from the mouth. Some of them were operable. Many were not. Last week one of his patients delivered a fetus that had developed literally inside out. It's tiny heart had fluttered against the injustice for only moments. Luckily it died. But the Calder baby? A child designed by a madman. Its brain was exposed. Feet grew where the belly should be. All mouth and teeth . . . he hoped to God it would die, and soon. They didn't baptize neoplasms at Lorimar Medical Center. But neoplasms didn't cry either.

He walked past the nursing station on the Gynecology wing, 3 North. He'd left orders for Mrs. Calder and two other patients on the section—two other patients who'd lost their babies. He never put his miscarriage patients on the Obstetrics ward, as some obstetricians did. It was heartless. 3 North was not a constant reminder that there was no baby to tend.

Obstetrics, 3 West, adjoined the GYN wing, and Greer glided silently down the long tiled hallway. He felt more at home on 3 West. He knew all the staff. And tonight he had to check on the nursery.

Luckily, Genevieve Byrd was on duty. When he slid into the white isolation gown and strode through the rows of isolettes in the nursery he was glad to see her face. Dr. Greer rarely entered the warm, humid arena of the newborn nursery. He left that to the pediatricians. But tonight he had to speak to Genevieve.

She sat at the charting desk with a stack of metal clipboards in front of her. "Hello, Dr. Greer," she said. She didn't smile. But, then, Lawrence Greer couldn't remember when the woman *had* smiled. He knew her from years of service on Obstetrics, and what he cared about was that Genevieve ran a ward like a private flower garden. She knew everything about a particular patient. She made it her business to find out every detail and maintain a crisp, professional distance at the same time.

Greer inclined his head toward a door behind the charting desk. The door led to the supply closet for the nursery. "How's it going in there?"

Without looking up Nurse Byrd flipped open another chart. "They should *never* come here to the nursery, Doctor. They belong in Pathology. The crying is getting on everyone's nerves."

"I understand—"

"Do you?" Her hazel eyes flashed at him. "It doesn't really cry, you know. We're used to babies crying in here. It moans—or something. It should have gone into formalin—not an isolette."

"You're probably right." It never paid to argue with Genevieve Byrd. "But there was nothing else to do."

Her mouth was rigid. "You don't have to explain it to me," she said briskly. "But let's see if you can clarify the situation for Father Leo. He's been here for an hour waiting to baptize the Calder—whatever it is." She didn't say baby. "I told him he'd have to speak to you."

The priest, awkwardly gowned in a white nursery drape and puffy green paper cap, sat in the viewing area. Under the gown his royal blue ecclesiastical shirt was visible. In one hand he clasped a purple vestment and a silver bottle that looked to Dr. Greer like a miniature canteen.

"I'm Father Leo from St. Mark's," he said to Greer when the doctor left the nursery to talk to the priest. "Are you Dr. Greer?"

"Yes, ah—" Greer stammered. "But—ah—"

"I'd like to baptize this child and get it over with. I've been here an hour already. Mrs. Calder called me from the Emergency Room this afternoon—I really don't understand why the parents' request for baptism is being denied." He glared at Nurse Byrd. "So, if you don't mind, could we get on with it—before it's too late?"

Too late for what? Dr. Greer wondered. He nodded toward the door of the supply closet. "I won't stand in your way, Father," he said. "You do what you have to do."

Genevieve led Father Leo into the crowded storeroom. Stacks of cloth diapers and diaper padding lined with blue plastic, white flannel blankets, and tiny ribbed shirts sat packaged in plastic wrap. Rows of saline, sterile water, rubber tubing of various sizes, swabs, and boxes of latex gloves lined the shelves from floor to ceiling.

Father Leo looked around uneasily. An isolette had been pushed far back, near one wall. "Am I too late?" This was not, after all, the usual place for a newborn infant.

"Oh, I don't think so, Father," Genevieve said wickedly. She hurried to the isolette and pulled the blanket away from the small lump of churning matter that lay there.

Father Leo kissed the fringed vestment, placed it around his neck, and edged nervously toward the infant isolette. He dribbled water from the silver bottle into the cup of his hand. "In the name of the—" The blood drained from his face to his toes. "What *is* that?"

"I'm afraid we aren't sure either," Genevieve answered.

Water dripped from the priest's hand onto the tissue. The malformed mouth sucked at the droplets of water. Dr. Greer turned away.

". . . the Father—and the Son—and the Holy Spirit," the priest finished shakily. "And may the Lord have mercy on your soul."

Amen, agreed Lawrence Greer. If there was a soul in there somewhere. He caught Father Leo when he fell backward in a dead faint.

On 3 North Elaine Calder lay deep in the grasp of a morphine sleep. She could not remember the pain now. It was very faint, as if it had happened a long time ago. But in her vaporous dreams she heard the strange words, like a chant, a primitive chant. *Tera Toma.* Something magic. A curse or a blessing. A drumbeat. A heartbeat. It pounded unmercifully in her mind.

Something evil, she thought. Something evil had taken over her baby. She must not have prayed hard enough.

When Kate Campbell arrived home that day, fifteen minutes later than Doug and Robbie, she found them perched on the redwood deck sharing crumbs from their lunch boxes.

"Where were you?" Robbie demanded. "Doug had a bloody nose and everything, and you weren't here!"

Kate appraised her elder son. His skin was mottled and a thin ribbon of blood clung to his dark hair in front of his right ear. "Well, it's stopped now. Come on, we'll get you cleaned up."

"I didn't hit him or nothing," Rob assured Kate. "His nose just started bleeding when we got off the bus. But I didn't hit him, Mom."

"Methinks you protesteth too much, me lad," she joked.

"What does that mean?" Robbie demanded, looking totally bewildered.

"It means Mom thinks you *did* hit me, stupid, because you said you *didn't* so many times," Doug explained.

"Does that mean I'm in trouble?" Rob asked.

"No—I assume you didn't hit him." Kate unlocked the front door and herded the boys ahead of her.

"Does that mean we can get the hamster then?" Robbie quizzed her hopefully. "Because I didn't hit Doug?"

"I've thought about it," she said. "And I decided we'll go to the pet store and get a hamster tomorrow. Okay?"

"Okay!" the boys chorused. Dougy washed his face and ear and then the two boys retired to a corner of Doug's bedroom to discuss the forthcoming hamster. Where would he sleep? What would he eat?

Katie put together a simple supper and tried to find Elaine Calder's phone number to check and make sure Elaine had arrived home safely. She'd written that number on the back of an envelope—but where was the envelope? Supper came and went, and Alan did not arrive home. That wasn't terribly unusual. Katie supervised homework and had a long bath herself. She dozed on the sofa in the family room and waited.

4

 Alan wasn't home at midnight when Kate, too exhausted to wait for him any longer, crept into bed, and he wasn't home at one thirty when she awoke long enough to glance at the clock and realize his side of the bed was still empty.

It was nearly two A.M. when he dropped his clothes in a pile on the bedroom floor and ran his fingers through his hair as if the clothing itself had been too heavy a burden to bear.

"You're very late," Kate said sleepily.

"Bad night at the hospital." His lank body, downily glazed with red hair, looked as if it might come apart at the seams at the least provocation, like a rag doll too hastily constructed. "Katie?"

She rolled over on her back, squinting at him in the dim light. "What?"

"Isn't Elaine Calder a friend of yours?"

"Elaine?" Kate sat up. "Why? What happened?" Suddenly she was quite awake.

"Dr. Lawrence Greer operated on her this afternoon.

I was called in to assist. She's stable." Alan's shoulders drooped even more, a fact Katie did not think possible. "A ruptured uterus."

"What about the baby?"

"There wasn't any baby. She had a neoplasm. A teratoma." He went into the bathroom. She heard the water run in the sink.

Kate pressed her hands tightly over her face. She wished she could cry. She wanted to scream. Not Elaine, not lovely, delicate, innocent Elaine. Not her baby. "I'm sorry," she managed to whisper, a small consolation for Elaine Calder's child and the weight of her own helplessness.

The shower in the bathroom ran for a long time. It was no ordinary shower. Three pulsating nozzles had been installed to jettison a person's skin into hypercleanliness. And a redwood bench sat against the far wall of the shower. Katie knew Alan sat there and let the water thunder down on him. Katie rarely showered, preferring the peacefulness of a soak in the bathtub filled with four inches of water. And in a day of severe California drought her guilt level would not allow the long shower Alan Campbell took as his right after a long day's work. Katie lay awake listening, trying not to think, until Alan finally slid into bed beside her.

"Alan?"

"What?"

"Why did this happen to Elaine?"

"I don't know, Kate. Go to sleep."

Neither of them slept. At the very edge of sleep Alan's nerves shot messages to every muscle, jerking him awake. He got up once and had a shot of Scotch, straight up. Katie lay on her side, curled up. Tears wet her pillow, and she turned it over once. Her mind raced. What had happened? It was one thing to protest radiation leaks. A baby deformed by something unknown was an entirely different matter. All that insecticide on the fruit . . . she considered. Antibiotics and steroids in the meat. EDTA in green beans. Calcium propionate in bread. Lead in the air. Mercury in a salmon dinner . . .

The next day was Friday. On the way to see the pediatrician, Dr. Silver, about Doug's nosebleeds, Kate spotted the For Sale sign on the Vickerses' lawn.

"I didn't know they were moving," Kate said to Doug. They'd lived in the lovely brick house for as long as Kate and Alan had lived on Portola Road. Jim Vickers was an engineer at Hewlett-Packard. Linda, his wife, was president of the Parents' Club at school. "Has Todd said anything about moving?" Todd and Doug had been friends ever since first grade.

"He says his dad's sick."

Kate nearly stopped the car. "He is? What's wrong?"

Doug shrugged. "I don't know. Just sick, I guess."

Kate promised herself she'd stop by and see the Vickerses soon.

The worst part of seeing a pediatrician was sitting in the waiting room with a dozen other children who were all sneezing and coughing or had rashes all over their bodies. That Friday, the waiting room was crowded, but quieter than usual. A little girl sat huddled against her mother. The child's eyes were glazed and dull. She could not seem to sit upright.

"Now, sit up, Mandy," the woman said. "You'll get Mama's new suit all wrinkled."

The child lifted her gaze to her mother. "It hurts," she whimpered.

"Mandy has to be a big girl now," the mother crooned.

Katie was getting irritated. The child was clearly ill. "What's the matter?" she asked the child.

"Tell the nice lady what's the matter with you, sweetie. She asked you a question."

"Is she a doctor?" Mandy asked her mother.

"She's just asking how you feel. Answer her!"

"My back hurts," the child stammered. Her face jerked nervously with the effort.

"And the doctor will make it better," Mama intoned.

The child intoned the expected response. "The doctor will make it better—don't move, Mama. It hurts when you do that."

The mother was clearly repelled by the illness of her daughter. Some people don't deserve their children, Katie thought, enraged at the woman's insensitivity. Or cruelty.

Another woman cuddled an infant who neither moved nor made a sound. When she jingled a rattle in front of the baby, no hand reached out.

"Must be a lot of flu around," the baby's mother said nervously. "I don't know what's the matter with Mikey . . ."

When they finally got into the examining room, Dr. Silver said nosebleeds were quite common in growing children and not to worry. Kate worried anyway. She was an expert at it.

They picked up Rob at school and drove to El Camino Pet Center to get the hamster. It was not clear to Katie how she had made the decision to let the boys have a hamster. It hadn't been a conscious decision on her part, but nevertheless, there they stood at five thirty on a Friday afternoon studying the furry creatures in metal cages.

"I want that one!" Rob squealed.

The hamster pen was lumpy with brown hamsters,

brown and white hamsters, a few black ones, fat hamsters, not-so-fat hamsters . . .

"A very nice choice, young man," the clerk said. He had probably not seen his twenty-first birthday yet, and had some sort of futuristic haircut, half crew cut, half permanent wave . . . "I see you know how to pick out a terrific hamster."

Robbie beamed. He'd chosen a rotund, beady-eyed brown and white animal.

"Is it male?" Katie asked. "We only want a male."

The clerk scooped up the small creature from the cage. "As a matter of fact," he said, turning the animal over in his hand, "it is. It certainly is."

Doug scowled at Robbie's selection. "I'd rather have that black one." He pointed to a small black hamster with glittering onyx eyes. "He's cuter."

Robbie peered into the pen again. "He is *not* cuter, is he, Mom?"

Neither hamster held much appeal for Katie. "Cute" was not an applicable term for a rodent. "They're both cute." As far as she was concerned, buying a hamster was the same as importing a rat into the house. And rats carried bubonic plague, among other hideous, fatal diseases. Katie shivered.

"You know," offered the clerk, "males are much better with a little company. Now, this isn't true of females, but the males seem to prefer living with another hamster. They curl up together at night—it's really sweet. I would certainly recommend you buy *two* hamsters. This fluffy one, and this one." He snatched the black hamster from the pen. "Two males. Yes, sir, and aren't they cute together?"

The boys grinned happily. And Kate didn't feel up to a debate with either the boys or the clerk. Besides, two hamsters could hardly be much more trouble than one.

"We'll need a cage for them," she surrendered. "And some food."

Thirty minutes later they left the pet center laden with two hamsters, one clear plastic cage with a bright yellow running wheel, add-on yellow tubing that would lead to a rest area and a feeding area when assembled, three boxes of food, including hamster "treats," a water bottle, and several rodent toys, for diversion, Katie thought dismally. She also purchased a large bag of chlorophyll-scented sawdust for the cage.

Katie and the boys spent two hours that evening assembling the "mouse town house," as it was called. Kate occupied herself with making sure the removable lids were not all that removable.

"I hope they like it in there," Rob said when they were finished and had spread a comfortable layer of sawdust on the floor of the cage.

Frank and Fluffy, as the two hamsters were named, took to the new habitat just fine. Fluffy immediately sat in the food dish and glared at Frank, who entertained himself on the noisy running wheel. Alan found some grease in the garage and applied it to the axle, but that didn't help much. The wheel clacked and clattered on its merry rounds.

"Fluffy's a stupid name for a hamster," Doug said to Robbie. "How'd you like to be called Fluffy Campbell? No one'd know if you were a boy or a girl."

"I like the name Fluffy," Rob defended stubbornly. "He's my hamster and I get to name him anything I like. Besides, I think Frank is a dumb name for a hamster."

"Stop with the arguing," Alan scolded them mildly. "Frank and Fluffy are perfect names. We all know they're boys, so I guess it's okay."

"I want Fluffy in my room," Rob said.

"That wheel will keep you up all night, Rob." Katie

could hardly bear to think of a near relative of a rat sleeping in the same room as her son.

Doug frowned. "You can't have them in your room! Frank is my hamster, I want him in my room."

"I don't want Frank. I just want Fluffy to sleep with me."

"No one except you is going to sleep in your room," Katie decided. "No one."

"You realize that hamsters sleep all day and play around all night," Alan explained. "Maybe we should find a place for them in the family room."

"They sleep all day?" Rob asked in disbelief. "Do they really, Daddy, or are you just kidding?"

"I think you two had better do some reading about hamsters." Alan found the article about hamsters in the children's edition of *Encyclopædia Britannica.*

The boys pored over the information while Fluffy and Frank settled down in their town house for a nap.

"They bite if you surprise them," Rob finally announced. "And they get indigestion."

"Not indigestion," Doug corrected him. "Gestation. That means they can have babies."

Robbie's blue eyes widened. "Can they? Frank and Fluffy can have babies?"

"No," Katie said decidedly. "They can't. To have babies there has to be a female hamster and a male hamster. We have two males, so they can't have babies."

"Why not?"

She knew Rob would ask that question. "Because only female hamsters can have babies. The male hamster only fertilizes the female, but the male can't have babies himself . . . luckily," she added softly.

Rob was apparently satisfied with her explanation. "Oh," was all he said. "Do they bite *hard,* Daddy?"

Alan blanched and shook his head as if he were clearing his thoughts. Then he grinned. "Yes, I'm afraid they do. So don't stick your hands in the cage and scare the hamsters— Now, guys, where shall we put these magnificent specimens?"

After much debate and trial placements, Frank and Fluffy took up residence on a utility table near the kitchen door.

Kate was miserable. "I don't want them in the kitchen. It's just not sanitary."

Although the cage was far enough from the table and food preparation areas, Kate hated the idea of rats in the kitchen. It was bad enough that they had to be in the house at all. Her own mother had spent months trying to get rid of mice. She'd entice them into those horrible traps with bits of cheddar cheese or a glob of peanut butter, and here Kate had spent fifty-two dollars for a town house for the little creatures and was being convinced that they should sleep in the kitchen.

The utility table, at long last, came to rest on Kate's desk opposite the end of the cupboards. It was a compromise solution. Katie and Amanda couldn't see the hamsters when they were working in the kitchen, but the hamsters were clearly in the kitchen. After ten minutes of watching Frank and Fluffy sleep, Doug and Robbie went to the family room to play a game of Block-Out before starting their homework.

"Call us if they wake up," Robbie said.

"I certainly will," Kate assured them, knowing Frank and Fluffy would certainly wake up soon, but she wouldn't say a word about it. It was one of those small indecencies of motherhood, lying without hesitation.

Kate poured herself a glass of Chablis wine and wandered off to find Alan. He'd cloistered himself in the study with a stack of medical journals.

"You get tired watching Frank and Fluffy sleep, too?"

Katie sank into the armchair upholstered in buttery soft black leather. She curled her feet under her and sipped the wine. "No, I wanted to talk to you—about Elaine Calder. How is she?"

"She's doing fine." Alan straightened the pile of journals.

"I'd like to go and see her. Do you think it's too soon?"

Alan shrugged. "Give her a few more days. She'll be a lot more cheerful."

He fidgeted with the open top journal, and Kate knew he wanted to be alone to study. More and more he closed himself off from her and the boys in order to read and study. Not that she minded terribly that he had to keep up in his field. But the journals on his desk were not the usual surgical bulletins. Now he was reading pathology and oncology material.

"Are you coming to bed early?" she asked him.

Already deeply absorbed, Alan looked up as if he were surprised she was still sitting there in the study. "I don't think so. Don't wait up for me."

That night the dream returned to Alan Campbell. Katie woke to find him rigid and moaning beside her.

"Alan," she called to him, "Alan, it's all right."

He groaned and rolled over. Kate dozed for what seemed only moments and woke to a scream, a high, organic scream.

"Alan!" she cried, shaking his shoulder roughly.

He stared at her, uncomprehending and pale. And then he stumbled to the bathroom and locked the door.

"Alan? Are you all right?"

She heard him vomit, again and again, retching miserably until she was sure he must have turned his stomach inside out. She sat on the edge of the bed and waited.

Was it the flu, perhaps? Or worse, something he caught from those hamsters? Just what were the initial symptoms of plague? she wondered. The trade-off for teaching her children responsibility with a couple of pets surely wouldn't be a husband who vomited half the night. But Katie knew the difficulty lay with the dreams, those night terrors of Alan's.

She heard him open the vanity drawers in the bathroom and rifle through the contents. He turned on the tap water, and finally, he opened the door to the bedroom. His blue eyes were glassy. They were rimmed with red and unnatural-looking. She couldn't say exactly what it was. But it wasn't flu.

"I want you to do something about the dreams, Alan," she said firmly.

He lay down on the bed and pulled the covers around his shoulders. "I don't know what to do, Katie. If I knew, I'd do it."

"I think you should see someone—talk to someone. Talk to a psychiatrist. Find out what these dreams are all about."

Alan laughed, a dry, amused chuckle. "I just can't see myself talking to a psychiatrist about my—my—dreams. He'd want me to describe them—I can't. He'd wonder how my mother potty-trained me. And whether I was getting it off with my wife—"

"Stop it. Just stop it." Kate flopped back down on her pillow. "I don't understand how you can be a doctor and still be so narrow-minded."

"You know what I think of psychiatry." He closed his eyes. "One step above voodoo."

Katie listened to his short, irregular breathing even out. She knew almost nothing about dreams, rarely remembering her own in the morning. Her expertise was in concrete areas like peanut butter sandwiches and hamster pellets. And ECHO viruses and streptococcus organisms a long time ago. But it didn't take an expert to know that something was eating at Alan.

"Promise me you'll talk to someone," she whispered. But he was asleep and did not answer.

Sunday afternoon was balmy and bright, the air sweet-scented by the smell of new grass and mock orange. Fred Amans stood in the doorway of Elaine Calder's hospital room. Fred was a fat man and then some. He was greasy. Every pore of his body secreted an oily sweat, the odor of which he lightly disguised by aftershave lotion. His clothing, a super-sized pale blue suit, blue plaid shirt, although pressed, seemed to be in need of a thorough laundering. He wore a black string tie.

"Elaine, my dear," he said cheerily, "I am so glad to see you lookin' so good." In his arms he carried a large bouquet of red roses mingled with white baby's breath. "I brought you a little something. Just to cheer you up. You know, we're all thinkin' about you down at the store. Yes, sir, we *do* miss our little clerk down there."

Elaine pulled herself up on the pillow with some difficulty. "Dick said you were coming this afternoon. You really didn't have to—"

"Well, I just want you to know I am real sorry about all your trouble. I waited till I thought you'd be feelin' up to a visit from your old boss." He held out the roses. "Now where can we put these so you can see them?" He looked around for a vase, but there wasn't one, so he laid the flowers on the sink. "We'll just have to get ourselves a nurse in here to find a vase for these pretty things, now won't we. And aren't they lovely, though? Why, I give my wife roses every year for her birthday. Yellow ones. She's real partial to yellow ones. But I figured you might like red. Big red roses."

"They're lovely," Elaine agreed. Actually she did like roses, but not roses from Fred Amans.

"Well, I didn't come to run on about roses." He chuckled, and his belly kept tempo. "I came by to see how you were doin', and have a little chat with you." He pulled a chair close to the bed and sat down.

Elaine wished Dick were there. And she wished Fred Amans would stop talking like John Wayne. She knew for a fact that Amans had been raised in upper New York State. He turned on that ridiculous cowboy accent for some kind of imagined effect.

"I been talkin' to your husband these last few days— you know, seein' how you were doing and everything, and I can tell you we are very concerned about you." Amans's graying eyebrows contracted deeply over his narrow eyes. "You know, Amans Appliance takes care of its own. We are well known for that."

Elaine caught herself nodding dutifully. That's how she had always behaved around Fred Amans. If he told her to clean out those old ovens, she'd always nodded and cleaned ovens. If he told her to demonstrate beef bourguignon in a microwave oven for a group of customers, she did just that. And if he said other things— he'd made other kinds of requests of her and other female employees—she'd acquiesced to them, too.

"I been in business in this area twenty-six years," he was saying. "And that shows a good business head. And one of the things I do is take care of my employees, especially when trouble comes knockin' at their door. I always say, 'Take care of your own.'"

"We all appreciate that," Elaine said softly. "But Dick is afraid I lost the baby because of all those chemicals I had to use—on the ovens."

"Bull—" he sputtered. "You and I know those chemicals couldn't hurt nothin'. Now, don't we? Why, that's just soap and a little water. And a little bit of grease remover."

"No, it was sodium hydroxide," Elaine corrected him. "And some other chemicals. It wasn't just soap, Mr. Amans."

"Now, that's just my point." He smiled at her. A top row of yellowed teeth gleamed at her. "I don't know where you got that idea. Why, sodium hydroxide would eat the enamel right off them ovens, and I know what I'm talkin' about. There's not a drop of sodium hydroxide, or any dangerous chemical, on my premises, so where you got that notion I really do not know."

"It was in that white drum in the back room."

"There ain't no *white drum* in the back room." He sounded irritated, but his voice mellowed abruptly. "Well, there *was* one, but that was paint. And I sent it back to the company just the other day. Not good enough for Amans Appliance. Yes, sir, we believe in only the best for our customers. And our employees," he added.

Elaine forced a smile.

"Now, as I was sayin', your hubby and I have had some long conversations about you, and we agreed that nothing at the store did you even the littlest bit of harm. *But*—" he said, before she could object, "we are still bound and determined to do our best by you. You understand what I mean, honey?"

As if on cue, Dick Calder stepped through the doorway. He was grinning foolishly. Elaine hated him when he smiled like that.

From a vaguely tainted jacket pocket, Fred Amans pulled several slips of folded paper. Elaine glanced at Dick, who had moved to the end of the bed. Dick was still grinning.

Fred Amans snapped a check, long, green, and new,

in front of Elaine's face. She read the numbers and gasped. "What? I don't understand—"

"Now, don't you go sayin' thanks or nothin' like that," Amans said. "This check is just our little token of sympathy to you and your husband."

Elaine picked up the check from the blanket where Amans had laid it. "That's a lot of sympathy." Five digits' worth, in fact. The names were correct. Elaine and Richard Calder. The date was yesterday. And the signature was none other than Sherman P. Dettler, Jr., of Dettler Industries, Inc., the fifth-largest producer of kitchen appliances in the country. "This check isn't from Amans Appliance," she said, still dazed.

"No, it isn't. Why, when I told Sherm Dettler about your sales record, he was mighty impressed, let me tell you. Yes, sir, mighty impressed. And when I went on to tell him about all this trouble you're having, well, he felt we could get a little check to you. Just to show our concern."

In Elaine Calder's experience the parent company of Amans Appliance had never before shown either concern or sympathy for its employees. The health insurance was just one fine example. She found it difficult to believe that Dettler Industries had experienced some heartwarming conversion in the past few days. "I really don't understand why—"

Dick Calder plucked the check from her cool hands. "It's really very simple, sweetheart. Mr. Amans, here, feels you deserve some consideration for all your service to his company. Isn't that right?"

Fred Amans nodded furiously. His stiff, wavy gray hair shuddered with each forward thrust of his large head.

"And in exchange we'll sign the form that says we do not hold Amans Appliance or Dettler Industries re-

sponsible, in any way, for what happened." Dick Calder
was still smiling. "It's that simple."

Amans shoved the release form at Elaine. Dick had
already signed the document. The language was plain. It
stated that the Calders relinquished any claim against
the two companies for damages of any sort. It was an
umbrella agreement. Dick handed her a pen, and Elaine
signed her full name. The scrawl was almost unreadable.
She thought it must have been because of the pain medication, which the nurse brought in a syringe every three
or four hours.

Amans slid the release form from beneath her hands
and tucked the paper in his suitcoat pocket again. The
smile was gone now from his heavily jowled face. "Just
one more thing." The accent had disappeared also.
"You are not to talk to any of my other employees. Your
husband and I agreed that you will be moving out of the
area very soon. Do you understand?"

Her understanding of the entire past few days was
only a vague memory. She'd lost her baby, signed a release form for Mr. Amans, and the last time Dr. Greer
saw her he said they'd be getting more X rays on Monday. Something about her throat. She was having some
difficulty swallowing. But all of it was much too unclear
for Elaine, at the moment.

Fred Amans did not say good-bye. He strode out of
the room with only a quick nod at Dick.

"We're going to get you out of here," Dick whispered
to her, leaning down close to her face. "I've made arrangements for a private nurse for you."

"I'd like to go home," she said, and smiled up at
Dick. She felt so tired. She wanted to close her eyes and
sleep.

"We won't be going home exactly—I found us a new
place. A nice new place. You'll like it. And we can de-

cide how to spend our money. I hear there are still some wonderful bargains in real estate in the Southwest—Arizona or New Mexico. You'll like it down there."

"What about the X rays—on Monday?"

"You look fine to me. You can have those X rays after we get situated. We'll find a good doctor."

Elaine allowed her eyes to close. "Do me one favor?"

"Anything, babe."

"Throw out those roses."

5

The Pathology Department and laboratory at Lorimar Medical Center were in the basement of the east wing of the hospital. It seemed unfair to Dr. John Lacey that Pathology always ended up in the basement. It was as if the dead were already buried in the brightly lit concrete hallways and autopsy rooms.

Dr. Lacey's name was on an office down the hall from the Chemistry Department. One wall of the office was a bank of windows that looked out on an outer office of desks and file cabinets populated with secretaries, several spider plants, and a Brew Master coffeepot. Strains of "Blue Hawaii" drifted through the speakers in the halls and offices. He resented the music. In fact, he'd managed to damage the speaker in his office so that he not only did not have to listen to "Blue Hawaii," but he didn't hear pages either.

John Lacey was a tall man, lean and elegant in his crisp surgical greens. An interior man with assessing eyes, he walked the long basement hallway, which was painted yellow. That was one other thing he resented. Sometime in the past every wall in Pathology had been painted the same unconvincing shade of sunlight. A basement was a basement, after all. Calling it the first floor didn't help either. Pale, shivering Boston ferns hung beneath the fluorescent lights in a small alcove. Their slow and patient dying mocked any decorating efforts in a department of the hospital where death was a reality, and life, at times, was indistinguishable from its darker, more fearsome opposite.

Dr. Lacey reached his office and sank into the swivel chair, turning it immediately away from the view of the secretaries. He hated feeling like an overseer. None of the secretaries glanced up at him. He knew that, in actuality, most of them kept an eye on him through the windows. It was just one more annoyance. He made a mental note to try to get drapes up on those windows.

Besides all that, it was Monday morning and the histology sectioning of the Calder teratoma had not been pleasant, to say the least. Dr. Julia Young, the Pathology resident, had looked positively green, even after six months experience at the autopsy bench.

She'd worked beside him that morning. Her mouth had quivered as the circular saw bit through cartilage and soft bone. Wafer sections of tissue sandwiched off the blade, squealing and whining when it hit the row of teeth. Bits of hair clung to the burnished steel blade.

The helter-skelter arrangement of limbs and organ systems was not a human child. It was clearly a teratoma, and yet, he admitted there was something chilling about bisecting the head of the neoplasm to find a partially developed eyeball staring up at them from a pocket of cerebral tissue.

Dr. Young's blue eyes had been wild by that time. "Do we have to do it this way?" she'd asked.

"Yes." He sectioned down into the remnants of a peritoneal cavity. Limbs, stiffened by formalin, were whittled away, micron by micron. And when he looked up Julia Young had left the histology area. He'd asked her to come to his office to talk.

"I'm sorry," she said when she walked into Lacey's office a short while later.

"You'll get used to it."

She shook her head and a wealth of sun-streaked brown hair streamed around her head. "I don't think so."

"Believe me, you will." He knew from experience that emotions could be jaded, dulled to the point where only good technique became the most interesting part of the work.

"Was that ever a baby?" she asked, nodding in the general direction of the histology room.

John Lacey picked up the tissue report from Elaine Calder. The tumor was classified as an intrauterine neoplasm. A teratoma.

Tumors or neoplasms were a common occurrence in Pathology. The distinguishing characteristic of the teratoma was the presence of embryological tissue. There was some question whether the structures present were an abortive attempt at twinning, or possibly the teratoma was the result of parthenogenetic development of an ovum. Some of the structures were organized, such as teeth, brain, and mucosa. The examination of the outer surface showed two fairly developed arms and rudimentary legs. The head was conjoined with the thorax and an undifferentiated slit in the anterior region was the only distinguishable facial feature. Tissue consistent with lung, cardiac, muscle, and intestines was present in varying quantities. "Perhaps it was a baby. We don't really know. Something happens to the chromosomal structure between the second to tenth day after conception—at least in intrauterine teratomas. Generally, we see so few of these it is merely a matter of passing interest."

Dr. Julia Young frowned. "It looks like the parts of a baby thrown in a pot and stirred." That was a very apt description. "And we're seeing it more frequently, aren't we? Certainly more than the statistics would indicate."

Dr. Lacey sat back in his chair and thought for a moment. Statistically the overwhelming majority of teratomas in humans occurred at birth or during the first year of life. The development of this particular kind of neoplasm in children and adults had certainly been on the increase, according to the data in the pathology journals. How many had he seen in the last months? Three? Five teratomas? Or was it more like fifteen or twenty?

Composed of at least three germinal layers, most teratomas originated in the genital organs, retroperitoneum, and mediastinum, probably arising from embryonic tissue along the primitive streak and notochord after an escape from the normal governing influences. Left to themselves, they took on the bizarre, jumbled appearance of human tissue without human form. And were they seeing the phenomenon more often? he asked himself silently.

His fingers sought out the small, tender spot on his ribs, and he winced. The sensation jarred his thoughts back to Dr. Young. "I don't know," he said, finally answering her question. "I'll check on that. Perhaps we *are* seeing more neoplasms as a result of environmental pollution—things like that." He knew he sounded evasive. "Did we get tissue cultures from the Calder teratoma?" he asked Julia.

"I'm afraid not. The baby—or whatever it was—died

during the night. It was in formalin before anyone thought to get cultures."

"That's unfortunate, but purely academic, at this point. It's possible the teratoma was a normal fetus that failed to segment. Or maybe it was a multiple fertilization of a single ovum."

"Or parthenogenesis." Dr. Young had done her homework. While a normal ovum had an XY or XX sex chromosome pattern, chromosomal studies of teratomas sometimes showed a configuration of XYXYXXX-YYY sex chromosomes in males and XXXXXXXXX or XXXX, or some variation of such, in females, which led researchers to believe the teratoma was the result of inclusion of many cells into one by some process completely foreign to normal reproductive processes.

Julia Young's color had faded to a putty gray. "I saw one once—it must have been a man with a teratoma. I was twelve, and we were at a carnival. My girlfriend dared me to go in and see the freak show—the tent where they had two-headed dogs and things like that." Her voice weakened. She spoke as if she were twelve years old again. "They had this 'man with no bones.' That's what they called him. It must have been a teratoma—like pudding with eyes and a mouth and hair."

"Most of them don't survive beyond birth," he told her.

"Some of them do. This Calder one did, for a few hours, at least." Julia Young stood and walked to the door. Her thin shoulders looked pinched together, as if she'd been hung out on a clothesline to dry.

"Unfortunately, you're right. Some do." He knew Dr. Young would conquer her aversions and be a very good pathologist. He had graver doubts about himself. Why had it taken a resident to point out the increase in teratomas at Lorimar? He should have noticed that.

Neither Dr. Lacey nor Dr. Young had mentioned the tissue slides from the Calder teratoma. Minute particles of cotton thread had shown up in the mouth area, and starch crystals were present in the lung tissue. John Lacey knew what that meant. Suffocation. But was it possible to murder a tumor by suffocation? He didn't think so. It wasn't a human life as far as he was concerned. Its death was as mournful as breaking an egg in a skillet. But he hadn't mentioned those cotton threads or starch crystals, and he'd thrown away the slides that showed them clearly.

He was too busy to think about theoretical murder. He had the research work in virology that was not going well. They'd just begun the work with interferon when one of his research assistants resigned and took another job. He had to find someone else to take over the work, and soon. Unfortunately, he knew exactly whom he wanted for the position.

When Dr. Young had left the office John Lacey opened the bottom drawer of his gray metal desk. There were old research papers in that drawer, a phone book, two notebooks, and several journals he'd meant to read —and a picture. He turned over the tarnished silver frame and stared down into the face of a woman.

I am such a fool, he thought, nearly saying it out loud. Quickly he turned over the photograph, extracted the hospital phone directory, and began to search for a number.

After an arduous set of tennis and a long, cool shower, Katie Campbell and Phyllis Latimer had lunch at Palermo Country Club, Los Altos's finest.

The club had once been a Jesuit seminary, and consisted of three long, sand-colored stucco buildings clustered around a central courtyard fronted by a great, soaring structure that had once been the sanctuary. The roofs of all the buildings were glazed red tile that shimmered in the sun, and trimmed pines, red geraniums, and beds of snowy alyssum sat in well-tended areas along the walkways of the courtyard. A sauna and cool splash pool were tucked near the west wall of the courtyard and were surrounded by small redwoods. A golf course stretched out beyond the building, out beneath live oaks with their wild arms flung against the sky, and farther, toward the green hills.

In the renovated sanctuary women in a Crayola assortment of tennis wear lunched on cold shrimp in silvered dishes of ice, romaine lettuce salads, zucchini hot dishes with melted Monterey Jack cheese, and thick sandwiches of sliced turkey breast and cilantro. The wine, while unblessed, was of the best vintage and plentiful.

Phyllis sipped her second glass of French Colombard. Her cheeks were livid. "It's a wonder Angie and Vera didn't beat us this morning with your arm on the fritz. That Vera Marker has a fantastic backhand. I mean, really fantastic. I hear she runs six miles a day and can bench-press two hundred and sixty pounds."

Katie tried to listen to Phyllis, but today it was difficult. Usually lunch at the club was a great treat. She could almost feel holy sitting there in that cavernous dining room, decked with maidenhair and asparagus ferns draping their long fronds gently to the tables below like pious fingers from on high. With a bit of imagination she could still catch a hint of monks in rough brown cowls hovering around the high, silent pillars, pillars now artfully disguised as salad, cocktail, and dessert bars. The very walls seemed to be infused with ancient hymns.

"Kate?"

"What?"

"You aren't listening to me at all. You're a million miles away." Phyllis looked pouty. "I'm sitting here chattering away about our tennis games, and you're thinking about something else entirely."

Kate grinned sheepishly. "You were talking about Vera's backhand." Katie took several spoonfuls of the thick lentil soup she'd ordered. It was quite good.

"I was talking about your arm! How is it now? After a hot shower?"

"Better, I think." She rotated her shoulder slightly. "I don't know what happened. I don't remember hurting it, but I must have pulled a muscle." The tennis game had been a misery, in fact. "Maybe you'll have to find a new tennis partner for a few weeks."

Phyllis looked indignant. "Don't be silly. A few days' rest and you'll be good as new."

"I hope you're right."

Phyllis forked a portion of her crab salad, glistening with plump, red cherry tomatoes. It was served with a whole-wheat muffin.

"You'd better be careful about that crab, Phyl," Katie said. "You know seafood is not inspected. I understand some of it is full of salmonella."

Phyllis eyed the crab on her fork. "Really? I hadn't heard that." She laid the fork on the plate. "Let's not talk about food. I want to talk about Elaine." Phyllis drained the wineglass.

"You know what happened to her was a genetic accident," Katie said. "One-in-a-million chance. But I think it's bigger than that. I think we're seeing the evidence of the chemical stew in our air." Katie felt a stab of cold pain streak from her neck down her arm.

Phyllis's skeletal hand fingered the empty wineglass. "If you ask me, I think there's something strange going on at the hospital. When I called Lorimar, I was told Elaine couldn't have any visitors. I sent a card and flowers from MANA. But if you ask me, they're trying to cover something up."

Katie took any criticism of Lorimar personally. "She's undoubtedly upset. You know how much she wanted that baby."

"I heard that baby lived. I know a nurse who works in the nursery at Lorimar. She said they put it in the supply closet. They didn't feed it, and it cried for a long time. And this isn't the first time. There's been other monsters born there."

Katie's annoyance warmed to protective indignation. These environmental issues were striking uncomfortably close to home, especially when Alan was involved. "It wasn't a *baby*, Phyllis. And it wasn't a monster. Alan assisted in Elaine's surgery. He wouldn't have allowed that to happen to a *baby*."

Phyllis shrugged. "This nurse said—"

"That's how ugly rumors get started," Kate interrupted. "I don't think you want to spread an awful story like that. Elaine had a teratoma. Alan told me." She reached for her water glass, and her hand hit the peeled pear in a crystal dish, spilling the pristine fruit onto the white tablecloth. A wet spot spread slowly beneath it. A pain, exotic and definite, shot through her shoulder and neck, nearly taking her breath away. "Ow!" she cried. "That shoulder really hurts."

Phyllis's leathery face creased in a deep frown. "Maybe you'd better have Alan take a look at it. You may have done more than pull a muscle."

Katie took a deep breath and blew it out slowly. "It's okay. It doesn't hurt now—unless I move too fast." She extended the arm slowly this time.

"I'm sorry if I upset you," Phyllis apologized. "I certainly didn't mean to."

Katie shook her head. "I've been upset for days, Phyllis. Dougy's having nosebleeds, Alan doesn't sleep at night—he promised me he'd see someone about the nightmares, but you know what he thinks about psychiatrists! I got talked into buying *two* hamsters who are living in my kitchen—and now this awful thing with Elaine—I don't know . . ." She blinked away unbidden tears. "And then John Lacey called this morning. I didn't tell you before because I wanted some time to think about his offer."

Phyllis's blue eyes narrowed. "Every time I see John he asks about you."

"I can't imagine why," Kate mumbled. "He called to offer me a job—viral research assistant. I almost said yes, but Alan would be furious." She fussed with the white linen napkin in her lap.

"Maybe it's time you went back to work."

Despite the ethereal coolness of the dining room, pastel in the golden light from clerestory windows, Kate felt the beads of perspiration on her face. Once more the pain radiated from neck to shoulder. She gasped.

"What's the matter?" Phyllis asked.

"It's just the shoulder." Her breathing was shallow and desperate. "It's like something's—biting me." Slowly the pain eased.

"You'd better get that checked, and right now. Sounds like a pinched nerve. You want me to drive you to Lorimar?"

"No—no, really. I'm fine. I'll have Alan look at it tonight. I'm sure it's just a muscle cramp—or something." She needed to get home. It was nearly three o'clock already, and she didn't feel up to another one of

Robbie's lectures concerning her neglect of maternal duties. "I think I'll just go home and lie down."

She slid a twenty-dollar bill toward Phyllis. "That'll cover my bill."

"Are you sure you're well enough to drive?"

"Yes, it's only a few miles. I'll be fine."

"Let me know what you decide about the job."

"I will."

"And if you see Elaine, tell her I'm thinking about her."

Katie drove home carefully, keeping her mind on that stretch of 280 North that was also called the Junipero Freeway. It was decked with oleander, blooming with abandon this time of year in bright pink, white, and red blossoms. She passed Lorimar Medical Center, visible off Marr Road. Lorimar was a series of gray buildings without any particular unifying architecture, but the aura of medicine hung over it like an antiseptic sky. Even the grass around Lorimar looked hygienic. She knew the center well from the two years she'd worked there before she married Alan. But today she didn't want to think about the virology lab in the basement. And she didn't want to think about the supply closet where a baby was left to die. She wanted to get home. Home, in the safety of those redwood fences and the sunny kitchen.

Her foot bore down on the accelerator. She mentally inventoried her neck and shoulder, and they seemed fine. The speedometer edged toward sixty-five before Kate heard the whine of a siren behind her. Brilliant red light flashed in the rearview mirror.

"Damn," she swore softly. And she pulled her car off to the shoulder. "This is *all* I need."

* * *

Alan carefully probed her neck and shoulder muscles, and Katie winced once.

"I think it's a pulled muscle, but I can't tell for sure without an X ray," he said. "Stop over at the hospital tomorrow and we'll get a look at it."

Katie gingerly slid back into her pink robe. "I'm going to Lorimar tomorrow anyway to see Elaine."

"Elaine Calder? She went home."

"She did? Then she's feeling better? Phyllis said the nurse told her Elaine couldn't have visitors."

Alan fidgeted with his journal. "She checked out against medical advice—but her husband said he had a private nurse at home for her."

"Well, I'll see her at home then. And if I have time I'll stop by Lorimar for that X ray."

Alan laughed softly and shook his head. "Some patient you are . . . 'if you have time'?"

"It only hurts if I move fast," she explained.

"Well, let's check that out . . . only I'll make the fast moves, if that's okay with you." He reached for her and she grinned and settled into bed beside him.

That night Alan dreamed of a dark field, stubbled with grass and the rotting carcasses of wild animals. At every step he held his breath. His feet sank through the mushy rib cages of the bodies that littered the grass. His heart clawed at his rib cage as he followed a dreadful sound across the field. A child joined him. A child dressed in a clown suit with a purple, ruffled collar. Beckoning him forward, the child led him toward a deep hole in the earth. It looked like the ground had collapsed, or perhaps imploded on itself and then sunk. Even the rocks were screaming.

Alan covered his ears, but that only intensified the wailing, wave after wave of mindless, monotone screeching from the pit. He knelt and looked deep into the hole.

The costumed child also peered over the edge. Something was down there, caught in the rubble. Something terrifying and dangerous. The child crept closer and slipped. Alan reached out to catch the boy, but the blue, red, and purple clown suit came away in his hand.

"Don't," he cried in his sleep.

But the body of the child fluttered downward. Alan grabbed for him. The earth shuddered, like a prehistoric beast waking far below. And Alan fell, too. Pitching forward, he plummeted into thin, reeking air. His own cries blended in a terrible discord with the howling animal and the frightened mewling of the child.

He woke, every muscle taut, his chest heaving helplessly. The darkness of the room threatened to suffocate him.

"Alan?"

He'd awakened Kate.

"Are you all right? Was it another dream?" Her voice was blurred with sleep.

He wished she wouldn't wake up. He couldn't explain the dreams to her. He didn't want to try. "Go back to sleep, Katie." He was shivering, but the coldness came from inside.

"Please, Alan," she begged, "do something about the dreams—before they—"

What? he wondered. What will dreams do? "I will," he whispered into her hair, gathering her close to him and breathing in her sweetly fragrant scent. "I promise you. I will."

He closed his eyes, and the sound returned, that high discordant sound. A near scream, but not a scream. He remembered the set of bagpipes Gordon Campbell had bought. Silver and African blackwood, and an elk-hide bag that smelled sickly sweet of leather and honey. Gordon Campbell had tried to play, but the sound was terrible. Wretched bleats and piercing wails. Was that the sound in his dreams? he wondered sleepily. Just the awful sounds of an untutored bagpiper who happened to be his father?

Sleep folded him deep and safely away from any further thoughts. Alan and Katie slept entwined until dawn.

6

 Mountain View, California, lay to the northeast of Los Altos. Mountain View was a community unprepared for the great influx of residents during the sixties and seventies, and now sat in the sprawling Santa Clara Valley like a mother startled or possibly puzzled by the unexpected growth and number of her offspring.

Kate drove to Mountain View in fifteen minutes. Her shoulder seemed to be fine, and driving gave her a bit of time alone to think. John Lacey wanted her back at the lab at Lorimar. But could she submerge herself again in the white world of viral cultures and electron microscopes? She didn't know. She hadn't even discussed it with Alan. She had to find the right moment.

Kate missed the turnoff at Kilkenny Road to Albany Avenue where the apartments stood in low beige rows, all identical with brown shutters and hipped, shingled roofs. After several trips around the apartment development she found the address. She'd been there only once before, for a MANA meeting. Elaine Calder's apartment was part of a smaller complex, and Kate felt immediately grateful.

The central courtyard of La Hacienda Apartments looked like a motel. A teacup swimming pool, three or four tattered yellow plastic lawn chairs, and redwood tubs of anemic plants dotted the grassy circle.

She found number thirty-two easily and knocked. She'd called the apartment that morning, but there was no answer. Where was that private nurse? Could Elaine reach the phone? Surely she wasn't alone in the apartment.

Kate knocked again, harder this time.

"Can I help you, lady?" a man asked behind her. "I'm Vern Gannon, the manager. You here to see the apartment?"

Kate turned to a small, wiry man in blue jeans and a khaki shirt. He seemed to be crouched in his clothing.

"I'm looking for Elaine Calder."

"Moved, I think. Rent's paid till the end of the month." He jammed his hands deep in his pockets.

"When did they move?"

"Couple of days ago. She a friend of yours?"

Kate turned away from him and checked the number thirty-two on the door again. "Yes." How could a woman four days out of abdominal surgery move from her apartment? And why didn't they have the phone disconnected? "Where did they go?"

"Don't know. They didn't say. The husband packed up and moved out some of the stuff. Left a lot. People are funny, you know." He spoke in a low monotone. His narrow eyes scanned Kate. "You wanta see the apartment, or what? Won't be available till June, of course."

Without waiting for an answer he sidled past her and stuck a key in the door lock. Kate followed him inside. The Calder apartment was a tumble of newspapers, odds and ends of dishes on the kitchen counter, a chair badly in need of reupholstering . . .

"They certainly did move," she said after a quick look around.

"Except for this mess," Gannon told her, "they were good tenants. Paid the rent on time. That's what I call a good tenant."

Kate found herself nodding at Gannon and edging toward the door. "I'm sure."

"Not like some of them!" the apartment manager continued. "I got a couple of them I ain't even *seen* for a month or two. One old lady slides a check under the door if I bang on it loud enough and threaten to call the cops." He followed Kate to the door. "You know what the cops do? Nuthin'! Ab-so-lutely nuthin'!"

Once outside Katie took a deep breath. "You don't know where the Calders moved? You're sure they didn't mention it?"

"No idea. Sorry."

"Maybe some of the neighbors might know," Kate suggested.

"I doubt that. The Calders weren't the friendly sort, if you know what I mean. You can talk to Mrs. Rubins— widow lady in number thirty-four."

"Do you mind if I try?"

"Not a bit, lady."

Kate knocked gently on the door of number thirty-four. There was no sound from within the apartment. After several repeated raps, Kate glanced over her shoulder at Vern Gannon.

"She put a rent check in the mailbox a couple days ago. Funny she don't answer." He fished for his keys hanging on the wide leather belt around his waist.

Before he unlocked the apartment, he hammered with his fist on the painted door. "Mrs. Rubins?" he called. "You in there? It's Vern. I got a lady here wants to talk to you. Mrs. Rubins?"

"Maybe she's out," Kate offered uncomfortably. "It's all right, I—"

"She ain't never out." He unlocked the door and swung it open.

The rush of a smell so putrid made Kate stumble back. It reeked of rotting potatoes, or wet walnuts, slightly sweet . . .

"Goddamn," Gannon swore. "That's the worst smell I ever—"

The apartment was dark, but in the eerie dimness a figure lay huddled on the floor.

"Mrs. Rubins?" Gannon crept over to the woman cautiously. "Hey—are you okay?"

Kate steadied herself by holding on to the door frame. She was unable to move or breathe. The smell of death was as heavy as lead. And yet she couldn't tear herself away.

Vern Gannon switched on a floor lamp, spotlighting the body. He rolled Mrs. Rubins over. Her arms flapped at her sides. Her head lolled on the gold carpet.

"Oh, shit!" Vern said. "I gotta call the cops."

She wore a green velour robe with food stains on the lapels. One pink slipper was on her foot. The other lay several feet away. On her emaciated ring finger a dulled gold wedding band dangled.

The face was purplish gray, the swollen tongue of the woman protruded. Her neck bulged. Broken capillaries webbed the skin of her face. Kate knew enough to guess that Mrs. Rubins had strangled. Certain nausea threatened Katie. Her hands began to shake.

"Will you look at that?" Gannon's eyes were incredulous. "You ever seen anything like that?"

Katie crept closer. Gannon pointed to the woman's

mouth. It wasn't a tongue that jutted from the gaped lips. It was a cheesy mass of hair. And something else.

"What is that?" Gannon's voice was choked.

Two small fingers of a hand were just barely visible protruding from the swollen mass in her mouth. Not just a mass, Katie knew. She began to shake uncontrollably. It was a teratoma. Kate dashed for the kitchen sink, reaching it in time to vomit miserably.

"Are those fingers?" Gannon crept closer to the body of Mrs. Rubins. "I'll be damned! Growing right outta her mouth!"

"Why didn't she go to a doctor?" she finally asked Vern Gannon. She ran water in the sink and took some small comfort from the fact that at least one aspect of the apartment functioned as expected, even if it was only the plumbing. "Maybe they could have done something."

Katie leaned heavily against the kitchen counter. Obviously Mrs. Rubins was not poor. The kitchen had a dishwasher and microwave oven, there was a ripening cantaloupe and pear apples in a crystal fruit bowl, and a fancy food processor that actually looked used.

"Guess she couldn't eat much, huh," Gannon observed after calling the police. He picked up a pear apple and bit through the yellow-green peel. Juice dripped down his hand. "Guess it'd be pretty hard to swallow with somethin' like that in your mouth."

Katie gagged. She refused to think about Mrs. Rubins trying to eat.

Gannon turned the half-eaten apple pear over in his hand and studied it closely. "You think it might be catching? Whatever she had?"

Kate shook her head. "No, it's a tumor. That's not contagious."

He nodded, apparently reassured, and took another

hearty bite. "This is a little overripe . . . you sure it's a tumor?" He dumped the core in a trash bag by the sink.

They heard a police siren screaming in the distance. Gannon wiped his hands on his trousers. "Well, I gotta go help those cops find the apartment. You better stay here. They might want to ask you a couple questions."

Katie waited outside, leaning against the rough brick wall of the apartment complex. This is a nightmare, she said to herself, over and over. This isn't happening.

Later that morning Katie parked in the lot near the east wing of Lorimar Medical Center. Numb and frightened, she studied her face in the small rearview mirror. She was pale, dreadfully pale.

Alan would still be in surgery, but it wasn't Alan she'd come to see. Instinctively she used the back door of the east wing that led down a flight of stairs to the laboratory and Pathology.

Little had changed in the ten years since she'd worked there. The plants all looked pallid, the walls were that same awful shade of yellow . . . had it really been ten years?

"I'm Kate Campbell," she said to one of the secretaries in the Pathology office. "I'd like to speak to Dr. Lacey."

The woman turned slowly in her chair and glanced at John Lacey's office. "He's not in his office at the moment. Do you have an appointment?"

"I don't—but could you page him? I'd like to talk to him."

"Is this about a job?" The secretary scrutinized her warily.

Katie was on the verge of tears and another bout of nausea. "I'm Mrs. Alan Campbell—my husband is a surgeon here at Lorimar." She hated pulling rank, but it seemed expedient at the moment. "And—"

John Lacey sauntered into the Path office. "Katie!" He reached out for her and then stopped, self-consciously. "Are you all right? You look like you've seen a ghost."

Kate managed a smile and extended her hand politely to John, primarily for the sake of the sullen secretary. "I came to talk to you—about that job."

"I hope you're going to take it. We really need you here again."

He gently steered her out of the Pathology office into his own cubicle. Kate felt the stares of the secretaries.

"You want a cup of coffee? Tea?"

"No—nothing—I—" She struggled with the tears. "I'm sorry—I don't know what's come over me—something awful happened this morning."

"Katie," he said soothingly, "just tell me what's wrong."

She grabbed several tissues from the box on his desk and dabbed at her eyes. "It's nothing, John. I cry when I'm upset—and this morning I saw a woman. She'd died —of a tumor. It was horrible."

John Lacey leaned forward in his chair, sheltering her from the straying gazes of the Path secretaries.

"A tumor in her mouth—a teratoma," Kate continued, letting the words rush on. "It killed her. And there were hands. And hair. Suffocated her. I don't—" A sob interrupted her voice.

He let her cry, handing her fresh tissues every few minutes and moving the wastebasket within easy range. When she finally looked up his face seemed even more gaunt.

"You looked pretty frightened when you came in here," he said. "You feel better now?"

Katie nodded. "I *did* come to talk to you about the job, actually. But this woman this morning—upset me." She sniffed loudly and sat up straight in the chair. "I'm sorry. I'm okay now."

"Couldn't have been better timed," he said. "We're seeing an enormous increase in teratogenic neoplasms. Almost pandemic in this area. Part of the research we're doing is with the cause of this tumor. It is my suspicion —only a suspicion, mind you—that the increase in teratomas and dermoids may be due to a virus. So far the cultures have been negative, but we're close to something, Katie. We're very close to understanding how a virus upsets the genetic patterning of the cell."

She had managed to compose herself, keeping her attention riveted on the technological theories and the cool, unemotional surroundings of John Lacey's office.

"I'll take the job," she said suddenly, surprising herself.

"What?" A smile brightened his face. "You will?"

"Yes. It's time I got back to work." She'd have to break the news to Alan. And the boys. Maybe Amanda could come four days a week instead of two . . . But it was Alan's reaction she was really worried about.

"Good, Kate. Stop over at Personnel and fill out the forms. Can you start next Monday?"

Katie stood. Her shoulder and neck ached, and she remembered she was supposed to get that X ray. "Give me a couple of weeks to get things arranged," she said. "I'll let you know. You see, I haven't told Alan yet."

"Well, it'll be nice to have you back at Lorimar— whenever that is," he added as she left the office.

Katie went directly home. She'd get the X ray later, she decided. Right now she needed a long soak in the tub and a nap to get herself together before the boys came home from school.

* * *

Dr. Viktor Straub was a well-known psychiatrist who had pioneered an existential therapy based on the moment in life when an individual becomes aware of good and evil. He liked to call the moment an "omega" point, or the loss of an innocence that could never be recovered and on which all decisions and delusions were predicated. That was as much as Alan Campbell knew when he managed to find Dr. Straub's office in San Francisco on Norwich Street, overlooking the moody bay. Alan was ten minutes late for the appointment because he had to park on the street and walk to the office.

Alan had debated about seeing Dr. Straub. That part of Alan Campbell that was a scientist scoffed at psychological therapy, even though he had seen clearly positive results in some of his patients whom he recommended for therapy. The part of Alan that was a healer, a medicine man, was stronger than the scientist. If talking to someone would help, Alan was willing to try it.

Straub's office was a suite on the first floor of a lovely old Victorian house. The door stood ajar and Alan looked in. Dr. Viktor Straub sat at a huge rolltop desk polished to a soft gleam. He swiveled in his chair and studied Alan mildly.

"Dr. Campbell?" he asked. His accent was German.

"Yes." Alan eased himself through the door and into the room, touched with late afternoon sun through many narrow windows.

Dr. Straub stood. He was a huge man, one of the giants of the race, standing at least six feet four or five and weighing well over three hundred pounds, Alan guessed. The doctor's hair was silvered and curly, frosting his head with somewhat unruly swirls. He was about fifty-five years old. But Alan was more struck by the psychiatrist's face, a face roughened and exquisitely gentle at the same time. It was not a new observation for Alan. Those men and women who worked with schizophrenics, in particular, often seemed to take on an "otherworldliness," a rare and absorbing compassion.

Dr. Viktor Straub filled up the room, existed in every corner, on every shelf of the library that lined two walls of the office, in the lush greenery at the windows and in the many fine paintings on the wall.

"Sit down, won't you?" Dr. Straub indicated one of the two chairs, tapestried in black with multicolored silk threads in an inscrutable pattern.

Alan felt almost too tired to be awed by the famous psychiatrist. "I appreciate you taking the time to see me."

Viktor Straub lit a finely carved meerschaum pipe. Ribbons of smoke coiled over his head. He did not ask Alan if he minded the smoke. "I see very few patients these days. Mainly, I teach. But I understand that you are in a difficult position." He struck another match and relit the pipe. "It's not possible for you to talk to a colleague. And you have bad dreams. Correct me if I'm wrong."

"I'm here because my wife insisted I talk to someone. I checked around, and you come with unqualified recommendations." Alan tucked his tie deep inside the gray vest.

"On the contrary," Straub said evenly, "you are the one who is coming here. My qualifications are not in question."

"No—no, of course not—I only meant that—"

"I know what you meant."

Alan felt a flush of irritation with the psychiatrist. "If it's too much trouble I'm sure I can find someone else." He stood up abruptly. He wasn't used to being insulted.

He'd driven an hour in heavy traffic to get there. And he hadn't slept well the night before.

Viktor Straub removed the pipe from between his teeth. "My dear fellow, please sit down." His voice was level and even slightly amused. "I assure you it is no trouble. I only tell you that I teach because it will affect our appointments from time to time. Next month I must be in New York for ten days. And in Zurich the following month. I want you to understand."

Alan remained standing, as awkward as an errant schoolboy in front of the principal. Or before his father. Straub nodded at the chair, indicating that Alan should definitely sit down. He sat down.

"Now, before you jump up and run out of the office, Doctor, do you or do you not have bad dreams?"

Talking to Viktor Straub was a little like cozying up to a bulldozer. "Sometimes," he answered. "They aren't really dreams. Or I don't remember them after I'm awake."

"Nothing?" Straub probed. "You remember nothing of the dreams?"

"A child in a clown costume . . . and a well . . . or something."

"How do you know they are *bad* dreams?"

"I remember a sound." He felt the sweat start.

"What kind of sound?"

"Someone screaming."

It was after nine by the time Alan arrived home that night. Katie was curled up with a book on the sofa, and the boys were in bed. The house smelled of lemon furniture polish, chicken stew, and cold wood ash all blended together in some kind of delicate vapor that reminded Alan of that old farmhouse in Illinois, and the days of rushing home, buzzy with hunger, after school.

"Hi, Katie." He kissed her lightly. "How's it going?"

"Fine." She closed her book. "The boys went to bed ten minutes ago. I told them you'd tuck them in when you came home."

Alan wound his way through the darkened living room and down the hall to the boys' rooms. Robbie, tousled and toasty, lay askew in his bed, the soft blue blanket threaded in and out of his sturdy legs. He mumbled something incomprehensible.

"Shh," Alan whispered, straightening the blanket and tucking it around the boy. "Go to sleep."

In Doug's room he touched his son's dark hair, not enough to awaken him. Doug slept like the dead. Even when he was a baby Alan remembered all the nights he and Katie had tiptoed into the room to check his breathing. Doug rarely moved when he slept. It was unnerving. It still was, a bit.

Alan rejoined Katie in the family room, making a short stop at the bar for a Scotch and water. "I saw Dr. Viktor Straub tonight. In San Francisco."

"Dr. Straub? Who's he?"

Alan sank into a recliner chair and sipped his Scotch. It rekindled that familiar fire in his stomach, spreading its warmth out toward his toes and fingertips. He held the lead crystal glass to the lamplight. Prismatic rainbows shone through the leaded glass. "He's a psychiatrist. A very good one. He says I should stop drugging myself to sleep. Only two ounces of Scotch a day."

Katie watched him silently.

"Straub survived the Nazi concentration camps. They say he never got over being starved. Food seems to be his one obsession. The man is absolutely obese." Alan finished his drink in one long, cool gulp.

"What did he say about the dreams?"

"Nothing."

"Nothing?"

"We talked about other things. I'm not even sure I remember exactly what—but he didn't say much about the dreams."

"Are you going to see him again?" Kate heard the strain in her voice. Had she expected miracles from one visit to a psychiatrist?

"A couple times a week. We'll see how it goes."

Katie nodded. Her eyelids felt heavy.

"Kate? Are you all right?"

"Just tired."

"I left an order in X ray for you, but they told me you didn't come in today."

"I guess it slipped my mind, Alan—some other things happened—" She traced the edges of the textbook in her lap. "I was reviewing my virology tonight. John Lacey called and offered me a job at Lorimar—research assistant."

Alan leaned his head back in the chair and laughed softly. "That's just like John. He never gives up."

"Whatever do you mean?" she snapped.

"John Lacey has never recovered from the fact that you married me instead of him." He frowned suddenly. "You didn't accept the job, did you?"

"As a matter of fact, I did. It's a good job. I need to get back to work."

"You took it without talking to me first?" Alan complained. Alan slammed the crystal tumbler on the coffee table. Shards of glass shot off in several directions.

Katie opened her mouth to say something and decided to remain silent. Alan dashed to the closet and grabbed a broom and dustbin. He cleaned up the breakage in silence, picking slivers of glass from the carpet.

"Are you coming to bed?" he asked.

Katie laid the virology book back on the shelf. "Yes, I'm coming."

He didn't shower that night. He liked the faintest odor of smoke from Dr. Straub's pipe on his body, and that night the sex was long and arduous.

He heard Kate's sharp, surprised breaths. "Alan—please—don't—" she moaned. Or begged.

He held on to her, forcing his greedy body on her. He needed something. Something powerful. Something she could give him. And, finally, he rolled away from her, spent, and ready for sleep. He lay on his back. Katie had curled herself beside him, but without touching him. He reached over and turned off the lamp.

Alan remained very still, willing himself into the void of dreamless sleep. He listened to Kate's breathing. It was quick and uneven. "Honey?"

She didn't answer. He knew she wasn't sleeping. Was she crying? "Katie, I'm sorry."

He shivered, even though the room was warm. She didn't know what it was like. She had the boys, he thought. She had her friends, her house, and now a job. All he had was her and his work. And work was slowly becoming a waking nightmare.

He heard her breathing deepen. The line of her shoulder softened in the moonlight creeping through the shutter. She was sleeping. It was hours before he sank into some form of numbed oblivion.

7

 Jennifer Wynn was twelve years old on Saturday, June sixth, and her parents, Dan and Amy Wynn, bought her the new ten-speed bike she'd wanted for two years.

"It'll be good for her," Amy had argued with Dan for three weeks before the birthday. "Have you noticed how she walks lately? She hunches up her shoulders and kind of leans to one side. The most exercise that child gets is turning up the volume on the television set and opening the microwave oven door."

Dan Wynn was objecting to the price tag on the bike, not the exercise habits of his daughter. "Her old bike is still in pretty good shape. I don't see why she needs a four-hundred-dollar ten-speed. From France, for heaven's sake."

"All the kids have them," Amy persisted. "And there are plenty of hills in Los Altos. When was the last time you tried to get up San Sebastian Road on a three-speed?"

Dan knew she was right. More right about Jennifer

–than about San Sebastian Road. The child had gone from being an eleven-year-old charmer with long black braids and red hair ribbons to a sulky twelve-year-old who slouched around the house wearing frayed, bulky sweatshirts and letting her hair hang down her back in long, greasy strings. After school and on weekends she seemed to gravitate between the television set and the kitchen, where she dined exclusively on quick pizzas, fifteen-second hot dogs, and chocolate ice cream.

"I think Jenny's self-conscious," Amy told Dan. "About her development. Her breasts . . . it just seemed to happen so fast with her. The bike will help. She'll get out with her friends again."

So they purchased the bicycle, a powder-blue French racing model, and Jennifer was thrilled that Saturday morning.

"Oh, thank you," she chirped. "It's just what I wanted."

Dan saw once more the sparkle in her wide, dark eyes, and the return of a jaunty tilt to her head. Four hundred sixteen dollars for the bike was probably worth it, he consoled himself.

Jenny straddled the bike and crouched low over the handlebars. "It's perfect." She wore an old blue sweatshirt, blue jeans faded to the color of ice water, and her blue and white Nikes.

"Keep your shoulders straight," Dan told her. "Otherwise it's too hard to raise your head."

"Raising my head increases wind resistance," Jenny objected.

Dan Wynn placed one hand gently on his daughter's shoulder and the other hand on her back. He pulled her shoulder straight and then let go of the girl so fast it even surprised him. He looked at his hands.

"I get it," Jenny said. She had her feet in the stirrup

pedals and shot down the long concrete driveway before Dan could stop her.

"Jennifer!" he called, but she didn't stop. Or she didn't hear him call. "I'll get the car."

"Dan?" Amy had been admiring the two of them, her dark, handsome husband and the child who looked so like him. And then she'd seen his face change from pleasure to a kind of agony. "What's wrong?"

"I'm not sure. I felt something—on her back. There's something wrong with Jenny."

They saw her flying down the long drive, past the stand of Monterey pines and live oaks. Dan had to squint against the sun, so he could never be sure of what exactly happened next. It was like one of those stunt acts on TV.

She must have been doing forty miles an hour by the time she hit the low curve that led out of the driveway to San Sebastian Road, but *she* didn't curve. The road did. Leaning wildly to one side, she continued in a straight line, and the bike wobbled off in the opposite direction. Her body skidded and bumped to a stop in the middle of the road.

"Oh, my God," Dan cried, and set off on foot, running like he never dreamed he could. He never completed the three-mile course at Madrone Hills Park without feeling he was going to die on the spot, but the moment he saw Jenny on the road, he ran like an Olympic sprinter.

Jennifer Wynn didn't move. Gravel, darkened by blood, was ground into one side of her face and head. Her eyes were closed. Dan moved her just enough to get her out of the way of any oncoming cars.

"Jenny," he whispered. "Hang on. Everything's going to be all right." And once more he touched the place on her back, a bulge he was certain shouldn't be there.

Now it felt mushy. No wonder she wore those loose shirts. Dan Wynn could have kicked himself. Why hadn't he noticed before? Why hadn't he asked her if she was okay? Or Amy? And maybe that's why Jennifer had become so moody lately. Maybe she was in pain. Maybe for a long time now.

Amy Wynn, tear-stricken and pale, hurried down the road. She brought a pink blanket. "I called 911," she panted.

It took ten minutes for the red and white ambulance to arrive, lights and sirens jangling the serenity of the warm spring day. Jenny's breath came in short gulps. Her shirt had ripped away when she hit the rough pavement, leaving her arms bare. Bright red weals crept up her neck and face, spreading like hives.

"What is that?" one of the paramedics asked. "She allergic to something?"

Jennifer Wynn trembled violently despite the blanket and the eighty-three-degree temperature that day.

"She fell off her bike," Dan explained as the paramedics gently slid her to a stretcher.

"Which hospital?" Dan asked.

"Lorimar."

The eight miles to Lorimar Medical Center took forever. Dan raced back up the drive and climbed into the Wynns' station wagon. Amy rode with Jennifer, and Dan followed the streaking ambulance as best he could, but he was blocks behind by the time they hit 280 North. He could hear the siren wailing farther and farther in the distance, and never in his life had he been more frightened.

By the time Alan Campbell saw Jennifer Wynn, two hours and twenty minutes after she'd been brought into

Lorimar wrapped in a pink blanket, the girl was stabilized and on a kidney dialysis unit.

"Catastrophic renal failure," the attending pediatrician, Dr. Lea Beaumont, explained, reading from the admitting notes. "A temporal-parietal concussion and internal bleeding. She fell off her bicycle, but it is unlikely that the fall produced this kind of kidney trauma."

Alan and Dr. Beaumont turned Jennifer Wynn's body over slightly. Her entire back, from shoulders to thighs, was a mass of deep purple bruises.

"You think it was child abuse?" Alan asked.

"No, I don't think so." The pediatrician set up a row of X-ray films on a light box mounted on the wall. "We found a mass on her lower back on admit. It's hard to detect now because of all the swelling and bleeding. But the X rays show bone fragments—here—and here." She pointed to the spots on the film. "One of them looks like a rib cage, Alan. It's the most puzzling thing I have ever seen in my life."

It was true, Alan saw as he studied the X rays. A small series of bone fragments were amazingly similar to the arrangement of the human rib cage.

"That's why we called you in."

"It might just be bone fragments caused by the accident," Alan said, thinking out loud.

"Yes, it could be, but there's more. Her blood type is A positive. And she has an immune Anti-B antibody and positive direct Coombs, although, according to the parents, she has never received a blood transfusion."

"That's impossible." Alan picked up Jennifer's chart. "She must have received type B blood products of some sort." The way an immune antibody formed was by introduction of an antigen, in this case a blood product that was type A1.

"She didn't get any blood in the ER by mistake?"

Alan asked quietly. It was not a question he wanted to ask.

"No—no chance. She came in with urticaria, elevated blood pressure, fever, dyspnea, and kidney failure. Whatever she got was well into this immune response before she arrived in the Emergency Room."

"In the ambulance? Could she have received any blood products in the ambulance?" Alan asked Dr. Beaumont.

"They don't carry blood."

Alan scanned the notes again. "You did do a pregnancy test . . ." Jennifer Wynn was twelve, and she looked like a pretty little girl, though it was difficult to say for sure at the moment.

"Yes, it was negative." The pediatrician was staring at him anxiously. The case of Jennifer Wynn was an intricate tangle of facts and speculation.

Alan had to come up with some answers. And fast. Jennifer Wynn was looking worse by the minute.

Dan and Amy Wynn waited first in the Emergency Room, and then they were told Jenny would be going to the Pediatric Intensive Care Unit on the fourth floor. So they waited there.

"Do you want a cup of coffee?" Dan asked Amy.

She sat staring straight ahead. Her hands were knotted in her lap. "She was so pretty. Have you ever seen a prettier child?" Amy Wynn's eyes were glazed. Her voice was flat. "I can't go home and see that chocolate cake she and I baked for her birthday still sitting there on the table. You know how she liked to bake things—I can't go home—without her—"

Dan comforted her as best he could. "Jennifer is going to be all right. Kids fall off their bikes every day. And you have to stop talking like this."

Her gaze shifted slowly to him. She could have been talking to a complete stranger. "She can make a better chocolate cake than I can. It really is better."

"Please don't worry, Amy," Dan soothed her. "It's going to be all right."

Alan Campbell took the large folder of X rays along when he went to the waiting room on 4 West so he could talk to the Wynns. It was important to explain to them what was happening to their daughter, and that was going to be difficult, since Alan, Dr. Beaumont, and the rest of the staff at Lorimar didn't know exactly what had occurred inside the twelve-year-old. What Alan knew for sure was that Jennifer needed to be in the operating room soon.

Within moments of entering the Pediatric waiting room it was clear to Alan that he had to convince Dan Wynn of Jennifer's dire circumstances. Mrs. Wynn sat numbed with shock. Alan wasn't sure she heard much of what he said.

"How is Jenny?" Dan asked immediately.

"She's stable, at the moment. We have her on kidney dialysis. That will take about two more hours."

Alan sat down in a chair across from the Wynns. Amy Wynn's eyes followed his movements like a panning camera. "I know how worried you are about your daughter. I want to assure you we are doing everything possible for her."

Amy Wynn blinked.

"I'll tell you as much as we know at this point and the treatment proposed." He fished out several of Jennifer's X rays and taped them up on the window. It was a poor substitute for a light box. "We're finding bone fragments just behind the kidneys—I don't know if you can see these small white areas." Alan traced several of the areas. "They may be slivers from the iliac crest—it's hard to tell. And here we can see the outline of one kidney. That's very good news. We were afraid she might have ruptured both kidneys." He let the information sink in for a moment. "You saw the accident—was she hit by a car, or did she fall off the bicycle?"

"She fell—the road curves, and she just kept going straight—" Dan told him. "Did you notice that lump on her back?"

"A mass was noted by the admitting physician—but she has extensive bruising along one side of her back."

"I put my hand there—on her back," Dan said. "And it felt strange. Like a lump, only softer. I hadn't noticed it before. She always wore those sweatshirts—I just hadn't noticed it before." There were tears in his eyes.

Alan glanced at Amy. She sat very straight. "Mrs. Wynn, had you noticed anything unusual about Jennifer lately? Had you noticed the lump on her back?"

She spoke slowly, like a windup toy. "She walks strange—lopsided. I tell her to stand up straight. But she always leans to one side. They're awkward at twelve. We shouldn't have given her that bicycle."

"Amy—" Dan Wynn's voice cracked.

"It's all right," Alan told him. "We don't feel the accident is the sole cause of Jennifer's problems, Mrs. Wynn. We think there's something else, and whatever you can tell us might help."

Amy Wynn nodded mechanically. "She walks strange. That's all."

Alan rubbed the side of his nose thoughtfully. All day he'd regretted that this was his weekend on call for surgery. "Is it possible she was pregnant?" He tried to make the question sound routine.

Dan Wynn shot him a terrible scowl. "At twelve?

Jenny didn't even date. Why would you ask a question like that?"

Alan didn't really blame him for his defensiveness. "I'm sorry I have to ask. Jennifer has an antibody that is produced by exposure to incompatible blood products. That exposure could occur during a pregnancy."

"She wasn't pregnant," Amy whispered. Large tears stood in her blue eyes.

"We'll have Jennifer in surgery by three," Alan told them gently. "We'll know a great deal more when we can get a look at what's going on inside her. You can wait here if you'd like. Just let the desk nurse know where you are."

Dan Wynn extended his large hand to Alan. "Thank you, Doctor."

And Alan shook the father's hand and even smiled a little, although there wasn't much to smile about.

"Shit!" Alan Campbell's hand clenched a retractor. He could have counted the bones in his hand through the latex glove, the way those metatarsals were outlined around the surgical instrument. He ripped the white mask away from his face and felt a cool rush of air against his skin. It was ten minutes before five.

Dr. Noel Kastler, the anesthesiologist, slowly removed the black plastic mask from the child's face. He did not look up. He let his own surgical mask drop from his face.

Dr. Michael Graham had assisted in the surgery. "It wasn't your fault," he said. "You did a brilliant job, Alan."

"She's dead anyway," he said. "She shouldn't be dead, not from something like that." He took a very deep breath. He was afraid he might vomit. That hadn't happened since his internship. The first radical bowel he'd seen sent him crashing out of the OR and straight to the sink. "How am I going to tell the parents?"

Dr. Kastler nodded. "Alan, she went into cardiac arrest. There was nothing more you could do."

Alan picked up the stainless-steel pan full of blood and tissue—a human soup. "She died of this! It killed her."

The scrub nurse backed away from Alan. Her brown eyes widened with uncertainty.

Alan scooped up the dripping tissue from the pan. Blood and bits of bone splattered to the floor. In his hand he held the shattered mass extracted from Jennifer Wynn's twelve-year-old body. It could have been human. And most certainly was not. "Look at this!" he demanded.

The scrub nurse backed up farther.

"It's a teratoma. And it just killed that child. Its blood type was different from hers—don't you find that extraordinary?"

"Of course we do," Dr. Graham assured him warily.

"And this isn't the first patient we've had with these—these killer tumors. Am I right?"

"Alan," Dr. Graham said gently, stepping between Alan and the frightened nurse. "Calm down. It's okay."

Alan saw Noel Kastler circling around behind him. "No," he said, "it isn't okay." They thought he was crazy, he knew. He slapped the tissue back in the pan. Blood spurted halfway up his forearm.

"We'll get Dr. Beaumont to talk to the parents—you don't have to do that." Noel Kastler reached out for Alan, who averted his grasp.

Good, Alan thought. Let Beaumont explain to the Wynns that their daughter died of cardiac arrest in surgery. Beaumont could assure them they'd done everything possible. Alan slammed through the doors of the operating room to the locker area.

The teratoma inside Jennifer Wynn had developed adjacent to the left kidney. When it burst, B positive blood had spilled from the dense hematopoietic tissues of the neoplasm into the bloodstream of the girl, causing the formation of an Anti-B immune antibody.

Alan stripped off his greens and turned on the shower. What Dr. Beaumont wouldn't be able to tell the parents was *why* this had happened. Why the teratoma had grown inside the too young body, eating away at her for months. Before it ruptured and killed her.

Alan stood in the hot shower a long time, letting the water run over his head and shoulders, drumming away the thoughts, pounding out the memory of Jennifer Wynn. Noel Kastler was sitting in the locker room when Alan emerged, naked and dripping. Kastler threw him a towel.

"You all right?" he asked. He didn't look at Alan.

"I'm all right."

"You know Phil Morrisey's contacted CDC about these tumors," Kastler said. Philip Morrisey was chief of staff at Lorimar.

Alan mopped himself off and listened to Kastler. "So?"

"*So,* they will be able to figure out what's causing them, I'm sure. It's not just here, Alan. We're not the only ones seeing this epidemic, you know. The cases in southern California are just as high."

"I know—I've seen some of the data . . . but I've got a son just about the age of that little girl we operated on—"

Kastler nodded. "I know. Every time my kid sneezes I suspect he has a nasopharyngeal tumor. And then the nurse on 5 West . . ."

Alan looked up slowly. "What nurse?"

"I can't remember her name—I guess she complained of shortness of breath—she collapsed and died before they could do anything for her."

"A heart attack?"

"No—she had a tumor. Attached to the thymus and lungs . . . a bad way to go."

"At least she wasn't only twelve years old."

"It wasn't the first time," Alan told Dr. Viktor Straub the following week. They sat in the cool, dark office Thursday evening. While the Santa Clara Valley baked in a sticky heat, quickly browning the hills and drying up the wild California poppies that flourished in the fields, San Francisco was foggy and temperate. Alan leaned back in the chair and stared at the ceiling.

"Ten years ago I lost a patient because of a tera—toma." His tongue stumbled over the word. "An infant. I'll never forget his name. Terry Cox."

Dr. Straub was an unmoving hulk on the other side of the room. He sounded bored. "What about Terry Cox?"

"He was born with a buccal teratoma. I operated on him when he was two days old—but—"

"But what?"

Alan listened to the sound of his own breathing in the quiet room. "There were questions about the surgery. Anesthesia is very difficult with a two-day-old infant. And—there was some question about whether we operated on a child or on a tumor. To this day, I'm not certain." His hands were sweating. He felt a mask of perspiration across his nose and cheeks. "Maybe we should have sent him to the University of California here in San Francisco—maybe they could have salvaged him."

"And the baby died?"

"I think so. It survived the surgery, but the teratoma was extensive."

"So you lost the baby. But was there anything you could have done, Doctor?" The psychiatrist filled his pipe, tamping down the tobacco and searching for matches.

"I wasn't thinking about the baby—the mother committed suicide. She'd been under psychiatric treatment before the pregnancy—it was more than she could handle."

"So you lost two patients, is that what you're telling me?"

"Or three. Possibly as many as five." The smell of pipe tobacco filled the room. "The pathology report on the tissue removed from Terry Cox said it was a trigerminal teratoma. They found cerebral matter, bone tissue, and rudimentary cardiac structures. Three of them, as a matter of fact. The pathologist felt we may have removed a parasitic twin—or two."

"It was a moral question," Straub murmured. "You had to perform surgery on that infant. Is that correct?"

"We could have let him die. That's what the parents wanted, I think." The office was very dim now. The black leather chair in the room looked like a crouching lion to Alan. "They'd been told that the baby was severely deformed and they refused to sign the surgical release. We got a judge to order Terry Cox a ward of the court in order to do the surgery."

Viktor Straub reached up and switched on a small green lamp on his desk.

Alan shivered in the light. His shirt stuck to his back, despite the cool temperature. "The baby had no mouth. It would have starved to death. We were ventilating through an endotrach tube—" He swallowed hard. "After removing the teratoma we had to form a mouth

from the tissue that remained—and open the esophagus. It wasn't pretty. Only one eye was salvageable."
Alan swallowed hard. He felt sick from his earlobes to his toenails. "I think I'm going to be sick," he said, his voice shaking.

"There's a wastebasket beside you," Straub said. "Feel free to use it."

"I'd rather not—"

"Think nothing of it. Some people cry. Others throw up. It's all the same to me."

Alan checked for the dark mouth of a gray metal wastebasket near his chair. He was determined not to vomit in there. "I think I'll go home."

Straub laid his pipe on the desk. "You may leave at any time, Alan. I won't stop you, but I'd like you to stay with me a few more minutes. I want to understand what happened after the surgery."

Alan clenched his teeth. "The surgical review board at Lorimar decided I had removed the patient from the teratoma, instead of vice versa. And a news reporter got hold of the story and convinced one of the nursery staff to take a picture of the baby. My name was not mentioned, fortunately—not until the day after the story appeared in the newspaper. Mrs. Cox—I can't remember her first name—Nancy?—she called me at my office." Alan took several deep breaths. He was nauseated. The room swam dizzily. But he spoke the words with careful deliberation, as if each one were an indictment or a defense. "She said she was going to—kill herself. And she did. I heard this explosion on the other end of the phone. She—shot herself—through the head."

"Uhh," Straub moaned softly.

"The reporter managed to find out we'd been unable to anesthetize the baby. That information could only have come from one of the staff in the operating room that morning."

"You operated without anesthesia?"

Alan's voice shook. "Yes."

"And what does an unanesthetized infant do during a surgical procedure like that?"

"We didn't know until it was too late." Alan stared at the psychiatrist. "There wasn't any mouth! Don't you see? How could we have heard anything?" What Alan saw in Viktor Straub's eyes in that strange, suffused light might have been a reflection. Or it might have been tears.

"I ask you again, Doctor. What did the child do?" His voice was harsh.

"It screamed." Alan leaned over and vomited into the wastebasket.

8

The home of Jerry and Maria Great-house was a perfect illustration of the physicist's theory that atoms are in continuous movement. The house vi-brated with children, dogs, cats, mu-sic, and laughter. Even the rocks in the backyard, huge boulders hauled in from the rockery on Monterey Road, seemed to oscillate slightly.

"If you put your ear on this one," Sean Greathouse told Doug, "you can hear its voice. It kind of sings."

"Rocks don't sing," Doug told him uncertainly. Sean was a year older than himself. Maybe eleven-year-olds knew things that ten-year-olds didn't. He put his ear on the warm, roughened surface of the red rock and lis-tened. "I don't hear anything."

"Well, maybe it's too noisy outside," Sean suggested. "I only listen to the rocks at night—you know, when it's real quiet outside. We'll try it after dinner. You'll see. It really sings."

The boys went to find the rest of the Greathouse chil-dren and Robbie. It was not an easy task in a sprawling house with thirteen rooms. The house was very old, with lovely old, dark oak floors, ceilings of twelve feet, and doors that towered eight feet in height. There were four bathrooms in the house. With five children and two adults, and, more often than not, a visitor or two residing with the family, four bathrooms were just about one less than needed.

Sean and Doug looked into Maria Greathouse's studio, a white room where a huge loom stood and baskets of wool surrounded it. A half-finished weaving stood on the loom. The colors were blue and green and a muddy color of purple.

"What's she making?" Doug asked.

"Stuff. She weaves stuff. It's very nice—I just don't know what you call it exactly."

"What does she do with it?"

"She sells it mostly. There's a bank that has one of her weavings on the wall." Sean was obviously proud of his mother.

"She sells it to banks?" Doug sneezed. The air in the room smelled like the blanket that used to be on Doug's bed. "I might get a nosebleed if I sneeze too much," he said. "I'm allergic to wool."

They exited the room quickly. Sean closed the door. Doug tried another door, but the doorknob refused to turn in his hand.

Sean looked up quickly at the edge of the door. "That one's locked. See that feather up there?"

Doug looked. A small white feather was barely visible stuck between the door and the jamb. "What's it for?"

"This is a secret room. Nobody goes in there except my father and the chief, when he comes. He stays in this room. I'm not allowed to go in there," Sean explained. "If the feather is gone my dad'll know someone went in."

"How come it's secret?" Doug asked, feeling uneasy and yet extremely curious. There were no secret rooms in the Campbell household.

"I don't know—it just is. They have meetings in there —you know, meetings that are secrets."

The boys heard voices down the hall and went to investigate. Rob, encircled by the four Greathouse girls, was looking miserable in a playroom full of dolls and dollhouses, a rocking horse nearly as tall as Rob, stuffed animals . . .

"I don't want to play with dolls," he was complaining.

The girls giggled, interrupted by Sean and Doug, much to Robbie's relief. Joanna, the youngest of the girls, was only three. She waddled around in saggy diapers, mimicking the older children. Sarah was the oldest; she was nearly thirteen. Jennifer and Jill were twins, seven years old, with raven-black hair and dark brown eyes.

Sarah laughed at Robbie. "These aren't dolls—exactly. They're namesakes. We all have Indian names. The dolls explain our names."

"I'd like to have an Indian name," Rob said, doubly relieved he did not have to play with the dolls. "How come you do? You're not an Indian."

"My dad is," Sarah said, looking to Sean for reinforcement.

"Yeah, our dad is," Jennifer and Jill chimed.

Sean had red, curly hair and slate-blue eyes. "I'm not Indian, but I have an Indian name. We're all adopted. That's why we're Indian in a way."

Rob found the whole explanation much too perplexing. He'd looked forward to swimming in the Greathouse pool that had a long rope tied to a tree. The children climbed the tree, swung out over the pool on the rope, and dropped to the cool water below. The first time Rob had done it he'd begged Alan for a month to construct a swing over their pool.

"Tell you what," Sean said. "Tonight, after dinner, we'll have a naming ceremony and we'll give Doug and Rob an Indian name."

The twins clapped their hands and volunteered to make the headbands for the two adoptees. "We'll find some flowers—"

"Boys don't wear flowers," Robbie sniffed.

"We'll find some weeds," Jennifer decided. "They'll look pretty."

"Do we have to have headbands for the naming ceremony?" Doug asked. "I think I'm allergic to a lot of weeds."

"We'll make yours out of paper then," Sarah told him sympathetically.

So it was agreed that the moment they could escape the adults after dinner they would meet in the woods at the rear of the Greathouse property.

Maria Greathouse and Katie were in the expansive kitchen finishing the cooking, which consisted of platters of greens and vegetables with a spiced sauce of cilantro and peanut oil, rice pilaf prepared with walnuts and pea pods, baked chicken, and a dark, fragrant fruit soup. There was also a chocolate cake, Maria admitted guiltily. The children had insisted.

"They're afraid your children will think they're strange if we don't have something chocolate for dessert," Maria said. Her long brown hair was tied back loosely, revealing her finely boned features and purple-blue eyes.

Katie laughed. "My kids think chocolate is one of the major food groups," she told Maria. "It's a full-time job making sure they eat enough vegetables and carbohydrates."

Maria nodded and gave the fruit soup a final stir. She ran her household with such ease, Katie thought. Granted, the decorating scheme would not have won any awards in *House Beautiful,* but comfort and character seemed more important than whether the wallpaper and drapery had been coordinated with the upholstery. Several of Maria's tapestries hung on the walls, and there were original watercolors and paper collages from her art school days.

"Oh, that . . ." she said nonchalantly, in reference to one of the paintings. "I did that years ago. I was experimenting at that stage."

Katie wished she could paint or weave or do something creative. Cooking didn't qualify, and she didn't do much of that with Amanda around. Like Amanda, Maria Greathouse had little time for extravagant kitchen aids.

"I don't like the way those food processors grate things," she told Katie. "Too fine. Coleslaw ends up looking like green sawdust—I prefer doing it the old way, I'm afraid."

The children, all seven of them, rushed into the kitchen to see if there was time for a swim before dinner, and there was, which pleased Robbie enormously. Alan and Jerry Greathouse supervised the wide arcs the children made from the rope swing, on hand in case a plunge into the pool proved too much for one of the kids. Rob's spidery body hung suspended in the hot, still air for a breathless moment before he plummeted into the cool water. Doug, on the other hand, clung to the rope and made several long passes over the pool before he dropped, howling, into the blue depths. Jennifer and Jill floated down together, lightly buffeted for only seconds before they slipped beneath the water, hardly making a ripple. Sean whooped and splashed in, and Sarah, thinking herself a bit grown up for this kind of fun, dived like an arrow.

Then they splashed Alan and Jerry, who splashed back until everyone was wet and had to change quickly because dinner was ready.

Katie hoped the boys wouldn't comment on the fact that there were walnuts in the rice or the obvious similarity of the prunes to certain body wastes. Luckily, Tamran, the Greathouses' Lab mix dog, sat beside Dougy and ate anything he cared to slip her, including walnuts and prunes.

"This is delicious," Katie said, after sampling the fruit politely and discovering it had a delicate flavor as well as aroma. "You'd never know there were prunes in there."

"What?" Jill asked, her eyes widening. "There are prunes in the soup?"

Maria and Jerry Greathouse rolled their eyes simultaneously. "Spare us your description tonight," Maria said.

"You know we hate prunes," Jennifer said. "They're all gooshy—"

"And brown," Jill added indignantly.

"They're like Tamran doo-doo," Jennifer said, giggling.

"Jen . . ." Jerry warned her, but he was having trouble keeping his laughter under control himself. "Behave yourself. And you, too, Jill."

"But it does! Look at it."

And everyone automatically peered into their soup bowls just before Jerry began to laugh because Tamran was looking quite guilty by hanging his head and staring at the floor. The laughter bubbled up around the table until everyone was hooting, and then Sean choked a bit and calmed things down.

Alan, despite his strong sense of decorum, had laughed as hard as anyone. In fact his stomach muscles ached from the unaccustomed heartiness. He sighed. "Where I grew up—in Illinois—my father would have sent me to bed without another bite of supper if I'd said that."

"Not that you didn't *think* it, I'll bet," Jerry said. "I used to analyze every mouthful. Sometimes I'd pretend I was eating moths or poisonous mushrooms just to prove how tough I was."

"Ewe," Sarah squealed, "you pretended you ate moths? Uck! I'd rather eat prunes."

And everyone laughed again. And everyone ate their prunes, even the twins, although they ate them last, just before the chocolate cake was served. It was unlike any family dinner Alan had ever known. Everyone talked and ate. Sometimes at the same time. Slowly, ever so slowly, he began to relax. When he saw Doug feeding Tamran the last of the cake, he didn't say a word. In the Greathouse world even the pet dog was an accepted part of the whole.

The children cleared the dishes and faded out the back door.

"It's nice they get along so well," Maria said quietly.

"This is a wonderful place to get along in," Kate said. "Rob said there's a whole woods out there to explore."

Maria nodded and began to load the dishwasher, which she did with precision. "This used to be a farmhouse. When we bought it—for a song ten years ago—there were still orchards on either side. And a pasture down the road. We've kept ten acres—but it's hard to ignore all those new condominiums they're building where the pasture used to be."

Katie nodded. Still, it was like being out in the country. It's what they had dreamed about finding in Los Altos.

Maria finished loading the dishwasher and started it. She dried her hands on a blue plaid dish towel. "Come and I'll show you my latest weaving. My studio is upstairs—Jerry and Alan are in the family room. We'll join them in a moment."

Alan and Jerry had propped themselves in deeply cushioned chairs in front of a screened view of the backyard. Jerry had slipped off his shoes and sat with his feet up on the coffee table. They each had a cup of coffee. Alan would have given his birthright for a Scotch, but there was no alcohol at the Greathouses'. Jerry had fought a long battle with alcohol addiction, and he'd won. From the time he and Alan were medical students together Jerry had drunk too much. Something drove the man, drove him in fits and starts, and used to lie just below the surface of his skin like a coating of gunpowder waiting to explode. That was gone now. The pressurized push of the man had been diverted into his clinic where he cared for the poor and elderly and minorities that lived on the east side of San Jose. The frenzied activity of Jerry Greathouse had been gentled by five adopted children and a wife who stood firmly by him now that he had licked his alcoholism.

"Before Maria and Katie come back," Alan said hesitantly, "I wanted to tell you that I'm seeing Dr. Viktor Straub in San Francisco—insomnia, and those nightmares have returned."

Jerry studied him thoughtfully. "Dr. Viktor Straub . . . the psychiatrist, am I right?"

"He's supposed to be good."

"You don't sound convinced. As I recall you always

thought psychiatrists were just doctors who couldn't stand the sight of blood. So what convinced you to go talk to one?"

"Katie. She's tired of the bad dreams." Alan knew that wasn't the whole truth. "I just feel like there's something wrong with me, Jer. Like I can't handle things anymore—not like I used to."

Jerry Greathouse whooped loudly. "Oh, yeah, I know that problem. It's called getting older, old man. Happens to the best of us."

"No—it's not that kind of thing. It's more than that— the dreams—" He shook his head, trying to translate the feelings and frustration into words. "I don't know. I've always been able to deal with the dreams before— but now, they're worse somehow."

"Sounds like you need a little session in the sweathouse," Jerry said, adjusting his feet comfortably and settling back. "Tell me about these dreams."

Alan laughed awkwardly. "I can't. Most of them I don't remember. I start to sweat just thinking about them." Sure enough, Alan's forehead was damp. And the evening air through the screen was cool and dry.

"So, is the shrink of any help?" Jerry asked with his usual grace.

"I don't know. How do you know what helps? The lack of sleep has begun to affect my work—that's pretty scary. I really blew my cool in surgery a couple days ago —a twelve-year-old with a malignant teratoma that burst after a fall from a bicycle." The sweat began on his nose, across his cheekbones, and down his back.

"A teratoma?" Jerry sat up straighter.

"I wanted to ask you about that. We've been seeing an increasing incidence of these teratogenic neoplasms at Lorimar. I wondered what you're seeing at the clinic."

"Teratomas? Man, I haven't seen one since medical school, let alone lately. Do you know what's causing them?"

"Not a clue—probably just coincidence."

"Not likely, Alan. You know that. Have you checked with Stanford and U.C. in San Francisco? If anything was going on, they'd be the first to know."

"No, but I'll do that. I know CDC is investigating."

"Ah, the big guns have been called in . . . well, they'll probably figure it out. Like they did Legionnaires' Disease. It'll be some new bacteria—or virus."

"In the meantime, Jerry, we've got a lot of cases of teratomas on our hands. And most of them don't make it."

Katie and Maria came downstairs and carried mugs of hot coffee into the family room.

"Maria was showing me her weaving. It's gorgeous, Alan." Kate snuggled up to the sofa. "If I weren't going back to work, I'd be setting up a loom in the guest room!"

Maria looked surprised. "I didn't know you were working, Katie."

"I'm going back to the research lab at Lorimar, just as soon as the boys are out of school for the summer and Amanda can arrange to spend more days at our house. Doug and Rob are going to summer school—they don't know that yet, I'm afraid. But I think it's high time I picked up my career. It's been ten years."

Jerry Greathouse was only partially listening to the conversation. He removed his feet from the coffee table and sat up very straight. His dark eyes narrowed and he looked around the room at Alan, Maria, and Katie. "Does anyone else smell smoke?" he asked.

* * *

Sarah made the naming dolls quickly out of two twigs lashed together with twine—she would have used ribbon, but she thought Doug and Rob would object to that. Doug's naming doll had a small, red stone tied in the center of some rosemary and a few other interesting weeds Sarah had found in the small woods behind the house. Rob's naming doll had some braided grass and a gray pigeon feather. She would have liked to find a nicer feather, but there wasn't time. Jennifer and Jill constructed hasty headbands from red ribbon and oak leaves. Doug's was made out of newspaper and green ribbon. Even they were satisfied, although they both thought a few flowers would have been prettier.

"What's my Indian name going to be?" Rob asked Sarah, who was putting the finishing touches on the dolls.

"I don't know. Sean is meditating right now—he'll discover your names and tell you. When he's ready he'll build a fire in the fire ring."

"A real fire?" Doug asked her. "You mean, with matches and wood and everything?"

Sarah laughed softly. Joanna grabbed for one of the naming dolls. "No—these aren't to play with, Joanna. Come on, we'll go see if Sean is ready."

They traipsed single file through several rows of oak, pine, and willow trees to a large clearing where a small fire blazed in the center of a ring of rocks. The sun was still a warm, golden glow in the west, but it would be dark soon.

"This is really spooky," Rob whispered to Doug.

"Shh," Doug told him. "It's not spooky a bit."

Sean, in a leather headband and beaded necklace that lay against his bare, pink-white chest, was sitting quietly waiting for them.

"Sit down," he said. "I have been told your Indian names."

"Who told you?" Rob asked him, sitting cross-legged, just like Sean, on the ground.

"The Great Spirit," Sean said. "It doesn't matter whether you're really Indian or not. There is an Indian name for everything in the world. You just have to discover its name."

Sarah ceremoniously placed the headbands on Doug's and Robbie's heads. Doug felt like sneezing, but he didn't because this appeared to be a very solemn occasion to the Greathouse children.

Sean fed the fire a few more sticks of wood and it leapt higher, devouring the dried fuel.

"Is it okay to have a fire out here?" Doug asked.

"Yeah, it's fine. We do it all the time."

"Make it bigger," Jennifer and Jill teased their brother. "Make the fire the biggest ever." Often it was impossible to tell which of the twins was speaking. They began and finished sentences for each other like a well-rehearsed orchestra.

Sean tossed on two logs and grinned at the twins. Smoke curled from the logs, and flames spurted toward the darkening evening sky. Sarah gathered Joanna into her lap and they settled down by the fire. Sean brought out a small skin drum and began a faint, hollow drumming that sounded to Doug and Rob like a heartbeat, but far away.

The fire spouted both flame and gray, heavy smoke, and Doug watched it dance and weave. "Are you sure about the fire?"

"We can't have a naming ceremony without a fire," Sean told him crossly.

"Then what's my Indian name?" Doug asked. "My dad'll kill us if he finds out we lit a fire."

Just then there was a crashing and stumping sound coming through the woods. Before the children could leap to their feet Jerry Greathouse and Alan stood over the campfire.

"What's going on?" Jerry demanded in a loud voice.

"A naming ceremony," Sean explained softly. "We were giving Doug and Robbie their Indian names."

Jerry frowned and squatted down beside his son. "You know, the naming ceremony is very important—it's not a children's game."

Sean's gray-blue eyes were level. "I know it isn't a game. Doug and Rob do, too, don't you?"

Doug and Rob nodded. The twins nodded solemnly. Joanna shook her head up and down. Even Sarah joined the head bobbing.

"But you're not even Indian," Alan told his boys.

"But I *wish* I was," Robbie said. "I really *wish* I was an Indian."

Jerry Greathouse, transformed in the flicker of fire and the deep shadows of night, rose slowly, gathering himself into a fierce, towering figure. "Then go ahead with the naming."

Sean's voice squeaked when he began the story. "When Black Bear was created he had no eyes . . ."

"So he sat, doing nothing," Jerry continued, taking over the story gently. "And when White Rabbit saw him, he said, 'What a great being you are, Black Bear.' But Black Bear didn't know he was a great being, because he had no eyes."

Kate and Maria joined the silent circle around the fire.

"So brother Rabbit gave his eyes to Black Bear. It was a very generous thing to do, because now Rabbit was blind. And Black Bear could see. 'You are my Great Brother,' Black Bear told Rabbit. 'I know of a secret place, and I will lead you there.' So Black Bear led him to a tall tree. 'Climb up to the top, and you will find the secret place.' But Rabbit could not climb the tree. So Black Bear led Rabbit slowly to the edge of Great River. 'Can you swim, Brother Rabbit? At the end of this river there is a secret place.' But Rabbit shook his head sadly. He couldn't swim. Then Black Bear led Rabbit to Tall Mountain. 'At the very top of this mountain is a secret place where you will be safe. Climb up the mountain.' Rabbit tried and couldn't climb up high enough. The rocks kept slipping out from under his feet. Rabbit was quite discouraged.''

Sean picked up the story. "Black Bear looked around and saw that he and Rabbit were in beautiful Green Valley. 'This is a beautiful place,' he told Rabbit. 'Stay here, and you will be safe.' But when Black Bear left him alone, Rabbit was frightened. Because he was blind. He sat trembling with fear."

Jerry took over again. "Suddenly Rabbit heard a voice, far off, like the beating of wings in the air. 'Jump, Brother Rabbit,' said the voice. Rabbit jumped, but not very high. 'Jump higher,' the voice called to him. 'Jump higher than you have ever jumped.' So Brother Rabbit took a mighty leap into the air." Jerry moved his hands in wide arcs, as if he were conducting some unheard symphony. "And when Rabbit jumped the Wind took hold of him. The Wind carried him high over the valley, higher still to the top of the mountain. Far above the world. Rabbit opened his eyes. He could see!"

Sean spoke softly to the enchanted audience around the fire. "Rabbit had become a great bird. An eagle! And the Wind said, 'Your new name is Eagle.' And that's why there's the white part on eagle feathers."

Only the crackling fire was heard for several minutes as they sat and watched Sean, who gave Rob the small twig naming doll. "Your name is Little Elk Nose," he said.

Robbie took the naming doll, a bit self-consciously. The ceremony had been transformed by the presence of the adults. At first it had seemed like a game. Now it was serious.

"You will discover what your name means, Robbie," Jerry told him quietly. "The Elk is a powerful animal. You must think about it and listen to your dreams and your heart."

Rob nodded. Little Elk Nose sounded like a dumb name to him. Then it was Dougy's turn.

"Your Indian name is Red Dawn," Sean said and handed him the doll with the stone lashed to it.

"Red Dawn . . ." Doug repeated. "What's it mean?"

"It means many things," Jerry said. "It is a great image—a red dawn."

In the distance they heard the sound of sirens.

"Uh-oh," Sarah said, "I'll bet somebody called the cops again about our fire."

Sure enough the sirens converged on the Great-houses'. Sean poured a bucket of water on the fire, which sizzled and smoked. "Sometimes the neighbors are afraid when we have a fire," he explained. "They call the police or the fire department."

"Why can't you have a fire in your own backyard?" Katie asked Maria. "That's silly. You can have a barbe-cue grill."

Maria shrugged. "There are fire ordinances. We pay a lot of fines . . . This particular one, I believe, will come out of the weekly allowances."

"Aw, Mom . . ." the Greathouse children complained in unison.

"I'll help pay the fine," Doug volunteered. "I have fifteen dollars saved up."

"I have two dollars," Rob added.

"Thank you," Maria said gently. "That's very kind of you, but Sean and Sarah knew they shouldn't start a fire without telling us. We could have had the naming ceremony around the wood stove. It's still a fire."

"It's not the same," Sean said. "It's better outside. I'm not even sure it was a real ceremony—I mean, there wasn't any singing or dancing."

"It was real," Maria assured him.

Jerry explained to the officer what had happened with the children, and after inspecting the fire pit surrounded by twenty feet of packed bare earth and reprimanding the children, he waived the citation and left.

Alan and Katie piled the kids in the car, reluctantly, because it had been an evening of real refreshment for both of them. Alan, once he relaxed, was astonished at the life-style of Jerry and Maria and their children.

"We'll see you soon," Maria called to them.

"And if Viktor Straub can't figure out those dreams, Alan, we'll go into the sweathouse. It's a remarkable experience."

Alan grinned. "Thanks, Jerry. I think I'll pass for now. I'm not sure I can afford the fines—there's probably a *steam* ordinance out here."

The last week of school was a thorough waste of time, as far as Kate could tell. She baked two batches of cupcakes and drove for Doug's class swim party and picnic. And she signed both the boys up for summer school over their objections.

"All I want to do this summer is teach Fluffy some tricks," Robbie complained. "Why do I have to go to summer school?"

"It'll be fun," Kate told him. "I'll be at work and you'll be at school. We'll both be having fun."

"What about Fluffy and Frank? Summer's not going to be any fun if they're alone all day," Rob argued.

"Fluffy and Frank sleep most of the day. They'll be up and running around just about the time you get home." Kate decided she'd heard enough objections. "You don't have to like it, Rob, but you have to go to summer school."

The swim party was at the home of one of the fourth graders, and the kids paddled and some of them played water basketball. A lot of them sat and watched, suffused in listless boredom.

For lunch there were hot dogs and potato chips, iced grape sodas, and large cartons of ice cream. Katie didn't think she ever wanted to see another hot dog for the rest of her life. The smell of them sizzling on the grill made her stomach pitch until she had to sit down and rest for a minute. Renee Benson, Doug's teacher, came over and sat down beside her.

"Are you feeling okay?" she asked Katie.

"Yes, I'm fine. Just a bit tired."

"There's a weird virus going around—a lot of the kids have it. So many of them aren't here today," Renee said. "I wanted to ask you how Doug's been feeling. He's been awfully quiet lately."

"Has he?" Katie tried to think about whether Doug had been more quiet than usual. "He's fine, I think. Oh —except he had a nosebleed one day after school. Although Rob may have hit him."

Renee Benson looked very serious. "You know, Doug's schoolwork has suffered the last month. I don't think it's anything to worry about—we'll see how he does in summer school. It's just puzzling when a good student like Doug suddenly performs well below his potential. And he's not the only one . . ."

"I didn't know his schoolwork had slipped. He studies. I know he does his homework."

"Yes, well, it's probably just an end-of-the-year slump." Renee stood up. "Keep an eye on him, though. He could be coming down with something."

While Katie served cups of grape soda to the children she did notice a certain lethargy among some of them. It wasn't anything definite. Just an odd sense of fatigue. And Doug was one of those children. Why hadn't she seen it before? she scolded herself.

And perhaps she, too, had a virus. Maybe that's why she'd been feeling so distinctly lousy almost every day for weeks.

"I can deal with only so much calamity," she told Alan that night. "Tumors, viruses, radiation leaks, air pollution . . ."

"The end of school . . ." Alan added.

"Going back to work . . ."

"Nightmares . . ."

"No, you have to deal with the nightmares," she told him. "I'm not going to do that." They sat together in companionable silence. The night air was just cooling, and the crickets had begun their evening concert. "You know the Vickerses sold their house. Did you know Jim Vickers has cancer? And he's only thirty-six? They're moving to Arizona."

Alan didn't say anything. Kate didn't know if he was surprised by the news of Jim Vickers, or if he knew something he didn't want to tell her.

"There are so many houses for sale in our area—have you noticed that?" she asked him.

"Not particularly. It's the time of year people try and sell."

"No, I don't think so. Pamela and Larry Doren—you know where they live, on Magnolia Avenue? They're selling that house. After all the work they put into it. And Larry's business. I don't understand it. Pamela said they just had to get away from the Bay Area."

Alan noticed the soft, subtle change in his breathing. "Maybe it was all this traffic—and the schools. I don't know. But it's not a bad idea. If you hadn't taken that job, you and the boys could spend the summer with your mom and Karl in Colorado."

"I don't want to be in Colorado this summer," Katie said. "I want to be here."

"I'm not sure this is such a good place to be at the moment." He didn't elaborate. Katie didn't ask him to.

The virology research laboratory was isolated from the other lab areas at Lorimar. The clinical labs were adjacent to the Pathology offices. The morgue, autopsy rooms, and storage areas lay in back of the lab in a catacomb series of hallways. And the virology lab was located down a long concrete hallway, commonly called the "dog run," ending in the three areas that served as a research lab. Research did not have a high priority at Lorimar since it generated more prestige than income, and laboratory administrators understood income better than prestige.

John Lacey's work with interferon and retroviruses, however, was relatively safe from the annual budget cuts because of the national concerns about the AIDS virus and hepatitis C.

"We're working with a retrovirus," John explained to Katie, who had come in for orientation and a refresher course at Lorimar before she started work. "It's RV128,

RV541, and RV67. Most of our recent work has involved only RV128. You met Deena Crist—the geneticist?—she's brilliant, I must tell you. You'll learn a lot from her."

Things had changed considerably in the ten years since Katie had left the field to marry and raise children. Ten years ago the retroviruses were an interesting phenomenon, but not particularly useful in the research arena. Chick embryos used as inoculation media were exactly that, small tissue bundles inside an egg. Now, chick embryos were embedded in a protein broth, the cells of the embryos categorized by function, so that effects of a virus on cardiac, nervous system bone, and circulatory cells . . . were much more easily defined. One room of the lab was a clean room with an air lock and an elaborate gowning and masking requirement. The air in the room was filtered three times to prevent contamination of growing specimens and to prevent the accidental contamination of the environs around the lab with viruses.

Katie could barely contain her excitement. "What will I be working on?" she asked John when they had finished the tour and were sitting in his office.

"Before Henry Baden left—he was my research assistant—we had begun studies of an artificial interferon. It was a very exciting phase of the research, and you'll be continuing his work. I think you'll like it. It's mainly categorizing the effects of the interferon on cell growth that has been exposed to RV128. Time permitting, we may get some work done with RV67. Deena is working exclusively with RV541."

John went on to explain that most of their funding came from MacKenzie Pharmaceuticals, which had developed the synthetic interferon, PreVent, nearly a year before, but the results of testing had been inconclusive. They were hoping for better results from Lorimar.

"It's wonderful to have you back," John told her. "It'll be like the old days . . ."

Not exactly, Katie thought. In the old days she and John would spend the day working together, have dinner together, and sometimes spend the evening together. Sometimes the night. Until she met Alan. It would never be like the old days, not for her.

"I'm delighted to be back, John," she responded lightly. "I'm not sure Alan is as happy about all this as I am."

"He'll adjust—most husbands do," John said. "I'll see you Monday morning, Kate. And once again, welcome back."

She didn't tell him she'd been feeling rotten lately. Besides, at the moment she felt fine. Even her shoulder and arm were better. She'd skip the X ray.

9

 Hilda Jobs stopped worrying when Waif came to live with her. Waif was a retriever mixed with probably mastiff, and he was acquired from the local pound when he was only a year old. That was right after Mike Jobs, Hilda's husband of fifty-six years, died. It wasn't that Hilda missed her husband. She just missed someone in the house. She'd never lived alone. And she didn't like it one bit. Not until Waif.

How many nights had she lain awake, afraid to open a window to let in a bit of cool air because burglars might creep in that very window when she was asleep? She was fanatical about keeping the front door locked and paid nearly seven thousand dollars to have an elaborate burglar alarm system in her Saratoga home, arming every window and door with a sound device that would send out a screaming message in case of illegal entry. Even that didn't make her feel safe.

And Saratoga, a city of broad trees and narrow streets, antique shops, overpriced houses and wealthy widows, seemed like a burglar's paradise to Hilda. Not that she'd ever been robbed. And the fact that her sprawling house was located at the end of a dead-end street did little to comfort her. Waif was her only consolation.

"What a sweet dog," she'd croon to him while she warmed up his dinner at night. "My pretty Waif . . ."

But lately, as Hilda's eyesight failed, Waif seemed to fail, too. Not in his task of guarding, of course. He just never bounded through the house anymore. She had to coax him to eat. And his fur was rough and matted. He hated to be brushed.

That Sunday afternoon Hilda was in the glassed sun room enjoying the summer heat. She was glad it was finally hot. She felt better in the heat. All the doors and windows of the house were open. Waif was outside, drinking from the garden birdbath, but Hilda didn't seem to notice. His mouth dripped saliva and birdbath water, and he returned to the sun room with a strange limping gait and flopped down beside Hilda. Waif was not beautiful. His head was very large and covered with dense brown fur that had some gold and gray color mixed in. His ears drooped and his jowls were heavy. The powerfully muscled body weighed about a hundred ten pounds—a serious deterrent, in Hilda's mind, to wrongdoers.

"Hello, Waif," Hilda said. She didn't pet the dog. She touched him lightly on his back, and he let his head droop to his paws. "Have you scared off all the robbers in the backyard?"

Waif didn't move. In fact, all he'd ever managed to scare in his eight years with Hilda was the mailman, a couple of children, and the squirrels and blue jays that frequented the yard. Lately, Waif wasn't very interested in any of them, either.

"Are you hungry?" Hilda asked him. "I'll bet you're starving, aren't you."

As a young dog, he had pranced through the house on those huge puppy feet, upsetting lamps and chairs with equal glee. He ate his food in huge gulps, chewed holes in the garden hose, and slept beside Hilda's bed, a relentless sentry. Now he prowled all night, but Hilda didn't notice. She slept in perfect confidence that Waif was on duty.

"I wonder if May will come this summer," she said out loud. Surely it was all right to talk to the dog. She knew talking to herself could be viewed as senility at her age. She never talked to herself. She talked only to Waif.

May was Hilda's daughter. She lived in Los Angeles and came only once a year. There were phone calls, of course, but that wasn't nearly as good as having May in her old bedroom again. Even if it was only for a few days. May was the one who went to the Humane Society and picked out Waif. Much to the dismay of Hilda's son, Lenny.

Lenny Jobs, ten years younger than May, had done one great thing in his life. Educated beyond his abilities in several engineering schools, he designed and patented a new type of windshield wiper for cars in 1962 that had been used in most American models of automobiles since that time.

"A better mousetrap . . ." he liked to say with studied modesty about his invention.

Lenny Jobs had more money than he knew what to do with. Luckily, his wife didn't have that difficulty. And he seldom visited his mother. This was a good thing, Hilda decided. Lenny, even as a child, had not been pleasant.

"God, he's ugly," he told his mother every time he saw Waif. "Isn't he ugly? Just look at that face . . .

ugly. I'da bought you a poodle or something if I'd known you wanted a dog . . . not some ugly hound."

Hilda Jobs didn't think Waif was ugly. But then, she didn't need him for aesthetic reasons. A poodle would never have let her sleep as well.

"Are you hungry?" she asked the dog again. The most she could tell is that he made no obvious response. He didn't get up and meander toward his dish. He hadn't been eating very well these last few weeks. Perhaps it was the liver, she considered. She prepared Waif's dog food from beef liver, ground round, garlic, and cornmeal. Maybe she'd feed him some steak for his supper. He liked it raw.

Hilda rose from her cushioned chair and started for the kitchen. She put out her hand, touching all the familiar objects as she moved slowly. Everything looked quite blurry to Hilda. It hadn't happened overnight. Her vision had slowly disintegrated at the edges and worked inward until her world was reduced to half images that had only the vaguest of boundaries. Her favorite wing-back chair was a kind of yellowish haze near the television set. There was the beloved Gustav Klimt painting from the early 1900s that hung in the living room. Now it appeared as only swirls of color to Hilda, unless she got very close, which she did sometimes to refresh her memory of the woman's pale face. To Hilda, Waif was a large brown hulk. Hilda Jobs never noticed that he walked with a distinct limp. And one of his eyes bulged. She never leaned down that close to him.

Her own dinner would consist of a can of stew heated on the new kitchen range with halogen elements, a gift from Lenny. Hilda's kitchen contained every convenience, thanks to Lenny. Still, she was afraid that with her poor vision she was missing things—things like ants or spiders. She hated spiders. Almost as much as she hated being alone. Before she went to bed she'd spray the house one more time with insecticide. Just to be sure. If anyone knew she was almost blind she figured they'd put her away in a rest home. Or worse. No, she was able to fool everybody. Even herself, most of the time.

"Come on, Waif," she called to the dog.

He did not move.

Sunday afternoons at the Campbells' were usually the most peaceful time of the week, but since Doug and Rob had decided that the two-day weekend was the sum of their summer vacation they were determined to teach the hamsters a trick or two, build a tree house in the backyard, and eat anything they wanted. Chocolate ice cream and pizza were at the top of the list. Kate, however, was trying to get the week organized because she started work Monday morning.

"This isn't your summer vacation," she'd explained at least a dozen times to the boys. "I want you to get your rooms picked up right this minute."

"Well, when *is* summer vacation then?" Rob demanded.

"Every afternoon! And we're going to Disneyland next month, and after summer school you're signed up for two weeks of camp. And after that to Grandma and Grandpa Jenkins for a few days. And then we'll take a little trip—don't ask me where. I don't know yet. Somewhere fun."

"Can Frank and Fluffy go, too?" Doug asked. "I'm not going if they don't go."

"I don't know—we'll decide that later. Now get those rooms cleaned up so Amanda can vacuum in the morning."

Alan had wandered around the house all morning,

reading the newspaper and eating toast, and had finally gone off to the hospital to see his patients.

Katie wanted to get a head start on some meals and make sure Alan had shirts and the boys' shorts and T-shirts were clean for school. Otherwise Amanda would have her hands full trying to organize everything. Amanda had agreed to come two full days a week and the other three days she'd be there from two to six. Without Amanda, Katie'd be lost. She knew it. But Sunday afternoon she was feeling exasperated with Doug and Rob, who were behaving like guests in the house, and Alan's assumption that Kate would take care of all the details. And the other thing that was gnawing away at her was her desire to live like Jerry and Maria Greathouse—simply and pleasantly. With the woods beckoning at the door. And Indian names. And brown rice. And prunes. It was so wholesome.

"I have to go to the market," she called to the boys, who had given up on hamster tricks and moved on to the tree house. "I'll be back in an hour." She toyed with the idea of buying brown rice and prunes, but decided to opt for a rolled turkey roast, a mountain of greens and vegetables that Amanda would transform into delicious salads and soup, and a frozen lasagna, or whatever looked easy. "Your dad'll be back soon."

"Okay, Mom," they called back to her. "Be sure and get chocolate ice cream . . ."

"When the Pacific Ocean freezes over . . ." she mumbled to herself.

It took longer than an hour at the Safeway. Kate rarely shopped on weekends and met up that Sunday with an army of highly efficient working women who raced up one aisle and down the next. They were able to grasp six cans in one hand and steer their cart with unerring accuracy. They never said "excuse me" when they moved the cart they'd thoughtlessly left in the center of an aisle. Katie seemed to be the only person who even knew that phrase anymore. They didn't look at anyone. They mumbled to themselves, and they each had a well-organized shopping list. Katie sighed and thought she'd probably end up like that. For now, she took her time checking the labels to determine the sodium level of beets and just how much sugar *was* in that package of breakfast cereal.

It was two thirty before she got home. Alan's car was not in the driveway. He must have been held up at the hospital. She'd get the boys to help her carry in the groceries.

"Doug? Robbie?" she called as she walked into the house.

"Mom!!"

She dropped a sack of groceries on the tiled entryway floor. "Where are you?" she said, willing herself to be calm. On the wall she saw a bloody handprint. A small bloody handprint. Adrenaline shot through her. "Doug? Rob?"

"In the bathroom—" came the answering cry.

She threw open the bathroom door. Doug was leaning over the sink, blood dripping from his nose. Rob was crying.

"I can't stop it from bleeding," Rob sniveled. "I didn't hit him—he just started to bleed."

"It won't stop—" Doug said in a thick nasal voice.

"It'll be all right," she comforted both of them. "It's just a nosebleed. When did it start?"

"After you left. We were getting boards out of the garage—and his nose just started to bleed."

Shaking and shivery, Katie dampened a towel with cold water and put it on the back of Doug's neck. She applied some gentle pressure on the bridge of his nose.

He winced. Fresh blood squirted out for a moment and then subsided. "This sometimes helps to stop the bleeding." Her heart was still racing wildly. And her voice sounded ragged.

The blood was congealing in the sink and Doug's shirt looked like something off an Iraqi refugee. Katie's dismay translated into instant nausea, and she breathed through her mouth to stop the gag reflex. It's just blood, she thought sternly. Just blood.

The bleeding finally stopped, and Katie let Doug tip his head up once more. He looked very pale and sweaty. And something else. Something she couldn't quite describe. He looked different, somehow.

"There, now," she said. "I think it's over. You'll have to be quiet for a little while—just to make sure."

"Okay." Doug didn't move his head. "What if this happens at school? Maybe I shouldn't go tomorrow?"

"Oh, you'll be fine. You remember what Dr. Silver said—nosebleeds are perfectly normal in growing kids."

"Will I get nosebleeds, too?" Robbie asked in a dubious tone of voice.

"Not necessarily," Katie reassured him. "Everybody doesn't get nosebleeds. Now, I'm going to unpack the groceries. Doug, you take it easy—while Rob helps me carry in those bags."

Katie and Rob went to the car, and when they returned with their arms full of bags, Doug was in the kitchen, looking into the freezer.

"He's dead," he said, extracting something small and black from the freezer. "I think he's frozen to death."

"What is?" Katie asked him.

"Uh—nothing—we were—" Rob stammered.

"The fly," Doug told her. "I put it in the freezer to see how long it would survive. Then my nose started bleeding and I forgot about it."

"You put a fly in the freezer? Doug, flies are filthy things—they carry diseases."

"He didn't look dirty." Doug turned the frozen fly over in his hand. "I put him in the microwave first. It was a kind of scientific experiment—you know, how long do you have to zap a fly to kill it—"

Katie sighed.

"Yeah, it kept flying around," Rob said, now that the story was out. "For three whole minutes."

"Well, sometimes it stayed in the corners," Doug said. "And then there was this funny glow—it was pretty."

Kate would have to scrub down the microwave. That's all she needed at the moment. "No more flies in the microwave. Or the freezer! No more experiments! And don't run the microwave when it's empty. Okay?" And where was Alan? she thought angrily. Why wasn't he here on a Sunday afternoon?

"Okay," they agreed. Only Rob looked the least bit guilty.

"But I don't see what's so bad about killing an old fly," Doug mumbled. "You do it all the time with the flyswatter."

"That's different—I don't torture the poor thing."

"No, you just squash him dead!" Doug dumped the dead insect into the trash compactor. "I don't see any difference."

Katie didn't care to argue with him. She had the groceries to put away, the bathroom to clean, and now the microwave and freezer had to be disinfected. "Did you clean up your room?" she asked as they were leaving the kitchen.

"No," Doug answered. "We didn't. Red Dawn doesn't clean. Neither does Little Elk Nose." He grinned at his mother.

"Well, maybe Red Dawn and Elk Nose don't, but Doug and Rob *do*!"

Monday morning began with at least three minor disasters before Katie arrived at work. Alan left the house at seven fifteen after she'd hastily ironed a shirt for him. That was the first disaster: no ironed shirts. The second catastrophe was that Frank was not in the hamster cage that morning. He was finally discovered in one of Doug's tennis shoes, which was lying on the floor of the dining room. The third mishap was that Katie threw up twice after she'd eaten breakfast. If it hadn't been the very first day back at Lorimar she would have stayed home in bed.

She drove the boys to school with their lunches full of conciliatory junk food. She noticed the SOLD sign on Pamela and Larry Doren's house on her way to the medical center. She was ten minutes late. But it didn't seem to matter. John Lacey was nowhere to be seen and Deena Crist was bent over the lab bench.

"Give me about fifteen minutes," Deena said about ten times that morning. "Then I'll be able to show you your work area."

Katie settled down with Henry Baden's notes from the past year's work on the effects of artificial interferon on RV128. Luckily, Henry Baden kept meticulous notes, and by noon Katie had learned that the interferon, called PreVent, had had little effect on chick embryos inoculated with RV128 from the eighteenth hour to the twenty-sixth hour after fertilization.

Deena Crist promised she'd have a couple of hours free that afternoon, and John would probably be out of the post room, so they'd be able to go over the research protocol. Katie had lunch in the cafeteria and suddenly remembered she had to call Phyllis Latimer about their tennis game and lunch.

"Phyllis?" she asked when she called and a woman answered the phone. "Is that you?"

"Katie . . ."

"Are you all right? It's nearly one o'clock. I can't believe you're still in bed."

"Just a little under the weather . . ."

"I wanted to tell you I'm back at work at Lorimar and won't be able to play tennis this summer—I'm sorry."

There was a long silence. "It's all right. I'm not really feeling up to tennis anyway. Have you seen the paper this morning?"

Kate felt her breathing rise sharply into a shallow pant. "No—I didn't have time. What's happening?"

"It's the water supply—they discovered hydrocarbons in the water supply in Mountain View, Almaden . . . and Santa Teresa. Hydrocarbons from the semiconductor industry. Do you get bottled water, Kate?"

"We had a reverse osmosis unit installed."

Phyllis's voice was winding down like an old gramophone recording. "That's good . . . I'm glad. Thanks for calling, Kate."

"You take care of yourself—get some rest."

"It's probably just a virus."

"Yes, probably just a virus."

The inoculation of chick embryos suspended in a protein broth was relatively simple. The tubes of cells and media were categorized by hours since fertilization, called the HSF, and kept frozen in a large walk-in freezer in the clean room. Kate tottered around getting used to the bulky clean suit and hood she had to wear. How could she learn to manipulate a syringe with a heavily gloved hand? she wondered. It had been a lot easier ten years ago before they'd had all this equipment. Of course, the results had often been altered by contaminants in the air. Deena laughed softly at Katie's first few attempts to manage the door latch on the freezer. Her hands slid around maddeningly.

"The only good thing about that lock is that it's nearly impossible to lock yourself in," Deena said, her voice sounding tinny through the hood speaker. "But just in case you do, there's an alarm inside. It's minus seventy-five degrees in there, and you'd be amazed how quickly that kind of cold works on joints and brain tissue."

Katie looked dubious and shivered at the thought of being trapped in the gray metal room. "How long does it take? How long can you be in there—safely?"

"Seven minutes and thirty seconds."

"Noted," Kate answered.

After the embryos were inoculated they were allowed to grow in a thirty-seven-degree incubator for varying lengths of time. Then the cells were separated, teased apart, and then each cell was grown on incubation plates so that the individual genes were visible under the electron microscope. It was tedious work, and demanding. The timing was critical.

About three o'clock her stomach growled and she exited the clean room through the air lock. The woven paper clean suit was disposed of in a closed red bag and the hood cleaned in an air shower and left on a shelf. Katie stood in the air shower herself for the required two minutes. Her stomach grumbled again. John Lacey was waiting for her in his office, Deena told her. And Deena winked.

What in the world did that mean? Katie wondered on the way to John's office.

"Yo, Kate," John said, "how's it going? Sorry I

couldn't be there this morning, but Deena says you have things well in hand."

"It's all pretty new—"

"Of course it is—don't worry—in a couple of days it'll seem like you never left research. Sit down—"

"Could we go get a cup of tea—and a cookie?" she asked, feeling impulsive and foolish. But she was starving.

John's left eyebrow twitched slightly. "Well—sure, why not."

"I'm famished—and I had lunch!" She laughed softly. "I guess I'm not used to all this work."

The cafeteria at Lorimar Medical Center was on the first floor. Decorated in rust, pale blue, and cream, it was a relatively attractive place, if you were willing to ignore the atrocious modern prints on the wall and the fact that no amount of pastel paint changed the taste of hospital food.

"I'll never know why we can't get this kind of paint job in the lab," John commented as they went through the line and picked up tea.

Kate settled for a muffin instead of cookies. They found a table on the patio in the shade. And Kate polished off the muffin in about three bites and washed it down with tea.

"I'm sorry—" she apologized. "I don't understand why I'm so hungry."

"Nerves," John said. "Everything work out okay at home? I mean, where are your children? And what about Alan? Is he taking this okay?"

"Alan? Of course. He'd never stand in the way of my career." She wished she'd taken two muffins. She also didn't like the sound of the word "career." She'd thought of herself as a wife and mother for too long now.

"Good—good. Well, I for one am very glad you're back. I've missed you—"

"You have Deena. She seems very competent."

"Oh, don't get me wrong—Deena's a whiz. But she's doing her own research. You'll be overseeing *my* brain-child—PreVent. You've read Henry's notes . . . what do you think so far?"

"I think he should have allowed much longer incubation times for the cerebral cells—twenty-four hours might not be enough for differentiation."

"We discussed that—Henry felt it was long enough. He was stubborn. Hard to work with."

"Really. Well, he kept superb notes, thank goodness . . . I'd like to get a look at the protocol. Did you bring it along?"

They pored over the research procedures and goals, and Kate got a better idea of what her specific work would be in the lab. For one thing, the time of inoculation and time of incubation had to be varied and plotted against genetic aberrations occurring in the embryos. She could do that, she knew. The new computer program was capable of scanning photographs of the cell growth on the incubation plates and reconstructing the karyotype for each kind of cell. The only complication was that Kate had to learn to use the computer. She'd always thought of herself as hopeless in the face of any computer technology more advanced than Pong. Oh, well, she thought, she had her work cut out for her. Beginning Tuesday morning.

Alan's receptionist, Mindy Warton, buzzed him impatiently about two o'clock when he was in with Mrs. Ma-son, on whom he had performed a textbook cholecystectomy, using the new laser techniques.

When the buzzer bleated at him the third time, he pushed the intercom button to talk to Mindy. "Yes? Mindy?"

"Mr. William Anderson is on the phone—he's called three times in the last ten minutes and I've told him you're busy, but he insists on talking to you." She sounded exasperated.

Alan remembered William Anderson—Bill. He'd had an uncomplicated bowel obstruction and reconstruction. "Put him on hold. I'll talk to him—no, better yet, have him come in. Can we squeeze him in this afternoon?"

"No, but we will," Mindy said. "Him and Mrs. Powell, who's been here since eleven this morning."

Alan sighed. You'd think he was running an emergency room the way patients stacked up demanding to be seen. The afternoon dragged on. Alan talked to Mrs. Powell and listened to her lungs and heart. Everything seemed fine. She was complaining of difficulty breathing. Four months ago Alan had operated on her to correct an esophageal vera—a small tear in the esophagus.

"Everything's humming like a top in there," he said. "I don't know what's causing your shortness of breath. I'd like to get an EKG and a chest X ray."

"Yes," Mrs. Powell wheezed.

"You don't have asthma, do you?"

"I don't think so."

"Allergies?"

"All kinds of them—pollen, grasses, chocolate, strawberries . . ."

Alan took the stethoscope ends out of his ears. "More than likely, Mrs. Powell, your allergies are causing this wheezing. But we'll get the EKG and chest film —and go from there."

And at three thirty he opened the door of an examining room and Bill Anderson, a retired postman, jumped off the examining table and grasped his arm.

"I've got cancer," he said. "I'm sure of it. You've gotta do something before it's too late."

Alan eased him gently over to the table. "What makes you think you have cancer, Bill? Are there any unusual growths? How are you feeling?"

"I'm feeling *fine,* just *fine*! But that's typical of a cancerous tumor, isn't it? You feel just fine until it's—curtains." Bill Anderson's blue eyes were wild. "I read in the paper where there's hydrocarbons in the water—I live in the Santa Teresa area!"

Alan reminded himself to be patient. "Generally, Bill, you don't get tumors from the water you drink . . ."

The man clutched Alan's arm. "No, no, you don't understand—see, there's these poisons that are leaking into the water—and they're dangerous—real dangerous —and according to the article in the paper, there's been a lot of tumors in our area—why Jerome Watts—he lives down the street from me—he was just fine and then one day—bam! He falls over in his backyard. He had a brain tumor. He died since then."

"But that doesn't mean *you* have a brain tumor, Bill. I think you're scaring yourself with all this newspaper stuff."

Bill Anderson scowled at Alan. "You still don't get it, do you? It's too late by the time you feel anything from the tumor—"

Alan took the prescription pad from his lab coat pocket. "I don't think you have a tumor, Bill. You'd notice some symptoms if you did."

"What symptoms? What would I notice?" Anderson demanded. "I have to know what to watch for."

Alan laughed softly. "Let me do the watching, okay?

That's what I went to school all those years for. We'll give you a physical, if that would make you feel better—you can schedule it with Mindy. In the meantime . . ." Alan wrote a prescription for a mild tranquilizer. "I want you to take this. It's a very mild tranquilizer. Just until I see you for a physical."

Bill took the prescription skeptically. "That's all you're gonna do?"

"No, I'm going to recommend you go fishing—take a walk, do some gardening—something to get your mind off this. You don't have a tumor, Bill."

"You're sure?"

"Reasonably sure."

"Okay—okay. I'll stop worrying. But I'd be a lot more convinced if you ran some tests—just to be sure?"

Alan had his hand on the doorknob. "No tests, Bill. Just schedule that physical. Okay?"

Bill gave him a thumbs-up. "Okay, Doc."

Alan knew he'd see a host of patients who'd read that newspaper article about the water contamination in the valley. Each one he'd have to calm down. He could do that for his patients, he considered. He couldn't do it for his wife. Katie was still convinced that possible radiation leaks threatened them all. He finished his afternoon patients, stopped back at Lorimar to check on the surgical patients from that morning, and then he went home.

10

"Frank's hiding in the corner of the cage," Doug told Katie. "Fluffy is always running on the wheel. He never gives Frank a chance."

She was trying to get dressed for the Country Club Dinner Dance, which was proving to be far more difficult than usual. At eight o'clock she was still in her robe, trying to find the blue shoes that matched the blue dress and the earrings that she'd bought last month to go with the dress. . . . Alan was complaining about the amount of starch in the tuxedo shirt.

"If I have to wear all this fluffy chiffon, a little starch isn't too much to endure for one night," she teased him lightly.

"I know, but chiffon doesn't make you itch," he told her. "How about if I wear the dress and you put on this silly shirt?"

"That's what we'll do for the Halloween Dance," Katie said, getting a quick mental image of the two of them in each other's clothes.

The one disturbing fact about the blue chiffon was the wide, tight belt, which seemed to fit last month, and was distinctly uncomfortable this month. Kate made a dash for the bathroom scale to see if all those muffins had been converted directly into adipose. They hadn't. The belt, however, was not influenced a bit by the information on the scale. Well, she thought, I just won't breathe all evening. It'll be fine.

Janie Hoover arrived to watch the boys while Alan and Kate went to the dance. At ten, Doug didn't like the sound of the word "baby-sitter," but Janie was a neighborhood teenager who knew both the boys and came over to "hang out," as she put it. They planned to watch a movie, *The Rescuers on Top of the World,* and maybe teach Frank and Fluffy a few tricks. That was Rob's idea.

Fluffy, a rotund hamster at least twice the size of Frank, had proved rather more adept at simple tricks than Frank, who mostly cowered and groomed his roughened fur. Janie and the boys were peering into the cage when Kate, at last, cinched on the belt, said goodbye to oxygen for about four hours, and came into the kitchen to talk to the boys.

"Wow, you look really fancy," Rob told her, his blue eyes wide and admiring.

"This is a pretty fancy dance tonight, Rob. We won't be home until late—but you two have to go to bed by ten—or so. Whenever the movie is finished." It was Saturday night. Kate knew it would be eleven before the boys were asleep.

"We're gonna make popcorn," Rob said. "And flavor it with cheese. Janie knows how to do that."

"Sounds delicious." Katie hastily transferred the contents of her purse into the delicate black satin evening purse and ignored the strange lurch of her stomach at the thought of popcorn drenched in Parmesan cheese.

"And we're going to teach Fluffy to jump through a hoop," Robbie added, trying to make it sound as exciting as possible in case there was any chance his mother would opt to stay home for an evening of hamster fun.

Janie laughed her husky, amused laugh. "I don't know, Rob—that Fluffy needs to go on a diet. We'll have to find a pretty big hoop for him to jump through."

"He's hungry a lot," Rob said in defense of his hamster.

"He's a pig," Doug said.

"He's not!"

"He is too!"

"Huh-uhhh . . ."

"Uh-huhhh . . ."

Katie went to help Alan. They were already fashionably late for the dance.

"Hold your breath and throw your chest out," Kate told Alan because the shirt was creasing in strange places.

"I can't do that all night!"

"Sure you can. We'll both be blue by ten o'clock."

The membership in the Palermo Country Club, once a prerequisite in Los Altos, was now a luxury, but one both Katie and Alan enjoyed. Kate liked the tennis and luncheons better than the elegant dance and dinner that was a yearly fund-raiser. Alan played golf now and then on the deep expanse of green that was an oasis in the midst of a drought. Their friends and neighbors all belonged to the Country Club. There'd been some debate in the Campbell household about continuing the membership, but every year they swallowed hard, wrote the check, and renewed.

That Saturday night the converted Jesuit seminary

twinkled with tiny white lights in all the trees, the light of floating candles danced in the pool, and the wealthy and leisured class of Los Altos gathered for their gala affair. No amount of twinkling lights could detract from the designer frocks and diamonds suspended from the necks, ears, and arms of the women.

"It's enough to give Lloyd's of London heartburn," Alan whispered to Katie.

"Don't be such a reverse snob," she told him. "If you've got 'em, wear 'em!"

He looked at her strangely, as if he were seeing her for the first time. "I thought you didn't want diamond earrings."

"I don't," she said. "I'd probably lose them—you know how easily I lose earrings." Actually she was thinking about Maria Greathouse. Somehow, she just couldn't imagine diamond earrings in Maria's ears. Not because they wouldn't look lovely with Maria's tawny skin but because diamonds seemed like a contradiction to Maria's artistic ideals.

Alan slipped his hand in hers very softly. "But maybe it would be nice to have a pair anyway."

For all his scientific coolness, Kate was deeply moved by that moment of Alan's insight into the feminine part of herself, the part that would love to have diamond earrings and chose not to have them more than once. It was nice to know he understood her apparent contradictions as part of who she was.

"Let's dance," he said to her when they had found a table right next to Lawrence Greer and his wife Cheryl, and Teddy Severin, the assistant hospital administrator at Lorimar.

"This seems to be the Lorimar corner," Severin said, nodding at several other physicians and spouses at surrounding tables.

A swing band was playing on a small stage encompassed by the shining oak dance floor, already crowded with couples. The saxophone wailed and an ice sculpture nearby wavered, sending the waiters into a frenzy relocating it.

"The annual bash," Lawrence Greer said. Clearly, he'd already been working on an alcoholic binge. His eyes seemed to have difficulty focusing. His wife sat beside him, oblivious as an oyster to its shell.

"Hello, Cheryl," Katie said. "I haven't seen you for a while."

Cheryl Greer turned her small, blond head about a quarter of an inch toward Katie. "I hear you've gone back to work. I hope that was by choice."

"Of course it was." Katie suddenly remembered why she carefully neglected the company of Cheryl Greer at other times of the year.

"Your new boss—or should I say your old boss?—is here. Alone," Cheryl said.

"You mean John?" Kate looked around.

"Over there . . ."

John Lacey sat looking totally comfortable in a stiff-collared shirt and black tuxedo. Just as Katie searched visually for him in the crowd he looked up and caught her eye. He smiled. Kate smiled back, hoping the expression on her face wasn't a grin.

"His ex-wife is here, too. On the arm of Milford Everet—you know, the attorney." Cheryl dabbled with the swizzle stick in her Manhattan. "I don't know what John ever saw in that woman. You two were something of an item for a while, weren't you?"

Katie realized John Lacey was still looking at her, with that long, cool gaze of his. She looked away quickly.

"An item? Cheryl, come on. John and I were never an

item. I think we saw two movies together—twelve or thirteen years ago. I hardly remember. I'm surprised you do!"

Cheryl looked nonplussed. "That's not what I heard . . ."

"Alan," Kate said loudly, "if I don't get something to eat soon, I'm going to keel over."

Alan was talking to Teddy Severin. "Okay," he said to her. Then to Severin he said quietly, "We'll talk about it later."

Alan and Katie threaded their way through the tables, greeting many of the people they knew. A long table of appetizers, oysters Rockefeller, black and white caviar, pickled pigeon eggs, crackers, stuffed mushrooms . . . all appealed to the pampered predinner appetites of the guests. Alan quickly filled one of the small glass plates set on a silver slaver of ice. Katie had two crackers on her plate.

"I thought you were hungry," he said.

"Nothing looked good to me." Her stomach was rumbling uncomfortably. "Maybe my belt's too tight."

Alan and Kate sat huddled at their table. Kate had made sure her back was turned to John Lacey. She nibbled her crackers.

"Let's have that dance, then," Alan suggested, having neatly devoured the plate of hors d'oeuvres. "Just as soon as they play something *really* slow. Maybe a waltz."

Katie laughed softly. "I don't think you'll hear a waltz tonight, Alan. Better brush up on your fox-trot."

Oddly, the band, called Bent River, launched into a lovely waltz. Alan offered her his hand and winked at her. "I have some influence . . ." he joked, "with someone . . ."

Alan Campbell was a prince on the dance floor. His back and head held high and stiff, he suspended Kate securely in his arms and moved with such grace Katie forgot her distress for a moment. And she moved with him, following his lead effortlessly. This was how it used to be, she thought. Only atoms moving through space and Alan's soft breath on her cheek. And then the music stopped.

"Thank you," Alan whispered into her hair. "Maybe that will perk up your appetite."

Dinner was served and Kate nibbled at the rice. "I don't know what's wrong with me. I was starving thirty minutes ago. Now I feel like I just ate three Thanksgiving Day dinners."

Kate *felt* John Lacey at her left shoulder before she saw him.

"Alan . . ." he said nicely. "Kate, I wondered if I could have this dance with you?"

"She hasn't finished her dinner yet," Alan said. "I don't think she's feeling well."

"Perhaps she can talk for herself," John said, and grinned at Katie. "How about it, Katie?"

"I might as well dance," she said. "I certainly don't feel like eating. If you don't mind, Alan . . ." It made her angry with herself asking Alan if he minded. She wasn't a child, after all. She just didn't want any trouble. How could she refuse to dance with her boss? Why should she?

John Lacey took her in his arms, and they danced. He held her away from himself, but the sense of familiarity passed between them like magnetic current. Katie willed herself not to blush. What was John feeling? she wondered.

"Please don't make things difficult for me," she whispered to him.

"I don't intend to. This is just a dance, Kate. Nothing more. A dance of a boss with his research assistant."

When the music ended John led her back to Alan. "Here she is, safe and sound," he said. "No harm done."

Alan did not look up at the two of them. Alan was nursing a glass of wine.

"Thank you," Katie said to John. "That was—nice."

John Lacey replied with a crisp bow. "It was my pleasure." He walked back to his own table.

"What did you talk about?" Alan asked her when she was seated again.

"He didn't say a word. I chattered like a magpie." The waiter had removed her untouched dinner.

"I'll bet."

Kate located Phyllis Latimer with her husband, Donald. Phyllis, usually bubbly and animated, sat dull-eyed over a glass of wine. Her eyelids were swollen. Donald excused himself and left the two women alone.

"How are you feeling?" Katie asked her, slipping into a chair beside her friend.

"Oh, not bad, really. Just a bit under the weather." Her hollow stare rested on Katie. "And how are you? You look lovely tonight."

Katie smiled. "I missed the MANA meeting—what happened?"

Phyllis sighed. "We are considering a widening of the horizons, Kate. The public is apathetic—mostly they don't understand that they are being bombarded by all sorts of toxins." Her voice faded, and she looked weary and old.

"Are you all right?"

"Yes, I just don't feel like myself. I get these head-aches—and I'm so tired. I went to the doctor. He said I have sinus congestion. Gave me some pills that don't help."

"Find another doctor," Kate told her.

Phyllis laughed. "That's easy to say. Most doctors look at me—fifty-two years old, menopausal, tired—they figure I'm depressed."

"Are you?" Katie asked her. "Do you think this could be depression?"

"No. It's something else." Phyllis's eyes glowed for a moment with the old energy. "I just don't know what. Do you remember the news about the hydrocarbons in our water supply? Think of all those years we drank that water and never thought about it. All those years of taking in poisons."

Kate nodded. "When I was a student at Berkeley we demonstrated against police brutality and for free speech, and we drank the water right out of the tap and didn't give it a thought—unless it was fluoridated. Remember the flap over fluoridation?" She shook her head remembering the passionate rhetoric. "And a lot of us were still smoking cigarettes!"

Phyllis smiled wryly. "We were young."

"Yes, of course we were. And we were also naive. I know what you're saying about the water contamination is true, Phyllis. But I can't get that truck driver at the Lawrence Livermore Lab out of my mind."

"The deli truck . . ."

"Do you remember what he said to us?" Katie leaned toward Phyllis and spoke in a low voice. "I can still hear him. He said it's the things we *don't* expect that are dangerous.

"Sometimes it all looks like a huge trade-off to me. You know what I mean? You can have clean air but you lose clean water in the process. Or if you work to get the antibiotics out of the hamburger, someone slips EDTA into your green beans when you're not looking. It's some kind of cosmic irony."

Phyllis and Katie looked up to see Donald Latimer returning to the table.

"I know," Phyllis said quickly. "It's like I spend my life trying to save people from exposure to radioactivity and get cancer myself!"

"Don't say that," Kate scolded her. "Don't ever say that. A headache doesn't mean you have cancer."

Donald Latimer arrived with two more glasses of red burgundy. "You two look positively conspiratorial. What are you doing? Cooking up another revolution?"

Phyllis frowned at him. He set a glass of wine in front of her.

"Alan and I have the only two wives in the valley who smell like tarmac most of the time."

"That's not funny," Phyllis complained.

Katie tried desperately to lighten the tension. "Maybe we could start a new line of fragrance—for the politically active woman. Eau de tarmac. It has a nice ring to it."

Phyllis finally smiled, and even Donald Latimer grinned happily.

"I better get back to Alan. Phyllis, I'll call you next week. Let me know if you need anything." Kate stood up and patted Phyllis's shoulder gently.

"Was she telling you about all her aches and pains?" Donald asked, clearly disgusted. "That's all I've been hearing about—*this* hurts. Then *that* hurts . . ."

"It's probably a virus," Katie offered.

"Yes, a virus," Phyllis agreed.

When Katie returned to the table Rick Connors, a veterinarian in Los Altos, was sitting in her chair. At the sight of her, Rick jumped up and relinquished the seat.

"We were just talking shop," he said apologetically. "I don't get much chance to talk to these guys."

"Don't let me interrupt," she said, and sat down.

"Well, I was telling your husband I've had some interesting cases lately."

Katie looked over at Alan. His face was pale.

"Cats who come in with large, well-differentiated tumors . . . it's got me stymied, let me tell you," Connors continued. "I was just wondering if Alan here had any ideas."

"Do they drink tap water?" Katie asked.

Alan frowned.

"The water in some areas of the valley isn't safe," she said. "And then there's the Lawrence Livermore Lab. And the fumes from local dry cleaners . . ."

Rick Connors glanced at Alan. "Actually, I was thinking in terms of a virus. I hadn't really considered environmental causes. The reason is that most vets in the San Jose area are not seeing these tumors—you know? The cats they see have the usual kinds of ailments."

"Are they teratomas?" Alan asked. "Are there three layers of cell development?"

"As a matter of fact, they are, usually. Trigerminal—teratomas."

Fred Amans belonged to the country club because he paid his annual membership dues, not because he fit into the social and intellectual atmosphere of the club. Fred didn't even play golf. It always looked like a silly game to him—hitting a ball with a stick. He had better things to do these days.

Katie spotted Amans at the dessert table and hurried over to him. "Mr. Amans?"

He turned and smiled at her, looking her up and

down. "Why, I sure am, pretty lady. What can I do for you?"

"I want to find out what has happened to Elaine Calder—she worked for you. And she lost her baby." Katie's voice sank as she realized everyone in the dessert line was listening.

"Elaine . . . Calder . . ." Amans sampled the cheesecake while he thought. "I don't seem to remember anyone like that. Maybe you got the name wrong?"

"No—Elaine. Elaine Calder." Katie repeated the name carefully. How could a boss forget an employee in a couple of weeks?

"Sorry. You could come to my office on Monday—Amans Appliance? You know where that is? An' I keep a list of my employees. We take care of our own at Amans, let me tell you. If your friend—what's her name again?"

"Elaine."

"Elaine . . . worked for me I *would* remember."

Kate felt her face flush angrily. "Two weeks ago, Mr. Amans, Elaine Calder still worked for you. She was pregnant—or she thought she was pregnant—and it was a tumor. Now she's disappeared off the face of the earth."

"I'm very sorry to hear it." Amans tucked several chocolate truffles into his mouth. He turned away from Kate.

She grasped the sleeve of his silk tuxedo. "You know about it, don't you!"

Amans's face, when he turned to her, was livid. He brushed her hand away from her arm as if she were an annoying fly. Kate realized the others in the dessert line had also turned to listen.

"I don't know nuthin' 'bout no Elaine Calder—"

Alan, alarmed at the fuss Kate was making, stepped in. "What's going on here?"

"He knows about Elaine Calder," Kate said, forcing back tears. "And he won't tell me."

"Is this your wife?" Amans asked Alan. "If it is, I suggest you take her home. She is mighty upset about something."

Alan put his arm around Kate and she leaned against him. "My wife, sir, generally doesn't get upset without a reason."

"I *will* find Elaine Calder," Katie told Amans, her voice shaking with rage. "With or without your help."

"I hope you do, lady." He gorged on a slice of fruit pizza, and a wedge of kiwi fruit, escaping the maw of his mouth, settled on his white shirtfront.

Alan steered Katie back to the table. Kate felt the sudden stiffness of his arm. "We're going home," he said through his teeth.

"There's no reason for that—"

Lawrence Greer stood up and wavered slightly beside the table. "Everything all right, Alan?"

"Just fine, Lawrence. Everything's just fine."

"That Fred Amans"—Greer grinned feebly—"he's quite a guy."

Kate collected her satin purse from the table. "How do you know Amans?" she asked Greer. "Didn't Elaine Calder work for him? *You* remember Elaine Calder, don't you?"

"Course I do." Lawrence Greer made loud biting sounds with his front teeth. "I remember those teeth—"

Cheryl tried to pull him back into his chair, but Greer wobbled and glared at her.

"Lawrence," Alan said, "I think you've had too much to drink. Cheryl—you'd better get him home before he says much more."

Alan and Kate brushed past the Greers and several waiters who had nervously stood by in case there was trouble. Kate knew Alan hated any kind of public scene. The valet took ten minutes to bring the car around, and Alan stood waiting in fuming silence.

"I'm sorry if I embarrassed you," Kate said levelly when they were in the car and on their way home. "I certainly didn't mean to."

"You'll have to learn to keep your political activities separate from *our* relationship." He didn't look at her. He kept his eyes on the road. They turned off onto the freeway.

"I know you're angry—and I'm sorry about that," Katie said. "But I have a *life*, Alan. It's not as neatly compartmentalized as yours. It's just my life. And Elaine Calder was part of it until she disappeared."

"I didn't know you'd become a part-time investigator of missing persons."

There was no talking to him in this mood, she decided. He could always out-argue her. She'd learned that a long time ago. And he was capable of maintaining silences through weeks if necessary to prove his point. Kate hated the tears that welled in her eyes. The sticky lump that stuck in her throat.

"Elaine was a friend of mine," she said. "I stand by my friends."

"You'd better figure out how to stand by your husband." He inhaled sharply. "I've got a lot on my mind. These tumors . . . I have patients coming in who think they have a tumor for no reason except they've been drinking tap water! That's what all your scare tactics have produced—*scared people*!"

"Maybe they should be scared—a little bit," she argued. "I think about it as being informed."

"Informed?" he snorted. "Informed about what?

That the drinking water has some contamination? It's always had *some* impurities. That there could be radiation leaks at some lab twenty-five miles away? You call that informed?"

"Yes, I do. I think the public has a right to know what the dangers are of all this technology—"

"Aw, Kate, that was the philosophy of the 1960s—grow up."

Katie felt the tears in her eyes ebb. It was physically impossible to be frightened and angry at the same time. "You're not the only one who has to deal with these tumors!" she nearly shouted. "You're not the only one!"

That night, Alan Campbell had another nightmare. He dreamed he was running down a long road and something chased him. Something huge and dark. It screamed at him. He ran until his lungs ached, until his breath was a fountain of steam from his mouth. He ran until his legs were liquid with pain and fatigue. The screams followed him. At last he dropped, felt the gravel rocks scrape his face and arms. And the dark thing behind him screeched and reached for him—

"Ahhh," he moaned, waking up drenched in sweat. Another dream. Its substance faded into the darkness. He changed into dry pajamas as quietly as possible and went to the bathroom. In the second drawer was a small bottle. He shook out two pills and swallowed them. Seconal. There were no dreams with Seconal. He went back to bed.

11

 Hilda Jobs found Waif's leash in the drawer next to the telephone. It had been a long time since she had taken the dog on their old walk, a walk both she and Waif knew by heart. Hilda's hands shook a bit as she felt for the choke chain on Waif and clipped on his leash. She did almost everything these days without the aid of her eyes. Or it was as if her hands were her eyes. She could fool almost everyone, she thought.

The reason she was taking the dog for a walk was that Eulipia Simpson, next door, had said to her, "Why, Hilda! We haven't seen you out and about for some time . . . not ill, I hope?"

"Actually, I've never felt better," Hilda informed the neighbor woman. "Never better."

Clearly, it was time to provide the neighbors with some assurance of her health and sanity.

Waif bit and growled at the leash.

"Why, Waif, what is wrong with you? Don't you want to go on a nice walk?"

Waif snapped his head from side to side and Hilda felt the light spray of saliva.

"Of course you want a walk . . . you poor dear . . . it's high time you had your exercise."

It was Sunday morning. There wouldn't be many children at the park this early. And she wouldn't meet many people on the road. If she was lucky she wouldn't meet anyone, but she knew the neighbors watched the road from their windows. If they waved, of course, she wouldn't see them. But that was understandable when you were walking a dog the size of Waif, she decided, encouraging herself.

It was already warm at nine thirty A.M. and she had just a bit of trouble getting Waif out the front door ahead of her. He kept biting the leash.

"Bad dog!" she admonished him. "You stop that biting."

Terror or something worse caused Waif to salivate in foamy strands that clung to his jowl and trailed down to the matted fur on his chest. Flies drove him crazy, and flies adored him. The moment he was outdoors they circled him hungrily.

Waif and Hilda walked down the little sidewalk along the side of the garage and out to the road. There were two bushes to avoid. Waif negotiated them easily.

"Good, you remembered," she said to him. "Good, Waif."

They went to the right down the road, the way they had always gone in the days when a walk was a daily activity. There were no sidewalks in the incorporated areas of Saratoga. Saratoga's snobbery meant its residents walked in the streets. First, Hilda and Waif encountered a car parked in the road. Waif wove to the left and Hilda followed him. The car looked like a maroon boulder. If she weren't so nervous, she thought, she might actually enjoy this. The park was only two blocks. They could surely walk two blocks and keep out of harm's way.

"Hilda!" someone called.

Hilda froze and Waif jerked her forward. She yanked on the leash and he growled, but stopped. "Hello!" she called back in the general direction of the voice.

"Isn't it a lovely morning? I'm trying to get these roses trimmed—before they take over the yard."

That would be Mary Painter.

"Why, Mary, your roses are always beautiful—it's probably all the trimming you do."

"And the fertilizer," Mary said. "You can't neglect the fertilizer for roses."

"I'm taking Waif for a walk," Hilda called. "I'll talk to you later."

And the woman and dog jolted off again down the road. Hilda hoped she had managed to keep the nervousness out of her voice. She counted the steps, knowing they were passing the old Argus house. She still missed her old friend Louise Argus. At least three other families had lived in the house since Louise died. She had never met the present owners. In some respects that was a comfort to Hilda. They, at least, didn't think it was odd that they never saw her out and about.

The fourth house was on the corner of Sheridan Road and Challenge Street. They turned right again. Now it was only a block to the park. Waif moved steadily ahead. Except for the occasional lashing of his head, he was behaving quite well, she thought. Quite well, indeed.

"Good dog."

She heard voices and squinted. There were vague shapes ahead. The shapes moved. Waif stopped. The leash was taut. Oh, no, she thought, not bicycles! Waif hated bicycles. She heard the soft clatter of the bicycle wheels—at least two of them. Waif strained at the leash.

"Waif!" she said severely. "No—back."

"Lookit that dog!" a child shrilled. "Yuk!"

"Andy—" an adult female voice warned. "Look where you're going—"

"But, Mama—"

Then the bicycles were safely past them. Hilda felt a slight shiver of indignation. Children had no manners these days. Waif might not be beautiful, but he'd always been a handsome dog.

They walked on, Hilda measuring her steps gingerly now. They were nearing the park. Unfortunately, she heard voices and the bounce of a ball on the basketball tarmac. The ball whooshed and clattered on the backboard. Several young voices of boys cheered. Waif seemed confused. Generally, they turned right and circled the small park. Maybe they should turn left.

"Hey!" one of the boys yelled. "Look at that dog!"

The ball was silent. Waif and Hilda stood still. Suddenly someone ran up to her.

"Hi—I'm Mark," he said. He held out his hand, but Hilda didn't see it.

"I'm—Hilda," she said uncertainly. "This is Waif. I'm just taking him for a walk."

"Yeah—I can see that. My dad's a vet—Dr. Fields? You know him? He's down on Lexington—just past the stoplight?"

"Yes," Hilda said.

"I was wondering what's wrong with your dog's eye—"

Hilda willed herself to stop shaking. "His eye?"

"You know, how it's bulging out? It looks pretty bad."

Waif's eye was bulging? She reached out to touch his head and he growled at her.

"It must hurt him. I'd take him to see my dad if I were you."

"I will. I guess I hadn't really noticed his eye—uh, thank you for telling me."

The basketball was bouncing again. Mark's voice moved steadily away from her.

"I'd take him in real soon, lady," he said.

"I will—thanks." Hilda was shivering. If they turned around now they could be home in five or six minutes. "Come on, Waif. Let's go home."

She had to pull him around, and he growled at her again. "Something's the matter with your eye? Poor baby—maybe that's why you haven't been eating. Well, we'll see to it."

The boys had stopped bouncing the ball.

"I heard she's a witch," one of them said. "A real one."

Hilda wanted to correct those boys. How dare they think she was a witch!! She wasn't. She was just old, and you'd think that was a sin, she fumed. She was dragging Waif along at her side. This *wasn't* their usual walk. She retraced her steps, hoping Mary Painter had finished her pruning. She didn't want to meet anyone else. Waif finally figured out they were going home, because he moved out in front of her, and that was better. Once more he led her back down the road, around the two bushes, and up the sidewalk to the front door.

"Oh, good dog," she said, breathing deeply. "Good dog."

She opened the door and let the dog in. He moved slowly, and he still whipped his head from side to side occasionally, but he'd been doing that for a couple of weeks now. She thought it was the flies that bothered him.

"I'll get you something nice for your breakfast," she

told him. "I'll even warm it up in the microwave for you." She closed the front door. "You'll like that. I know you will. And you must be starving after all that exercise."

That was the last time Hilda Jobs would take Waif for a walk.

Kate and Alan slept late that Sunday morning. Kate was still indignant, and Alan had refused to talk about it further. When she awoke, his side of the bed was empty. It was ten thirty. She'd promised the boys French toast for breakfast. Kate wrapped herself in a flowered cotton robe and shuffled out to the kitchen. The doors and windows were open. It was going to be a very warm day.

Alan sat hunched over the Sunday paper in the breakfast nook.

"Where are the boys?" she asked.

"Outside. They said they wanted to work on the tree house." His voice was flat. "Rob said something was wrong with the hamster."

"He always thinks something's wrong with the hamster," she said, still feeling irritable. She went to dig through the refrigerator to see if there were enough eggs for French toast. There weren't. One wouldn't do. Katie sighed and went to check on the hamsters.

"I'm going to the hospital," Alan announced and left the kitchen to Kate.

Good, she thought. Go to your precious hospital. She had some reading to do, she'd have to run to the market, and there was the matter of the ironing in the laundry room. She bent down and peered into the hamster cage.

"Oh, my God," she said softly.

Fluffy was lying on his side and breathing heavily.

Frank was crouched in the corner, his black eyes glittering.

"Are you hurt?" she said out loud, prying off the yellow lid of the cage. She stuck her hand down into the cage and attempted to prod Fluffy slightly. Fluffy lunged, sinking his teeth into Kate's hand.

"Ouch!" she yelped and withdrew the injured hand. There were two small pricks on her finger. "You didn't have to do that. I won't hurt you."

Katie replaced the lid. Any hamster who could lunge like that wasn't too sick, she decided. She washed her finger with soap and water, poured hydrogen peroxide over it, and put a Band-Aid on. Already it throbbed painfully.

Doug came through the family room into the kitchen. "Hi," he said to Katie. "Did you look at the hamsters?"

"Fluffy bit me. I put my hand in the cage without thinking."

"Did he bite you bad?" Doug asked, looking skeptically at the bandaged finger.

"No, not too bad."

They watched the hamsters together for a moment. Fluffy circled around in a nest of sawdust. Frank remained in his corner.

"I don't think they like each other," he said. "Maybe we should get another cage. That way they wouldn't have to live together."

"They'll be fine," Katie assured him. "Listen, I've got an idea. I have to go to the market—you can come along, if you like."

"Can I pick out the cereal?" Doug asked.

"Sure—as long as it's not sugared."

After buying groceries and hamburgers and french fries at McDonald's Kate and the boys returned home.

They carried in the sacks and set them on the kitchen counter. Alan had left for the hospital.

"Mama!" Rob cried, looking into the hamster cage. "There's blood everywhere!"

Katie pushed the boys away, feeling her own blood drain away to her feet and knees, leaving her head reeling. The clear plastic sides of the cage had splatters of blood, and inside Fluffy hunched over the sawdust nest.

The nest, of course, she thought. Hamsters have babies. Except Fluffy is a male. And so is Frank.

In the nest lay a mass of gelatinous lumps. "Oh, my God!" she cried.

Fluffy, clearly not a male, was licking her belly clean of blood and debris. In the nest the malformed babies to which she had given birth wriggled and undulated. They were pink and hairy. Mostly they were headless. Katie's stomach spasmed.

"What's wrong with Fluffy?" Rob sobbed.

"You boys go—and get a box in the storeroom—find a box to put Fluffy and Frank in—no, *two* boxes. One for each hamster. I have to get them out of there."

Frank was creeping over to the nest. His eyes darted between Fluffy, who was occupied with her grooming, and the glistening mass in the nest.

"Go—" Katie ordered the boys, knowing she did not want them to see any more of the drama inside the cage.

Doug could hardly tear himself away, but he finally followed Rob, whose small shoulders jerked in short sobs, to the storeroom. It'd take them fifteen minutes to find the boxes, Katie prayed. Fifteen minutes. If only she could scoop the nest out of the cage. She got a large spoon and removed the yellow lid of the cage.

Frank screamed, a high feral screech, when Fluffy attacked him at the nest. He had one of the monstrosities in his paws. His mouth was red where he had bitten it.

Fluffy charged at him, ripped at his shoulder, and more blood flew.

Kate was feeling dizzy. I've got to separate them, she thought dizzily. Otherwise they'll kill each other. She jammed a cookbook between the hamsters, isolating Frank in one end. He still clutched one of the babies, which had stopped moving.

Fluffy, in a feeding frenzy, stuffed her mouth full. Kate gagged. My God, she was eating all of them. How could she do that? Blood dripped from the hamster's mouth.

One fetal mass lay in the nest. Kate took the spoon and ladled the small lump out, gagging once more when she saw there was no head, just feet and a belly and a thumping heart. Fluffy leapt for the spoon and crashed down again. She lay there, poised for the spoon in case it should threaten her again.

Kate heard the boys coming down the hallway. Quickly she dumped the malformed fetal hamster into a plastic bag and stuffed it into a drawer. Doug's eyes were wide when he came through the kitchen door. Each of the boys held a box. Doug had a shoe box. Robbie had a box that a mug had come in for Christmas.

"Is this big enough for Fluffy?" he asked, holding out the box to Kate.

"It'll do fine—just until I can clean out the cage."

The boys crept closer to see what was happening inside the hamster cage. They didn't ask about the cookbook stuck between the plastic sides.

"Frank's bleeding, Mom," Doug said quietly.

"He's not hurt too bad—he'll be okay. We have to get Fluffy out first."

"His mouth is bleeding—" Robbie's voice was choked again.

"Fluffy is *not* a *he*!" Kate told him. "He's a female—a girl hamster. And he—she—just had babies."

"Where are the babies?" Rob peered at Fluffy and the empty nest. "I wanna see the babies."

"She has them in her mouth." Katie tried to sound calm. Where was Alan in a crisis? she ranted silently. Why wasn't he here when she needed him?

"Is she eating them?" Doug asked.

"I'm afraid so. Hamsters do that if there's—something wrong with the babies." She didn't want to say any more. She was feeling very light-headed. She leaned on the table.

Rob's eyes were wide.

"I have to get Fluffy out of there—and then Frank—" Kate slid into a chair.

"You look funny . . ." She could hear Doug's voice, but it was very far away, floating over her head.

Everything went black, and Kate slumped to the floor.

When she came to, Linda Vickers was bathing her face with a cool, damp towel. Katie tried to scramble to her feet.

"You fainted," Linda said calmly. "Doug ran over and got me—you just stay there for a few minutes. Jim's coming."

Jim Vickers was tall and lanky and quiet, and Katie didn't know him very well. He walked in the front door with a wire cage.

"How're you feeling?" he asked Kate.

"I feel fine—a little silly," she said from her prone position on the kitchen floor. "Alan's at the hospital—really, Linda, I think I can get up now."

"Sit up first," Jim said, and expertly placed his hand on her back to help her sit up on the floor.

"I feel so stupid . . ."

"Fainting's not stupid," Linda said. "I'm just glad you're all right. Doug thought you were dead."

The boys were crouched beside her, their eyes wide with alarm.

"I'm fine," she assured them. "Really."

Linda helped her stand and then sit in the chair. "Robbie said the hamsters had babies—and then ate them."

"I'm afraid so. I was trying to separate them—and—I fainted."

Jim looked into the cage. "I'll get the big one into the wire cage. We'll use the box for the smaller one."

"That's Frank," Doug said. "He's mine. But Fluffy bites."

"He does not!" Rob objected.

"All hamsters bite," Jim pronounced and silenced both boys.

He reached into the cage and grabbed Fluffy from the back. She bared her teeth, but couldn't turn to bite his hand. She landed in the wire cage with a soft plop. Frank went into the box without a show of teeth.

Linda kept an eye on Katie. "How're you feeling now? Shall I call Alan at the hospital and have him come home?"

Katie laughed softly. "No—don't do that. I'm really all right."

"You aren't pregnant, are you?" Linda asked. "When I was pregnant with Todd I passed out three times."

Katie held her breath. What she had been afraid of had been spoken out loud. "I don't know—" she said quietly.

"Well, you'd better check." Linda Vickers was not one to beat around the bush.

Kate thought about the fetal hamster she'd stuffed in the drawer. She wanted to get a closer look at it. Without fainting. "I will," she told Linda and Jim. "And thank you for getting Frank and Fluffy out of that cage. And for coming over."

"Anytime," Jim said. "Better get another cage and keep those hamsters separated."

Katie stood carefully, and discovered she felt fine. She reached over and closed the kitchen drawer where the plastic bag was just visible.

"I wanted to ask you about your house—I couldn't believe it when I saw the For Sale sign."

"Time to get out of this valley," Jim said, sounding irritable. "Too many people, too many cars—"

"The fact is, you know, Jim's not been well—"

Jim Vickers interrupted her. "Oh, don't start on all that again. I'm sure Kate doesn't want to hear about it, Linda. Let's just go home and let her rest."

Linda rolled her eyes. "He doesn't like to talk about it."

Jim took her firmly by the arm. "It's not that—I have a growth. It's inoperable. They think I have six months. There—I said it. Now, let's go home, Linda." He looked at Katie with large, sorrowful eyes. "If you need us, you just call, or send one of the boys."

"Thanks," Kate stammered. "I'm—sorry—I—"

When they were gone Katie hugged Doug and Robbie. "You did just the right thing," she said. "I'm sorry if I scared you."

"Boy, did you ever," Robbie told her and hugged her tightly.

"How come Todd's moving, Mom?" Doug asked her. "It isn't fair. First Mitch moved, then Peter, and now Todd. I'm going to lose all my friends."

"People move from this valley," Katie told him. "It's just a fact of life."

"Is Mr. Vickers gonna die?" Rob asked.

"Everybody's going to die someday," Kate answered.

"But not for a long time. You aren't going to die for a long time . . ." Rob was reassuring himself. "Isn't that right?"

Katie tried to sound cheerful. "That's right, kiddo. I'm planning to be around here for a very long time. So you'd better clean out that cage."

Doug looked miserable.

"Come on, Red Dawn, you're brave," she coaxed him. "You'll make new friends. Maybe someone really nice will move into the Vickerses' house."

Katie and the boys cleaned out the cage, dumping sawdust into the garbage can and hosing out the cage in the backyard. They let it dry on the picnic table. Kate knew Linda Vickers could be right. With all the fuss of starting a new job and worrying about Elaine and Phyllis and arguing with Alan, she had totally lost track of her periods. When was the last one? Two months ago? Or was it three months ago? Dr. Robertz would want to know the exact date. How many women kept a little black book of their menstrual dates? she thought irritably. She'd guess it was two months ago. She'd go in to see the doctor tomorrow—if there was time.

When Doug and Rob went to swim with their friend Tammy, two blocks away—Tammy's mother was once an Olympic swimmer—Kate retrieved the plastic bag from the drawer. Steadying herself against the kitchen counter, she opened the bag.

What lay in the bag was a purplish mass with bits of hair and legs protruding from an enlarged belly. It looked like a raw oyster, except it was purple and red. And it was dead.

She took a deep breath, checking herself to see if there was any evidence of dizziness. There wasn't. The only thing she felt was a ringing alarm. What had happened to these hamster babies? In her own kitchen on a sunny Sunday afternoon?

"I had another dream," Alan told Dr. Viktor Straub. Straub yawned.

Alan glared at the psychiatrist. The drive to San Francisco had been particularly tedious that afternoon, the room was too cold for Alan's comfort, and he'd left Kate in a foul mood. "I don't get it," he said to Straub. "I thought that this is what I'm here for—to examine these dreams I'm having. If there's something else I should be doing—I expect you to tell me."

"Do you, now?" Straub drawled, adjusting himself in the black leather chair where he sat during each session. "A fine surgeon like you—surely you can decide what you want to do here for an hour. Can't you, Alan?"

"I thought I was—I want to tell you about this dream —I'm remembering more of them now. It seems to me that's rather important." Alan stood and walked to the windows, framing a sweep of the San Francisco Bay and the wharf area.

"It is my feeling you are obsessed with these dreams . . . they have become self-serving."

Alan laughed softly and turned back to Dr. Straub. "I thought psychiatrists were always interested in dreams —or am I wrong?"

"Dreams are a part of the analysis, certainly," Straub said, "but your dreams have become the central issue."

"They are the central issue—that's why I came here."

"I'd like to hear about your daily life—tell me about your children, your wife, your friends . . ."

"I don't want to talk about my children or my wife or my friends—I want to understand these dreams that take up a third of my life! I don't see that as unreasonable."

"Perhaps the dreams are a camouflage for your depression." Straub stared at him.

"Depression? You think I'm depressed?"

"I do. You give every evidence of a man in the grip of a depression. I think you should try a medication—"

"I'm not taking meds—I don't believe I'm depressed." Alan heard his voice shake with fury. It was so difficult to be angry with a shrink, he thought.

"I'd like you to try Protocol—it's new—"

"I have no intention of taking medication." Alan returned to his chair and sat down heavily. "I cannot afford to do anything that would jeopardize my work. How would you feel if your surgeon was taking an antidepressant just before he operated on you?"

"I might think he was a very wise surgeon," Straub said.

"You might think differently if there were complications in the surgery . . ."

"Protocol has very few side effects—"

"I'm not taking it. I do understand your opinion on this—but I assure you I am not depressed."

Straub shrugged and his eyebrows suggested his skepticism. Alan shivered. He'd had enough. He headed for the door.

"You're not going to tell me your dream?"

"No."

"Will you return next week? Perhaps we could talk about it then."

Alan turned to look at the doctor. "I don't know. I have to think about it."

"I'll keep the hour open—there's some issues we need to deal with—your father, for one, Dr. Campbell. You think about it . . ."

"I've thought about it—" Alan tried to keep his voice level. "I won't be back."

* * *

When the door closed behind Alan, Dr. Viktor Straub sighed and lumbered heavily to his desk. In the top drawer was a large plastic bottle of Prolixin. Dr. Viktor Straub swallowed two and went back to his chair to wait for his next patient.

That night Alan dreamed he was in a room where the orange flames of a great fire were visible through the windows. The fire was getting closer and he tried to escape through one of the doors of the room, which was only painted on the wall. He ran to the windows, one after another, only to discover that each was a creation of paint on plaster. Now the flames licked at the corners of the room. Bright orange fingers of fire crept up the side of the walls. Smoke and heat engulfed him. There was no escape. And that's when he heard the sound again, high and panicky. He'd never get out of there alive.

He awoke panting. Kate rolled over and looked at him, but he could tell she was not really awake. His pillow was soaked with sweat. Alan squeezed his eyes shut, but sleep did not come until he swallowed two Seconal. He dived into the white oblivion of drugged sleep.

12

Amanda was busy in the Campbell kitchen making an exotic chicken stew with corn, shrimp, and Tabasco sauce. She was born and raised in New Orleans, and her cooking reflected her heritage. Now and then she glared at the two hamster cages on the utility cart in the kitchen.

"Shouldn't be no rats in the house," she murmured to herself. "Unhealthy . . ."

Frank and Fluffy eyed each other from their separate containers. Frank was still in the wire cage, and Doug had been protesting the clear discrimination for days.

"Half a mind to let 'em loose outside . . ." Amanda continued. "Let them cats at 'em. Make short work of rats, them cats . . ." She stirred the soup.

At two thirty the boys arrived home on the bus. Rob bounded in the house and said he was going swimming at Tammy's. He dumped the remains of his bag lunch on the kitchen counter and ran off to his room for swim trunks and a towel. Doug wandered into the kitchen.

"Hi, Amanda," he said, poking through the bread drawer where cookies had been known to hide out.

"Hello, Dougy," she said. "And how was your school today?"

"Doug doesn't like it much."

"You mean Robbie?"

He looked up at her. His dark hair swept over his forehead, and she brushed it out of his eyes. His skin was pale and damp next to her browned, dry hand.

"No, I mean, I don't like it. It's hot and boring. Doug hates school in the summer."

"Isn't that odd, little boy? Talking about yourself as if you was someone else?"

"What? I'm not someone else . . ." He stuffed two oatmeal cookies into his mouth and chewed absently.

Amanda shook her head. Sometimes it was hard to figure out these children, she thought. Her own were grown up, all five of them. Lucky thing, too. Too hard to raise children these days.

"You wanna go swimming?" Robbie was already in his swimming trunks and had a towel over his shoulder. "Tammy's mom said it was okay."

Doug shook his head. "Naw—you go ahead. I'm gonna watch TV or something."

"Not on a beautiful day you're not wasting your time in front of no TV," Amanda told Doug. "Not good for little boys."

"I'm not a little boy, Amanda. Doug is going to be eleven."

She laid aside the spoon. "You feeling all right, little boy?" She placed an experienced hand on his cheek. "You not hot or anything? I could call your mama, if you feeling sick. Your nose not bleeding, is it?"

"No," Doug said. "I feel fine. I just don't want to go swimming with Rob and Tammy. They're such babies—

they splash water at each other and go down the slide and scream—I'm too old for that."

"I don't scream," Rob interrupted. He was still in the kitchen doorway. "Tammy screams a lot. But I don't. It's no fun unless you come, Doug."

"I don't feel like it—"

"You never feel like it! You're just an old poop out! I think you get a nosebleed or a headache on purpose. That's what I think."

"Dougy has a headache?" Amanda asked him.

"Not much . . . just a little."

"The teacher was real mad at him today," Robbie told Amanda, eyeing Doug suspiciously the whole time.

"Why she mad at you?" Amanda stirred the soup again.

"I don't know—she gets mad real easy. She said I wasn't paying attention."

"And was you?"

"I was paying attention—but not to her."

"And what was you paying attention to?"

"Doug thought he heard something—you know, something real big. Like an earthquake coming. Sounded like a giant rolling over, except the sound came in waves—you know, like the ocean. Or maybe bagpipes."

Amanda silently stirred the soup.

"I think it was bagpipes." He finished the last bite of oatmeal cookie. "Have you ever heard bagpipes, Amanda?"

"Nooo," she crooned.

"Well, they kind of sound like an earthquake starting. They sort of rumble and screech at first. Someday Doug's going to play bagpipes. My dad said so."

She'd better talk to Kate, Amanda decided. Something wrong with that little boy. Could be he was scared of another earthquake. Could be something a lot worse.

"Can I put a hot dog in the microwave, Amanda?" Doug asked her.

"No, you cannot, child. Amanda doesn't trust that contraption. Here—" She helped him extract a hot dog from the package in the refrigerator. "Amanda'll fry it up for you nice and brown. Just like my mama used to do."

Mrs. Ramirez, Doug's teacher, called at the lab and asked Katie to call her back when she had time. Kate took the message and read it three times. Was something wrong with Doug? Another nosebleed? She called the school, but the school secretary told her Mrs. Ramirez was in class and couldn't be disturbed.

Kate spent the afternoon inoculating a new batch of tissue cultures. Deena Crist had the day off, and John Lacey wasn't in his office for the day. Kate had the lab to herself, which was relaxing. There was only the hiss of the air filter in the clean room, and now and then the freezer room hummed into high gear. She did not like the freezer room. She had visions of the door closing behind her every time she went in to get more frozen chick embryo cultures. Even clad in the protective suit and headgear, she was extremely cold whenever she walked into that stiff gray compartment.

Her work at the lab was going well after only three weeks, and she was getting used to the hours. She tried not to think about the boys. Did they miss her when they came home from school? At least Amanda was there . . .

The afternoon dragged on. Kate had inoculated the eight HSF cultures, separated one inoculum of four HSF cultures into individual cells, a task assisted by a

450 power microscope. And she'd reincubated the individual cells. Tomorrow she could begin the photographing of the genes in the cultures. In a couple of weeks she would start the addition of artificial interferon to the tissue cultures to see if the interferon had any effect on the viral mutations of the cell genes. It was interesting work, but seemed to progress slowly. She sighed. That's how research actually progressed. Slowly.

She'd called and made an appointment with Dr. Robertz that morning. She had an appointment at four forty-five.

And at three thirty she took a break and called Mrs. Ramirez at the school. There was no answer, so she tried the second phone number Doug's teacher had left.

"Hello?" a voice said.

"Mrs. Ramirez? This is Katie Campbell—I got your message to call."

"Oh, Mrs. Campbell, I'm so glad you phoned back. I'm really very worried about Doug. I wondered if you'd noticed lately how he talks about himself in the third person." There was a long silence.

Katie hadn't a clue what Mrs. Ramirez was talking about. "I'm afraid I haven't . . ."

"He's stopped playing with the other youngsters. He daydreams through the morning and says he has a headache most of the time. I know he has nosebleeds—but, Mrs. Campbell, I think something is bothering that child."

Kate felt her heart beating in her throat. "What do you mean? What could be bothering Doug?"

"I don't know—he said some hamsters died—he seemed upset about it."

"Yes—the hamsters had a litter of—" A swell of nausea threatened her. "Well, they all died. It was quite upsetting—for all of us. But I'm sure Doug will get over it."

"Well, you may be right. I hope so. But I strongly recommend you get him to a child psychologist. I know some good ones—"

"A child psychologist?" Kate felt like an echo. "You think it's that serious?"

"I do, Mrs. Campbell. I really do."

At four thirty Kate left the research lab and walked to the office building where many of the physicians at Lorimar had their private offices. Claude Robertz had delivered both Doug and Robbie, but still Kate felt anxious sitting in the waiting room. She paged through a copy of *Parents* magazine. Bright infants with popping blue eyes stared back at her. But what she saw was quite different. Her head swam.

"Well," Claude Robertz told her after he'd run the pregnancy screening test right there in his office. "You *are* pregnant, Kate." He was grinning at her.

"Yes, well—I suspected as much. I almost bought one of those pregnancy kits at the druggist—but I decided I'd rather hear it from you."

"Good girl. Take your vitamins. Get plenty of rest. And come back in a month." He turned back to her. "I imagine Alan will be pleased?"

"Oh, yes." Katie tried to beam. "Very pleased."

"Good. See you next month. If there's any problem you let me know." He had his hand on the doorknob.

"Dr. Robertz—Claude?"

"Yes?"

"What about these teratomas? What are the chances that I'm carrying a—tumor—not a baby?"

Claude Robertz frowned and thought for a moment. "There may be a correlation between stress and molear pregnancies," he said. "There is some evidence that stress causes genetic mutations in laboratory animals. We don't know yet if this is true in humans. The best I can tell you, Kate, is to avoid the obvious—alcohol, toxins around the house, smoking, drugs—even aspirin."

"Yes—but I was wondering—"

He smiled. "We'll talk about it next month. And your due date. Don't you worry about this baby. If there's anything to worry about, I'll tell you. Agreed?"

"Yes, of course." She was feeling slightly foolish and very pregnant suddenly. The desire to throw up had been replaced by the desire to cry. She'd forgotten what an emotional roller coaster those first three months of a pregnancy could be.

Except it hadn't been an emotional roller coaster for her before. She'd actually enjoyed her pregnancies, and hadn't had many of the discomforts her friends complained about.

That evening she nibbled on her dinner.

"Are you okay?" Alan asked.

"Fine. I'm fine."

"You're not eating much."

"I'm not hungry—I guess it's too hot. I think I'll just have my iced tea." Hadn't they talked about another child? she wondered absently. Hadn't the plan been to have one more, hopefully a girl? She should tell Alan the news, but the words wouldn't form in her brain. Maybe she'd wait awhile. Just in case.

"Isn't it strange," Jerry Greathouse mused, "that we are only seeing this rare tumor in upper-middle-class areas? Has anyone looked into that aspect of the epidemic?"

Alan glanced up at him from the article he was reading in the *New England Journal of Medicine*. "A tumor that selects by income? A yuppie neoplasm?" Alan muttered. "I, somehow, doubt that. Besides, how do we know it's only in upper-income populations? Elaine Calder, for one, wasn't exactly a millionaire."

Jerry buried himself in his copy of the medical journal. "I don't know—it just seems like whenever it's mentioned it's somebody from Berkeley, or Palos Verdes, or Scottsdale, Arizona. I don't see any mention of Harlem in New York or Watts or . . ."

"Okay, okay—maybe you're right . . . Tell me what rich people do more than poor people?" Alan kept his finger in his place in the journal.

"Almost everything except breathe." Jerry laughed wickedly. "Golf! How about all those fertilizers they put on the greens? Or cholesterol? Or stress? Or ultraviolet rays in those tanning booths . . . the list is endless."

"I doubt this is a strictly regional epidemic, although the cases reported seem to be from the West Coast—in well-heeled communities. So what do the *western* rich do that the *eastern* rich don't?"

"Eat yogurt?"

"You're not taking this seriously." Alan went back to reading.

"I am. I'm just trying to think creatively about all this. It seems to me the article is bogged down in statistics that probably don't mean much."

"Maybe there is a delay factor—poor people don't see a physician as often as rich people. Maybe the rates will increase in the middle incomes and lower with time. Maybe you're looking at a couple of neoplastic teratomas in your practice, and you just haven't recognized it yet."

"It's possible—entirely possible." Jerry stretched his feet out on the leather sofa and leaned back into the buttery softness of the cushions. He took a sip of his iced coffee.

Doug wandered into the study and stood looking at his father and Jerry.

"Hey, big guy, how come you're not playing with Sean and Sarah?" Jerry asked him.

"I don't know—they're in the tree house. I got a headache." He flopped down into a comfortable wing-back chair.

"You're probably hungry," Alan told him. "I'll bet your mom has dinner about ready."

"No—they're just drinking tea and talking." Doug curled up in the chair. "Besides, I'm not hungry."

Alan studied his son for a moment. Doug did look a bit peaked. Probably coming down with something.

"Dougy, did you know you can move your headache around in your head?" Jerry asked him. "Look—if you press over your eyebrows—" He touched a spot on his eyebrows near the bridge of his nose. "The headache moves. Sometimes it goes away."

Doug sat up and watched Jerry. Then he pressed his fingers into his own eyebrows. His mouth opened slowly as he pressed. It looked as if he were going to yell. Tears sprang into his eyes and brimmed over.

"Doug?" Alan asked, slightly alarmed at the boy.

Doug groaned and stopped the pressure. "It makes it worse," he told them in a small voice.

Alan got up from his desk and went to Doug. "Let's have a look," he said. He turned Doug's head and the boy grimaced. "Does that hurt? When you turn your head?"

"A little."

"I think you'd better lie down for a while. I'll bring you some Tylenol—"

Doug got off the chair and left the study without a word.

"It's probably the flu. Or a cold," Alan said.

"I don't like the way his left eye is swollen," Jerry observed. "Has he had a physical lately?"

"Kate has him at Dr. Silver's office about once a week —he has nosebleeds—you know how mothers are . . ." Alan left to get Doug a Tylenol and a glass of water.

Jerry stayed in the study for a while, enjoying the quiet of this Campbell house, so unlike his own. It was nice for a few minutes, and then it was eerie, like finding yourself alone on a dark country road in the middle of the night. Finally, he went to the kitchen to see how the women were doing with dinner, and where this tree house was in the backyard.

Dinner at the Campbells' was more formal than the Greathouse children were accustomed to, even though Kate tried to keep it family style.

Jill picked up a cloth napkin from beside her plate. "What is this?" she asked.

"Your napkin," Maria told her, blushing. "You'd think they'd never seen a napkin before."

"But it's not paper! It's cloth!" Jennifer chimed.

Jerry grinned at the kids. "Kate's being ecologically correct. Cloth napkins are better than paper because you can use them over and over. The paper ones you have to throw away. Just think about it. A tree gives up its life so you can wipe the spaghetti off your mouth."

"Can't we get cloth napkins, too?" Jill begged her mother.

"Please?" Jennifer added.

"Yes!" Maria said, grinning. "Yes! Cloth napkins— we'll make dozens!" Clearly she wanted to change the conversation. "How's Dougy feeling? Better?"

"I gave him a Tylenol," Alan said. "He's lying down. His left eye is a bit swollen."

Rob attended to his plate of spaghetti with all the industry he could muster. He didn't look at his father.

"Did anything happen outdoors that would cause Doug's eye to swell?" Alan asked.

"Nope," Rob said after a particularly uncomfortable silence.

"No," Sean agreed. "He said he had a headache."

"He didn't fall—or get hit with something?" Kate asked. She hadn't noticed the swelling of his eye. It'd probably be black and blue by morning.

Rob shook his head. "I don't think he fell. Or got hit. He hardly ever feels like playing anymore. I wish those old headaches would go away." He tackled his salad.

"I play," little Joanna Greathouse piped up, sucking a strand of spaghetti into her mouth. And everyone laughed at her.

Katie laughed the hardest at the youngster. Secretly, she couldn't keep her eyes off Joanna. She knew it was because she hoped to have a daughter. Not that another boy wouldn't be perfectly all right, but a little girl was different. She loved Joanna's chubby little hands and bare feet. Yes, a girl would be delightful.

When Katie finally told Alan she was pregnant they agreed not to talk about a new baby around the children yet. Not until Katie was well enough into the pregnancy that there was little chance of a spontaneous abortion and the subsequent explanations that would entail. Better not to put the children through any unnecessary trauma.

"Jerry and I are going to run over to Lorimar after dinner," Alan said, eyeing Kate, "if that's all right. There's something I want to show him. Some records."

"That is, if you can spare us from washing the dishes," Jerry added. "We won't be gone long."

Kate wasn't happy about it. She felt that men and women should not segregate at a dinner party. "As long as you come back and don't spend the rest of the evening closeted in the study."

"We won't. Scout's honor." Jerry held up two fingers in a Cub Scout salute.

"What records do you need to look at?" Maria asked. She expertly whirled a forkful of spaghetti into her mouth.

Alan and Jerry looked at each other.

"Surgery records," Alan said. "It's very dull. Do you really want me to explain it?"

"Yes," Maria said. "I'm interested."

"It's about the geographical occurrence of a very specific tumor. There was an article this month in the *New England Journal of Medicine*—and we just wanted to check some of our own statistics against it."

Jerry nodded. "It's very strange—I haven't seen any of these tumors in my practice. And Alan's had eight. Or ten, isn't it, Alan? In five months."

"What kind of tumor?" Katie asked. Her throat had closed up momentarily.

"Teratomas," Jerry said, nonplussed. "It's quite rare, so it's surprising that Alan has seen so many."

"That's what Elaine Calder had." Kate laid her fork on the table and put her hands in her lap, hoping she was a match for the nausea that whirled around her insides.

"Oh, Kate, I'm sorry we mentioned it," Alan apologized. "Elaine was a friend of Kate's."

"Please don't talk about her like she's dead," Kate said, looking around at the children. "She moved away. But she's not dead. Or anything."

Maria patted Katie's hand reassuringly. "Of course not. I don't think that's what Alan meant."

"No, I didn't. Elaine came through the surgery fine. No reason to think she didn't move to Arizona or Idaho. Or somewhere." Alan quickly dabbed at his mouth with the napkin. "Now, if it's all right, Jerry and I'll go and get back before you even miss us. If you're okay, Kate . . ."

"I'm fine," she told him. "Just not terribly hungry. Will you have more spaghetti, Sean?" She saw him looking around the table hungrily. He'd already polished off one huge plate of pasta. Is this what she had to look forward to with teenagers? she wondered.

Sean helped himself to the spaghetti, and Alan and Jerry left. Rob told the girls about the baby hamsters who'd been eaten. Jennifer and Jill squealed and declined more spaghetti.

"That's quite normal," Maria explained to the children. "Mother hamsters get rid of babies who probably wouldn't survive anyway."

"Yes, but it's *gross!*" Sarah objected. "Especially after we've just eaten."

"*Gross!*" Joanna mimicked happily.

Alan and Jerry went directly to Alan's office when they arrived at Lorimar Medical Center.

"It's been a while since I've been in here," Jerry said, admiring the shining tiled floors and clean, painted walls. There were framed paintings and collages on many of the corridor walls. "Artwork!" he exclaimed. "Will you look at this! I'd kill for a framed print in my clinic!"

Alan's hospital office was on the third floor in an older wing of the hospital. The bookshelves were built in, the windows were wide and washed, and a beige tweed carpet covered the floor.

"Nice . . ." Jerry commented.

"If you're done admiring the decor, let's check this list in Medical Records. I think you'll find my tumor patients were from all areas of the valley."

"Maybe—" Jerry conceded. "Maybe not."

Alan pulled the surgical reports from his desk. They were arranged by months, so he had seven months available. In Medical Records he handed over a list of patients' names and chart numbers to a young woman sitting at a desk neatly organized with a spider plant, several pens, a telephone, and memo pads.

"It'll take me a minute," she said.

Alan nodded and she hurried through a door. The phone rang and she rushed back out. "I'm the only one here this time of night," she explained, picking up the phone. "Hello? Medical Records . . ."

Alan and Jerry waited patiently through the phone call, and then much longer while the woman went to the files to retrieve the requested records. She returned empty-handed.

"I'm sorry—none of these records are available." She frowned. "I don't quite understand it—maybe someone's doing a patient review—sometimes the residents request a lot of files."

"*None* of the records are available?" Alan was irritated. "Can I find out who has them?"

"I could check the request file—" The phone rang again. She answered it, darting quick glances at Alan and Jerry. "I can't talk right now," she said, and hung up the phone. "Let's see—the request file . . ." She typed something into the computer. "Yes—here it is. Let's see—what were those names?"

She typed and frowned at the computer screen. Finally, she said, "Two of these patients' files are in Patient Review—that's Dr. Spender—no—he returned them—I think . . ."

"I thought computers were supposed to make this kind of thing simpler," Jerry quipped quietly.

Alan gave him a black look. "Usually it isn't this much trouble."

"Well, I'm sorry," the young woman apologized, clearly getting annoyed with Alan and Jerry. "I'm the only one here—and—"

The phone rang again. She answered several questions in a brusque manner and hung up the phone.

"And I'm very busy—as you can see. I'm sure they can find these records for you tomorrow."

"I need them tonight," Alan told her abruptly. "Can I speak to your supervisor?"

"I'm the supervisor on evenings—but I can't control what happens in here on days. Someone hasn't recorded the requests or returns on these files—maybe they're behind on their inputting—"

"I'm sure." Alan turned and walked out of Medical Records. Jerry followed him.

Before they were halfway to the elevator the young woman came trotting up behind them. "I found this," she said. She handed Alan a slip of paper with a name on it. "I don't think he's a doctor. But he requested a lot of files. He may have the ones you want."

Alan read the name on the paper. "Lt. Col. Stephen Reynolds? Who the hell is that?"

The woman shrugged. "Beats me."

"I'm pregnant," Katie told Maria. "We planned this —we hoped for it. But I don't want it now."

Maria sat and studied Katie's face calmly. "Is that

why you're not eating? Do you think you can starve it away?"

Katie took a deep breath. "No, I don't think that. I'm just not hungry. If I take a bite, it sticks in my throat."

"Are you taking vitamins? Drinking milk?"

Katie nodded. She tipped her head back to prevent the tears from spilling. "I don't want this baby, Maria!" She thought she must be going mad. "I want an abortion!"

"I can't agree with that—don't ask me to agree with that."

"You don't understand—this baby—what if it's not a baby?"

"Not a baby?" Maria repeated slowly.

"What if it's a tumor? I couldn't bear it—I can't stand thinking about it. Sometimes it feels like that—like a growth that's sucking at me—" Katie let her head droop miserably. "You don't know how scared I am. I can't trust my own body now."

Maria folded Kate in her long, slender arms, and held her for a few moments. "It'll be all right. You wait and see. Everything will work out."

"No," Kate finally said, pulling away from the tenderness of Maria. "I don't think it will."

Jerry and Alan went back to the Campbell house. The evening air was just beginning to cool and even the dust smelled like summer. Alan was in a foul mood. He drove, formulating in his mind what he would do the next morning: He'd go directly to the chief of staff and find out who the hell Lt. Col. Stephen Reynolds was and why he was allowed to sequester patient files at Lorimar.

"Alan," Jerry said, "I meant to ask you—if you don't

mind. How's it going with the great head doctor in San Francisco?"

"At the risk of sounding like a resistant patient, it isn't *going* anywhere. I don't think I'm going back."

"What about the dreams? Hey—whoa—slow down, will you?"

Alan had swerved sharply around a car. He slowed down and took a couple of deep breaths.

"You know, dreams are just a different path—a different way to understand ourselves." Jerry listened to Alan's breathing. It was leveling out. "When I was a boy, the first thing my mother asked me in the morning was 'What did you dream?' She was a Lakota Indian—a very beautiful woman, but I didn't know it then. I just thought of her as my mother."

Alan was relaxing. Jerry could tell by the muscles in his arms and the way he gripped the steering wheel.

"Tell me one of your dreams. I can show you another way of understanding them besides psychoanalytic technique."

Alan glanced quickly at Jerry. "None of my dreams make any sense."

"That's okay. None of mine do either if you look at them rationally. But I don't. Tell me a dream. We'll slow it down and look at it."

So Alan told him the dream about the sheep. "I was in a foreign land—I don't know where—but it was hot and sandy. There was a tree there and a sheep tied to a branch of the tree. A young man was dashing the sheep against the tree trunk in a strange ritual—I didn't understand it. I wanted to rescue the sheep. So I insisted that the young man stop torturing the sheep. But when I looked into the animal's eyes I sensed this calmness . . . this resignation . . . a kind of peace. And I knew I was interfering in something that was none of my business. So I left. I walked away. Even though I knew I could have killed the sheep quickly and painlessly—I let the torture continue. I walked away."

Jerry sat and listened to Alan tell the dream. "That's quite a dream," he finally said, after a rather long silence. "What do you think that dream is telling you?"

"I don't know, Jer. If I knew it wouldn't bother me."

"Guess. Take a guess about what it means."

"A guess? Well, it means—I am a participant in some plan or ritual I don't understand."

Jerry nodded. "That's a start. And what is the dream asking of you?"

Alan took the Madrone Road exit. "What's it asking of me? I don't know."

"If 'I don't know' isn't an answer, what is the dream asking of you?"

"It isn't clear." Alan laughed softly. "Do we have to play these word games? What do you make of the dream?"

"It's not my dream, pal. It's yours. You have to figure it out. Think about it. Come out to the house some evening and we'll go into the sweathouse. It's a good place to think. And relax. There's no phone. Sometimes things are clearer there."

"I'm a scientist," Alan explained softly. "I'm trained to think about things in a certain way. My mother never once asked me what I dreamed. She asked me if I put on clean underwear—in case I was in an accident on the way to school. I can't change the way I deal with things overnight."

"I'm not asking you to do anything overnight—just think about it. Okay?"

They pulled into the Campbell driveway. "Okay. I'll think about it."

* * *

Hilda Jobs was asleep when Waif made the first attack. She did not hear him lumbering down the hall to her bedroom that night. It was a very warm night, and she slept with only a sheet and a light green cotton blanket. She left the air conditioner on in the living room and listened to the radio news for a while before she fell asleep.

She woke only momentarily when Waif barged through the door. He was whimpering. He shuddered with the pain. He stopped, whined, and bared his teeth, hurling his great head from side to side.

"What's the matter?" she asked sleepily, reaching for him in the dark.

He bit deeply into her hand, wedging his teeth between the metatarsals of the wrist and the many sinewy bands that held muscle and nerves in place. Hilda shrieked, trying to pull her hand away. He held on, whipping the hand in his teeth. She stretched out her other hand for the telephone beside the bed, but she couldn't reach the receiver. Blood, spurting in steady red throbs, soaked into the sheets.

"Waif!" She wept, her voice shaky with shock and terror. "Waif, let me go!"

In the dark she saw the flash of his maddened eyes. They were huge. He must be sick, she thought, her mind beginning to reel in slow gray circles. Very sick. A dog doesn't bite the hand that feeds it. Wasn't that what they always said?

"Help!" she called, barely able to get the words out. "Help me!" Then she fainted.

When she was finally quiet Waif started on her feet. By dawn he had reached her knees. And he kept going. At six fifteen Hilda Jobs's heart fluttered for a few seconds and then stopped.

* * *

On Wednesday Lewis Kotura, the postman, reported the fact that Hilda Jobs's mail had not been collected from her mailbox for three days. He asked Eulipia Simpson if she'd seen Hilda since Monday and if she'd mind checking on the woman.

There was no answer at the door when Eulipia knocked. She listened and thought she heard a low growl. Probably that awful dog, she thought, and decided not to try to open the door. It wasn't odd not to see Hilda for weeks at a time. Eulipia closed the screen door.

Besides, it wasn't her responsibility. She marched home. If the mail was still there tomorrow, she'd call the police and ask them to check on Hilda. And why weren't her children checking on her? she wondered, exasperated. Perfectly grown-up children who hardly ever showed up. But what if she was sick? What then?

When Eulipia arrived home she closed the door to her bedroom and quietly called the police.

Captain Eric Newman was the first one through the door of Hilda's house.

"Ugh!" he grunted and slapped on a face mask with a carbon filter. The smell in the house was distinctive. Someone was dead.

"Hilda?" he called. "Mrs. Jobs?"

Officer Alexis Carpenter followed Newman into the kitchen and living room. It was in the living room they heard the low, rumbling growl.

"Must be a dog," Newman said to Carpenter. "Hilda? Hilda Jobs? Are you here? This is the police?"

Only the snarl answered them. Carpenter jumped and pulled out her revolver. Newman gestured her behind him. He started down the hall.

They heard a scream, or a whine. It wasn't clear. And footsteps. Four-footed steps.

"Hilda?" Newman said.

Waif crashed through the door of the bedroom and stood facing the two officers.

"Holy shit!" Newman wheezed through the face mask. "Would you look at that?"

The dog's face was covered with blood. One of his eyes had bulged to twice the size of the other. The white of the eye had hemorrhaged. Waif stood very still for a moment. And then he lunged for Newman.

Officer Carpenter stopped the dog in its tracks with one bullet in the head, which exploded like a casaba melon. Waif folded in half, midair, and sank to the floor. He lay very still.

Newman approached him cautiously. He'd seen stunned dogs before. He'd seen cunning dogs before. He didn't take chances. He nudged Waif with the tip of his boot, and the dog didn't move.

"He's dead," he said.

They stepped over the body and looked into the bedroom. It looked like a butcher shop. Hilda Jobs had been gnawed. Then ripped. And gnawed some more.

Alexis Carpenter gagged, ashamed and helpless for an instant, before she regained her composure. Eric Newman called for an ambulance and the animal disposal team. It was a "no lights, no siren" call, so they knew it would take a while.

"Something's really wrong here," she said, pointing to a picture on the bedroom wall of Hilda and Waif, the dog's head resting comfortably in Hilda's lap. "Someone's pet doesn't just get up one morning and eat their owner."

"The dog was probably sick—"

"I know, but when my dog gets sick he lies on the

couch and watches television. I mean, he doesn't come and chew me—" She gagged softly again. "Maybe the dog was mistreated—you know, it went wild—"

Eric pulled a blanket up over the body on the bed. "Let's go wait outside. Nothing we can do in here."

They looked around the apartment. Carpenter admired the Gustav Klimt original and the other prints that hung in the apartment. The furniture was old, but classic. Why'd she keep a great big ragged dog around? Carpenter wondered. She touched the collection of glass paperweights on a small table.

"No accounting for taste," an ambulance driver quipped savagely when they finally arrived.

Carpenter leaned over and threw up in the flowers.

13

 Alan sat in his office thinking about Kate. And a new baby! Hopefully it would be a girl this time. The pregnancy had come as a mild surprise to both of them, which he didn't like admitting even to himself in the day of efficient contraceptives and socially responsible family planning. It was just that Claude Robertz gave Kate a one-in-a-thousand chance to conceive another child after Robbie was born, so they'd been quite casual about birth control. It'd worked for eight years.

Alan was waiting for a phone call from the chief of staff. Alan had gone back to Medical Records to collect surgical files and found they were still in the hands of a Lt. Col. Stephen Reynolds. He wanted to know who this guy was, and what he was doing with the medical files.

The phone rang. It was Dr. Philip Morrisey, the chief of staff.

"Philip? Can you tell me who this guy—Lieutenant Colonel Stephen Reynolds—is? He has most of my surgical files, and I want to know why."

Philip Morrisey had the job of chief of staff because he was diplomatic, Alan knew. But that afternoon he wasn't behaving up to his usual standards.

"Reynolds? Yes, well, he's here—at Lorimar—on a—special assignment."

"What kind of special assignment? Why does he have access to the records?" Alan was furious, but he kept his voice level.

"Because I gave it to him. It's rather important—a matter of military importance . . ."

"Military importance?" Alan said. "What could be of any interest to the military in my patients' records?"

Morrisey paused. Alan could hear him breathing softly into the receiver. "I'm afraid I can't tell you that, Alan. I don't know myself. I'm certainly sorry if this has caused you any inconvenience—"

"Inconvenience? My patients' records are confidential, Philip. I don't want *anyone* snooping through them —not anyone, and especially not the military. Not unless I know the reason."

"I'm sorry you feel that way, Alan. I'm afraid we have no choice in the matter. The orders come from the very top—"

"Who?" Alan demanded. "Who gives that kind of an order?"

"The Surgeon General of the United States."

Alan sat back in his chair. "Oh, really—the Surgeon General?"

Morrisey didn't answer. "It's a national study—that's all I can tell you."

"Tell me where I can find my patients' charts," Alan growled into the phone. "Where is this Reynolds fellow?"

"I don't think it's a good idea to contact him. Let me speak to him—"

"Just tell me where he is, Philip. I need my charts."

Morrisey paused. "He has an office on 5 North."

Alan slammed down the phone. He glanced up at the map he'd taped to his wall. It was a map of the Santa Clara Valley, and red stickers had been placed in areas where the teratomas had occurred in the last year. Alan had gleaned most of the information from the morbidity reports from Pathology, and the addresses of the patients were available through Admitting. But it was a laborious undertaking. And, already, the red stickers were clustering. What if Jerry Greathouse was correct? That the incidence of the teratomaceous tumor was higher in certain areas? Had anyone looked at this aspect of the phenomenon?

Alan found the office on 5 North. It was the only one. 5 North was the old TB ward, from the days when TB was originally a menace. Now it stood largely vacant except for sleeping rooms for the interns and residents. Those rooms had large, unfriendly coded locks on the doors. The office area, at the end of the long hall, also had a lock. He knocked. No answer. He knocked again.

"Come in . . ." someone said.

Alan opened the door and looked in. A young fellow was bent over the desk. He wore a yellow golf shirt and a linen jacket that was the color of coffee with cream in it.

"I'm looking for a Lieutenant Colonel Stephen Reynolds," Alan said, glaring at the clear-eyed, sandy-haired man who was smiling at him.

"You've found him," he said. "Come in."

Alan had been prepared for a military officer, not this boy who looked like he couldn't be more than a year or two out of college. He spotted the stacks of medical records on a long table in the office.

"I'm unable to get a number of patients' files from

Medical Records," he told Reynolds. "Dr. Morrisey told me you had them. I don't know what's going on, but I can tell you—"

Reynolds stood up straight. A smile still played around his mouth and eyes. "I'm sorry if I inconvenienced you, Doctor. That is clearly not my intention. If you tell me the names of your patients I will return the files."

"Can you tell me what's going on? What's this study at Lorimar?"

"I'm afraid I can't. I would if I could. The military has an interest in certain kinds of cases in this country—"

"What kinds of cases—if I may ask?"

"I can't answer that," Reynolds said. "I can only tell you that the study is of vital national security. It's important, Dr.—what was your name?"

"Dr. Campbell—Alan . . ."

Reynolds thrust out his hand. "Lieutenant Colonel Reynolds . . ."

They shook hands. Alan noticed that Reynolds's hands were very strong and warm.

"I need access to my patients' files," Alan reiterated. "I don't know what the military would find of interest in them—but it's essential that I am able to retrieve them when needed."

"As I said, Doctor, you just give me the names, and I will not detain the records any longer."

Alan pulled the folded list from his lab coat pocket. "I happen to have the list right here." He handed it to Reynolds.

"Is this a study of the teratomas?"

Reynolds glanced at him coolly. He didn't answer. "I will have these files back to Medical Records by sixteen hundred hours."

"Thank you. And if you're interested, I've got a map

on the wall of my office. These tumors seem to be clustering. Very unusual."

"I doubt I'll be interested in your map." Reynolds turned back to his desk.

But Alan knew he was deeply interested. And he knew that Reynolds was also studying the teratomas. Most laymen had no idea what the word meant, and they asked. Reynolds had simply ignored him. He made his way back to his office, across the street from the Medical Center. Why was the military interested? he wondered again and again for the rest of that afternoon while he examined patients, removed sutures, and wrote prescriptions.

At four o'clock he requested eighteen patient files from Medical Records, assuming that Lt. Col. Reynolds had returned them. A transport service would deliver them by nine A.M. the following morning. Alan sat staring at the map on the wall at six thirty that evening. The last patient had left, and the office area was finally quiet.

He heard footsteps. "Hello?" he called.

Dr. Lawrence Greer stuck his head in and grinned at Alan. "I thought I saw your lights still on—" Lawrence Greer's office and examining rooms were next door to Alan's.

"I'm just sitting here thinking. Come in and look at this."

Greer came in and looked around. "What? You redecorated?"

"No—the map. On the wall."

Lawrence Greer sank into a chair. "Sure—it's a map all right," he joked.

"Those red stickers are the areas of the valley where we're seeing the teratomas, Lawrence. I don't have all the data—but already there are clusters. Peculiar clusters."

Greer studied the map for a moment. "So, there are clusters . . . I don't think you can draw any conclusions from ten stickers, Alan. Not good scientific technique."

"I'm going to contact Dr. Banos at Stanford to see if their teratoma patients are showing the same pattern—and Dr. Oliveras at the University of California, San Francisco. I think we may be onto something here."

Greer smiled. "I wish *I* had time to play with red stickers, Alan . . . it sounds like fun." He stood up abruptly. "Listen, are you going to the Medical Association meeting tonight?"

"I plan to," Alan said.

Greer nodded and shifted from foot to foot. "Well, I guess I'll see you there. Uh, Alan, I really came in to—apologize to you for the other night—at the country club." He grinned sheepishly. "Had a bit too much of the brew, I'm afraid. Cheryl tells me I behaved badly—so I'm apologizing."

"Apology accepted," Alan said nicely. "And I'll see you tonight. Oh, one more question . . . have you met this fellow, Reynolds, at Lorimar? Lieutenant Colonel Stephen Reynolds? He's doing some kind of research for the military—Army, I believe."

Lawrence Greer thought for a moment. "Can't say I've met the gentleman. Why?"

"Because I think he's studying the teratoma rate. And I'm curious why the U.S. military would be interested."

Greer was halfway out the door. "How do you know he's studying teratomas?"

"Because all the files I need, he seems to have in his office. And he wouldn't tell me exactly what he was studying. So, I'm drawing my own conclusions."

"I think you're studying oil slicks in mud puddles," Greer said. "I'd better get out of here—Cheryl and I are having dinner before the M.A. meeting. I'll see you later." He sauntered out of the office.

Alan heard his footsteps recede down the hall. He wanted to go home himself and have his dinner and a shower. The Santa Clara County Medical Association meeting would be a chance to talk to some of the other surgeons in the area. Someone else may have noticed this odd clustering of tumor cases.

Kate was shaken by her discovery in the lab. She'd taken the small plastic bag containing the frozen body of the baby hamster she'd saved from Fluffy's litter into the lab and dissected it that afternoon. Clearly, it was a teratoma.

Kate was lying down in the darkened bedroom when Alan arrived home. She thought maybe she could figure everything out if she could just think about it alone for ten minutes. The hamster babies who were monsters . . . teratomas. Doug's strange behavior these days. And Alan. And John. And Phyllis . . . Katie's heart lumbered along in her chest. She gave up thinking and tried to sleep, but that was impossible, too.

She heard Alan come into the house, stop, and then start down the hall to the bedroom.

"Katie?" he asked softly. "Are you okay?"

She sat up and raked a hand through her short hair. "Oh, Alan, it's been the day from hell!"

He shucked off his shoes and socks and unbuttoned his shirt. "What happened?"

"Alan—no, first I have to tell you that Amanda thinks Doug is acting strangely. She said he's talking about earthquakes and bagpipes and he doesn't want to play after school."

Alan slipped out of the white shirt. "That's hardly pathological for a ten-year-old boy." He tossed the shirt into the clothes hamper.

"And that litter of hamsters Fluffy had?" Katie continued fiercely. "They were teratomas, Alan. I had John look at them."

Alan frowned. She knew he didn't want her to even mention John Lacey's name. "Okay, so hamsters have genetic problems. What else happened?"

"You're not taking this seriously." She grabbed a pillow and hugged it tightly against her.

Alan unbuckled his belt, slid it out of the belt loops, and hung it over the wingbacked chair by the window. "I am, Kate. Believe me. It's just that I don't think this is good for you. It's not good for you to get upset over nothing."

"What do you expect me to do? Ignore it? For God's sake, Alan, this tumor is happening right under our noses—how can we ignore it?"

"It's just not uncommon for hamsters to have malformed litters."

Katie shook her head, furious with him. "I don't think so, Alan. I think you're wrong about this. Did you read the paper this morning? A dog *ate* a woman! It had a brain tumor! You think it's not uncommon for a dog to get a brain tumor and eat its owner?"

"I have to take a shower, sweetie. I've got a meeting at eight." He unzipped his suit pants.

She buried her head in the pillow. "Oh, sure, we can talk about it a month from now! Or a year. How will that be? Will that fit into your precious schedule?"

Alan, stripped down to his underwear, sat down beside her on the bed. "Katie, I'm sorry. I know you're upset. I'm sorry I don't have time to talk about it just now."

"But what about radon, Alan?" She knew she was pushing the subject. "I've been thinking, if we have radon in our house it could cause tumors, couldn't it? Maybe we should test again for radon."

Alan stood and left her alone on the bed. He picked up a fat pink towel from the bathroom. "We don't have radon, Kate. Besides, radon causes lung cancer. Will you quit worrying about every little thing?"

Alan closed the door to the bathroom behind him. She heard the shower running. He opened the door again.

"Katie—"

"The *water's* running!" she whined at him.

"It's just getting warm." He sounded defensive. "Look, I'm worried you aren't feeling up to this trip to Los Angeles for the convention."

"I'm up to it. The boys have been ready for a week."

"Did you tell them we'll go to Disneyland?"

"Yes, I told them." She felt she'd been defeated by Alan's expertise, and the obvious priority of his work. It wasn't fair. And they'd made the plans to go to the California State Medical Convention months before they knew Kate was pregnant.

"Please don't treat me like one of your patients," she said, her voice husky. "I'm your wife." She stormed out of the bedroom and slammed the door behind her.

"I won't have time for dinner," Alan said after a long shower. "I'm not very hungry."

"Dougy's not hungry either," Doug said absently. He was sprawled on the love seat in the family room watching television.

"You mean, *you're* not hungry—" Alan corrected him.

Katie was still furious and not entirely sure why anymore. "He's been talking about himself like that. I think he picked it up from Amanda. She's always referring to herself as Amanda—'Amanda will finish the ironing.' "

Kate didn't want to bring up the subject of counseling for Doug again. When she'd mentioned it to Alan he'd thought it was ridiculous.

"Well, get rid of Amanda," Alan told her. "I won't have some illiterate woman in this house teaching my kids bad grammar!"

"She's certainly not illiterate," Katie shouted at him. "She's the best housekeeper I've ever had—and I'm *not* going to get rid of her!"

"Fine! Then at least tell her not to talk to the boys!" Alan ranted and left the house.

Doug and Robbie watched him leave.

"I won't talk to Amanda, if that's what Dad wants," Robbie vowed.

"That's not what he wants, Rob. He's just mad right now. Amanda is a fine person—you talk to her all you want."

They ate their dinner in silence. Amanda had fixed lamb chops braised with carrots, zucchini, and mint, and she'd left it simmering on the stove for their dinner. Kate could hardly choke down a bite.

That evening when the boys were in bed, she wandered the house and finally opened the door to the small room across from their bedroom. She turned on the light. The room was stuffy, but clearly Amanda had cleaned it lately. In fact, the beautiful maple crib stood in the corner. Who had set it up? Amanda? Alan? Angrily she marched to the garage, picked out a couple of screwdrivers and a wrench, and then went back to the nursery and went to work on the crib. By ten thirty it was apart and stored in the garage again.

* * *

The Santa Clara Valley Medical Association met at the Fairmont Hotel in San Jose. The weather, that last week of June, had turned hot and quite humid, but in the ballroom of the hotel the air conditioner kept the temperature at a cool, refreshing seventy degrees. Alan breathed a sigh of relief and poured himself a cup of hot coffee. Dr. Banos, a tall, dark-haired man with a handsome face, was head of Surgery at Stanford University Hospital. He believed he had an aura around his head. Alan had never seen it, but others attested to its presence. He picked up iced tea. Banos was presenting a paper on the rate of teratomaceous tumors in a three-county area. The residents hung around him like drones around a queen bee.

Marty Kane, one of the cardiologists at Lorimar, showed up in madras shorts and a hot-pink Pierre Cardin shirt. His sunglasses rested on his black hair, which had been mowed around his ears and left long on top.

"What a peacock," Banos announced loudly.

Marty looked around innocently. "Was he referring to me?" he asked Alan. "A peacock? Me?"

The laughter was uneasy, but Alan pulled Marty into a seat beside him. "Just sit down. You know Banos. If you're not from Stanford you have no taste."

"I'll have you know I paid a hundred and twenty-five dollars for this shirt!" Marty grumbled.

"You were robbed," Alan said, grinning. "But it looks sharp."

"Thanks," Kane said, settling into his chair. His legs were tanned and had a layer of curly, bronzed hair.

The first report of the evening was given by Dr. Josef Lang on the rosette test for fetal-maternal bleeds. Everyone sat patiently through it, although there were some murmurings in the ballroom from small groups of physicians. With the new requirements for continuing education, the Medical Association meetings had become primarily educational events. To remain a member in good standing a physician had to attend three times a year.

Dr. Banos gave the second report of the evening. He had a monotone voice and darkened the room so he could show some slides.

"At Stanford we have seen an increase of six hundred percent in the rate of teratomaceous tumors in two years," he droned. "Two years ago we had six cases. Last year we had one hundred and thirty-six. Of those, eighty-two of the tumors were terminal, sixteen were superficial, and thirty-eight were removed surgically. Of the thirty-eight, twenty-two have had a recurrence of the teratoma within six months. This is an epidemic of major proportions. We have studies from the San Gregorio Institute in Los Angeles confirming our own findings. The causative agent of the tumors remains a matter of debate. We know that X rays and certain chemicals and drugs can be mutagenic, but neither of these agents can possibly account for the increasing incidence of this particular tumor. Interestingly, the incidence is much higher on the West Coast than in the Middle West or eastern parts of the United States." There were rumblings of conversation throughout the ballroom. Alan felt the sweat begin on his forehead despite the coolness of the room.

"Unless we discover the causative agent, it is likely this tumor will continue to be a virulent threat," Banos said. "There are a number of studies by the Centers for Disease Control and the State Department of Health, and I understand a definite paper will be presented at the California Medical Convention in Los Angeles next week."

The questions flew after Banos had finished. He had few answers.

"Do you think this could be the result of the holes in the ozone layer?" someone asked.

"I don't really know," Banos answered.

"Food additives?"

"I have no idea . . ."

"Air pollution? Hydrocarbons in the water supply?"

Banos shrugged. "We just don't know enough yet . . ."

"Do you know if the United States military is doing one of the studies?" Alan asked.

"No, I hadn't heard that. But it's possible," Banos said.

"Have you mapped the incidence geographically?" Alan asked.

Banos shrugged. "No—"

"I have. And the incidence at Lorimar seems to show some clustering in high-income areas." Alan knew he was standing on shaky scientific ground at this point. The ground consisted of ten red stickers on a map.

The ballroom was silent.

"That's very interesting," Banos said. "How many cases have you mapped, Dr. Campbell?"

"Only ten," Alan said quietly.

There was some soft derisive laughter behind Alan. "I realize ten is not statistically significant," Alan defended. "But I urge all of you to keep track of the geographical data on your teratoma patients."

"I doubt that has any significance," Banos said, smiling benignly. "But if any of you have the time, by all means, map the cases."

Alan was sweating profusely. He was embarrassed, but he was also certain that the evidence in these teratomas was so important that even obscure information might be important. It was the plight of all research, he thought dismally. He looked over at John Lacey. John seemed lost in thought.

The third report was a psychiatric evaluation of a new drug called Restoseton.

Alan waited around after the meeting to talk to several other physicians, but mostly there was just the usual banter, tasteless jokes, and ego massaging. He asked Dr. Adam Shatner his opinion of the clustering of the teratoma rate.

"I don't have an opinion," the surgeon said uneasily. "If you'll excuse me? I have to make a phone call." And he hurried away.

Alan headed for the opened doors of the conference room.

"Peanut clustering?" he heard someone quip, obviously referring to Alan's statement to Banos.

"No, carob! You know how those 'high-income areas' try to hold their cholesterols down."

Annoyed and impatient with the refusal of his fellow physicians to face the problem squarely, Alan remembered Katie's accusations of his own denial. But that's different, he decided. There's no comparing hamsters and humans. It's apples and oranges . . . He strode down the hallway and took the elevator to the lobby of the hotel.

Larry Sullivan, an internist in Los Gatos, caught up with him outside the wide glass doors of the Fairmont Hotel. "Dr. Campbell," he said, "can I talk to you a minute?"

Alan stopped. "If you're going to tell me I'm wrong—"

"No, no, I'm not. I wanted to tell you I think you're right about the clustering. It's what's so puzzling. Did you know the U.S. Army thinks the West Coast may be being bombarded by radiation? Have you heard that theory?"

"No, I haven't . . ."

"Sounds like crap to me—still, something's happening here in California. Not just in this valley. All over. I'm afraid if the media gets hold of it, we'll have mass panic. What are you telling your patients?"

"Nothing, unless they ask. Then I tell them I don't know. It isn't much."

It was still warm outside at ten thirty, and he drove home slowly. He needed time to think. And he hadn't eaten. His stomach objected to even the hint of food. He'd have something light at home. Soup. He'd apologize to Katie. He reminded himself that she was pregnant. He had to be patient. He'd get those medical files in the morning and map the other known cases of teratomas. He'd tell Viktor Straub to take a hike. He'd take a Seconal tonight. With a plan in mind, Alan felt a little better.

The dreams had a way of circumventing the Seconal. Or waiting until the numbing effect of the drug on the brain had ebbed. Alan dreamed he had won a painting at a gallery. He was told it was painting number twelve. He searched the huge canvases, all of them modern with wild colors. Finally he found number twelve, but it had a hole in the center of it. The painting, itself, seemed to be made of tissue paper and was still wet. Alan thrust his hand through the hole. And his hand was bitten. He cried out in pain and tried to withdraw his hand, but it was held fast.

The sweat drizzled down his face. He called for help, but no one came. His arm was yanked through the hole up to his shoulder. When the hole widened, his shoulder slid through. He did not want his head to disappear into that abyss. He craned his neck, stretching the muscles until they cramped. Then his head plunged through the damp tissue paper into the darkness behind it. He screamed.

Alan lay panting in the darkness of the bedroom. Damn these dreams, he swore silently. He took another Seconal.

Deena Crist was a beautiful young woman, all legs and tucked-in waist and auburn curly hair that wreathed her thin, angular face and blue eyes. She had strong, graceful hands and an efficiency that Katie admired very much. Deena had worked in the research lab at Lorimar for seven years after getting her master's degree at U.C.L.A. Kate kept an eye on Deena and John Lacey to see if any relationship was developing between the two of them. They seemed so perfect for each other. But John treated Deena with cool, though not unsympathetic distance and she, in turn, returned the attitude.

By the beginning of July, Deena had finished the separation phase of her work, isolating those tissue cultures that showed genetic disintegration from those that did not after inoculation with a virus.

"I'd noticed that some of the chick embryos revert to normal after showing clear signs of chromosomal abnormalities," she told Katie one afternoon. It was cool and quiet in the clean room of the lab. "I was curious about why and how the organism could correct this aberration. I mean, how does the embryo recognize a mutation?"

Katie didn't know. "How does it?" She was working with the automatic diluter, making serial dilutions of PreVent that would eventually be inoculated into the tissue cultures.

Deena laughed softly. "I still don't know, I'm afraid.

But what I have discovered is that some of the embryos are not only able to recognize the mutation, but are able to isolate it from the growing organism and replace the genetic material it contained."

"You mean it self-corrects?" Katie asked her.

"Apparently—the problem is it only happens in one cell in about a hundred thousand. I have no means of predicting which embryos will revert to normal, so it has been a long process finding enough samples, purifying them, and getting them ready to test to see if the results can be duplicated."

Kate and Deena were in their white suits and head-gear. The air purifier wheezed softly.

"That's when Henry Baden came. He took over the work on the artificial interferon so I was free to study this genetic reversal." Deena's inoculating technique was flawless. She didn't waste a motion. "Since most of our funding comes from MacKenzie Pharmaceuticals for the interferon research, PreVent gets top priority, of course. And Dr. Lacey is adamant that our work is primarily with the interferon—I'm sure you've noticed that."

Kate nodded. John Lacey seemed to ignore Deena's long hours and steady, plodding work at the lab.

"He thinks I'm off on a wild-goose chase." Deena smiled. "If I can get this substrate from the original cultures to inhibit or reverse the genetic mutation of new tissue cultures, then, I think, I can get private funding for my work. And Dr. Lacey's approval." She grinned. "Given a choice, I'd rather have the funding."

Katie glanced at Deena quickly. "Money's always the problem in research." She removed a rack of test tubes from the automatic diluter and corked them with sterile cotton.

"It's more than money," Deena said. She removed

the tray of inoculated tubes and put them in the incubator, setting the timer. "A year ago Dr. Lacey was much more interested in the work here. But now?" She shrugged. "He doesn't seem to want to do much more than oversee the projects."

"He's recently divorced, isn't he? Maybe he's been upset because of that."

"I don't think so. I think something else is going on, Kate. And I wish I knew what it was."

Katie finished her tray of tubes and stretched. She had planned to begin inoculating HSF18 cultures, chick embryos that were eighteen hours postfertilization. They would incubate for forty-eight hours and then be examined for genetic damage from the RV128 virus. Those cultures that showed aberrations would be subjected to the artificial interferon at intervals of one, two, four, and six hours, to determine whether the interferon caused any effect on the aberrant growth.

"I've known John a long time," Kate told Deena. "I worked here before I was married to Alan—seems like eons ago."

Deena nodded. "Dr. Lacey told me that. He said you were one of the best research assistants he'd ever had."

Katie smiled to herself. "He does seem preoccupied —I'd guess it was because of the divorce."

"Did you know there is a picture of you in Dr. Lacey's desk drawer?" Deena didn't look at Katie.

"What? A picture of me? Whatever for?"

Deena was silent for several minutes. "I was in Dr. Lacey's office a couple of months ago, and he opened the bottom drawer. There was a picture of a woman. I assumed it was his wife—I knew they were divorced."

Katie felt her breath quicken, and her heart kept time, skittering inside her rib cage.

"Then when you came to work, I realized it was a

picture of *you,* not his wife." There was no insinuation in Deena's voice.

"Years ago," Katie said slowly, "before I met Alan, I dated John. Not for very long. He must have had a picture. I can't imagine why he kept it." She looked into Deena's eyes. "There's nothing going on between us, I assure you."

Deena met Katie's gaze levelly. "There may not be anything going on with you, but there's clearly something happening to Dr. Lacey."

The inoculation of the cultures would have to wait, Kate decided. "Deena—there's something you should know—I'm pregnant . . ."

Deena's blue eyes sparkled. "That's great! I'm really happy for you—"

"John—Dr. Lacey—" she said self-consciously, "doesn't know yet. I'll have to tell him."

"The sooner the better," Deena told her. "Good research assistants are very difficult to replace."

John Lacey was not in his office when Kate barged in to talk to him. Through the glassed windows Katie could feel the gaze of the secretaries in the outer office. She decided to leave a note, and reached over John's desk for a pen and notepaper. With her right foot, she tried to open the bottom drawer of the desk. It was locked. Good, she thought, maybe Deena is the only one who's seen a picture of me in that drawer.

The door behind her opened and John came in wearing his soft surgical greens. The shirt was loose, and far too big.

"Hi," he said. "Did you need something?"

"I was leaving you a note," Katie said quietly. "I just wanted to remind you that I won't be here most of next week—we're going to the medical convention in Los

Angeles. I've planned the inoculations so that I can finish what I've started before I leave."

John smiled and nodded. "Good. Very good. Maybe I'll see you there."

Katie paused. "I also need to tell you that I've just found out that I'm—pregnant."

John Lacey's face turned to granite.

"It wasn't exactly planned. I didn't know when I was hired here." She shifted uneasily from foot to foot and couldn't look at John. "Will you say something?"

"Congratulations," he said. "Just don't ask me to be happy about losing you. As my research assistant."

"I won't ask you to do that," she promised. "I'll stay as long as I can. The baby's not due until December—or so."

"Sure," he said, the restive smile pasted on his face. "Who knows? By December none of us may be here."

"And I want you to get that picture of me out of your desk drawer," she whispered. "Deena said she saw it."

John Lacey leaned against his desk and nodded. "I've meant to do that . . ."

When Kate left the office, John sank into his chair and bent forward to read the half-finished note she had written. He didn't want those nosy secretaries to see that he was upset. Or disappointed. Or despairing. Whatever this terrible feeling was.

His hand instinctively sought out the small nodules along his ribs. He counted them like beads on an abacus. Five, six . . . There was clearly a new one.

14

 "Dr. Robertz?" she sniffed into the phone. "I don't want this baby. I want you to schedule an abortion."

"I don't do abortions, Mrs. Campbell," he said stiffly. "Not after the twelfth week."

"I'm twelve weeks pregnant?" she squeaked in disbelief. "I can't be twelve weeks. It's only nine weeks. Ten, at the most."

"I believe you're twelve."

"I don't want this baby—"

"Come in and talk to me," he suggested. "We can talk about the problems."

"I have to go to Disneyland," she wailed into the phone receiver. "I can't come and talk to you!"

"Make an appointment for next week," he suggested. "Whatever it is, Kate, we can solve it. Okay?"

Alan relaxed on the plane. Two glasses of white wine on a very short hop between San Jose and Los Angeles helped. Kate was as tense as a jackrabbit. She wasn't allowed a glass of wine. Not good for *the baby,* she complained unhappily, but silently. *The baby* had become a lip-curling slur in the last week. Claude Robertz had convinced her she was twelve weeks into this pregnancy. An abortion was risky after that time.

The boys sat beside Alan, and Kate had the seat across the aisle. Doug and Rob were excited about Disneyland and talked incessantly about the wonders in store for them.

"Let's go on the Matterhorn bobsleds first," Doug tried to convince Robbie. "It's a real scary ride."

"I wanna go on the pirate ride," Robbie moped.

"We'll do that—we'll do that. But the Matterhorn first . . . Okay? Then the pirate ride."

"Okay," Rob agreed. He'd been studying the Disneyland brochure for two weeks.

"Are we staying in a hotel?" Doug asked. "Or are we going to camp out?"

"Camp out?" Alan laughed. "Your mother's idea of camping out is calling room service for the hot dogs. No, we're staying in the hotel where the convention is being held. You'll take a tour bus to Disneyland."

"Does the hotel have a pool?"

"Two or three, I think."

Kate leaned her head back and closed her eyes. She was seated beside a rather heavyset man who had claimed one of her armrests. She tried to keep her arms close to her body and relax at the same time. She kept her feet off the floor. There was some theory that that helped with the tension of flying. It didn't seem to be working.

They landed at LAX and took a cab to the hotel. The cab ride turned out to be just as exciting as any ride at Disneyland, Katie thought miserably. But they were finally established in the two-room suite.

"Gee whiz," Rob said. "Lookit this." He'd discovered a chocolate wafer on the pillow of his bed. "Somebody left their candy."

"The maid left it, dummy." Doug battered his brother lightly with his fist.

"Can I eat it, Mom?" Rob called to his mother in the next room.

Katie's mouth was full of luscious chocolate, which she'd wolfed down the instant she spotted the two wafers on the pillows. She ate Alan's, too. "Yes," she called back. "Go ahead."

Alan had unpacked and was checking the locks on the windows and doors. This was his ritual whenever they stayed away from home. If the doors didn't have deadbolts, Alan carried a sturdy rod that slipped under the doorknob and prevented unexpected entry.

Alan stretched out on the bed beside Kate. "How're you feeling?" he asked.

"Fine—a little dizzy after that lightning trip in the cab."

"Do you want a cup of tea?" he asked her. "I'll call room service. You rest."

Kate sighed. The tension of the past few weeks ebbed slowly. Alan was relaxed, thank God. He'd been as taut as a piano string lately, jabbering about geographical epidemics and the military poking around the hospital, and mumbling about the Medical Association meeting. But now, away from it all, he seemed more like the old Alan.

The tea cart arrived, with lovely mint tea and a plate of delicate crackers and small cookies, fruit punch chocked full of pineapple tidbits, kiwi, and oranges for the boys, and hot, black coffee for Alan. And there was a small package sitting on the tea cart. It had a red ribbon tied around it.

"What's this?" Katie held it up.

"Open it and find out." Alan was grinning.

"Is it for me?" She untied the ribbon and lifted the lid off the box. Katie gasped. "Oh, Alan—diamond earrings!"

"Do you like them?"

She gently removed them from the velvet-lined box. "Can we afford them?"

"First, do you *like* them?" He laughed at her obvious delight.

She took them to the mirror and held them up to her ears admiringly. "Of course I do. I love them. I just thought—"

"We can afford them, Katie. Don't worry—hey, what's a working wife for, anyway, if not for a few luxuries!"

Katie smiled and put on the earrings. "I'll just wear them for a while. Then we'd better lock them up in the hotel safe—just wait until next year's country club dance . . ."

Katie sipped her tea. The boys established themselves in front of the television set in their room to watch the most recent sequel to *Raiders of the Lost Ark.*

"You don't even have to pay for the movie," Rob told his mother reassuringly. "It's free."

"Heaven help us if they discover the ones that aren't free," Alan whispered to Kate when the boys were out of the room.

"I'm sure they've figured it out by now," she said. "I heard about one family—their kids ran up a three-hundred-dollar bill watching those pay-per-view movies."

They finished their snack, and Katie fell asleep for an hour. When she awoke Alan was still beside her. He had his long arms folded comfortably behind his head.

"Did you have a good nap?" he asked. "I've been

watching you sleep. And got to thinking, Kate, that it might be a good idea if you took the boys and spent the rest of the summer in Colorado with your folks." He saw her open her mouth to protest. "I know you have your job and all, but I'd feel better if you were out of the city this summer—away from all the stress and air pollution. The boys would have a wonderful time."

"Alan," she said softly, "I'm not going anywhere. Not unless you come along. Why are you asking me to do this? Are you worried about something?"

He shook his head. But he always denied worry, Katie knew.

"I just don't think the valley is a good place to be for a pregnant woman," he finally said.

"Are you worried about this tumor thing?"

"Sure, I'm worried. Kate," he began hesitantly, "maybe I shouldn't tell you all this, but the cases among pregnant women are very high—much higher than in the normal population. And there is this clustering geographically. There are cases in our own neighborhood."

"Who?" she demanded to know. She tried to think about who she knew who was pregnant in their area. Startlingly few people, she realized. It was a typical California suburb. She'd never met the people who lived in the houses behind them. She knew only a few of the neighbors.

"I can't tell you the names, Katie. You know that. Something's happening in the valley, and we haven't figured it out yet."

Kate lay back on the pillow. She listened to the muddle of sound from the next room, where the television produced a series of screams and gunshots. "I can't spend the summer in Colorado, Alan."

* * *

The Royal Arcadian Hotel was a lush expanse of holiday enticements, anything from golf to tennis to swimming in three heated pools surrounded by palms and exotic flowers. The dining room, with cool white tablecloths and hot and cold tables of lovely, spiced food, served the guests of the Royal Arcadian from six o'clock in the morning until midnight. And there was a row of elegant boutiques for shoppers.

Huge ceramic pots of calla lilies and flowing blue lobelia bloomed in every outdoor walkway, and feathery green ferns adorned the lobby of the Arcadian with its cool, black marble floor that looked like black ice. At night tiny white lights flickered in all the trees, giving the appearance of fireflies. A Dixieland jazz band was scheduled to play outdoors at the hotel one of the nights of the convention. Katie loved Dixieland jazz. She had begun to relax, away from the worries and busyness of their life in Los Altos.

Luckily, Jerry and Maria Greathouse and the children were at the convention, too, so Maria and Katie had each other for company while the kids swam in the pool. Rob was especially impressed with the long, cool waterfall, and came bursting through the curtain of water with a bloodcurdling whoop. The other children followed suit, except for Joanna, who was content to splash in the wading pool. The next two days they would all take the bus to Disneyland, and on Sunday the older children were going on a chaperoned children's day at the San Diego Zoo. That day Kate would attend several of the convention lectures with Alan.

"How are you feeling?" Maria asked Katie.

Kate laughed. "Pretty good—I'm not as young as I was with Doug and Rob. But I'm feeling okay. Except . . ."

"Except what?"

"Except I'm afraid this time."

Alan met Dr. Michael Senter that Thursday evening, before the keynote address. Senter was a fresh-faced researcher at San Gregorio Tumor Institute in Los Angeles. He was single and handsome, the latter of which he was hardly aware, and the former causing him some anxiety. He was a man with an edge, and he drew people to him with his unsullied warmth.

"Dr. Senter," Alan said, extending his hand. "I'm Dr. Alan Campbell—Los Altos, California."

Michael Senter was dressed in a crisp white shirt, gray slacks that had been pressed by a laundry, and a narrow black belt. He had not cultivated that southern California mystique in his apparel, at least. He had the build of a long-distance runner, lean and smoothly muscled. "Alan," he said, shaking Alan's hand. "Please call me Michael. Los Altos . . . do you know Lawrence Greer? I believe he is from Los Altos."

"Of course. We're colleagues at Lorimar Medical Center. How do you know Lawrence?"

"He's come to San Gregorio several times this spring —we have several of his patients. Or we did." Senter smiled sadly. "We're doing some incredible things—but it doesn't always work."

"I'd like to see it," Alan said. "Is there any chance of that?"

"Of course. On Sunday we're having an information seminar at San Gregorio. Come and see." He shook hands with Alan and was promptly snagged by another group of people who wanted to speak with him.

There was an undercurrent of intrigue at the convention. Alan could feel it like an earthquake waiting to happen. There were low rumblings now and then, questions that were asked that hinted at the concern over the tumor epidemic in California. And at the same time, the denial that any such difficulty confronted the golden life-style that prided itself on health was very evident.

"No one's talking about it directly," Alan said to Jerry Greathouse after the remarks by the opening speaker, Dr. Frederick Cope from the National Institutes of Health in Bethesda, Maryland. Cope alluded to the problem only indirectly, as a "threat looming on the horizon that will make the AIDS virus look like a case of acne."

"They're afraid of scaring the public," Jerry said. "But I wonder if there'd be this much concern if the tumor was mainly a problem for the poor."

And Alan knew he was right, unfortunately.

The Centers for Disease Control presented at least three papers that related directly to the epidemic. So far, they had little idea of the causative agent. The culturing of the tumor for virus identification was time-consuming, and had yielded little information. Environmental causes were certainly a concern, but the investigation of air pollution, for example, in relationship to an outbreak of a specific kind of tumor needed to be exhaustive. As far as CDC could determine, everything was safe.

On Friday, while Katie and the boys ventured into Tomorrow Land, Alan attended the workshops and seminars specifically designed for surgeons. He had signed up for Laser Techniques in Microsurgery. While he used microtechniques in many of his surgeries, the field had been extended into cardiac and neurosurgery. Microsurgery was less invasive, but it required precision and patience on the part of the physician. And Alan attended the seminar on platelet function in postoperative patients. With the AIDS epidemic, most patients did not submit happily to platelet infusions, and there was growing interest in performing surgery using as few blood products as possible. As platelets decreased in the body, however, there was the possibility of spontaneous bleeds, or "oozing to death," following surgery.

Even in the platelet function seminar there was talk of the teratoma. One doctor described a patient whose tumor produced an incompatible blood group and killed the patient when it ruptured. Alan shuddered and remembered Jennifer Wynn. So there were other cases like that, he thought. And no one was saying much about it. At least not openly.

Friday evening was the banquet. Alan picked at the prime rib and rice pilaf. By nine o'clock he was back in the hotel room. Kate and the boys had just arrived. Rob was decked out in a Mickey Mouse T-shirt and mouse ears. Doug had a year's supply of pencils with cartoon characters for erasers. The boys were tired but excited as they described every ride to Alan.

"You gotta go on Flight to Mars!" Doug told his father. "Can't you come with us tomorrow? It's really fun."

Alan grinned at them.

Kate was collapsed in a chair. "I think I never want to see another hamburger or cotton candy. Or ice cream bar! It's a wonder those two aren't sick."

"How are you doing?" Alan asked her.

"Well, I've had my exercise," she said. "And I rode on the Main Street Trolley—that was about the extent of it. But the electric parade—it was great fun."

"And tomorrow's another day," Alan told the boys. "Better get some sleep."

But it was nearly midnight before Doug and Rob were able to fall asleep. Alan lay in the darkened room listening to Katie breathe softly. He had not taken a Seconal. Surely he would not dream, not here where he was relaxed and away from the stress and demands of his practice. The dreams, however, had other ideas.

Alan woke once with Doug standing beside the bed.

"Are you all right, Daddy?" Doug asked, his eyes wide with fright. "Are you all right?"

"Just a bad dream. Go back to sleep, Doug." Alan took a Seconal.

The Saturday morning seminar was well attended. In fact, it was moved from the Sierra Room of the hotel to the auditorium, which seated a thousand people. Even then extra chairs had to be set up and crammed in the back aisle. Everyone wanted to hear the discussion of neoplasms and neoplastic etiology. Alan had a seat near the aisle.

Dr. Banos from Stanford settled into a seat behind Alan, and Marty Kane dropped into the cushioned chair beside Alan. Marty was wearing psychedelic shorts and a black T-shirt that said something about "skinny puppies."

"Who designs your wardrobe, Marty?" Dr. Banos asked loudly. "Your teenage son?"

"I'm only trying to break all of you white-shirt-and-maroon-paisley-tie folks out of your prejudices," Marty told him evenly. "It's a tough job. But someone's gotta do it."

Alan grinned at him. Marty's flamboyance was countered by brilliance in the operating room. He was one of the best cardiologists in the state, and had pioneered the repair of heart valves, a tedious surgery that most surgeons avoided, preferring to implant an artificial valve.

"I see I'm making inroads with you, Alan," Marty said. He plucked at Alan's white golf shirt.

"It was a choice between this or a T-shirt with Mickey Mouse on the front," Alan told him.

"You chose *wrong,* guy!"

"What're you doing in the neoplasm seminar, Marty?" Alan changed the subject. "I'd've thought you'd be off with the wizards working on that artificial heart."

Marty frowned. "That was yesterday. The thing still squawks and rattles—really hell on the patient."

The room had filled to capacity. Alan noticed a young woman with flame-red hair searching for a seat. In the end she opted to stand, her back against the wall.

When Michael Senter began his discussion of the etiology of the tumor known as the teratoma, Alan noticed the young woman raise a small camcorder. With hardly a sound two men were beside her. They stood directly in front of her, blocking her view. And then she was gone, as if she'd vanished into thin air. The two men had vanished also.

"Did you see that?" Alan leaned over and asked Marty.

"The redhead with the great legs?" Marty asked.

"Two men just—escorted her out. She was videotaping."

"Ah, a real no-no at a medical convention," Marty whispered.

"But who would care if she videotaped this session?" Alan asked himself as much as Marty.

Marty Kane shrugged.

Michael Senter was saying, ". . . I can tell you that in clearly defined regions of California, Nevada, Arizona, and Washington State, the mortality rate from this tumor has risen seven hundred percent in two years, and projections are in the neighborhood of two thousand percent by 1994. This means, ladies and gentlemen, that ten percent of the neoplasms that present to us will be teratomas."

The silence in the conference room was palpable. It was like a gasp. Ten percent was a very high figure for what had previously been a very rare tumor.

"Teratological pregnancies will probably be even higher. We are seeing alarming figures among certain populations—"

"What are these populations?" someone asked.

Michael Senter looked uncomfortable, but he smiled. "The tumor is showing a clustering in large cities, well above what would be expected in the general population. All I can tell you, sir, is that if I lived in Palos Verdes in L.A. or Queen Anne Hill in Seattle and I were pregnant, I'd worry."

Alan wiped at his forehead and found it was slicked with sweat. At least Michael Senter had vindicated his own unsubstantiated claim that this neoplasm was clustering in wealthy areas of cities. Alan turned and glanced at Dr. Banos from Stanford. Banos refused to meet his gaze.

"What possible causes are being investigated?" a doctor asked from the audience.

Dr. Willamena Forsythe, a renowned epidemiologist, rose to answer the question. "The study of causative agents is in the formative stages. We are looking into chemicals, viruses, air pollution, drugs, even communications. For example, a very high percentage of the known victims have cellular phones. Now, this may be a coincidence, but we do not dare to overlook even the most trivial of commonalities."

Alan found himself on his feet. "Can you tell me what

interest the United States military could possibly have in this tumor?"

Michael Senter and Willamena Forsythe stared at Alan in silence. There were bursts of conversation throughout the conference room, like an electric current coursing through a highly conductive medium.

"I have no idea," Forsythe said. "If they have an interest, I have not been informed about it."

"It's not unknown that the military will investigate unusual phenomena," Senter said hesitantly. "The danger of a sudden upsurgence of a tumor as deadly as this one is that the general public will become alarmed and react in ways that are both harmful and inappropriate. I'm uncertain, however, in this case, of the ethics of keeping our information away from the general media."

So the young woman had been trying to videotape the information for the news, Alan thought. And someone doesn't want this news published.

"The public often misconstrues medical information," Willamena Forsythe offered. "If you remember, in the beginning years of the AIDS epidemic, there was a great deal of false information given, and the general public reacted with a certain amount of fear and even violence against gays."

"But information has been our only weapon against AIDS," a woman said from the audience. "We haven't provided enough information to the right population— that's clear. And you're telling us that the teratoma is going to be hushed up now? Is that what you're saying?"

Forsythe bristled. "I am saying that we just don't have enough information at the present moment to responsibly release this for general consumption. It's a fact of life." She sat down.

"What do you advise us to tell our pregnant patients?" an obstetrician from San Francisco, California, asked Michael Senter.

"I'd tell them all to move to Iowa and live on a farm. We haven't had one incidence of the tumor in rural Iowa. Or New Hampshire." Senter surveyed the audience with a long, cool stare. "Now, if there are no more questions—"

"If you had to guess, Dr. Senter," Banos said in his booming, resonant voice, "what do you think is causing this tumor?"

"I don't know—if I had to guess I'd say it's something we have overlooked. Something that looks innocent and is as deadly as if we poured thalidomide into the water supply."

Alan resolved to insist that Kate and the boys go to Colorado for the rest of the summer.

Sunday afternoon was hot in Los Angeles, and the air hung heavy and thick. "An inversion layer," the weatherman said airily.

Doug and Rob were safely on the bus bound for a day at the San Diego Zoo with the Greathouse children and Maria, who opted for the zoo instead of one of the seminars.

"I can take Joanna," she said. "I'll keep track of Doug and Robbie. What's two more when I've got five?" She laughed her low, pleasant chuckle.

Katie thought if she spent one more day watching her children making dizzy circles on the Matterhorn or eating gobs of cotton candy, she'd go crazy right there on the spot and do something foolish, like cry. She had some hesitancy about sending the boys off alone for the day, because Doug had had one nosebleed and a headache Saturday night. Alan guessed it was all the excitement.

That Sunday morning they had a long, leisurely brunch in the hotel, and then picked up the rental car for the trip to the San Gregorio Tumor Institute, which was nestled in a hillside and surrounded by trees. The structure itself was stark, like concrete boxes wedged into the earth. There were no windows visible from the outside, and Kate felt her skin begin to prickle. How could anyone build a treatment facility without windows?

But inside the Institute Katie was pleasantly surprised. The exterior walls were built like the walls of a castle, and the actual buildings were glassed cubes set within those walls. Light poured in through those windows and everywhere she looked there was a view of small trees, flowers, ponds, and fountains. Ribbons of brilliantly colored koi fish swam in many of the pools. Dr. Michael Senter met them in the lobby. He was grinning. "How do you like it so far?" he asked the group. About fifteen other people had come for the tour.

Everyone thought the architecture clever.

"Every patient room has a view," he said. "We felt it was important to maintain some natural connections."

The first hour of the tour was spent in the laboratory and research areas of the Institute. Although it was Sunday, the work seemed to be proceeding as if it were any day of the week. Kate was particularly interested in the research work with viruses and a synthetic C2 receptor antibody that would bond to many viruses and prevent its replication in the body.

"If this works," Senter told his group, "it would mean we can literally vaccinate people against viruses."

"Will it work against the AIDS virus?" someone asked.

"We don't know," Senter responded. "We hope so."

* * *

Alan was more interested in the surgical treatment of tumors.

"It's a bit different here than anything you're probably used to," Michael Senter told them after taking them through the gigantic surgical department. "We operate at least three times on most patients with certain kinds of tumors. We have found that this provides the best chance for the body to recover its own immune status."

"Isn't that rather traumatic for the patient?" a physician from Sacramento, California, asked. "Most of my patients can hardly tolerate one surgical procedure."

"Actually, we find they do rather well. And you have to remember that San Gregorio is tertiary care for most carcinomas. For our patients, we are their last hope."

The wards at the Institute were semicircles of glass surrounding a nurses' station and large, comfortable lounge areas, where patients walked about or played cards and talked. It didn't look much like a normal hospital ward, Katie thought. In fact, it was sometimes difficult to distinguish the staff from the patients. Everyone smiled. The air of tension that pervaded so many wards was absent.

"On the other hand," Senter told them, after greeting several of the patients on L ward, "some of our patients are with us for a very long time. We have a ten-year-old boy, Terry Cox, who has been here since he was an infant."

Alan stiffened suddenly. Kate glanced at him. "Are you all right?"

"Did he say—Terry Cox?" he asked.

"Yes, I think so. Why?"

Alan shook his head. "Nothing—it's nothing."

The tour proceeded, but when Kate looked around Alan was gone. Katie went after him.

He was sweating in earnest. He walked through several wards and finally stopped at a nursing station. "I'm looking for Terry Cox," he said, hoping his voice was steady. "I'm a physician from Lorimar Medical Center in Los Altos, California—I was on the Cox case."

The nurse checked the computer. "He's in M ward—down that hall and around the corner."

"Thanks." Alan loped off. He was glad he had decided to wear dress slacks and a white shirt. He fit in.

M ward was very quiet. There was no one at the nursing station, so he quickly checked the row of patients' charts. Terry Cox was in room 6M.

The room was dim, as the horizontal blinds had been drawn. A woman sat in a rocking chair and held a blanketed bundle. She was singing softly.

"Oh, hello," she said. "Can I help you?"

"I—was looking for Terry Cox," he said. His heart thundered in his chest. "I'm Dr. Campbell."

"Well, this is Terry. He doesn't get many visitors, do you, sweetie?" She gathered up the blankets and laid him back in a crib. "Are you a relative?"

"No. I was his—surgeon—a long time ago. When he was born."

"Oh," she said quickly.

Nestled in the blue blanket was a lake of tissue, hardly resembling a child. Except one blue eye blinked steadily at Alan from a cranial lump. The stump of an arm protruded directly below the head, and one leg had developed at the caudal end of the tissue. Lungs and heart and digestive organs had been covered over with minute skin grafts, through which tubes had been secured for feeding and breathing.

"He's our star around here," the nurse said. She patted his small arm. "He's pretty tough."

The gaze of that marble blue eye never left Alan's face. A wave of dizziness passed through Alan.

"How much does he—?"

"Think? Feel? We don't know. We treat him as if he thinks everything a ten-year-old would think and feels everything any youngsters feels. I think he likes the Teenage Mutant Ninja Turtles, don't you, Terry?"

On the wall of his room was a large cutout of Leonardo. The blue eye blinked.

The nurse hooked up the breathing tube, and Terry's midsection heaved and then settled into a slow rhythm.

"Can I talk to you—outside?" Alan asked. His breathing was ragged.

"Sure. I'll be back, hon," she said and left the room with Alan.

"I was quite shocked to learn he was still alive. I know his mother died—shortly after he was born. How about his father—Paul Cox, isn't it?"

"He has been here twice that I know about." She fussed with the pens on the desk of the nursing station. "Terry's been through a lot. We don't keep him alive for the sake of research, Dr. Campbell. The breathing tube makes it easier for him, that's all."

"Does he show any signs—of—recognition, or emotion?"

"Yes, once you get to know him."

"Is he able to make any sounds?"

"He has nightmares," she said. "That's the only time he screams."

The nursing station grayed at the edges. Alan grasped the edge of the counter to steady himself.

"Are you all right, Dr. Campbell? Here, sit down for a moment."

Alan felt her guide him into an armchair. "Thank you," he said. "I felt rather faint there, for a moment."

"It's probably the heat," the nurse said briskly. "It gets everyone down, now and then."

"Yes, probably the heat . . . May I look at the chart? I can ask Dr. Michael Senter, if that's a problem."

"I don't see why not." She handed him a clear plastic board with a computer printout on it.

He paged through the massive computer printout of blood gases, glucose and electrolyte results, a dietary log, and handwritten nurses' notes.

"Terry's medical bills have been paid by the United States Army," she said. "Many of his records are confidential." She stood thinking for a moment. "But, if you ask me, I think it's because they want to cover up something." She leaned nearer to Alan. "We had three children here at one time. They were all about the same age. Two of them died—all teratomas. If you ask me, and I realize you didn't, I think they were running some sort of experimentation in the Army. That's only my opinion, of course."

"Of course," Alan said, greedy for more but afraid of pushing this nurse too far. "It's hard to say what happened to Terry." He saw the address of Terry's father, Paul, on the back sheet of the file. He memorized it, slowly and methodically.

"I feel so bad for him. It'd be better if he died. But he hangs on in there, poor little tyke. He's had over twenty surgeries."

Alan slipped the plastic clipboard back into its slot. "What did you say your name was?" he asked.

"I'm Emma. Emma Reese."

"I'm glad you're taking care of Terry, Emma," Alan

said, reaching out to shake her hand. "And thanks for the information."

"You won't tell anyone what I said about the Army, will you?" she asked. "I probably shouldn't have told you that."

"I've forgotten it already," Alan assured her. And he walked out of M ward. As soon as he was safely away, he reached in his pocket and found a pen. He wrote the address he'd memorized on the palm of his hand. It was an old trick left over from his intern days to prod the memory, especially in front of attending physicians.

His breathing had leveled out. By seven that night they'd be on the plane home. But how would he ever forget that one blue eye?

He wasn't sure where he was, but he had an eerie sense of being followed. He glanced behind him and didn't see anyone. He was in a long, cool hallway that he hoped would lead back to the lobby area of the Institute. But he was sure he heard footsteps. He rounded a corner and stopped to figure out where he was.

"I have lost my husband," Katie told a nurse at one of the stations she passed. "Have you seen him wandering through here? Red-haired? Tall?"

The nurse laughed. "We lose about one person every weekend, but not for long, believe me. They all end up back in the lobby. If I were you I'd go back and wait for him there."

A hand clutched Katie's sleeve.

A woman stared at her. She wore a thin hospital robe and floppy blue slippers on her bare feet. Her hair was dark and stringy. She held up a notepad. With a black marker she wrote the word "Kate."

"How do you know my name?" Katie stared at the

woman, searching for a clue in the face. Her skin was sallow, but her eyes blazed.

Elaine, the woman wrote.

Katie held her breath. "Oh, my God—Elaine. Is it you?"

Elaine Calder nodded and brilliant tears burned in her eyes. Her hand still clutched Katie's sleeve. Kate put her arms around her and held her tightly. She felt the soft sobs against her body, and held the woman until her breathing was steady again.

"You'd better go back to your room, hon," the nurse said to Elaine. "You know you're not supposed to be up too long."

Elaine clutched at Kate and shook her head no.

"I'll take her back to her room—I'm an old friend of Elaine's."

"Elaine?" The nurse frowned. "Her name's Norma Montrose. You must have made a mistake."

Kate glared at the nurse. "Her name's Elaine Calder! You're the one who's made the mistake." She took Elaine's left hand and read the name on the orange name band. Norma Montrose. Kate looked up at the woman.

Elaine Calder, the woman wrote on the pad of paper. *Come to room.* She maneuvered Katie down the hall. The nurse glared at them until they disappeared into the cool darkness of a small room, lit only by the shadowed light coming through the bank of windows. Elaine closed the door.

"Why can't you talk?" Katie asked her. "I don't understand why they think you're someone else. What's going on?"

Elaine Calder smiled, a half smile, and she put her finger to her lips to silence Katie. *Norma Montrose is Dick's mother. Very long story.*

"Tell me what's happening to you," Katie said softly. "I've been so worried."

Dying. They think I don't know.

"No—you can't be. Alan's here—he'll help you—I know he will—"

Elaine laid a gentle hand on Katie's arm and shook her head slowly. *Done everything,* she wrote slowly. *Except say good-bye to you.*

Kate began to cry, helpless, hot tears. "You can't be—you just can't." And with each protest she knew it was true.

Tell me about you.

"Oh, God—where do I start?" Kate sniffed. "I've gone back to work at Lorimar—research. And—I'm pregnant!"

Elaine gave her that brave half smile again and nodded her head.

"I'm so scared about this baby, Elaine. I can't tell you how frightened I am—and no one understands. Everybody thinks I'm just being ridiculous. But I feel something's wrong. Do you know what I mean?"

Elaine nodded.

"Something's happening, and I don't know what. I don't think it's a radiation leak at the Lawrence Livermore Lab. I don't think it's a virus. Or something in the water." Kate leaned close to Elaine. "But I don't know what it is. Or if it's too late already."

The nurse bustled into the room. "Time for your meds, Norma." She had a syringe on a metal tray.

"Her name's Elaine," Katie said nastily. "I don't care what's on her name band."

"Well, whatever she wants to call herself it's okay with me," the nurse chirped. She uncapped the syringe and plunged the needle into a heparin lock on Elaine's hand. "But around here we call her Norma. Norma Montrose. Isn't that right, hon?"

Elaine lay back on the pillows. She kept her gaze focused on Katie.

"She'll go to sleep now," the nurse said. "I suggest you come back another time."

Elaine blinked slowly. In slow motion she made a writing motion on the palm of her hand. Kate handed her the pad and marker.

Don't worry. Won't be here long. Good luck with baby. She laid the pen on the edge of the bed. Her eyes closed.

The nurse took Katie's arm. "You'd better go find your husband."

"No—I—" She was virtually dragged from the room.

"Can't you see she needs her rest?" the nurse barked.

"I just—" Kate's nose stuffed up almost instantly, and she blinked back tears. "She thinks she's dying. I wanted to have my husband take a look at her—"

"Well, there's nothing anybody can do for Norma anymore, except keep her comfortable. That's what we're doing. Just keeping the pain manageable." The nurse headed back toward the station.

Kate followed her. "Why can't she talk?"

"She had surgery. They removed several large tumors that were blocking the throat. In the process it was necessary to remove the tongue."

Kate stopped and shouted at her. "Don't talk about her as if she were a specimen! She's a person! It wasn't 'the' tongue you removed, it was *hers*!"

The nurse opened her mouth to say something and then closed it slowly. "You have to understand that we are seeing so many cases of this tumor—sometimes we hope a patient will die because it will open up a bed for someone we just might be able to save." The nurse smiled a little. "If I sounded callous, I apologize. It's just that I'm no use at all if I'm in tears all the time."

Kate felt instantly guilty that she'd complained. "I am sorry. I didn't mean—"

"Oh, I know you are upset—I don't take it personally. But I think you'd better go back to the lobby and find your husband." She walked quickly back to the nursing station and sat down at the desk. She did not look up at Katie.

Kate turned and retreated down the hall. She slipped back into Elaine's room and left a note. *It was good to see you. Do everything you can to get well. I'll write to you. Love, Kate.*

After several wrong turns, Alan figured out the system of numbering and ended up back in the lobby area, where Kate sat waiting.

"Alan," she said, obviously relieved when she saw him, "where'd you go?"

He grinned. "I zagged when I should have zigged, I guess," he said, trying to look sheepish.

The lobby of the San Gregorio Institute was cool and quiet. Pastel blue and peach upholstered chairs clustered in the wide expanse, forming sheltered areas for patients and visitors. One woman sat weeping silently. In another area a middle-aged man in a gray suit sat beside an old man staring vacantly into space. He wore a hospital gown and a blue terry-cloth robe. Katie looked away from them.

"I'm tired," she said to Alan. "Let's go back to the hotel."

"But you haven't seen the rest of the research labs," he objected. "I thought that's why you came along today."

"I've seen something else," she said, slowing, meeting his blue-eyed gaze. "Something even more important."

"What?"

"I'll tell you later."

They caught up with the tour group in a large conference room adjoining the research labs in the north wing of the Institute. Alan wanted to speak to Dr. Senter before they left.

"I had hoped to have a moment to talk to you alone," Alan told him, after apologizing for getting lost and having to leave early.

Michael Senter's handshake was warm. "I'm sorry there wasn't enough time. It seems like there's never enough time these days."

"I'll give you a call in a couple of days. We need to coordinate our work on these teratomas."

Senter nodded. "We're getting five requests a day for bed space at San Gregorio. I'm treating a number of patients on an outpatient basis who really need to be hospitalized." He jotted his phone number on a San Gregorio brochure.

"I'm sorry you missed seeing the rest of our research labs," Dr. Senter said to Katie. "I understand you work with John Lacey and Deena Crist at Lorimar."

"Do you know them?" Katie asked, somewhat surprised.

"I try to keep up on most of the research going on in the state. Deena is doing some exciting work with a reduction substance. John tells me she will present a paper in the fall. Are you involved in that project?"

"No," Katie told him. "My work is with an artificial interferon. We've just begun tissue culture testing."

"Dr. Sovan—you may know about her—did some preliminary work with interferon. About two years ago."

Katie wasn't sure. "I'm sure I've come across her name in the literature."

Michael Senter gave them a thumbs-up before they left the conference room. "Give me a call next week, Alan."

Katie glanced down several hallways on the way back to the lobby. The Institute was beginning to make sense to her. Patient rooms were in a wheel arrangement and the ancillary services ran in long spokes off the central lobby. The spokes were connected by short bridges that opened to outdoor gardens and patio areas. Every window had a view of a bit of greenery.

A large blue and white sign indicated X-Ray Diagnostics to the right when she and Alan turned left down the last hallway. She noticed a man in a hospital robe edging out of a wheelchair. The man's back was turned to her. He was being assisted by a nurse. Katie caught only a glimpse of the side of the man's head. She caught Alan's arm.

"Alan? Wait a minute—doesn't that look like—"

The man and nurse had disappeared through the doors.

Alan looked puzzled. "Who?"

"I don't know—John Lacey. It looked like John."

Alan was pointedly silent and walked on. Kate felt a small stab of guilt. Alan disliked any mention of John Lacey.

"I was probably wrong," she said when they reached the lobby and headed for the large glass doors at the entrance. In the parking lot the tarmac felt spongy underfoot. "I was probably seeing things back there."

"More than likely." Alan unlocked the car door and opened it for her. When she was situated, he slid into the driver's seat. His muscles bunched along his jawline.

"But I wasn't seeing things earlier, Alan. I saw Elaine Calder!"

Alan started the car and turned the air conditioner on high. "Elaine Calder? She's here?"

"She's dying, Alan. The tumor has recurred."

"You're sure it was Elaine Calder?"

"Positive. Except she's using the name Norma Montrose, for some reason. I don't understand it."

"Oh, Kate," he said, exasperation clearly evident in his voice, "I doubt it was her. Probably someone else you thought—"

"Don't patronize me!" she said, furious with him. "I may be pregnant, but I'm not stupid."

"I never said you were." Alan put the car into gear and they roared out of the San Gregorio parking lot.

On the final approach into the San Jose International Airport Katie closed her eyes and waited for the thud of the tires on the runway that meant they had touched down.

"Mom!" Doug screamed.

Across the aisle, Doug was a mask of blood. His shirt looked like he'd been recently murdered. Alan pinched the bridge of Doug's nose to stem the bleeding, and Doug gathered his T-shirt into a ball and pressed it against his nose. Alan and Katie exchanged glances that said "We have *got* to do something about these nosebleeds."

They were the last passengers off the plane. The stewardess handed Doug a wad of wet paper towels, and the Campbell family disembarked, finally.

15

Sherman Percival Dettler, III, sat in his circular office in the Plaza Town Center in Los Angeles on Monday morning. The son of Senator Sherman P. Dettler, II, who had died three years earlier due to clogged arteries complicated by his love of Jim Beam, he had always hoped to please his father by the rising success of Dettler Industries. As it turned out, nothing pleased the old man.

And nothing was pleasing the son that Monday morning, especially not the reports of a "rainbow glow" visible in the new microwave oven released just a year ago.

"A rainbow glow!" he howled, holding up the latest of the reports, along with a handful of new complaints from customers. "What the hell is a rainbow glow?"

Four men sat in Dettler's office. They were solemn-faced grownups in out-of-shape bodies dressed in look-alike gray business suits and muted ties. Jerry Colon was the youngest of the four. He looked like a virtual infant with his pudgy, florid cheeks and curly brown hair that crept down over his ears and forehead. Les Weller was the veteran. Lean and rangy, he had the reflexes of a snake and about the same mentality.

"Well, it's a funny kind of light inside the oven," Les told Sherman Dettler. "According to these letters. We've sure as hell never seen any glow in production. Or testing."

"Could be they put something weird inside the oven and turned it on," Jerry Colon offered. "I mean, people do some very strange things with their microwaves. I heard about a lady who gave her poodle a bath and then—"

"We've all heard the poodle in the microwave story," Dettler interrupted Jerry.

Bobby Anderson, a forty-year-old who used to be a handsome twenty-year-old, leaned back in his chair. "Then there were the stories about the clock radios . . . remember those? About three years ago? People swore they were getting messages from aliens on them? Turned out to be a bunch of lunatics."

"Yeah, I remember that," Jerry Colon agreed. "Yeah, a bunch of loonies . . ."

Sherman Dettler threw the letters at Jerry. "Well, find out if there's anything to this 'glowing' business. I want these complaints squelched. We've never had a serious product complaint in ten years. Rumors like a damn microwave oven glowing could get us sued in ten minutes."

"There was the butane ignition incident . . ." Bobby Anderson said quietly. "It turned out to be a bit more than a rumor."

"Shut up about that," Dettler roared. "I don't want to hear a word about any of that. You understand me?"

"Yes, sir," Bobby answered, feeling fairly warned.

"Now—" Sherman Dettler arranged the folders on his desk. "Let's get on with the rest of this." He paged through several long reports. "The communications division is reporting splendid sales this month of the XRJ cellular phone. Sales are up nearly ten percent from last month. Considering that the Japanese have been dumping their cellular phones on the market for two years, I think that is very good news."

Three of the four men brightened perceptibly. Good news lowered their blood pressures. The fourth man sat looking slightly bored. He studied his fingernails periodically.

"And the communications disks have been selling like hotcakes," Les added.

"That's because the price is lower than anybody's," Jerry Colon said. He was still clutching the microwave oven reports. "Those little devils sell as fast as we can get 'em to the stores."

"Need to raise the price . . ." Dettler was thinking. He leaned back in his black leather chair and gazed out the window at the panorama of Los Angeles sixteen stories below. It would have been more dramatic if the smog had not obscured most of the view. The air-quality rating was well over one hundred that July morning. "Make some kind of small improvement . . . I don't care what it is. Change the color of the paint—something. Get the engineers on it as soon as possible. Les, you take care of it."

"Yes, sir." Les took the file from Dettler.

"Anything else?" Bobby asked.

"Yes, as a matter of fact, there is." Dettler opened another file. "I am considering a new product. I just want you to listen, and then give me your comments."

Dettler eyed his management team with a critical stare. They all knew that meant they'd better be positive about this new product, but find one mild objection just in case it didn't work out and they needed an excuse.

"It's a home irradiator," Dettler said. "One of the newest ideas to hit the market in several years. Do you know what an irradiator is?"

Three of the men shook their heads.

"It passes a mild X ray through the food, destroying any bacteria, and the food keeps forever. I mean, it could eliminate the use of refrigerators!"

"Really?" Jerry looked quite surprised. "Will it keep the beer cold?"

"No, Jer, it won't keep anything cold—it's a preserver —more like a freezer. Think of it as a freezer."

"Oh—sure—a freezer."

"The unit is fairly small, shielded with a new woven lead material that is expensive, but readily available . . . I think it will revolutionize the American kitchen. Just think about it—milk that'll keep for weeks. Meat that can sit in the cupboard . . . no more mold on the cheese . . ."

"Amazing," they all agreed. "Have you got a prototype?"

"In the lab," Dettler told them. "Go out and take a look at it. I think you'll be impressed."

"Aren't X rays dangerous?" Les asked.

"The unit, when in operation, is completely sealed," Dettler told them.

"What about the price? Who can afford these things?"

"We have always targeted that group with extra money in their pockets—those up-and-coming executives with little wives at home in the kitchen. These are not for your run-of-the-mill households."

"Sure—I shoulda thought of that," Jerry said, smiling. He had begun that nervous twitch that shot from the top of his head to the side of his mouth. It made him look like he was winking.

"It sounds just great, Sherm," Bobby Anderson said. "Just great. The only problem I can see is getting product safety approval from the feds—you know how rigid they are."

"Tony'll take care of that," Dettler said, nodding at the fourth man in the office. "I don't think that'll be a problem. There are still friends of my father in Washington. We'll let Tony do his work there."

Tony smiled thinly. His wavy hair was brushed straight back from his forehead, leaving his face looking rather naked and spare. He was not a particularly handsome man, but there was something wickedly intelligent about his pale blue eyes. Educated and slick, Tony Horbit knew exactly what he had to do.

"Anything else?" Jerry Colon asked again. Clearly, he was anxious to get out of that office.

"Ah—" Les Weller hesitated. "I've been doing some thinking—about pharmaceuticals."

Sherman Dettler leaned back in his chair. "What about them, Les?"

"There's a great market for diet aids, aging creams, tranquilizers, antidepressants, vitamins . . ." He read from a typed list, proving he'd done more than just think about the subject.

"Not interested," Dettler said flatly. "Too many lawsuits in pharmaceuticals. Better to put some thought into auto parts—big market for auto parts. Now, I think we're finished."

Les, Jerry, and Bobby stood at the signal. "Les, you get back to me about that funny light in the microwave . . . you hear?"

"I will," Les promised, and the three filed out of the office, breathing easier.

When they'd gone, Dettler eyed Tony Horbit, who sat like a well-dressed sack of flour in the chair. Not a nerve in that man, Sherman Dettler thought to himself. Except for his eyes.

"Well, Tony, what do you think? Was that a management meeting or feeding time in the monkey cage?"

Tony didn't look up. "You are surrounded by idiots," he finally said. "You know it. I know it. The question is moot."

"I suppose so," Dettler conceded. "I've been thinking of bringing Dee Dee Fairchild into the management team. What do you think?"

"It's always nice to have a woman around to make the coffee." Tony was fussing with his cuticles.

Sherman Dettler laughed. "That day's over, I'm afraid. I like the killer instinct in Dee Dee. She's clever and gets what she wants, any way she can get it."

"Good. Let her handle the irradiator. Good job for a lady who isn't afraid to play with the big boys."

"Can you fix it in Washington—if I decide to go ahead with production of the irradiator?"

"No problem."

"You think we're going to have any trouble over these complaints about the microwave ovens glowing?" Dettler quizzed Tony.

"Nope. It's a tidal wave in a teacup, Sherman, my friend. Microwaves don't glow. But I'll check the safety tests to make sure."

Sherman Dettler felt much better. "Let's go get some lunch." Lunch always made Tony more talkative. He stopped talking in staccato sentences that usually made Sherman a bit nervous. Tony would take care of things. He had a law degree from somewhere. Sherman couldn't remember the name of the school. And Tony had saved him from several previous scrapes. The butane ignition, for one. When several people were burned by the explosion of the small butane ignition on a charcoal grill, Tony had been able to prove that reasonable caution had not been exercised by the unfortunate victims.

"Good old Tony," Dettler said, putting a manicured hand on Tony's shoulder. "I can always count on you, can't I?"

Tony Horbit stepped away from his boss. "Of course you can."

"I don't want to go to the doctor," Doug protested. "I'd rather go to *school* than go to the doctor."

Katie had her purse on her shoulder and was standing in the kitchen with Amanda. Rob had been sent off to school alone, under protest.

"He looks different, don't you think, Amanda?" Katie asked, tipping Doug's head upward a bit. "Don't you think he looks like his nose is broken, or something?"

"Looks to me like the little boy turning into the little man," she said. "Don't look much different than that."

"I've got a headache," Doug complained. "I just want to lie down. The doctor won't do nothing about a headache."

"Maybe not, but we have to go see what's causing all these headaches. And nosebleeds."

Doug trudged out the door behind his mother, and they drove to Dr. Silver's office, which was located in a medical complex near Lorimar Medical Center. Katie had called that morning and insisted that Dr. Silver take a look at Doug.

"This isn't just a normal nosebleed," she told the nurse. "Believe me, it's not."

So they'd promised to work Doug in that morning, which Kate knew meant an hour of sitting in the waiting room and practicing patience. Patience was a lot like knitting, as far as she was concerned. She could do it for a while.

Dr. Silver was clearly overbooked already, so by the time he strode into the examining room to see Doug, he was scowling.

"Another nosebleed?" he asked Doug. "Did you have to pack it?"

"No—it stopped, finally," Kate said. "But he's having these nosebleeds much too often, and often accompanied by a headache."

"I was in the plane," Doug said. "It just started to bleed. *Now* I got a headache."

Dr. Silver flashed a light in his eyes and pressed on the bridge of Doug's nose. "Looks a bit swollen there. Have we checked your eyes, young man? You may need glasses. You have any trouble seeing?"

"Doug sees okay. Sometimes it's fuzzy."

"Excuse me?" Dr. Silver frowned. "You mean, *you* see fuzzy sometimes."

Doug nodded very slightly. He kept his head still because then the headache hurt less. "I think I'm going to throw up," he said to his mother.

While he vomited miserably into the sink, Katie held his head and Dr. Silver got a wet towel to clean the boy's face. When Doug finished he lay down on the examining table and held his head. He was pale and shivery.

"We'll have to do some tests," Silver said. "I'll call the hospital. I want to get a CAT scan. And a CBC. The hospital will call you with the appointment."

"Can you do this soon?" Katie asked the pediatrician.

"As soon as possible . . . I don't think it's anything serious. Probably a capillary that will have to be cauterized. These things usually aren't serious in boys this age." He patted Doug's shoulder. "You take it easy."

Katie was faintly irritated with Silver, and she wasn't even sure why. It wasn't fair to expect preferential treatment for her children just because Alan was a physician. Still, her son was hurting, and that made her insides twist with anxiety. Pediatricians should all be women and mothers, she thought to herself while she trundled Doug back out to the car. He had regained some color, but kept his eyes closed all the way home.

"Do I have to go to school tomorrow?" he asked when he was home and lying in bed.

"We'll see. You just rest now. You can have another Tylenol in two hours. I told Amanda."

"Okay," he said. "Do you have to go to work?"

"Yes, Dougy, I do. You know that. Amanda will be right here. And when the hospital calls, we'll go over there for some tests."

"Dougy wishes you could stay home," he said. Tears glistened in his eyes, and he frowned.

"I know you do. I wish I could, too. But I'll be home by five thirty." And Katie left, feeling nearly as miserable as her son. He must really be hurting if he was begging her to stay home.

She'd better call Alan at his office and tell him what Dr. Silver had said. Nothing to worry about . . . a capillary that would have to be cauterized . . . nothing to worry about . . . she chanted on the drive to Lorimar.

John Lacey was waiting for her. "What's going on?" he barked. "You're gone two days last week, and you don't show up this morning. You don't make your own hours around here, you know."

Katie took a deep breath. "If you'd check with the office, John, I called and told them I'd be late."

"This work won't wait, Kate." He glared at her. "We're months behind, and the contract for PreVent is up in a month. Unless we've got some results, I think they'll pull it. You know what that means? No money."

"I'm doing everything I can—"

"I'm not approving any more vacation," he shouted at her. "And if you show up late one more time I'll find someone else to finish the project."

"My son is sick," she gasped, fighting back tears. Oh, dear God, don't let me cry now, she begged silently. "I had to take him to the doctor—"

"Let your precious husband take time off to do that!" John Lacey whirled around and stood with his back to her.

Kate could see he was taking deep breaths. It must be more than just the fact that she was late, she thought. Something else was wrong. "Doug has to have a CAT scan. The hospital will call with an appointment." She spoke softly, her anger at John Lacey dissolved. "I'm sure Alan will be there—but so will I, John. Don't make me choose between a job and my son. There's no question who will win."

He turned around and blinked at her. "I realize—" he started, and then shook his head. "You don't know how important this work is to me, Kate. Deena is off on this wild-goose chase with this Crist substrate. You're the only one I've got working with PreVent. Don't let me down. Okay? That's all I'm asking."

"I have no intention of letting you down. This afternoon I'm doing the timed injection of the PreVent, and plating will begin tomorrow. That's the best I can do."

"Okay, okay—I'm sorry I blew up. I didn't know your son was ill." He turned away from her.

Deena Crist had been given permission to proceed with mammal studies on the Crist substrate. She'd refined fifty milliliters of the substance and prepared vials

of varying doses for the rats. It was a fairly straightfor-
ward project. She would inject the rats with RV128
along with varying dosages of the Crist substrate. The
lowest dose she would use was 0.05 mg, and the highest
dose was 1.0 mg. In the chick embryo studies, doses
above 1.0 mg were toxic.

"Aren't they cute," Deena crooned at the cages of
rats in the lab. The animals were housed in the far end
of the main lab room.

"Darling," Kate agreed sarcastically. "I suppose
you're going to name them."

Deena looked slightly guilty. "Well, maybe a couple
of them." She had already injected ten of them that
morning. Six of them would be controls, receiving only
RV128, a guaranteed case of metastatic carcinoma, usually of the liver. "I'm not going to get attached to the
controls. The first time I did animal studies I cried
through all the dissections. It was terrible."

Kate was putting on the clean room jumpsuit.
"Deena, what would cause a hamster to give birth to
teratomas? Would a virus do that?"

Deena looked at her thoughtfully. "I doubt it. A hamster would have to be exposed to a fair amount of virus
—unless you poured a culture down its throat, I doubt
you'd get neoplasms from normal exposure. Of course,
it's possible. Just unlikely."

Kate slipped on the paper boots and belted in the
billowy white jumpsuit. Her waistline had clearly thick-
ened, she thought. "What else would cause it?"

"Lots of things—X rays, chemicals, inbreeding . . .
it's hard to say."

Katie slid into the helmet and snapped it into place
on her shoulders. She nodded at Deena and stepped
into the air lock between the lab and the clean room.
There was no intercom in the air lock, so she and Deena

couldn't talk while she air showered. But once inside the sealed room, she flipped on the intercom. Deena was singing softly.

"Do the same things that affect hamsters affect humans?" she asked Deena.

"Why else would we do mammal studies in the lab?" Deena answered.

Katie worked through the lunch hour, inoculating the chick embryo cultures with PreVent until her hands ached from the small muscle movements required and her neck felt stiff. At three o'clock she left the clean room to call Amanda to see how Doug was feeling and try to get hold of Alan. Doug was feeling better. His headache was nearly gone, and he was watching reruns of *Star Trek.* Alan was in surgery all afternoon, his secretary said. She'd have him call Katie the minute he came in to the office. Kate grabbed a sandwich from the vending machine. It was tuna fish. She hated tuna fish, but she ate it anyway. It tasted like wet sawdust spread between two pieces of cardboard. Half an hour later she threw up.

Everything will be all right, she soothed herself, drowning out any thoughts to the contrary. Nothing to worry about. Nothing at all.

The sign in Amans Appliance advertised the Sizzling Summer Sale, and Fred Amans was delighted with the brisk sales on a Monday. Nobody buys a refrigerator on a Monday, he mused, chuckling. They'd sold three that morning.

Donna Martinez was demonstrating the Liberty 5000 microwave oven, and she had a small crowd around her. They sampled the beef stew she'd prepared in twelve minutes flat.

"Delicious?" she asked, smiling broadly and tugging at the strap of her sundress. "Yes?"

Fred Amans liked to see Donna smile. But when she looked up and realized he was staring at her, the smile faded. He didn't understand that. He'd gone out of his way to be nice to her. Very nice. His "little clerks," as he liked to call the women who worked in the appliance store, stayed about three months, on the average. He was tired of that. He wanted Donna to stay.

Donna had noticed the young couple who'd watched two of her demonstrations already that morning. They stood very close together and hovered near the table where she was working.

"Darrell will help you," Donna said to them, pointing to a red-haired fellow in the refrigerator section.

"Oh, we'll wait for you," the woman said shyly. "We know exactly what we want."

"Okay." Donna laughed softly. "I'll help you." She wiped her hands on the towel and removed the green plastic apron. She was wearing a very skimpy yellow sundress that showed off her tanned legs. "You folks just help yourself to the stew. There are cups there—and spoons." She reached under the counter and brought out a stack of napkins. "And here's plenty of napkins."

Fred Amans stood watching. Damn that Donovan Mills, he thought. If he'd shown up for work, Donna could have gone on with the demonstrations. Demonstrations of food always attracted a lot of buyers. Maybe it was the smell of beef stew in the shop. Maybe it was Donna. Perhaps it was that yellow sundress.

The young woman's husband blinked steadily at Donna.

"Oh, I don't always dress like this for work." She laughed. Her deep chuckle usually made everyone around her want to laugh. "It's for our *sizzling* summer sale, you know."

"My husband's the minister at First Baptist—the one downtown in San Jose?" The young woman's blue eyes were large and clear. She held out her hand to Donna. "I'm Lydia Perry. And this is my husband, John."

"Glad to meet you," Donna said breezily, shaking hands. "Now, what can I do for you? You mentioned you'd already picked out something special."

Lydia Perry beamed. "We've saved up the money for the Liberty 5000. We were just married a month ago— June twenty-second."

John Perry said nothing. Now and then he nodded at his wife.

"Are you sure you want the Liberty? Why, it takes up so much room in the kitchen . . . if'n I were you, I'd buy the Sun JFB1100. It's such a nice model. Very—"

"*We* want the Liberty 5000," Lydia told her, implying that she certainly wasn't Donna. "It is on sale today, isn't it?"

"It certainly is," Donna chirped. "I'll write it up for you—how did you say you wanted to pay for it?"

"Cash," John Perry told her. He brought out a wad of bills. "We deal in cash only."

"Good for you." Donna hurried off to finish the sale. Fred Amans watched the transaction from his office. Then he wandered over to the demonstration table to sample the beef stew. When the Perrys were gone, their boxed microwave oven stowed safely in the trunk of their car, Fred Amans took Donna aside. He had hold of her right elbow, which was dry and patchy. He shifted his grip to the fleshy upper arm.

"Don't you ever let me hear you discourage a customer like that." Not a trace of his cowboy accent lingered. "Not ever, you hear me?"

Donna glared at him. "They're just a young couple—they'll probably have a kid—"

"So what?"

"Well, you know about that Liberty—you know the reports we been getting."

Fred Amans tightened his hold on her arm and felt her wince. "Whatever reports we get, miss, are for my eyes only. You been pryin' in my office again?"

"No—of course not—I answered the phone a couple times, that's all. People complaining about the funny-colored light in the Liberty—getting sick—"

"That's not none of your business."

When a customer strolled by, Donna wrenched away from Fred Amans.

"How about Elaine Calder? You remember her. And Glenda, before her. And Ruth Ann? How about Ruth Ann?" she whispered savagely.

"That was coincidence. That's all that was. Coincidence. Now, you get back to work, darlin'. You're just lucky I ain't put you on no quota system here, like Darrell and Jake. You push me, however, and I'll do that."

"You forget that I know too much," Donna shot back. Her brown eyes snapped angrily. "I'd go right to the *Mercury News* with what I know, believe me." She stamped off.

Fred Amans took a couple of deep breaths and returned to his office, where he closed the door.

Lt. Col. Stephen Reynolds sat in Alan's small office at the hospital and studied the map on the wall. "Very interesting. I didn't give geographical grouping much credence."

There were many more red markers on the map. All of them clustered in groups of three or four in a rim around the valley.

"The only similarity in these areas, as far as I can tell, is the income of the people who live there." Alan had another stack of charts on his desk. He'd planned to spend an hour finding the addresses of the newest tumor patients. Not just any tumor patients. Teratomas."

"I notice that many of the cases cluster around the semiconductor industries—Sunnyvale, Los Altos Hills, Palo Alto . . ."

"How do you know where the semiconductor industries are?" Alan asked him.

"I make it a point to know."

"But how do you account for the number of cases in the Almaden Valley? IBM is a good five miles away."

"Five miles isn't very far," Reynolds observed.

"I haven't seen any correlation with industrial locations," Alan said. "As a matter of fact, the tumor rate in Los Altos is as high as in the Almaden Valley. And there's no semiconductor industry there. I believe the only correlation is income."

"That's possible." Reynolds stared at the map again. "Then again, it may have nothing to do with any of that."

"I'd like to know why the Army's interested in these tumors."

"I assure you, Doctor, it's very routine." Lt. Col. Stephen Reynolds stood up. "Let me know if you come up with anything else."

Alan smiled. "I don't imagine you will return the favor."

Reynolds smiled back. "The United States Army doesn't do favors, sir."

"It occurred to me that since we have made friends with most of our enemies around the world, you guys might not have enough to do anymore. Poking around in hospital business might just keep you occupied."

Reynolds wasn't smiling anymore. "There are always men around, like Saddam Hussein, to prove you wrong, Dr. Campbell. If you think we don't have enemies, you are mistaken." He turned briskly, and left the office.

Alan sat back in his chair. He'd touched a tender spot in the Lieutenant Colonel. Whatever could that mean? Was the United States Army worried about a virus that could cause these teratomas? A virus released intentionally? But by whom? Or did they suspect gamma rays were bombarding the West Coast? Gamma-ray radiation was known to be mutagenic. . . . It would be quite a trick, however, to aim them only at neighborhoods where engineers and scientists lived. And again, who would do such a thing?

Everyone's looking for something fantastic, Alan thought. I think the answer is right under our noses. If we could just see it.

He sorted through two more charts, placed two more red markers on the map, very close to a cluster of other red markers, and then he had to leave to check on two surgical patients in the ICU.

16

 "Look!" Alan slammed several patients' charts down on the metal desk in the Medical Records Department of Lorimar. "These charts have been altered! Pages are missing. The diagnosis has been changed on one of them. Don't tell me I'm wrong. I know better. And I want an explanation."

The head of Medical Records was Marian Kettering. She had been a nun in some obscure order in California, but now she atoned for all that and ran her department as if it were the kingdom of God. She did not smile at Dr. Campbell. "I do not doubt your belief, Doctor. But I do, clearly, doubt your facts. And it isn't unusual, after all, to have a diagnosis change on a patient." She gazed serenely up at Alan.

"I want to know who has had access to these charts. Who requested them in the last two months?"

Marian Kettering took the charts. "I can find out for you—in a few days. We're swamped at the moment."

"I need to know right now." Alan sat down in a chair

across from Marian. "I'm not leaving until you provide that information."

Alan glared at the Medical Records librarian. His blue eyes met her own steely blue gaze.

"I don't see what's so important—"

"Just give me the information."

It took her no more than five minutes to extract the information from the computer. She typed in each name and proceeded to handwrite a list for Alan.

"Could you do a printout for me?" he asked. "I want to make sure all the names are there."

Marian Kettering's bottom lip narrowed visibly. She hit the print button on the computer keyboard, and a little daisy wheel printer sprang to life on the table. She ripped off the two pages and handed them to Alan. "Will that be all, Doctor?"

"For now," he growled. "I'll be back." Clutching the two pages, he returned to his office.

He expected several names, but one was listed simply as "Surgical Dept." There was no physician's name. Surgical Department? Why would a chart be requested like that? Lt. Col. Stephen Reynolds's name was on two of the three lists. But Reynolds had made no secret of the fact that he was reviewing charts. And one of the charts was on Jennifer Wynn. Alan had operated on that girl, and the original diagnosis of teratoma had been changed to nephrotic rupture. Who had changed it?

Kate returned to the obstetrician, Dr. Claude Robertz, that week. The morning sickness had subsided somewhat, but she still felt bloated and uncomfortable. And John Lacey was furious that she was taking the morning off to see the obstetrician.

From the moment Dr. Robertz walked into the examining room, tears covered Katie's face.

"It's okay," Robertz said, "it's the hormones. Makes you cry easily."

"It's not the hormones!" Katie railed. "My son has to have a CAT scan—he has these terrible nosebleeds and headaches. And I'm scared to death about this new baby. Something's not right. I can feel it—"

Dr. Robertz sank to the stool and listened.

"This isn't like the first two pregnancies. Can we do an ultrasound? Or an amniocentesis? Just to make sure the baby's all right?"

Robertz nodded. "We *can* do that, but I don't see any reason, at the moment. One pregnancy is not, necessarily, like the others, Katie. But the one thing you have to do is relax. I know, absolutely, that stress is bad for a pregnancy."

"How can I relax?" she wailed at him, embarrassed by the sound of her voice, which had distinct childish overtones. "Just tell me how I can relax?"

"First take a couple of deep breaths . . ."

Katie did, and felt a little better. The tears subsided to a slow drip.

"Better?"

She nodded. "I hate feeling like this—so out of control."

Robertz laughed gently. "You're not out of control. You're pregnant. There's an enormous difference."

He did a pelvic exam, and Kate lay there and willed the muscles into momentary tranquillity. It wasn't easy, but it kept her mind off the exam. She diverted any worry by thinking about how she'd design a woman, given half a chance. There'd be a zipper . . . she thought.

"I'd say you are about four and a half months," the obstetrician said, stripping off the latex gloves. "That'll

put the due date at the end of December. Or the beginning of January. A Christmas baby."

The tears started afresh. "I can't even think that far
ahead," she sniffed. "December sounds like the next
century."

"Well, you'd better start thinking about it," he said,
smiling. "Christmas usually comes right after Labor Day
these days. And come back in a month—unless you
have any problems in between—any spotting or unusual
discharge. Then just give me a call. And relax. Everything's fine."

Dr. Claude Robertz left Kate in the examining room
and went to his office with her chart. His smile faded
the moment he closed the door to the office. He looked
at Katie's chart for several minutes, made a few extra
notes, and laid the chart on his desk. He pulled a small
box of colored stickers from his top drawer and pasted a
green one on Kate's chart. He'd have to watch her, he
thought. Very closely.

Alan took the call from Dr. Viktor Straub. "I know
. . . I'm sorry . . . I should have called . . . No, I
don't think I'm so important I don't have to call you. I
said I was sorry . . . Fine, send me a bill!" He hung up
the phone and stared at it for several minutes.

He had no intention of going back to Dr. Viktor
Straub. And he had told him he wouldn't be back the
last time they had met. But, apparently, that was insufficient notice for the great psychiatrist, Alan fumed silently. Seconal worked better than any analysis. Except,
he knew he had to be careful with the sleeping pills.
And he was. He didn't take them every night. Not usually every night, anyway.

That evening he was home with Kate and the boys.
Katie was edgy and tried hard not to show it in front

of the boys. The CAT scan was scheduled for eight thirty the next morning. Doug had a wretched headache, and the Tylenol gave him little relief.

"Can't you give him something stronger?" Katie asked Alan.

"No," Alan told her. "I'd like to, but with the nosebleeds, sedation isn't a very good idea. If he had a nosebleed in the middle of the night, he might not wake up if he were sedated."

She nodded. "It's just so hard to watch him lie there in that kind of pain."

"I'll go sit with him," Alan said, and left Katie and Rob in the kitchen.

Dinner sat untouched on the stove. Amanda had left chicken cordon bleu and saffron rice, but no one was hungry. Rob cleaned out the hamster cages, scraping up the soggy old sawdust and replacing it with fresh-scented new wood chips. He didn't even complain about the fact that he'd done it three weeks in a row.

"Fluffy looks funny," he said, peering into the cage. "He looks all lumpy."

"Fluffy's a female," Katie corrected him. She walked over and looked into the cage. "Oh—dear—she does look lumpy." She had an array of bumps with red pustules on her back and sides. "I'll get your dad to have a look at her."

"Frank's okay." Rob had already cleaned Frank's cage, and the little black hamster crouched near his food dish. "I think Frank looks all right. Do you think Fluffy's sick again?"

"No—she's probably fine. I don't know much about hamsters. Except it looks like she has a sore, there on her back. Maybe we can put some antibiotic on it . . ."

Alan returned from Doug's room after about half an

hour. Katie and Rob were curled up together on the love seat watching television.

"Dad?" Robbie asked. "Will you look at Fluffy? I think he's—she's sick. She's got a sore."

Alan sighed and went to the kitchen to take a look. Hamsters were not his specialty, he grumbled to himself, but when he looked into the cage, it was clear that the animal was not well. A suppurative mass was visible on Fluffy's back. Alan reached into the cage, and the hamster screamed when he grasped her and pulled her out.

Fluffy was a bundle of small, distinct masses. When she opened her mouth to bare her teeth, Alan noted the protuberance on the roof of her mouth. Quietly he put the animal back in the cage. His hand shook slightly.

He got his bag and loaded a syringe with thiopental. Rob came into the kitchen and studied his father's face. He glanced at the syringe.

"What's wrong with Fluffy?"

"She's pretty sick, Rob. She has a lot of tumors. I'm going to put her down."

Kate rushed into the kitchen, and Robbie fell into her arms.

"He's killing Fluffy," Rob cried, horrified. "Stop him, Mom!"

"What's wrong with the hamster?" Katie asked Alan. "Is it sick?"

"Take a look at it—there are growths all over—even in her mouth," Alan said quietly. "Robbie, Fluffy is very, very sick. She can't eat, and she's probably in pain all the time. Would you want to live like that?"

"She does eat—she ate all, well, some of her food today." His voice was ragged with tears.

"And what about the pain? Do you want her to live in

pain? I'll let you make the choice. I won't put her down unless you tell me to. All right?"

Rob cooed at the hamster, who lay in the sawdust in the cage, baring her teeth now and then. Her sides heaved. Helpless tears coursed down his small, pale face. "I don't get it," he finally said, half choking. "If there's something wrong with Dougy, will they stick a needle in him and kill him, too? Just because you're sick doesn't mean you haveta die, does it?"

Alan pushed the syringe of thiopental out of sight, and gathered Rob to his lap. "No, lad, it doesn't. Most people, and most animals, get sick and then they get better. But Fluffy won't get better, Rob. Doug will. That's the difference. Fluffy will get worse and worse. We don't want her to suffer anymore."

"No," Rob sniffed. "Me neither. But I don't want to watch. Okay?"

Alan felt the sweat start. "Okay. I'll do it quickly. Fluffy won't feel any more than a pinprick, and then she'll be unconscious. There'll not be any more pain for her."

Rob nodded and went to his mother, who sat at the table unable to speak, crying herself. "Come on," she said. "We'll go see how Doug's doing."

Alan injected the hamster, filling the abdominal cavity with the barbiturate. Fluffy sagged, heaved several times, and lay still in his hand. Her teeth were bared. Alan wrapped the small body in plastic, and suddenly he was aware of a strange, burning sensation in both eyes, as if he'd rubbed his eyes with salt. He laid the hamster into a small check-blank box and closed the lid.

Later, Alan and Katie lay in bed and talked.

"Tears," he said to Kate. "There were actually tears in my eyes. I haven't cried in years."

"It's too bad Robbie didn't see you cry. I think he was

more upset about the hamster because of Doug. We have to be really careful not to ignore Robbie because Doug is sick." Her own tears stung cheeks already irritated from the previous crying. "If I weren't so scared, Alan—what if we lose Doug?"

He reached for her gently. "Lose him? You mean, if he dies? Doug isn't going to die, Katie. There's probably just an artery that enlarged at the back of the nose—nothing more complicated than that. It's easily repaired. We do it all the time in the hospital."

"Then why do I think he has a tumor, Alan? Why can't I get it out of my mind?"

"I don't know," he soothed her, lost in his own thoughts for a moment. "I don't know."

"The worse thing is feeling so helpless. Every day I get up and work and take my vitamins and buy milk and bread at the supermarket and drive the car just like everything's normal. I sometimes think I'm denying it all. Just continuing on and hoping for the best."

"I call that an act of bravery," he told her, kissing her lightly.

They bundled Doug into the car at six thirty the next morning. His headache was better. Amanda had come early to be with Rob until he went to school. When the car left the driveway, Amanda and Robbie went back into the kitchen, cool with early morning air and the scent of mock orange, to finish breakfast.

"He's having a cat scan," Rob told Amanda as he stirred the banana slices into his cornflakes and milk. "Cats have to walk all over him all morning. That's why he couldn't have breakfast. Because if a cat smells food on your breath it might bite you or something."

Amanda laughed softly. "Oh, I don't think so, little man. A CAT scan is one of them fancy medical tests.

Dougy takes a ride through a big tube. I've had one o' them tests. It doesn't hurt a bit."

Robbie opened his eyes wide. "You had one? And there weren't cats?"

"No, no, just a shiny tube. That's all. Doug will be fine. You'll see."

Robbie relaxed. A big tube didn't sound as bad as cats walking all over Doug.

"I have to bury Fluffy," he told Amanda. "My dad had to kill her last night. She has something bad. I can't remember what it is."

"Your mama told me. Would you like to do that this morning, before school? We could do it together. I'm pretty good at buryings."

"Are you? Can we bury her under the oak tree?"

Amanda nodded. "You finish your breakfast. I'll find the spade."

"Will it hurt?" Doug asked his father.

"No, you won't feel a thing. You just have to lie quietly."

"How come?"

"They're using a computer to get a look at your bones and muscles," Alan said. They were waiting in a small room with only a bench and a shelf for Doug's clothes. He had on a blue hospital gown that made him look younger than his ten years. Alan looked at the boy's bare feet, dangling from under the gown. They were tanned and squarish, shaped like Alan's own feet. Something squeezed tight in Alan's chest, and he quickly looked away from Doug.

"How long will it take?" Doug asked him.

"Not too long . . ." Alan glanced at Katie, who was fighting tears again.

She stood up and walked to the window.

"How come Mom's crying all the time?" the boy asked. "I wish she wouldn't cry."

"Well, Dougy, better get used to it. Women cry easier than men. It's a fact of life. We men somehow learn that crying isn't all right, but women know better."

"You think it's okay to cry?" Doug sounded incredulous. "They call you a sissy at school if you cry."

"Do they? Well, that's too bad—but crying doesn't make a person a sissy. Believe me. Some of the bravest men I have ever known cry."

Doug looked up at his father, and at that moment a bright flash of red blood gushed from his nose. Katie dashed to the desk to get a towel, which, of course, was not easily available. Two towels later, Doug, looking pale and shaken, his gown stained with blood, was wheeled off to the scanner.

"I have to go check in with the OR," Alan told Kate. "I'll be back in about half an hour. Are you all right until then?"

"I thought you could be here," she whined.

"I will—I'll be right back. But I have two patients waiting this morning, and I need to see them. I won't be long."

Kate nodded and sat down in one of the chairs. "I'll be fine."

She watched him leave. She could go down to the lab and talk to Deena, but somehow it seemed disloyal to Doug. The separation of several walls and corridors was like a thousand miles at the moment. It's only an artery, she soothed herself. They'll cauterize it. That's all it is.

Alan came back once, and Doug was not out of the scanner. He left again, promising to return in moments, which turned into thirty minutes. Kate tried to keep her breathing even and slow. Her bottom lip quivered periodically. She looked at two magazines and saw nothing in them, not even the pictures. The act of turning pages was all she could handle.

At ten minutes after ten, Doug emerged from the scanner area. He was asleep, his dark hair damp on the white pillow. He had a clean gown on, and he'd been sponged off.

"Hi, I'm Becky," the young attendant said to Katie. "Are you Doug's mom?"

Katie nodded, afraid if she spoke the tears would start again.

"He can go home in about half an hour," Becky said. "We'll keep an eye on him in the outpatient observation —you can go along."

"How was the scan?" Katie asked.

"It went well—he's a very sweet little boy." Becky maneuvered the gurney expertly down the narrow halls, past other patients and staff.

"I mean, what did you find out?"

"Oh, I don't know that—Dr. Silver will let you know."

"How long before they know—how long do we have to wait to find out?"

"Not long. If you don't hear from him right away, that's good news."

Katie sat with Doug while the nurses checked him over.

Alan came in and ruffled Doug's hair. "How's the kid?" he joked. "Feeling okay?"

"Tired," Doug said. "I want to go home."

"I talked to Dr. Silver," Alan told Katie quietly. "They're looking at the scan right now. We'll know something soon."

Kate drove Doug home. He stretched out in the back seat of the car with a pillow and blanket, and Alan went back to his surgeries. Then Katie waited for the phone to ring. Amanda fixed a cool shrimp and avocado salad for lunch, and Katie ate two bites. She wrote a card to Elaine Calder at San Gregorio. Doug was still asleep at one o'clock when she got in her car and returned to the hospital to work. The timed tests were due to be read and recorded. It couldn't wait.

"How'd the scan go?" Dr. John Lacey asked her, eyeing her warily.

"We don't know a thing yet. I don't know what takes so long—it shouldn't take this long to read a scan."

John Lacey started to reach out for Kate and then drew back, allowing the extended arm only to adjust a chair for Kate to sit down. "It'll be okay. Kids are tough. You know that."

"I'm not so sure, John. I'm really not so sure this time. I think something awful is going on—and it isn't only Doug."

John Lacey sat down across from Katie in the lab. Deena was in the clean room. "Listen," he said quietly, "I'm sorry I blew up about you taking the morning off. You take whatever time you need. We'll manage here."

"Thanks, John," she said, and meant it. "I really appreciate that."

He nodded. "Even if I don't always sound like it, I've got the priorities straight around here. And—" he said hesitantly, "if there's anything I can do, I'll do it."

"Can you go get them to speed up that scan reading?" Kate asked him.

John Lacey grinned. "I'll go try. Okay?"

"Okay—and I've got some work to do. I may leave at four—if I get it all finished." Kate stood up slowly. "Oh, and one more thing, John. I'm missing several boxes of PreVent. I had fifteen in the freezer before I left for Disneyland. I used one box last week, but there's only twelve there. I can't figure it out. Deena isn't using any of the interferon, is she?"

"No—not that I know of . . . You didn't miscount?" John stood up and frowned slightly.

"I don't think so. I'll have to check the last shipping list."

"I'm sure it's all there," John said.

Dr. Silver came to the lab at three thirty to talk to Kate. John Lacey stood behind him, acting like a petulant shepherd.

"I already talked to Alan," Silver complained. "But John insisted I tell you—"

Kate caught hold of the edge of the counter. "What's wrong—what did you find out?"

"There's a nasoseptal mass," Silver said easily, as if he were talking about the weather. "It has extended into the hypothalamus region—"

"A tumor?" Katie demanded. "Does he have a brain tumor?"

"Well, not exactly." Silver explained, "There is some cerebral involvement, but it is not extensive. We'll do a biopsy first. And then remove the mass. That's what's causing the nosebleeds. And the headaches."

Katie wanted to scream at him. Why hadn't he done this scan months ago? "When?" she asked. "When will you do the biopsy?"

"Next week—"

"Tomorrow," John said. "You can do it tomorrow, can't you, Ben?"

"Uh—tomorrow? Possibly—I'll have to check the OR schedule."

"Tomorrow," John Lacey said firmly. "There's no reason to wait."

"No, of course not—maybe Alan can help me get an operating room cleared for the afternoon." Dr. Silver was glaring at John Lacey. He wasn't used to being pushed around.

"Tomorrow then," Katie said, feeling much stronger. "We'll bring Dougy in. Where do we go?"

"Outpatient Surgery—where you were this morning," Silver told her. "I'll call and let you know what time."

The pediatrician left abruptly, but not before a final dagger glance at Lacey. When he'd left, Kate thanked John.

"I don't know how you did that, but thank you. I don't think I could bear to wait a week."

John Lacey leaned close to her. "The sooner we get Doug healthy, the sooner you can concentrate on the research," he said. "I'm doing this for strictly selfish reasons. Besides, I hate to see you in tears all the time."

Kate leaned into him. It wasn't intended to be a hug, but his arms circled her, and she allowed it. There was a moment of familiarity about the smell of him, a cinnamon toast smell, that swam around her. She reached out and held him, her arm around his back. And that was when she felt it, the small nodules on his back. She stiffened. John Lacey straightened up sharply.

"Sorry," he said, "it was just a friendly hug—nothing more." He hurried out of the lab.

Alan was on the phone late that afternoon. The patients were gone from the waiting room, and the receptionist and his nurse had also left for the day. He sat and stared at the directory in front of him. It was a listing of his medical school colleagues, all two hundred ten of them. He'd marked off the ones who might remember him. And he began to dial.

"This is Dr. Alan Campbell," he said when the phone was answered. "May I speak to Dr. Jim Lawson."

He made one call after another, undeterred by the

silences at the other end of the phone line when he asked about the teratomaceous tumor rate. Clearly, most of his classmates in the western states had seen the sharp increase, and equally clearly, they were reluctant to comment on it. Some of them, however, had no idea what he was talking about. Those physicians, invariably, worked with clinics in lower-income areas. By seven o'clock, the pattern was clear.

Alan finally hung up the phone. His ear ached. He needed to get home to Kate and the boys. What was happening to their idyllic life? he wondered, feeling helpless and vulnerable. What was happening to all the plans they'd made?

His nurse, Sharon, who served alternately as counselor and ready listener, came into the office. "I hate to trouble you, Dr. Campbell," she said. "But I wondered if you'd look at something."

Alan agreed. He figured one of the plants was dying in the waiting room. Or she had an idea for repapering the exam rooms and had samples for him to look at.

Sharon was a good-looking woman, and when she unwound the bright blue scarf from her neck, Alan got nervous.

"Uh—" he said.

She unbuttoned the top two buttons of her shimmering white blouse. "I've got this strange lump."

Alan stood up and gently palpated the mass located between her breasts. The sternum was slightly protruded. "When did you notice this?" he asked.

Sharon looked a bit sheepish. "About a month ago— except I didn't think it was anything. But with all these tumor cases, I got to worrying about it."

"I think Dr. Wang should take a look at it." Alan tried to keep his voice level. She'd read volumes into even the slightest emotional cue.

"Do you think it's serious?" Sharon's gray-blue eyes were calm.

"I don't know, Sharon. Have you noticed any other masses?"

"Yes," she said quietly. "This morning. There are two in the—groin area. That's why I thought I'd ask you."

"Call Dr. Wang's office in the morning. I'm sure he can tell you more." Alan refused to care for the medical needs of his staff. In his experience that wasn't a good idea.

"You don't think it's a tumor, do you?" She was talking in her nurse voice, but beneath it was a sea of fear lapping at every syllable.

"I doubt it," he lied.

17

Amanda brought a battered tweed
suitcase and moved into the guest
room of the Campbell house that
evening. Katie was more grateful
than she could say.

"I called my mother," Kate told Amanda. "She and
Karl wanted to fly out, but I asked them to wait until we
know more."

Amanda nodded solemnly. "I'll sit up with the little
man tonight, jus' to make sure nothin' bad happens, so
you can sleep."

"I'm so tired I can hardly stay upright. But Robbie
has to get into that bathtub and actually get wet," she
vowed, sinking into the rocking chair in the guest room.
"And I'm terrified Doug will have another nosebleed."

"I be there. Don't you worry. Amanda'll watch him."

Kate yawned. "He can't have any water after midnight. Not even a sip."

"No, ma'am. Not even a sip."

Katie closed her eyes. Her muscles twitched, and she

bolted awake. "You'd better rest a bit now, Amanda, if you're going to stay up all night."

"Oh," the woman crooned softly, "Amanda doesn't need much sleep these days. I'll get Rob into the bathtub."

"I'll go talk to Doug." Katie heaved herself out of the rocking chair. "I think he's worried about the biopsy tomorrow."

Kate found Doug in his bedroom. He'd had a shower, and his hair was still damp. It was one of those rare humid evenings in California, so Katie had turned on the air conditioner.

"Will Dad be there?" Doug asked, looking up from his comic book.

"He won't actually be in the operating room, Doug, but he'll be in the area. He's doing two surgeries himself tomorrow morning."

Doug nodded. "I didn't think he'd be there. I just thought I'd ask."

"It'll be all right. You'll be asleep during the whole procedure, and it's very quick. By three or four o'clock you'll be home again."

"I know, I know. You already told Doug that." He concentrated on the comic book.

Katie sat on the edge of the bed and watched him for a moment. He wore only a pair of striped cotton shorts, and his sturdy arms and legs were tanned to a golden brown.

"You know *I'll* be there," she told him. "Not in the operating room, but just outside. And the minute you're awake they'll let me see you. You know that, don't you?"

Doug nodded and looked up at her. "The headache's a lot better—couldn't we wait?"

"No, Dougy, we can't wait." She rubbed her hand

lightly over one of his bare legs. "But it's going to be all right. I promise."

"Unless it's a brain tumor," he said. "Then it won't be all right."

"What makes you say that?" A river of cold fear ran through Katie like a faucet turned on in her spinal column. "Even if it is a tumor, they can remove it."

"How can they remove it?" he asked.

"Surgically. They do that all the time—all the time. They're very good at it."

"Doug doesn't think so." He turned back to the comic book.

Panicky tears welled up in Katie. Where was Alan when she needed him to explain this to Doug? Why wasn't he here tonight? Doug would believe Alan. Alan was the one who made the world safe for her sons.

"I can only tell you what I know," Katie said quietly. "And that's that you're going to be fine. And that I love you."

Doug didn't look up.

The biopsy left Doug's face swollen and bruised. He looked like he'd been battered in a fistfight when Katie saw him in recovery.

"Oh, that's normal," the nurse told her briskly. "It'll fade in a week or so."

Doug mumbled and thrashed his way to consciousness that afternoon. Alan came in about noon, looking wan and exhausted.

"How's it going?" He leaned over Doug. "Dr. Silver says you did fine."

"I have to throw up," Doug said, and promptly vomited into the emesis basin beside him.

"When will we know about the biopsy?" Katie asked.

"A couple of days—unless you can get your friend

down there in Pathology to speed things up. I know I have no clout in the basement."

Katie knew he meant John Lacey. Alan had heard about John Lacey pulling Dr. Silver to the research lab to talk to Kate after the CAT scan. "I'll see what I can do."

And when Kate went to see John in the lab he was already in Histology supervising the frozen sections, so she didn't get a chance to talk to him. She left a note that she'd be in to work the next morning.

But Dr. Silver decided to keep Doug in the hospital overnight because the tissue in the area of the biopsy was so swollen it blocked the breathing passages. And if the boy had a nosebleed before the swelling went down he would be unable to breathe. Doug seemed to accept the overnight stay, and the nurse promised him ice cream for his supper.

"I'll see to it personally," she said, a wide smile dancing on her young face.

"I like chocolate," Doug told her sleepily.

The frozen sections were inconclusive, they learned three days later, but the sections of fixed tissue, hardened in formalin and then sectioned into thin slices, showed clear areas of embryonic cells and the wildly mixed cellular growth consistent with a teratomaceous tumor. Dr. Silver scheduled the surgery for the fifth of August. Kate was horrified. Three weeks? They had to wait nearly three weeks?

The problem was that the neurosurgeon was not available until then. He was on vacation until the first of August, and he had no time on his calendar until the fifth.

"Unless you want another surgeon," Silver said to Alan. "It's up to you."

Alan was furious. He'd call Stanford and see who was available there. He knew several surgeons at the University of California, San Francisco. Surely someone was available sooner.

"My wife is pregnant," he told Dr. Banos at Stanford. "Waiting three weeks is going to be very hard on her, as well as my son."

"Send me a copy of his medical record," Banos told Alan. "I'll get it to Nelson Fell—he's the best around."

"Nelson Fell, of course," Alan said, grateful, his breathing easing a bit. Dr. Nelson Fell was one of the top neurosurgeons in the country. "Thank you—I'll fax those records in the morning."

Alan went directly to Medical Records to get Doug's chart, but was told it was not available.

"It's probably still in circulation," Marian Kettering told him in a cool, languid voice. "You know it takes a couple of days for us to get it. I suppose that's not as efficient as your Surgical Department . . ."

"No, our patients probably wouldn't make it with that kind of inefficiency," he barked at her.

"It's not my fault," Marian Kettering said. "I've got these CDC guys breathing down my neck, and surgical review, and—well, it just isn't my fault."

"No, of course it isn't. It never is." And Alan turned and left the Medical Records Department, vowing to speak to Philip Morrisey about the problem.

It was just after two A.M., and the Surgical Department at Lorimar was finally quiet. They'd done an emergency appendectomy, set three compound fractures on a multiple trauma case, and Dr. Lawrence Greer had been called in for surgery on a possible ectopic pregnancy.

Dr. Greer sat in his small office in an area that used

to contain the old operating amphitheaters, but was now used only for routine outpatient surgical procedures and offices for residents and surgeons. His office was one of the smallest. It contained no windows, being a subdivided room. He hated that office. It seemed more like a prison cell to him. And the green color of paint did little to convince him otherwise.

He sat bent over patients' records, a stack of them. The desk was cluttered with surgical reports, anesthesia reports, pathology reports . . .

The door opened, and Greer bolted upright. His heart hammered in his chest.

"Jesus, you scared the hell out of me," he said to Lt. Col. Stephen Reynolds, who was standing in the open doorway. "What are you doing around here this time of night?"

"I often work late," Reynolds said. "Mind if I come in? I just happened to see your light on under the door."

"No—by all means, have a seat. I'm just finishing up a few reports." Greer laughed uneasily. "Seems like there's never time to get the paperwork done." Lawrence Greer carefully closed the chart and slid it into the pile beside him.

"It does seem like that," Reynolds mused, pulling up a chair. "I'm missing a number of charts. I just wondered if you had any of them."

"Well, I should be finished with these by tomorrow. I'll return them to Medical Records."

"I'm particularly interested in this latest case of teratoma—the young Campbell boy? Dr. Alan Campbell's son?" Reynolds leaned toward the desk.

Greer nodded. "Very unfortunate. Must be hard on Alan and his family. Do you know Katie Campbell? She's John Lacey's new research assistant."

"No, I'm afraid I haven't met her. But, about Douglas Campbell—I don't suppose you have his records there in your stack, do you?"

Greer glanced at the medical records. "I doubt it—these are all gynecology patients, I believe."

"Yes, you aren't involved in the Campbell case, are you? There'd be no reason for you to have the chart."

"No, no reason . . ."

"You don't mind if I look then . . . it's possible it got misplaced with the files you requested. Isn't that possible?" Reynolds eyed Greer coolly.

"I suppose it's possible, but unlikely. I haven't seen it. And I'm afraid I do mind if you browse through these files. I see no reason why it can't wait until Friday."

"I have a reason," Reynolds told him, standing up. "It's because I have found alterations on a number of patients' charts—just small things, you understand, but critical information that has been deleted or changed. Now, that's a criminal offense, and Dr. Morrisey and I are trying to figure out who would do such a thing. And why."

Greer blinked blandly at the Lieutenant Colonel. "I haven't the slightest idea."

"I'm glad to hear that, Dr. Greer." Reynolds remained standing. "Some of the changes have been very clever. A Susan Veracruz—do you remember that case? She died of a hemorrhage due to a particularly malignant teratoma. The cause of death was listed as teratoma, originally, and later changed to anoxia. Isn't that curious? And a twelve-year-old named Jennifer Wynn? She died of an incompatible blood type exposure from a teratoma that ruptured when she fell from a bicycle. Even the surgical specimens have disappeared from the morgue. And her cause of death is now listed as nephrotic rupture. Very curious . . ."

"How odd," Greer agreed, fidgeting with his pen. "But why are you telling all this to me? Surely, you don't think *I* altered charts or death certificates."

Reynolds smiled thinly. "Did I say that? I certainly didn't intend any accusations here. It's just that those patients' charts were always requested by the Surgical Department. No doctor ever signed them out. The request is always just 'Surgical Department.' We began to wonder who that was."

"I request charts," Greer sputtered. "I've always requested charts, to update and add comments. There's nothing unusual about that."

"No, of course there isn't. I didn't mean to imply that there was . . . but I would like to check through that pile of charts to see if Douglas Campbell's is there."

Lawrence Greer stood up. "I'm sorry, I can't allow you to do that. These are confidential files—"

"Are you sweating, Dr. Greer?" Lt. Col. Reynolds asked. "I do hope you're not coming down with something. They say there's some nasty viruses around . . ." Reynolds turned smartly and left, closing the door behind him.

Greer slumped into the chair. He'd only wanted a look at the Campbell chart. It wasn't a crime to just look at it, he told himself. He unlocked the bottom drawer of the small desk and fished out a bottle of bourbon. He locked the office door, took several long pulls from the bottle, and felt better immediately. Nothing to worry about, he decided. Just some nosy military man. He'd return the charts by morning. He'd get Marian to erase the entry. Somehow he'd convince her to do that. My God, what a mess life is, he thought. And the money to finance the mess, that was worse. Cheryl, with her insatiable need for everything from cruises to new kitchen cabinets, had managed to deplete their savings and run

up charge accounts in the five digits. There was the matter of his small habit . . . it wasn't much. He only used
cocaine on weekends, and then purely for recreation.
Or escape, he thought dismally. And then the gambling
. . . If it weren't for that he'd be okay. He wouldn't
have to look around for extra money.

He took one last drink and locked up the bottle again.
The alcohol fire shot through his veins and stopped his
nervous twitching. He'd call Dettler in the morning and
tell him there were suspicions. Sherman Dettler might
have some ideas about what to do to get this army guy
off his back.

It had been so easy in the beginning. He just re-
arranged Elaine Calder's diagnosis. For a fee. Then a
few others. He raised his prices. It was so easy. And he
needed the money. And who cared if the diagnosis was
teratoma or ruptured uterus? Or carcinoma. Who
cared?

Greer nodded to himself and sat down at the desk
again. He pulled a chart out of the stack. It belonged to
Douglas Campbell. He opened the chart and began to
read.

That night Alan Campbell's nightmares were in earnest. He dreamed of a strange house where many other
people lived, besides himself. He thought his father was
in one of the rooms, but a long search proved useless.
He shuffled around a dream body, a heavy body pep-
pered with oozing sores that looked like small rats had
nibbled at his muscles and bones. In the shadows of the
dream house he saw the glint of black eyes staring out at
him. And there was nothing he could do. Mounted on
the wall of the house was a display of surgical scalpels
that he was unable to reach, no matter how many chairs
he stacked up. No matter how high he jumped to try to

catch hold of one knife. Rat teeth bit deep. He was sweating and he screamed.

Katie woke up and found Alan moaning.

"Alan?" she whispered, taking hold of his bare shoulder. "Alan, wake up."

"Aaagh," he cried out and pushed her hand away. He leapt out of bed, brushing away the nightmare as if it were cobwebs. He stood gaping at her.

"It was a dream, Alan," she said softly. "Just a dream."

Alan ran his fingers through his hair, stared at her, and finally shook his head. "A dream . . ." he mumbled.

"Come back to bed," she said softly.

Alan crept between the sheets and lay there, stiff and frowning.

"What about Dr. Straub?" she asked him. "Haven't you figured out anything about these dreams?"

Alan sighed. "Katie, the man was useless . . . I tried to explain. He wasn't interested in the dreams—and I couldn't remember many of them . . . I don't know. I just didn't go back after a while."

They lay there in silence. Only the sound of their breathing disturbed the warm, silent air.

"If you just guessed—I mean, if there were no wrong answers, what do you think the dreams mean?" Katie asked.

"Now you're sounding just like Jerry." He lay thinking, one long arm cradling his head. "I think there's something I have to do—something I should have done a long time ago, and didn't. If that makes any sense . . ."

"Dreams don't always make sense—logical sense." But she didn't know what sense they did make. "What do you think you need to do?"

"I don't know. If I knew, I'd do it."

"Have you talked to Jerry Greathouse? He has a very different idea about dreams. I talked to him once about it—"

Alan gave a short, strangled laugh. "Jerry thinks I should sweat it out in his sauna. Beat a drum . . . I don't know, Katie, it sounds like hocus-pocus."

Katie yawned. "I don't think it's magic . . . Jerry doesn't think it's magic. It's just a different way to look at dreams—like they're real."

Alan's eyes looked heavy. "Maybe I'll talk to Jerry— once Doug's okay. And the baby . . ."

"I can't do this by myself, Alan. I can't take care of Dougy, and you, and this baby—and myself, without your help. And if you're having nightmares, you're not much help. Do it for me, if nothing else. Go see Jerry. Will you do that?"

"Sure, Kate. I can do that."

"I'll call Jerry tomorrow . . ."

"*I'll* call him."

"You promise?"

Alan laughed softly. "I promise." He closed his eyes and felt the comfortable weight of sleep descend on him. He opened his eyes once. "When are you having an ultrasound?"

Katie opened her eyes. "I'm not sure. Why?"

"Nothing . . . I was just wondering."

"Dr. Robertz said there was no hurry. Probably next month."

"Okay . . ." Alan nodded off to sleep, and Katie followed shortly afterward.

Jerry Colon spent the Tuesday morning in the Product Testing Division of Dettler Industries. Product Testing was located in a satellite warehouse on Tucker

Boulevard in L.A. Jerry avoided Product Testing whenever possible because of "Lord Jim," Jim Everson, who was the head safety engineer. Jerry Colon didn't like Jim Everson, and Jim Everson clearly did not like Jerry.

The building was painted an odd blue-gray and had green doors. The windows had been sealed and looked like they had chicken wire on the inside that had been sprayed with a translucent coating. Low, dusty junipers did little to dispel the gloom of the exterior building. It was dismal, in Jerry's opinion.

But Sherman Dettler wanted the safety reports on the Liberty 5000 on his desk by that afternoon, or before. Jerry had phoned Jim Everson and told him to have the report ready. Everson had expressed several raw expletives and hung up on him.

So, Tuesday morning, Jerry parked in the executive parking spot and marched in to collect the report. Jim Everson was waiting for him in his office, which looked like a closet inhabited by a pathological pack rat. Belts, transistor tubes, red and white tubes of sealant, clipboards clutching mad reams of paper, and rolls of cloth duct tape clogged Everson's desk.

"Mr. Colon," Everson said menacingly.

The nervous twitch on the right side of Jerry Colon's face had begun in earnest, jerking the side of his lip spasmodically. He hoped Everson wouldn't notice. "I've got to have that safety report," he said. "The one I called you about."

"Dettler had that report a year ago. What's the big deal now?" Everson swept a stack of manuals off the seat of his black swivel chair and sat down.

Jerry Colon shifted from foot to foot. Evidently Everson wasn't going to provide him with a chair. "The big deal is a couple of complaints that the Liberty 5000 glows when it's running."

"Glows!" Everson snorted. "Glows! Gimme a break. Glows, for Christ's sake? What the hell does that mean?"

Jerry's tic worsened. His right eye was nearly closed with the twitching. "It means, Everson, that we'd better have a clean safety report on the thing—by this afternoon. You seen any glowing when you tested the Liberty?"

"Nope. I'd remember something like that."

"How about leakage?"

"Nothin'. Zip. Nada. The Liberty doesn't leak."

"Then we ain't—haven't—got nothin' to worry about." Jerry's chest muscles relaxed a bit and allowed him to get some oxygen pumping through his lungs again. "But just to be on the safe side," he said, "can you show me a test? Just so's I can tell Sherm I saw it for myself. Should calm him down if I can say I seen it with my own eyes."

Everson glowered. "I'm sure your personal testimony will be invaluable."

Jerry knew he'd been insulted, but his response time for returning insults was about fifteen minutes. Everson heaved himself out of his chair and beckoned Jerry to follow him. In a corner of one of the end rooms, amid long tables of coiled electrical wire, meters, and shields used in testing appliances, a battered Liberty 5000 sat on a test tray. The shielding boards had been laid to the side. Everson put a plastic test cylinder inside the microwave and closed the door. He set the timer for two minutes and picked up a small black gauge. He pushed start and swept the gauge around the door seals.

"Nothin'," he said, handing the gauge to Jerry.

Jerry Colon, at least fifteen years out of any mathematics class, stared at the gauge. There was a red zone.

Evidently that was the danger zone. The small black needles wavered well below that red zone.

"Now if we had the right equipment, we could really test this baby," Everson said. "I mean, with a fluorescent detector I could tell you the exact wavelength of those microwaves. But my budget gets axed every damn year."

Jerry Colon felt a small stab of fear. "Does that mean that these tests are no good, Jim? You're not tellin' me that, are you?"

Everson grabbed the gauge from Colon's hand. "As far as they go, they're reliable. It's about the equivalent of testing for methane gas with canaries."

Jerry had no idea what Everson was talking about. "Uh-huh," he said. "Okay, well—as long as we meet the state guidelines—"

"We're well under the five milliwatts allowed by the *feds* for microwave ovens," Everson said pointedly. "If that doesn't satisfy the boss, tell him to come over here and I'll show him myself."

"And what about this glowing?"

"Never saw any."

The microwave oven shut off.

"Well . . ." Jerry heaved a sigh of relief. The tic was down to a tiny jerk in his eyebrow. "I guess that's it then."

"I guess so," Everson parroted.

"Can I get a copy of the report?"

"Can do," Everson said. "The one thing we can do here is put out great reports. Follow me. Portia Ramirez runs the kingdom of reports."

Portia Ramirez's office was the exact opposite of the testing division. Tidy, clean, and well lighted, the documents office was an enormous relief to Jerry. Portia Ramirez sat at a large beige desk. A computer gleamed on the desktop. Three printers on a side table were spitting out reports, humming contentedly.

"Portia, this is Mr. Jerry Colon," he said, indicating Jerry with a very generalized gesture in the man's direction.

Portia only nodded and went back to her work on the computer.

"I'm going to input a little data, and then I need a copy of the Liberty 5000 testing," Everson told her.

"Yes, sir," Portia said, never looking up. "You let me know when you're ready."

"She's a whiz," Everson told Jerry. "She can put out the best-looking copy this side of the California border. Buries data so deep in some of these files it'd take the feds years to dig it all out."

Jerry wasn't sure if that was good news or bad news. He waited patiently for Everson to feed in the new data into a computer console on the back wall of the office.

"Okay, Portia," he finally said. "Print her up."

The finished report, spewed out of a slightly intimidating laser printer, was, indeed, impressive. Jerry looked at the stapled report he held in his hands. He couldn't make heads or tails out of even the first page. "Okay, then, I guess that's it."

"You know how to get out of here?" Everson asked, implying the sooner the better.

"Yeah—shoot, I wasn't born yesterday. I know my way around pretty well."

Everson stifled a laugh. Portia continued with her typing. Not even a hint of a smile played on her lips. Jerry Colon tucked the report under his arm.

"It was nice meeting you," he said to Portia on his way out. "You might give 'Lord Jim' a few tips on neatness. I think he could use them." Colon closed the door behind him.

"Son of a bitch," Everson swore. "Portia, you know the thing about a guy named Jerry Colon?"

"His last name rhymes with asshole?"

Phyllis Latimer admired the deep tan she had achieved with no small effort in Hawaii over the ten days she and her husband spent there. She did nothing but sleep, eat, swim, and suntan, despite Donald's frantic efforts to get her to use sunblock. She wanted a tan. She wanted to feel healthy and vital once more.

It wasn't anything specific that seemed to be wearing her away, just a general tiredness, and, now and then, small disturbances in her vision. Sometimes she was dizzy and felt faint. Now and then she had a headache. The doctor had put her through every cardiac test known to man, or woman, and she'd passed them all. So she packed her bags and Donald's and bought two tickets to Hawaii. July was the low season, so the crowds were less and the plane tickets a bargain.

Phyllis stood in the bathroom and tried to see the tan on her back. She'd had a long, cool bath, and was wrapped up in a white Turkish towel. Donald popped his head around the bathroom door and stared appreciatively.

"You look gorgeous," he said. "What's taking you so long?"

"I'm admiring my tan." She twisted slightly and held up the small mirror to catch one last glimpse of the narrow, bronzed shoulder blades. A sudden wave of dizziness made her stagger. She steadied herself with one hand against the wall.

"You okay?" Donald asked.

"Fine—just tired, I think," she answered, hoping her voice was steady. Donald was not an easy man to fool. "I was thinking—maybe I'll drive to Sacramento tomorrow and spend a couple of days with Ginger and the kids."

Ginger was Phyllis's married daughter. She had two small children, Tommy and Alison, whom Phyllis adored.

"Sure, you do that, if you're not too tired."

"I want to show off my tan before it fades." Phyllis laughed softly. She had some reservations about driving alone, because the dizzy spells came on quickly. But she'd be careful. Besides, they happened only once or twice a week. And the drive to Sacramento was only an hour and a half. Good, she'd go, she decided.

She examined her face in the mirror. "Do you think I look different?" she asked her husband. "You know, a little puffy around my eyes. And my nose seems like it's flattened out."

"You look perfect to me," he said. "Quit staring in the mirror and come to bed."

The next morning Phyllis got up early, threw a suitcase in the trunk of the car, got some candy for the grandchildren, and stopped for gas before climbing out of the Santa Clara Valley on Highway 680. The traffic was light, and it was a beautiful, sunlit morning. With nearly five years of drought, the hills were a burnished gold under the relentless sun. Eucalyptus and stands of oaks relieved the landscape with their silvery greens, and she drove, singing along with every tune she knew on the radio.

She reached the outskirts of Sacramento and went north through Citrus Heights to Roseville, where her daughter and her family owned a home on a bluff overlooking Folsom Lake. Her daughter's white Volvo was in the driveway, Phyllis saw, relieved. She probably should have phoned.

Generally, she would have called first. But things

were different now. So many things were different. Never in a million years would she have brought M&M's for the kids, for example. Bad for their teeth. Today she had several sacks of the delicious little chocolates stowed in her luggage. Things had changed. She had a life to live, and she didn't think she had much of it left. Something was wrong. Something the doctors hadn't discovered yet. She knew it like she knew her eyes were blue. And after all the energy she'd put into a clean environment, it was slightly funny that something was wrong with her, personally. The nameless masses she'd defended were a blur. Only her own face stood out in the crowd.

Ginger and the kids were delighted she'd come. Phyllis's periodic visits provided her daughter a welcome respite from caring for children, a house, and working part-time as a pediatric nurse at Kaiser Permanente.

Tommy and Alison loved the candy, a quite unexpected gift from their grandmother.

The children were gathered around their grandmother's suitcase in the newly redecorated guest bedroom. As Phyllis went out to the kitchen, they followed after her.

Ginger was busy putting the finishing touches on lunch, which consisted of tuna-salad sandwiches, carrot and celery sticks, and vegetable soup.

"Excuse me?" Ginger commented, digging several brightly colored candies out of Alison's chubby little hand. "Is this candy? I'm surprised at you, Mom."

"A little sugar doesn't hurt them," Phyllis said. "Life is too short not to have any fun."

Ginger studied her mother. "Life is too long to spend it in a dentist's chair," she quipped.

Phyllis ignored her, pointedly handing Alison several more sweets. "For your information, that celery you just put on the table is full of aflatoxin. I'll bet you didn't know that, did you?" She gave several sweets to Tommy. "Besides, I want my grandchildren to remember me bringing them candy and dolls and airplanes."

"Dolls and airplanes are great, Mother," Ginger criticized mildly. "And what's wrong with oranges? Or banana chips?"

Tommy made a face and popped a handful of candy into his mouth. "Don't like banana chips," he said.

And Phyllis laughed. "Oh, Ginny, humor me, just this once. I won't bring processed sugar into your house ever again, I promise. But this one time . . ."

Ginger frowned. "Okay, but you're talking like you'll never see us again. Are you depressed?"

Phyllis beamed at her. "Depressed? Of course not. I've just had a wonderful trip to Hawaii—oh, I brought you a pineapple and a T-shirt."

Ginger grinned. "I don't suppose the T-shirt says C&H pure cane sugar, or anything . . ."

"No—it has fish on it, don't worry."

Ginger sat down across from her mother at the glass-topped table in the dining area. "I'm almost disappointed in you, Mom. What about all your work with MANA? I mean, you were so *dedicated.* Now it sounds like you're giving it all up."

"I *am* resigning as head of MANA," Phyllis told her daughter. "The issues are still important, honey. But I have other things I want to do." She wondered if she should drop a little hint that she hadn't been feeling well lately. She decided not to. "Before I get too old to do them."

Alison crawled up on her grandmother's lap and laid her head against Phyllis's shoulder. "More canny?" the child asked.

"No, it's all gone, sweetheart."

"You're sure you're not depressed?" Ginger asked. "I hear there's a direct correlation between depression and the amount of chocolate you buy."

Phyllis cuddled her granddaughter. "No, of course not. I've never been depressed in my whole life. Why start now?" She smoothed Alison's hair from her forehead.

"Gamma, our kitty died," Alison said sweetly. "Poor kitty."

"Yeah, Licorice had a great big old lump on her head," Tommy added. "An' she died."

Phyllis looked at Ginger, who had turned away. "Is that true?" she asked her daughter.

"I'm afraid it is," Ginger said. "The vet said he had a tumor. He—hadn't been acting quite right. His eyes looked a little bulgy—you know. And then we found him on the kitchen floor."

"He was dead," Tommy said. "We're going to get another kitty."

"Well, maybe not right away. The vet said there's some kind of epidemic with these tumors . . . I think we'll wait awhile before we get another cat."

Phyllis rocked her granddaughter quietly.

John Lacey sipped a martini in the living room of his condominium, recently redecorated in "warm" gray, as the decorator had called it. The room had a slightly pink glow to it in the early summer evening, and John put his feet up on the handsome leather hassock and leaned back into the deep cushions of the sofa. He wore only a pair of black silk boxer shorts. The air conditioner hummed softly.

John Lacey held up the crystal glass and looked through the slightly oily-looking martini. The world changed through that glass. Like my life, he thought grimly.

He wasn't supposed to have alcohol. Dr. Senter told him that alcohol significantly depressed the immune system and might compromise the effects of the new cholinesterase drug he was taking. And John needed his immune system, all those white cells and antibodies, plus the new drug to fight off the tumors. Dr. Senter was always cheerful when John showed up for his monthly weekend examination and treatment at San Gregorio. His hand strayed to the lumps that circled his ribs. A lot of good it had done, giving up all those drinks that smoothed out the edges of his panic. He'd discovered two new nodules in the last week, and had made another appointment at the San Gregorio Institute.

On John Lacey's expansive walnut desk sat a picture of himself looking young and fit, the breeze in his hair, a bright smile on his face. Hard to believe that was only a year and a half ago. He took another sip of the martini, and then a deep swallow. He waited for that inner glow that a martini always gave him. In the meantime, he ate the green olive.

John rose from the sofa, balancing the glass, and went into the kitchen for a refill. Beside the microwave oven sat the small brown plastic vial of pills. A new cholinesterase that interfered with a virus's ability to replicate. If it was a virus that was causing the tumors, he considered. He opened the vial and swallowed two of the purple pills, washing them down with his martini. He clearly wasn't feeling any glow.

"I don't give a shit," he said out loud, glaring at the immaculate kitchen. The geometric gray and maroon tile on the counters and the enameled gray and white appliance center, complete with food processor, coffee grinder, and toaster, gleamed back at him.

He finished his drink and leaned heavily against the counter. Maybe he'd double his dosage of PreVent, the artificial interferon Katie Campbell was testing in the research lab.

It had been a kind of personal experiment at first, taking a few bottles of the liquid drug and injecting them. No one had missed the PreVent. And when Henry Baden left his research position, John had free access to the drug. Now, Katie had begun to notice small shortages. Nothing serious, John decided. He'd say a box of the bottles broke in the freezer. He'd already written the drug company and requested more PreVent, telling them that several boxes were broken in transit. All a pharmaceutical company cared about were results.

John's head felt a bit buzzy. Yes, he'd double his dosage. If it didn't work at eight hundred milligrams a day, perhaps sixteen hundred would do the trick. But how would he cover the IV tracks from injecting the medication? Dr. Senter would be sure to notice. Maybe he could use the small vein between his toes . . . if that failed he'd try to inject under the tongue. He shivered and reached for his empty glass and peered once more through the crystal that fractured the careful pattern of the tile.

He thought about calling Katie, telling her that he was ill—very ill.

He imagined the conversation, the sound of Katie's sympathetic voice, his own nervous confession of his fear and his need for her. He shook off the fantasy. That was over. Katie Campbell was not a part of his life anymore. She never would be again.

Then there was Carol. She'd walked out on him last January. He's seen her several times and spoken to her on the telephone. Maybe he should try to talk to Carol. Maybe this time he could tell her that it wasn't her.

He'd just never loved her enough. She wasn't Kate. It was that simple.

Instead, he'd signed over the house in Los Altos Hills and the Jaguar, and the Tahoe skiing cabin. He mailed her a check every month. Unless San Gregorio could come up with a miracle, none of it mattered anyway, he thought.

A short letter arrived from San Gregorio addressed to Kate Campbell. Her unopened card to Elaine Calder was inside the envelope. The note said that Norma Montrose died on the twelfth of July. Kate folded the letter and placed it in her address book. She didn't cry until later.

18

 Alan wore his navy-blue swim trunks with the red and white stripes down each side seam. He changed into them in the Greathouse bathroom on Friday evening, in a house that was oddly silent. Where were the Greathouse children and Maria? he wondered. The house stood like a fortress around the traces of children and the memory of their voices and their life within its walls—a doll capsized on the sofa, five toothbrushes in a green plastic holder shaped like a frog, an abandoned Macy's shopping bag. . . .

Alan padded through the hallway to the back door of the house, which led to the pool and sauna. The sun had just sunk beneath the foothills to the west, and the sky drifted overhead like a luminous pink-gray umbrella.

Jerry Greathouse looked up from the fire he had built in the rock-lined basin near the pool. He straightened up and then smiled at Alan. Jerry was naked, and looked completely comfortable without his clothes. His movements revealed no self-consciousness. He laughed softly, a laugh that jiggled the generous padding around his belly.

"You'll be more comfortable without those swim trunks," he said. "There's no one around, except me."

Alan tried hard to look nonchalant. "I can't imagine being comfortable without some clothing on, Jer. I'm not used to it. . . ."

"Give it a try—trust me, you'll find out it's not a big deal." Jerry fed the fire with several good-sized logs. "When I was a kid we ran around naked most of the summer. I got a few sunburns in some pretty delicate places—I wasn't as dark-skinned as most of my cousins. But it's a wonderful experience of freedom—no restrictive clothing holding you back. All children should have that."

"I wore wool sweaters until June," Alan admitted. "But I think it's a little late to go back now and change my inhibitions."

"Never too late," Jerry half sang, standing back to assess the fire pit. He didn't look at Alan. He stood with his hands on his hips, staring into the fire.

Finally Alan slid out of the swim trunks and kicked them aside. "What the hell . . ." he murmured. The most delicious bath of air touched him, like being wrapped in loose silk.

"Try walking around a bit," Jerry said, striding across the grass to the huge oak that sheltered that portion of the yard.

Alan followed him. "Won't the neighbors object to the smoke from the fire? Will we have the cops here again?"

"Not likely," Jerry reassured him. "We are not inside the city limits here. I straightened that out with the officer last time. We are within the fire ordinances with the rock pit. And Darren Proudhorse is coming a little later. He'll watch the fire."

Alan looked skeptical.

"He will play the drums for us. You'll like him. He's a young fellow."

Alan trotted alongside Jerry for a few minutes while they circled the yard. "I don't know—maybe this isn't such a good idea. Couldn't we just take a swim and have a ginger ale?"

"We could, but I think you'll actually like this better."

"Okay, whatever you say." A sheen of perspiration slicked their skin, gleaming in the twilight.

"Nothing weird is going to happen, Alan," Jerry told him. "We're going to cool off in the pool, talk a little by the fire, and go into the sauna. Maybe you will sleep, maybe you will dream, maybe none of that will happen. It's okay. All you have to do is relax and let go of your expectations for a little while."

Alan nodded. "I can do that."

"It's not that easy. Most of us have spent our lives trying to live out our expectations. What I want you to do is give that all up. Just be here. You don't have to do anything else."

"It's hard to keep my mind off Doug, you know? Last night he asked me when I thought he'd be old enough to learn to play the bagpipes . . . he's always wanted to do that. Ever since he was six. I lied to him, Jer. I told him there was plenty of time. That he had his whole life to do that. I'm scared to death he won't have much more time—"

"If worrying did any good, I'd tell you to worry. But we both know it's a waste of time."

"And these tumors—it goes around and around in my head—"

"Give it up. Just for tonight. Tomorrow you can worry

about anything you want. But not tonight," Jerry told him.

They stopped jogging around, and Jerry settled by the fire. The pit was constructed so that it was possible to crouch near the burning logs, with one's feet comfortably roosted on a rock. Alan crouched down and felt the heat of the flames lick him. Jerry began a low, throaty song that had no melody. It was more like a series of vowel sounds that ended in a sharp rise of the tone. At first it was strange, and then relaxing.

"Is this like hypnosis?" Alan asked when Jerry stopped.

"Hypnosis? My singing?" Jerry said with a laugh. "No —it's nothing like hypnosis. It's more like opening a door. That's how I think about it. A door you might not have seen before."

"I'm getting really warm," Alan said.

"Good. Your muscles have to be very warm."

"Isn't there a danger of hyperthermia? I mean—"

"Will you let me take care of all that? You're not the only doctor around here, you know."

"Okay—sure—sorry."

Jerry took deep breaths and sat staring into the vermilion logs that crackled and sputtered in the pit. "Tell me a dream. The last one you remember."

Alan told him about the unfamiliar house where he was sure his father was living, except he couldn't find him. And the sores that felt like vermin eating at him. And the scalpels mounted too high on the wall. While he talked Jerry only nodded and hummed a tuneless song.

"And another. Tell me another."

So Alan told him a dream about flying like an eagle, and then suddenly dropping out of the sky into pitch-dark. Falling deeper and deeper, the darkness heavy and suffocating. Alan's breath became ragged.

"Keep falling, Alan. What do you see?"

"Nothing—nothing. Everything's black."

"Then you see black. Do you feel anything?"

"Scared—there's nothing to grab hold of."

"What do you smell?"

"Smell?" Alan tried to think.

"Yes, there must be a smell in a place that's all black."

"Like something dead—like the smell of the ground after a spring thaw—when the old grass rots. A putrid smell."

"Hold on to that," Jerry told him and stood up.

Alan, relieved to back away from the heat of the fire, stood, also, and took a deep breath.

"Keep the blackness inside and the smell of rotting grass," Jerry said. "We'll go into the pool and wash off —be careful not to drink any of the water. Even if you're very thirsty."

Alan couldn't imagine wanting to drink swimming pool water, but the moment he slid into the cool water he was clearly tempted to drink. He paddled quietly through the water, not sure where Jerry was, and not caring a lot. It was like swimming in a black pool. He enjoyed the flow of water over his skin and through his hair.

Alan turned over on his back, and suddenly Jerry's hands lifted him by the shoulders out of the water. He shivered and stood dripping. Jerry's dark eyes glittered in the firelight.

"So far, so good," Alan said lightly.

Jerry Greathouse didn't answer. His berry-brown body, reflected in the firelight, ran with small rivers of water as he walked toward the sauna. Alan followed.

When the door of the sauna opened, a cloud of steam and a strange, pungent odor engulfed both of them. Alan's head whirled for a moment.

"My God, what is that smell?" Alan asked.

"Aromatic herbs," Jerry told him. "Nothing more. They were my mother's secret."

Inside the wooden sauna there were two wide berths spread with brightly striped blankets. Five or six water pots stood near a pile of rocks that hissed loudly. The air was thick with steam and heat. Alan felt his lungs object to the air, but breathing was soon comfortable.

"Lie down," Jerry told him. "Try not to think about anything. If your mind wanders concentrate on your breathing. Or count. Or think about that smell of rotting grass."

The blanket was slightly scratchy, but Alan found a comfortable position. "I don't know if I can do this . . ." he said.

Jerry was silent. "Close your eyes. You don't have to do anything."

"Just be here . . ." Alan reminded him.

"Yes, you have to be here." He began a different song now, a much higher pitched song that seemed to come from the top of his mouth and nose more than from his throat. Sometimes his voice fell, in a series of little yips and grunts, and then it rose again, filling the wooden sauna, accompanied by the steamy hiss of the rocks. Alan thought about Dougy . . . then he counted his breaths. One, two, three, four . . . one, two, three, four . . . his mind strayed to Katie . . . he was very thirsty . . . he counted again.

Slowly his breathing deepened. He didn't feel so warm, even though he could feel the sweat on his face. This sweat was not produced by panic. It was different. He looked around the sauna, and realized it was very dark inside. The dark was almost palpable. He reached out a hand, and then pulled it back to his side, slightly embarrassed.

Outside, from what seemed like very far away, he heard a soft drumbeat. It paralleled his heartbeat, and he found himself lulled into a soft sleep by the steady, comforting sound.

He woke up and realized he was sitting up and talking, even though his tongue felt like it had swollen to twice the size of his mouth. At first, his thoughts did not match what he was saying; he seemed to be speaking in another language. But then, he realized he was just talking in very short sentences, and in a rather childish, abrupt tone.

"And what is the name by which you call the darkness?" a voice asked him.

"Death. Pain. Disease."

"Hold out your hand . . . do you see your hand?"

Alan saw his hand in front of him, even though he was certain both his hands rested on the blanket. "Yes."

"Beckon to the darkness. Call it to you . . ."

The hand in front of him waved slightly. Alan felt the drum beating in his backbone. Each beat jarred him slightly. Or was it his heartbeat? he wondered.

"Now push it away with your hand. See if there is any light behind that darkness . . ."

Streaks of blue light broke through the darkness in small rays, and then flooded his vision. He was standing in the backyard of the house where he'd grown up. On the ground was the dog, Lady, panting. Her eyes rolled up into her head.

"Don't . . ." he heard himself beg. "Don't shoot her." He looked up into the face of his father, whose wind-roughened face was wet with tears that brimmed over his ice-blue eyes.

His father was crying. Alan heard the gunshot, and then everything was quiet. His father stood over the dead animal, his face shining.

"My dad is crying," Alan said. "He's crying." He lay down on the blanket again and closed his eyes, but found they were already closed. He stretched out his hand and beckoned to the dark again, and it came to him like an ocean wave, dropping over him like a cool sheet. He opened his eyes. It was no longer dark inside the sauna. The drum was still. Jerry sat across from him, looking like he'd fallen asleep.

Alan sat up. "Jer?"

Jerry looked up. "Yes? I'll bet you're thirsty!" He grinned. He picked up a clay jug and handed it to Alan, who took a deep swallow of the sweetest water he'd ever tasted. The last of it trickled down his throat and chest.

"What time is it?" Alan asked.

"I'm not sure . . . probably midnight. You want to talk about what happened?"

"I never knew that my dad cried—I never remembered him crying when he shot Lady. I thought he was just a hard old man, but he wasn't. My idea of what happened wasn't quite correct. I missed something that was so obvious I overlooked it, or forgot it, or something. But I know now."

Jerry extended his long brown arms and tilted his head back and gave a loud whoop. "We're finished then."

Alan gasped when they left the sauna, after wrapping thick yellow towels around themselves. The night air was cool and dry.

Sean sat under the oak tree with a big skin drum between his knees.

"Darren Proudhorse couldn't come tonight," he said

sleepily. "He called, so I thought I'd better drum for you."

"You did very well," Jerry told his son. "I would have sworn it was Darren."

Sean smiled up at his father.

"But you'd better get to bed, Sean. Your mother will have my hide keeping you up so late."

Alan retrieved his swim trunks, noted that the fire was nothing but ash, and he and Jerry went into the house that was filled with shadows and stillness. "Was that an Indian ceremony?" he asked Jerry.

"No, not what you would usually think of as an Indian ceremony. It's something I learned from my dad, who was Irish, actually. And my mother. They kind of combined their cultures when I was growing up. They both felt dreams were very important, and not especially difficult to understand if you just relaxed and put yourself into them. And really looked at them."

"So you really didn't use anything but herbs in the sauna? I could have sworn it smelled like—"

Jerry grinned. "Nope—rosemary, tansy, wild onion, and tundura—it's a prairie grass."

"Your mother's secret?"

"Yes," he said quietly. "It was my mother's secret. But dreams were a different experience for her. In many ways she lived so close to her dreams sometimes it was difficult to tell when she was in this life or when she walked in the dream world."

"I don't admit to much understanding of dreams. I only know they've kept me awake for years. But this feels like some sort of handle on them."

"Oh, no, friend, you don't have a handle on your dreams—it's the other way around. They now have a handle on you, a conscious handle instead of an subconscious one. It's quite different."

They said good night, and Alan drove home slowly, savoring the peacefulness of the valley in the very darkest part of the night. At home Katie, Rob, and Doug were asleep. Amanda sat dozing lightly in the chair beside Doug's bed.

"Everything all right?" he asked her.

"Yes," she answered. "That little man's sleeping like an angel."

"The swelling should be down by now," Alan told her. "There's probably no reason for you to sit up every night with him. Should he have a nosebleed, he'd be okay."

"It's no trouble," Amanda crooned. "Amanda doesn't need much sleep these days. I don't mind at all."

Alan smiled warmly at her. "I don't know what we would have done without you this week, Amanda."

She only nodded at him.

Alan checked his messages at the answering service. There were two calls from Dr. Michael Senter from the San Gregorio Tumor Institute in Los Angeles. Alan decided to try calling Senter in the morning.

He crawled into bed beside Kate. The sheets were smooth and smelled like the outdoors. He took a deep breath and walked into the dream world that night without the fear that usually dogged his journey.

In the morning he tried the two different phone numbers Dr. Senter had left. There was no answer at either.

Jerry called him two days later. "Alan, I've seen my first case of this tumor. A twenty-two-year-old. He came in with what looked like swollen lymph glands. Turned out to be a series of malignant teratomaceous tumors."

Alan propped the receiver on his shoulder. "Do you have an address for him? We're finding the tumors are occurring in a few areas in the valley."

"He lived in his van. Worked as a cook in some res-
taurant—that was his latest job."

"Most of the cases have been in the affluent population—with exceptions, of course," Alan told Jerry.

"Maybe we should look closer at the exceptions,"
Jerry suggested. "It seems to me they are the key to this
puzzle."

"I hadn't thought of that—but they're difficult to
keep tabs on. Most of them move around, disappear—
or die."

"Well, this one's not dead yet. And he hasn't disappeared. He's recovering from the surgery at St. Joseph's
Hospital. He'll be there awhile."

"Good," Alan said. "As soon as he's able to talk, we
need to get a history from him. Maybe you're right.
Maybe there'll be some clues there."

"By the way, how are the nightmares?"

"You mean the dreams . . . I don't call them nightmares anymore."

Jerry laughed his soft, bubbly laugh. "Good for you,
man."

Fred Amans scowled. Amans Appliance had been
open two hours and Donovan Mills, the manager,
hadn't shown up for work again. In fact it had been
three days since Mills had come in, and then he'd left
early without any explanation.

Fred tried calling Mills, but there was no answer. "If'n
he's so goddarned sick, he sure as hell could pick up the
phone," he bellowed, dialing the number again and
crashing the receiver back into its cradle when there was
no answer again. "Son of a bitch, you'd think I was run-
nin' a goddamned hospital ward the way everybody gets
sick around here. Next, I'll need to hire our own private
doc just to keep these pansies on their feet."

Amans's receptionist looked up from her desk. "It could be the flu. There's been a lot of it around."

"Flu? What in the hell is flu?" he stormed. "You get the heaves and then you get up and go back to work. Isn't that the flu, Lucille?"

"Yes, sir, I guess so."

"You ain't sick, right? And I'm fit as a fiddle. So what's going on around here? I don't pay people to be sick. They can do that on their own time, far as I'm concerned."

"Yes, sir," Lucille agreed quickly.

"You get me Mills's address. I've a mind to go out there and talk to him, face-to-face. See just how sick he is. I can't run this business single-handed. That's why I hired that little faker."

Lucille paged through the Rolodex and found Donovan Mills's address. She wrote it on a slip of paper and handed it to Amans.

"I'll be back." He marched out of the appliance store to his black Cadillac in the parking lot and drove off, squealing the tires as he pulled onto Center Street.

Donovan Mills lived in a secluded condominium development, and Fred Amans got lost three times trying to find it. Despite the air conditioner he was sweating. July was not his favorite month. He finally did locate the low gray buildings tucked into stands of birch and elm trees. The grass was clipped and a long row of junipers had been carefully trimmed into bushes resembling bonsai.

"I'm paying that jerk too much," he said out loud, looking around at the make of cars in the parking areas. Peugeot . . . Beamers . . . Mercedes . . . hardly a Ford to be seen.

He knocked loudly on the door of number twelve. There was a doorbell, but Fred Amans pressed it only when his knocks failed to produce a response. The doorbell played a dizzying version of "Summertime." My God, what ever happened to a good old "ding dong," he thought, irritated and overheated.

"Dammit, Mills," he screamed. "Answer the fucking door."

He heard an electrical crackle and the PA system came to life. "I'm busy. I can't come to the door at the moment." It was Donovan Mills talking from inside the condo.

"You open this door, if you know what's good for you. It's Fred Amans. I gotta talk to you."

"I can't—I'm sick," came the response.

"You're gonna be sicker if you don't open the damn door."

The door lock clicked and Amans pushed his way into the dark condominium. Pewter-gray walls, gray cushioned sofa and a matching chair, and tightly shut gray blinds combined to create an oppressive atmosphere. The place must have been decorated by a damned undertaker, Amans thought to himself.

"Where the hell are you?" Amans bellowed.

"In the bedroom—to the left."

The door of the bedroom stood slightly ajar, but to get there Fred Amans had to negotiate a short, dark hallway. "If I can find the light switch . . ." he muttered.

No lights! Mills screamed. *Don't turn on the lights!*

But Fred had already located a toggle switch and flooded the living room with light. "I can't *see*! What you got against lights?"

He swung open the bedroom door and looked into a small dimmed bedroom. Donovan Mills lay clutching sheets around him. His eyes were narrowed, and his hair lay long and uncombed against the pillows.

"Holy shit, you look like a damned stray dog." Amans sighed. "I figured you just needed a little vacation— now, what's going on? Flu?"

Mills groaned softly. "Flu—that sounds so easy. No, I don't think this is the flu."

"Well, what does the doctor say?"

"Haven't been to one. I can't move—can't walk anymore."

"Shit, why not?" Fred Amans was tired of the guessing game. He reached over and turned on the lights in the bedroom.

Donovan Mills screamed. "Turn them *off*!"

At the sight of the man, Fred Amans's stomach lurched threateningly. Donovan Mills lay shaking under a thin, unwashed sheet.

"You want to see what's wrong?" Mills shrieked. "You want a look, Fred?" He ripped the sheet away from his naked body. "Well, get an eyeful."

Donovan Mills's testicles looked like two black, over-ripe cantaloupes.

"Jesus—what's wrong with you?"

"I don't know—an infection—"

"Have you seen a doctor?"

"No. No doctors. I hate doctors. I have some antibiotic in the medicine cabinet. I've taken that."

Fred Amans was feeling decidedly unwell, himself, at that moment. He wanted out of Mills's condo. "Well, you just rest—take as much time off as you need. You got any family in the area? Somebody who could come and help out for a few days?"

"A sister in Utah," he mumbled. "I just need something for the pain—you know, something strong."

"Something white and powdery?" Amans sniffed. "Ain't you got connections for that?"

"I did," Mills whined. "I did—but I can't get out of bed. No home delivery for what I need."

"I'll see what I can do. You just rest, okay, buddy?"

Mills nodded and tried to straighten the sheet. Fred Amans didn't help. His feet refused to move any closer to the rumpled bed where Mills lay.

"You just call me if you need anything . . ."

"You think I should see a doctor?" Mills asked.

"Naw—probably just a nasty infection. One of your girls, maybe? You check out your girlies, Mills?"

Mills nodded. "Always."

"Well, maybe one of 'em's been lyin' to you. I gotta get back to the store—we've got a big sale goin'."

"But you'll get me some coke first?"

"I'll send somebody. You let them in the door, you hear? And if anybody asks, I ain't never heard of cocaine."

Fred Amans didn't wait for a response. He was holding his breath, breathing only in short, gasping breaths, just in case the air in Donovan Mills's bedroom was tainted. Jus' no good with sick people, he thought, letting himself out of the door and taking a deep breath of the hot, dry July air. Never was no good with sick people, never will be. He hurried to his car and sat there a few minutes before he made a phone call. A drop would be made that afternoon. It was the least he could do. And it kept Donovan Mills from using his health insurance policy. There'd been enough of that already. The employees at Amans Appliance were considered bad risks, and the insurance rates had skyrocketed over the last six months. Every time somebody got sick, they raised the rates. It wasn't fair. Better to keep Mills stoked. And quiet. And out of the hands of the medical profession. He was a dead man, anyway.

* * *

Katie Campbell had a grueling schedule, trying to keep up with the work at the research lab and her family at home. Thank God for Amanda, she breathed silently. Katie had been getting dressed at midnight, driving to Lorimar, and working four hours, inoculating and screening the chick embryos. Then around five A.M. she'd go home, sleep until nine or ten, take care of Doug and Rob, when he came home from the school summer session, and then put in two or three more hours late in the afternoon at the lab.

Alan hadn't been happy with the change in scheduling, but he agreed that it was temporary and necessary. Katie actually found she liked those quiet, dark hours of the night in the lab. She could work uninterrupted. The phone never rang. And even the drive was quite pleasant with so few people on the freeway. Besides, she wasn't sleeping very well, anyway, and the work kept her mind off Dougy. And the baby.

There had been very little progress testing the PreVent on embryos that were infected with the retroviruses. As the wild growth in the cultures continued at four, eight, and twelve hours, PreVent seemed to have very little effect. It was discouraging, especially in the face of John Lacey's unequivocal faith in the new drug.

"More testing," he had advised Kate. "Just keep doing the testing. We haven't hit on the right sequence of time yet."

"I don't know, John," she answered. "I think it's a blind alley."

"No, it isn't," he barked. "Other labs have been able to show that PreVent ameliorates the malignant growth —I don't see why we're getting these negative results."

Clearly he believed she was at fault, but Katie couldn't discover why she was unable to replicate the new drug's miraculous results. Deena, on the other hand, was very excited about her work with the Crist substrate. Katie had seen some of the preliminary results and the paper Deena was preparing.

"In large doses, Crist does exactly what it does in small doses," Deena explained to Katie late one afternoon in the lab. "It reverts the organism to a normal growth sequence. You remember the earlier studies—the tissue cultures?"

Katie nodded, even though her head felt heavy and her eyes gritty from lack of sleep.

"Well, in the tissue cultures we had a reversion rate of nearly fifty-four percent. In the rat studies I'm getting sixty-two percent!"

"Sixty-two percent of the infected rats are reverting to normal growth patterns after getting the Crist?" Katie sat up straighter. "That's an amazing result rate. Twenty-six percent is considered successful."

Deena beamed. "I know. I think we're really onto something here—if only I could produce enough of it. The production of Crist is what takes most of my time. I really need a couple more staff people dedicated to production."

"Have you asked John about hiring a couple more people?"

"He had a fit, as usual. He thinks Crist is a flash in the pan, and that I'll never be able to duplicate the results quickly enough. And he's probably right—for the moment."

"Has he seen your results?"

"Yesterday."

Katie rested her chin on her hands. "We're not seeing much success with the PreVent. John's worried about the funding for the research lab unless we can produce something positive."

Deena shook her head. "Oh, he always worries about

the money. It's the life of a researcher. Why do you think he keeps his hand in Pathology? It's a lot more reliable paycheck than research."

"I suppose," Kate agreed. "We've just had a lot of problems with the PreVent. For one thing, two boxes of the drug were broken in transit. That's left me with only three hundred and sixty milliliters for the month. John said he wrote the drug company and asked for a supplement."

Deena looked up thoughtfully. "You know, I'm missing some of the Crist—at least, I think I am. I documented thirty milliliters frozen over the last two weeks, but I only have fifteen milliliters in the freezer. At first I thought I must have made a mistake on the log. Now, I think I must have lost track of some of the Crist in the freezer. Very strange. It's clearly labeled—it's not like anyone would pick it up by accident."

"I'll keep my eyes peeled," Katie told her.

Kate remembered the conversation that week when she could not account for another sixty milliliters of PreVent. She was sure four vials had been there, frozen. Now there were only three. Three was hardly enough to finish her work for the week, and there were still eight days before the August shipment would be received.

She'd have to talk to John about it. She didn't look forward to another clash with him. Generally he steered clear of the research lab in the late afternoons when she was there. When she did see him he always wanted to know about Doug. And John Lacey was looking more and more gaunt. His eyes seemed too large for his face, and she had felt those strange nodules on his back when he'd hugged her that one time.

"Nodules?" she said out loud in the isolation room of

the research lab. Her words seemed to echo inside the head hood. "Nodules—oh, my God."

If he had the tumor, surely he wouldn't be so foolish as to inject himself with the PreVent or the Crist? Surely he was smarter than that. But her stuttering heartbeat told her that she had probably stumbled onto the explanation for the missing drugs.

19

Alan tried both phone numbers Dr. Michael Senter left with the answering service. No one answered.

It was seven o'clock in the evening. Katie lay on the cool sheets in the bedroom trying to catch a nap before she went into the lab again that night. Dougy had a headache and was in bed. Amanda was busy with the washing, and Rob, as was his usual pattern, went to a friend's house to play. Finally Alan called the San Gregorio Institute and asked to speak to Dr. Senter.

"Dr. Senter," said the receptionist in a low, authoritative voice, "is unavailable at this time. If you will leave your name and phone number he will return your call."

"I've tried to get hold of him for three days," Alan explained. "This is Dr. Alan Campbell in Los Alamos— it's very important that I speak with him."

"Would you like to talk to Dr. Valdez? She might be able to help you."

"Yes, by all means. Let me speak to Dr. Valdez."

There was a series of clicks, and finally a woman answered, "Hello? This is Dr. Valdez."

Alan explained who he was and that he was trying to contact Dr. Senter.

"Your guess is as good as mine," she said. "We haven't seen him since last week. We even had his apartment checked by the police. He seems to have disappeared."

Alan heard the confusion and anger in her voice.

"Well, that may not be quite the word for it," the doctor hastily said. "Maybe he's taken an unscheduled vacation—but it isn't like him to leave without informing anyone."

Alan hung up the phone. Disappeared? How odd. But he'd disappeared last week, and he'd called Alan four days ago. That meant he probably hadn't called Alan from Los Angeles, or at least not from San Gregorio or his home. Alan looked at the two phone numbers. There must be some way to trace those numbers. He called the long-distance operator.

"I've got two phone numbers I want to trace," he said.

It took the operator only a minute to inform him that both numbers were from Monterey, California, from the army base at Fort Ord.

"I thought that closed," he said.

"I wouldn't know about that," she answered, and disconnected.

Fort Ord. Lt. Col. Stephen Reynolds might know something. If he was still working at Lorimar. Alan hadn't seen him for a while. Not that he went looking.

The next morning Alan checked the small office that Lt. Col. Reynolds used. He was sitting at the desk in full uniform. Alan blinked several times.

"Lieutenant Colonel Reynolds?"

He turned and smiled. "Dr. Campbell. How is your son?"

"We're hoping to get him into surgery soon—how did you know about Doug?"

Reynolds smiled again. "I heard about him. You know how it is . . ."

"There's been a mix-up in the Pathology report—originally they called it a possible teratoblastoma. Now the report calls it a papillary parenchymal cell growth."

"There's a great deal of difference," Reynolds said. "As you may be aware, there've been some alterations in patients' charts here at Lorimar. Small changes that could easily be done on a computer if you knew departmental codes—things like that. I suspect it's somebody on the inside."

"Why would anyone do that?" Alan felt a trickle of sweat begin.

Reynolds shrugged. "People do strange things under pressure. Or for money. I believe the alterations are meant to deter lawsuits without denying treatment."

Alan sat down in the chair opposite Reynolds. "Why are you telling me this? I thought the Army's investigation was secret."

"We have been undeniably concerned about the tremendous rise in the number of cases of teratoma in California—you're not the only hospital experiencing this phenomenon. We've been going over patients' charts to determine possible causes. I can tell you that it was our fear that someone was bombarding the coastline of this country with microwaves, which, on occasion, have been known to be teratogenic. But we no longer believe that is happening, so the covert nature of our investigation has been lifted."

Alan's shirt was sticking to the back of the chair. "What *do* you believe is happening?"

"I wish I could tell you. The reason I can't is because I don't know. But I'm sure it's not a foreign threat. These people are being exposed to a severely teratogenic agent. What that agent is, I can only guess."

Alan tried to think back to medical school and all the teratogenic substances in the textbooks. The most famous of all of them was thalidomide. "There was some talk about the increased cancer rate among people who lived near high-tension wires . . . could that be it?"

"A magnetic field . . . I doubt it. The rate of teratomas in those circumstances shows no increase. No, this is something more insidious. Something we have failed to see, so far. But we'll figure it out—hopefully, soon."

"Yes—but I really came to ask you a question. A colleague of mine called twice, and when I tried to return the phone call there was no answer. I traced the numbers and they are from the old army base at Fort Ord. I thought that was closed last year."

"We maintain several operations there," Reynolds told him. "Most of it is highly classified. If your colleague is involved in anything like that I'm sure he would not have phoned you from the base. That's about all I know."

Alan stood up uncertainly. Reynolds stood, ramrod straight, and offered his hand to Alan. "I wish you and your son all the best, Dr. Campbell. And if I were you, I'd watch my back these days. Especially when Dr. Greer is around."

The body had lain in the morgue all night, and the autopsy was scheduled for ten o'clock that Thursday morning. Dr. Lacey was on the Anatomical Pathology rotation that week, so he would perform the postmortem. Dr. Liz Uribe, the patient's assigned resident, was hoping to be there.

"What's so special about this guy?" John asked, flipping through the chart. "Holy—" He read quickly. "He only lived six hours after he came in? What's his name? Donovan Mills?"

Dr. Uribe was a beautiful young woman with raven-black hair worn short and softly shaped to her small, delicately sculptured head. She nodded and her dark eyes took on a sympathetic shine. "We tried everything. He was hemorrhaging when he came in, his blood pressure was eighty over sixty as I recall, and these growths—" She looked stricken. "I'd never seen anything like it."

The body was laid out on the post table and covered discreetly with a white sheet. John Lacey ran his posts like a surgical amphitheater. Residents and interns were gathering in the small glassed-in room to observe.

"The guy with the black balls," someone joked. The statement was broadcast over the intercom.

John Lacey glared at the small group. "You can cut the humor," he snarled at them.

Slightly shamefaced, they stared at their knees, or a few inches to the left or right of Dr. Lacey.

"Now, Dr. Uribe, you were saying—that our Mr."— he checked for the patient's chart—"Mills—Mr. Mills had these growths."

"It's a wonder he could stand all that pain—I mean, they must have been terribly painful."

"Didn't you do a toxicology screen?" John asked.

"Yes—he was full of cocaine."

"That's how he managed to stand the pain," Lacey said. "Although it's certainly not the first drug that would come to mind for pain relief. I'm surprised he hadn't gotten hold of morphine sulfate."

"He was just an appliance salesman," Dr. Uribe explained. "We gave him morphine twice during the night —after the tox screen was drawn."

John Lacey drew back the sheet. Donovan Mills's eyes were staring. From the umbilical area to midthigh he was bruised and swollen. The blood from some of the hemorrhaging had collected under the skin. The testicles were at least five times normal size, black, and grossly distorted. John Lacey took hold of the metal table.

"I, uh—" he stammered, "I have to—will you excuse me for a moment?" This had never happened. He'd never frozen up in a post. Like a damned intern, he thought. He escaped quickly from the morgue and went to his office. John Lacey intended to pick up his car keys and walk away. He never wanted to see another dead body. He didn't care if he ever walked down those stairs to the basement of Lorimar Medical Center or not. But if he did that, he considered, he would no longer have access to either the PreVent or Crist substrate. He glanced into the research lab on his way back to the morgue. Deena Crist was bent over the yellow counters, hard at work. John took a couple of deep breaths and swung open the post door. He grinned at Dr. Uribe, who stood looking forlornly at Mr. Donovan Mills. Even the room full of interns was quiet.

"Sorry," he said with a grin, donning the goggles and mask and apron. He slipped into two pairs of latex gloves. "When you gotta go, you gotta go."

Dr. Uribe smiled back at him. This was the Dr. Lacey they all knew.

When the autopsy was finished, John Lacey called Alan Campbell's office. "Just tell him we've got one more case for the records," he told Alan's nurse.

That evening, before he left the hospital, John Lacey

went into the clean room of the research lab, took out all three vials of the Crist substrate he found frozen. He took one more sixty-milliliter vial of PreVent, replaced it with sterile water in a used bottle, and left the hospital. All in all, it had been a good day. In fact, unless his eyes were deceiving him, he thought he detected a very small decrease in the size of one of the lumps along his sternum. He'd been injecting the Crist for only five days, taking as much as Deena froze and replacing it with a mixture of egg albumin and water. So far, she hadn't suspected. Once the rats began to die, she probably would. How long was that? he wondered. A couple of weeks?

He pulled a frozen pot roast dinner from the freezer and popped it in the microwave. He set the timer and started his meal cooking. It was the first time he'd been hungry in quite a while, he realized. Yes, something was clearly happening.

Nelson Fell, one of the more distinguished neurosurgeons at Stanford, called Alan Friday morning after he'd looked at Doug's medical records. "I see no reason to operate quickly," he told Alan. "This does not appear, from the tissue sections, to be a carcinoma. And I'm sure you realize these nasopharyngeal growths in children are not all that rare."

Alan hardly heard the last sentence. "Excuse me, Dr. Fell, but the histology report showed embryonic cells consistent with a teratocarcinoma."

There was a long silence. "I have the chart in front of me. I see no indication of that from Pathology."

"You don't? I have a copy of Doug's chart—wait, I'll get it. I'll read you the histology report." Alan retrieved the file from his desk drawer. He paged through it until he found the Pathology report on the tissue biopsy.

"Tetraploid embryonic cells suggestive of teratoblastoma, along with papillary parenchymal cells and normal squamal epidermal cells."

"I only have the papillary cells and normal epidermal cells reported, Dr. Campbell. This report says nothing about teratoblastoma."

"Shit," Alan swore. "I don't know what's going on here, but my son has this tumor—I have the Pathology report in my hands—and I can't get anybody to do anything about it."

"Well, maybe we could do another biopsy—make sure of the diagnosis," Fell suggested. "I'm sure there's some explanation. If you want to bring him in—"

"He's already been through one biopsy," Alan said hotly. "One is enough. I want him in surgery as soon as possible."

"I can schedule him after I see him," Fell said. "You understand—I can't just—"

"You can't take my word?" Alan yelled. "You think I'm making this up? For God's sake, man, this is my son I'm talking about."

Nelson Fell stammered out a response. "I realize your concern, Doctor, but we have to follow some protocol here—for your son's sake."

"Someone has tampered with these reports." Alan tried to keep his voice level. "I suspect there is some alarm about the number of teratomas we have been seeing—someone doesn't want that to show up in the morbidity reports. Now, I don't have any idea who that is—and I don't have time to find out. My only concern, at this point, is my son."

"I understand completely," Nelson Fell answered, smooth as a cooling salve. "I completely understand. If this child—Doug, isn't it?—were my son, I'd have him in surgery as soon as possible. If you need any further assistance, please let me know. As I said, I'd be happy to look at the boy."

"Thank you, Dr. Fell," Alan said. His neck felt hot. "I will get back to you."

He dialed the number of Dr. Silver and insisted he speak to the pediatrician. When Silver answered, his voice clearly demonstrated fatigue and irritation.

"What can I do for you, Dr. Campbell?" he said.

"I want Doug moved up on the surgery schedule. I don't think we can wait another six days."

Alan heard Silver sigh. "I've explained this before. We are waiting for Dr. Ramirez, and for the swelling to go down. You, of all people, should know that we can't operate in the nasopharyngeal area until that swelling has gone down." Silver sighed again. "Is the pain worse?"

"No—he had a headache yesterday—but that's not what is concerning me. There's been some mix-up in Pathology about the biopsy report. Nelson Fell, at Stanford, got a copy of Doug's records and the biopsy indicated a papillary adenoma."

"That's correct," Silver said. "So what's the problem?"

"Dammit, man, the original path report indicates a possible teratoblastoma. I have a copy of it."

Silver was silent. "Oh, I don't think so, Dr. Campbell. I know there was some question of that—but the final report indicated a nonmalignant growth."

"That was *not* a final report, Dr. Silver. What you saw was an *altered* report."

"Somebody changed the report?" Silver sounded incredulous, but there was a subtle change in his breathing.

"Exactly."

"Are you certain?"

"I am."

"Well, let's get hold of John Lacey and verify the report. And bring Doug into Lorimar tonight. I'll call and make the arrangements. Dr. Stan Shuck is on neuro service—he's very good."

"Has he done pediatric neurosurgery?" Alan asked, already knowing the answer. Stan Shuck operated almost exclusively on adults.

"I don't think so, Alan—but Doug's not an infant, after all—and what choice do we have?"

When Alan arrived home Katie lay on Doug's bed with the boy stretched out on a sheet, his head resting in her diminished lap. It took only one look for Alan to know that Doug was in enormous pain.

"He won't let me touch his head," she said, her voice shaking.

"He'll be admitted to Lorimar tonight, Katie. I talked to Dr. Silver. They can do the surgery in the morning." Alan sat down on the bed and touched Doug's arm.

He lay with his mouth open and his eyes closed. His breathing was rapid. Perspiration stood out on his forehead.

"It'll be okay, Doug," Alan whispered. "We'll take care of this."

"How are we going to get him to the hospital?" Katie asked. "If he moves, it hurts him."

"I'll carry him. We'll lay him in the back of the station wagon—and drive slowly. I'll get pillows and a blanket. You stay here with him."

It was like a dream, getting a bed ready in the car, telling Rob that Doug was being admitted to the hospital, and finally carrying the boy and laying him, as gently as possible, in the back of the car.

"Maybe we should have called an ambulance," Katie said, when she saw the pain on her son's face.

"He's in now. The pillows will protect him, and there won't be much traffic if we take Monty Way instead of the freeway. Get in, Kate."

The drive was excruciating. Every time the car bumped, Doug moaned. Katie rode in the back with him, crooning to him the entire way. Finally, they pulled into the Emergency entrance. Alan parked the car. Lorimar Medical Center loomed huge and reassuring against a pink streaked sky.

"I'll get them to take him in on a gurney," he said. "I think that'll be easier." But the Emergency Room triage nurse was clearly skeptical.

"He's a new admit? Why'd you bring him to Emergency?"

"Because he is unable to walk, and he's in too much pain to ride in a wheelchair." Alan's patience was as thin as a stretched rubber band. "Just get an attendant with a gurney."

She glowered at him. "We're extremely busy—"

"I want a gurney, dammit." He barged past her, pushed his way into the circular treatment area where a line of gurneys sat in a hallway that looped away from the central desk.

"Dr. Campbell?" one of the nurses in ER asked, when Alan pulled a gurney out of the lineup and headed for the pneumatic doors.

"I need a gurney," he told her. He had just begun to experience the frustration of most patients. Why was it such a problem getting a gurney? No one listened to an explanation. And he'd been on staff at Lorimar over ten years. For the average patient, this must be hell!

The evening was cool and heavy with the smell of newly cut grass and hot asphalt. On any other night

Alan might have enjoyed it. Tonight Katie sat sheltering Doug's head in the back of the station wagon. The nurse from the Emergency Room had followed him outside.

"Here, let me help you," she said quietly. She knew how to hold Doug's head so that the movement from the car to the gurney was not quite so painful. He even opened his eyes once.

Katie followed the gurney into the hospital and up the elevator that took them to the third floor, where Doug was placed in a room near the desk. He was expertly stripped of his clothes and slipped into a pediatric cantilevered bed, resting inside a suspended hammock that immobilized him about an inch above the mattress.

"We're going to be doing his admission workup," the nurse, Gloria Tam, told Alan and Katie. "It's probably better if you wait outside until we're finished. I called Dr. Silver, and he's on his way in. It won't be long, I promise."

Kate, who felt like she was being propelled by events that were beyond her control, leaned down to speak to Doug. "We're right here, sweetheart. Don't you worry about anything. This will be over soon."

His eyes squeezed just a bit tighter, so Katie knew he'd heard her.

"I think he's conscious," she told Alan. "I wasn't sure at home. He didn't respond to anything—unless I moved. My God, Alan, what's happening to him?"

They sat down in a small waiting room with two blue sofas, a coffee table stacked with magazines, and colorful posters of teddy bears tacked up on the walls. "I'm not sure, Katie. It's probably a change in the tumor."

"But it came on so suddenly. He complained of a headache, and then he went rigid with the pain."

Alan nodded. "We'll just wait and see what Dr. Shuck says."

* * *

When they saw Doug again he was resting more comfortably. His eyelashes lay gently over his pale cheeks, and his breathing was relaxed.

His room was a pediatric neuro room with a thermo-regulated bed with built-in monitors that blinked and flashed. There was a rocking chair and a straight-back wood chair, a small bathroom, and a sink beside the door. Katie pulled the smaller wood chair close to Doug's bed. She sat and held the boy's hand. She found a small callus on one finger. She hadn't really looked at Doug's hands in a long time, she realized. They were beautiful, long and sinuous.

Alan went to talk to Dr. Shuck. Katie stayed with Doug.

"Silver tells me there was some mix-up in Pathology," Shuck said matter-of-factly.

Alan nodded. "What do you think?"

Shuck shrugged. "We're looking at a noninvasive tumor, or we're looking at a teratoblastoma that may have broken through into the brain. In that case, we're in for a very tough fight. I'm sure you know that. And since the biopsy showed evidence of a blastoma, we'd better be ready."

"What time will you operate?" The next day was Saturday, not a regularly scheduled OR day.

"We'll bring him up about seven thirty—he's doing much better once we got the morphine sulfate started. He's more responsive—that's encouraging." Shuck finished reading the chart.

Alan noticed that a handwritten Pathology report had been appended to Doug's chart.

Shuck finally looked up. "We're going to do everything we can. I'll see you tomorrow."

Alan went back to Doug's room. Katie held Doug's hand and talked to him softly.

"Mom," Doug whispered.

Tears dripped down her face, and she sniffed. "I'm right here, Dougy. Right here."

They stayed until nearly eleven o'clock, and then went home to get a little sleep before returning to the hospital the next morning for the surgery.

"I want to see him before they take him to the operating room," Katie insisted on the drive home. "I want him to know we're there with him."

They waited in a stark white waiting room adjacent to Surgery for the entire three and a half hours, painful hours filled up with silence or mindless turning of pages in an unread magazine, or staring out the windows into the parking lot below. Kate watched people park their cars, get out, and walk to the hospital entrance. She envied them. She knew it wasn't fair. They probably had troubles of their own. Still, it seemed like their children were probably not in surgery that day. She watched a delivery truck negotiate the narrow lanes of the parking lot and pull out of sight.

"It's not fair," she said softly to Alan, who stood beside her at the window. "All those people still have a life. Their son doesn't have a tumor. And don't tell me life's not fair."

Alan put his arm around her shoulders. "Come back and sit down. I'll get you some tea." He guided her back to a brown Naugahyde sofa. "We have to believe Doug's going to be fine. Dr. Shuck is one of the best neurosurgeons on staff."

At eleven thirty Dr. Shuck emerged from the operating amphitheater and found Katie and Alan in the waiting room. He had slipped a white gown over his surgical greens.

"He's doing well," he told them. Kate's heart was syncopating from the moment the door opened and she saw Dr. Shuck. "The tumor—was quite large. Clearly a teratoblastoma. We got most of it."

Alan was on his feet. "Most of it? What does that mean?"

Shuck looked down uncomfortably. "We couldn't get at it all, Alan. There were some retinal attachments, it had invaded the orbits of both eyes, and entered the brain at the base of the cerebral cortex. If I'd taken any more tissue he might have lost all cognitive and language function."

Katie held her breath. She felt faint and leaned her head heavily into her hands. "This can't be happening," she said softly. "Dr. Silver told me the tumor could be removed."

"That's when we thought it was just a papillary tumor, I'm afraid, Mrs. Campbell." Shuck shifted uneasily from foot to foot. "We're just going to take this an hour at a time for today. We'll know a lot more by tomorrow when Doug wakes up. You can see him in recovery if you'd like. He'll be there at least an hour." He looked quite sympathetically at Katie. "We're going to hope for the best."

"What is the best?" Kate asked.

"That he'll wake up tomorrow and smile."

Saturday passed in an agony of small moments. Doug was in the Pediatric Intensive Care Unit and Katie and Alan were allowed in to see him for ten minutes every hour.

At five o'clock Phyllis Latimer came up to the third floor looking for Katie. "I just heard about your son," she said, wrapping her arms around Kate. Both women were crying. "I didn't know what to do except come and see if there's anything, anything at all, you need."

"No, no," Kate whispered. "We just have to wait now."

Phyllis extracted a large brown teddy bear with a floppy red bow from a shopping bag. "I saw it in the gift shop downstairs."

Katie hugged the bear. "Oh, he's beautiful. Doug will love him, I'm sure."

Alan suggested that perhaps Phyllis could drive Katie home to spend some time with Robbie and have a nap. Over protests and promises extracted from Alan to call the moment there was any change, Phyllis took Katie and gently led her to the elevators.

Alan sat alone in the waiting room of the Intensive Care Unit. He thought maybe he should go check on his own patients in the hospital. He'd made arrangements for rounds with Mark Kresky, who said he'd gladly look in on Alan's surgical patients. Since Alan had his beeper in his pocket, clearly all of them were doing all right.

So he sat there, alone, listening to the evening sounds of a hospital. Only it was quieter in Intensive Care. He could see into the open semicircle of rooms and watch the nurses move through and around the patients' beds. He listened for the bells of the elevator. He heard soft footsteps come and go. It had been a long time since he'd sat in silence, he thought. It seemed to him he should pray, or something. His father would have been down on his knees the entire day. Alan sagged on the sofa. Something strange washed over him. Something he had not felt in a long time.

He reached up and touched his face with the tips of his fingers. Tears. He was crying. He straightened up quickly and brushed away the tears. But they kept coming. He didn't sob, he just sat there and wept for his son.

And not only for Doug. For another child, too, ten years earlier, whom he had hardly remembered consciously. Now he remembered. And he knew what he had to do.

Katie sat quietly in the car with Phyllis. Phyllis did not start the car. "Do you want to talk?" she finally asked Kate. "I'm pretty good at listening."

Kate's eyes were dry. She stared down at her hands for a long time. "It sounds stupid," she finally said. "But I'm afraid I am being asked to trade my son's health for my baby's. I can't make that kind of a bargain, Phyllis. I want my son to live. And I want this baby to be healthy. But it seems like I can't have both."

"Of course you can," Phyllis tried to soothe her.

Kate looked up at her friend. "No, don't you see? I could have both if I were in charge of the world—but I'm not. I used to trust my body, at least—but now? Who knows what's happening to us . . . to all of us." She shook her head slowly. "Doug didn't do anything wrong . . . Do you know what I'm saying? His body did something it isn't supposed to do. It began to grow in a wild pattern. Hair and teeth and a stomach grew where it shouldn't. And something caused it. Now he's dying."

"No, Katie, Doug will be fine. You wait and see." Phyllis looked away. "He has to be okay."

"No, he doesn't. He doesn't have to be any more okay than Elaine Calder, or that little girl, Jennifer Wynn. She was only twelve. They're not okay."

Phyllis swallowed hard and started the car. "I don't think you should talk this way, Katie."

"I have to, Phyllis. I wish I didn't."

The car engine rumbled and then settled into a steady Mercedes purr. Phyllis carefully backed out of the space in the parking lot.

"These tumors—these teratomas—" Phyllis said slowly. "They're different than most tumors, aren't they? I mean, is it possible that they *think*? Or *feel*? On their own? Or is that crazy . . ."

"I don't know, Phyllis. I don't know."

"But what if they do? What if they grow and take over—you know what I mean? If there's brain tissue present, who knows if they can think."

Katie sat in numbed silence in the passenger seat of the car. The once familiar scenes of Los Altos streamed past the window. It all looked like Mars to her.

Phyllis cast several anxious glances at Kate. "Oh, I'm sorry. I shouldn't have said that."

They passed the 7-Eleven convenience store on Piercey Road. Phyllis was taking the back roads home. "It's okay, Phyl. I was just thinking . . . when Dougy was little I was so scared he'd fall and hurt himself. Or drown in the swimming pool. Or get hit by a car. I never dreamed he'd get a brain tumor. Now I don't know what to be scared of anymore."

Phyllis's voice was husky. "Everything will be okay, Kate. You have to keep believing that."

"I don't think it will ever be okay again." Katie closed her eyes for a moment. She'd been so hopeful that all of the tumor could be removed. But, clearly, Dr. Shuck had told them that was not possible. What could she tell Rob? Not to expect his brother to live? And if he did live, would the teratoma return, possibly more vicious than ever?

"You think that now, Kate, but it will get better. You'll see." Phyllis turned off Piercey Road at the stoplight.

"How can you say that?" Kate's voice sounded brittle. "Your son isn't dying in an intensive care unit. You're not carrying a child which may—be—" She couldn't finish.

Phyllis passed a Honda Accord and swung back into the right lane. "No, you're right. But I have something else to worry about. These headaches and dizziness—they keep getting worse. And the doctor doesn't seem to know what's going on."

Kate looked up at her. "You have headaches and dizziness?"

"For about a month now. I haven't said anything—because a lot of people have headaches and dizziness now and then. But this is something else, Katie. This is something gnawing away at me. It just doesn't have a name yet."

"Have you been to the doctor?"

"Three times. The last time he gave me pain pills. And they helped for a while. I'm going back next week."

"I'm sure it's nothing . . ." Katie heard herself say the old tiresome reassurance.

Phyllis glanced at her pointedly. "I wish I was so sure."

They pulled into the driveway of the Campbell home. The lights were on in the kitchen, casting a cheery light into the deepening night shadows.

"What's happening to us?" Katie asked, not of Phyllis, especially.

"I don't know, Kate. Maybe Jennifer Wynn was the lucky one—you know what I mean? I just have this awful feeling that it's going to get worse before it gets better."

"They're having healing meetings at St. Michael's," Phyllis said, a little sheepishly. "I don't usually go to church, but . . . You should see the number of people who show up." Phyllis sighed. "It's frightening, in a high

Episcopal church, to have healing meetings. I mean, it looks like the Middle Ages and the Black Plague."

"How do they propose to heal people?" Katie asked, clearly skeptical.

"I'm not sure how it's supposed to work. They put their hands on your head and say your name. And there's a long meditation and prayer. It isn't weird, or anything." She reached across the seat and touched Katie's arm. "I just wanted you to know that I'm praying for Doug. I don't know if God listens to somebody who hasn't said a prayer in years, but it's all I can think of to do."

Katie nodded, touched by her friend's desperation. "Doug needs all the help he can get," she said. "Thank you."

Kate left Phyllis, who assured her she was perfectly capable of driving home alone, and went into the house. Amanda and Rob were in the kitchen with a bowl of popcorn.

"Mom!" Rob called, running to her.

Kate hugged him. "Doug's out of surgery. He isn't awake yet, so your dad stayed with him. He should wake up tomorrow." Kate glanced at Amanda.

"We just made ourselves a bit of popcorn," Amanda explained. "Rob's been worried."

"I thought you'd be home before this," Rob said. "And then when you didn't come I thought something bad had happened—and then I found out something bad *did* happen."

"To Doug?" Kate looked to Amanda for a clue.

"No, to Frank. He's dead. I went to give him some food, and he just laid there. Amanda said he's dead."

"I put the cage outside." Amanda nodded toward the garage door.

"Poor Frank." Rob looked very sad. "And Doug didn't even get to say good-bye."

Alan came home at ten thirty that night. "No change," he told Kate, who had lain down on the sofa to rest. Rob was asleep, and Amanda had gone to bed.

Katie sat up slowly. "Do you want anything? There are some leftovers in the refrigerator."

Alan shook his head no and sank into the overstuffed chair beside the sofa. "I don't know, Katie. It doesn't look good."

"I know. I heard Dr. Shuck."

"We have to get ready—you know, just in case . . . And hope for the best."

"I'll never be prepared for Doug to die," Katie said. "It would take my whole lifetime to do that. Don't ask me to do that, Alan. I just can't."

"I know, I'm only saying—"

"If he dies I will cry and scream at God for taking him away. If he dies something in me will die. And I can't get ready for it."

"I understand. I wasn't thinking about that exactly." Alan's voice sounded weary. "I was thinking about if he lives . . . you know he won't be like he was before. If they have to go in and take more of the cerebral cortex he will probably be—impaired, in some way. And his eyes—he's going to be blind, Katie. I just wanted to make sure you understood."

"Did they take both of his eyes?"

Alan nodded, and Katie's face convulsed. Her mouth opened in a soundless cry, and she wept for her child.

Monday morning Fred Amans showed up in Sherman Dettler's office quite unexpectedly.

"Good to see you," Dettler said. He extended his hand to Fred. "What brings you to our fair city?"

Fred Amans did not shake hands with Dettler. He had wedged himself into a chair and looked like he was cemented into place. "I didn't come here for no chit-chat," he said. "I want the straight scoop from you bastards, and I don't want no beatin' around the bush."

Dettler pulled his hand back to his side and swore silently at this dirty little man who'd weaseled past his secretary. Who did he think he was, refusing to shake hands? "I haven't a clue what you're talking about. You'll have to fill me in."

"My manager died last Wednesday," Amans said. "And it wasn't pretty, I can tell you. Some kind of weird cancer."

"I'm sorry to hear that," Dettler said evenly. "But what's that got to do with me?"

"I don't know nuthin' for sure, you understand. But this isn't the first time one of my employees got sick and died. And a couple of 'em just got sick, and I don't know what the hell happened to them. And they all got the same kind of thing, Dettler. They all got these weird tumors."

"Uh-huh," Dettler said. He reached under his desk and pressed a small button.

"Now, it occurs to me that maybe something is wrong with these appliances I'm selling." Fred Amans held up both hands, palms extended outward. "And I'm not accusing nobody, but I want you to tell me, for sure, that there ain't nothing wrong with that Liberty microwave oven, or the convection oven we been selling for about a year. Or the freezers. And that communications dish. You been testing all those products?"

"Of course we do—"

"But you discontinued the Liberty 5000 model last

month, which makes me mighty suspicious . . . mighty
suspicious, sir."

Sherman Dettler shifted in his chair. "There's nothing
suspicious about changing a model. We do it all the
time. The public likes new models. You know that."

The door to the office swung open soundlessly and
Tony Horbit sauntered in. "Oh, excuse me," he said
nicely, his wavy hair shining in the early morning sun
that streamed in through the windows. "I thought you
were alone, boss."

"No—it's fine, Tony. Come in and sit down. Fred
Amans, here, has been telling me he thinks we have a
problem with one of our products. He thinks it may be
causing, uh, cancer." Dettler said the word "cancer" as
if he were talking about the delusions of a madman.

"I ain't stupid, Dettler," Fred said, fidgeting in his
chair. He glanced suspiciously at Tony Horbit. "I know
you think I must be off my rocker or something, but I
ain't. I jus' want you to tell me that everything I'm selling in my store is safe. Perfectly safe."

"I'm telling you that every Dettler product produced
today is perfectly safe," Dettler parroted. "You have my
word on that."

"Then how come my employees are dropping like
flies?"

"I'm sure I haven't any idea," Dettler told him.
"Maybe it's the flu."

"I don't believe it is the flu, sir," Amans said pointedly. He heaved his bulk out of the chair and straightened his rumpled blue linen jacket. "The other thing I
wanted to mention is that every employee who's been
sick has demonstrated the Liberty microwave oven. Did
I mention that?"

"No, you didn't." Sherman Dettler could feel his

blood pressure take a sudden surge. His temples pounded. "But I'm sure it's just coincidence."

"Well, I'm not so sure. I'm not sure at all." Amans headed for the door. "I am sorry to trouble you with all this, but I'm not takin' responsibility for your mistakes. No, sir, you can bet on that. I went along with you when that Calder woman got sick. You remember how I cooperated? No questions asked? No trouble?"

"I remember . . ." Dettler wanted the fat man out of his office. "A pregnant employee is always an enormous risk, Fred. I suggest you don't hire any more. They tend to sue."

"Dead employees don't sue." Amans had his hand on the doorknob. "Good ol' Donovan Mills, why, he can't sue nobody where he went."

Dettler looked blank. "I don't know what to say. All I can say is that—"

Fred Amans opened the door and whirled out with a surprising grace. He slammed the door behind him.

Sherman Dettler sat quietly for several minutes.

"This guy could ruin everything. All we need is another month or two to let that Liberty 5000 fade out of the market. It isn't like we've been negligent, has it, Tony? Every test indicates that the Liberty 5000 is perfectly safe. Am I right? Or am I right?"

Tony Horbit tipped back his head and stared coolly at Sherman Dettler. Horbit's ice-blue eyes were half-lidded. This kind of rhetoric from his boss did not demand a response.

"They can't get us on anything. Nothing. We're clean as a baby's bottom." Dettler was talking to hear himself talk. "We just need some time. Temporarily, we've got everything covered. All we need is time."

"I can snap my fingers and buy you some time," Tony said. "I can shut up guys like Fred Amans. No problem.

At least for a while." Tony Horbit stood up slowly and walked to the window of Dettler's office. He peered down through the peach-colored miniblinds and watched Fred Amans climb into his white rental car.

"You'd better take care of Amans," Dettler finally said. "I hate to do that, but what choice do we have? Keep it clean, okay, Tony?"

Tony Horbit nodded and had his portable phone out of his pocket before he reached Sherman Dettler's door. He murmured something about a white car into the phone.

It may be enough time, Dettler thought. If not, he had some insurance—a group of handpicked medical personnel who, for a fee, were willing to alter certain medical information to disguise any diagnoses that could be linked to microwave radiation. They were all panicky, short-term measures, to be sure. But necessary. What Sherman Dettler wanted badly was silence. No lawsuits. No complaints. Just quiet. With any luck at all he'd get that. And if those complaints continued, or the lawsuits began, what could they prove for sure?

 Katie sat beside Doug's bed and watched his chest expand with each breath. He was in a coma and remained on the respirator but had been moved to an end room of the pediatric wing. Katie was afraid that meant he would get less attention from the nurses, but Gloria Tan on the day shift and Amy Gilbert on nights checked on Doug regularly, giving him medication, taking blood pressure and temperature, and jotting notes.

Jerry and Maria Greathouse came Monday evening to sit with Katie and Alan. Alan decided to go home to spend some time with Rob and get some sleep.

Jerry touched Doug's shoulder. "Hey, Red Dawn," he said, close to Doug's ear. "It's about time for you to wake up."

Doug's eyelashes did not flutter. Jerry studied the child's face for any signs of consciousness. He continued talking gently to Doug, while Katie and Maria sat together by the window. Katie kept one eye on Doug.

"You have to take care of yourself, too," Maria was saying. "You have another child to think about."

Katie nodded. "I know. But I can't leave. He might wake up, and no one would be here."

"He won't wake up all at once, you know," Jerry told her. "There will be the fluttering of the eyelids, and hand movements, and small responses to voices."

"I know, I know—I just feel like I'm deserting him every time I leave. You can't imagine what it's like to have him lying there like that—"

Maria took her hand. "I can imagine. I wish you didn't have to go through this. Especially not right now. Are you feeling all right? Are you eating?"

Eating. Katie thought about the breakfast she'd been unable to swallow. Lunch had been a cup of soup in the cafeteria. The soup tasted like salty water. She'd had no more than three tablespoons. "I can't think about food at the moment."

"And Robbie? How's Robbie doing with all this?"

"All right. As well as you can expect. He has Amanda, who caters to his every whim." Katie sighed. "And my mother and her husband are coming—I'm not sure when—in a couple of days."

"Good—you need your family around you." Maria was nodding and rocking back and forth slowly.

"I wish they wouldn't. Is that terrible to say?" She knotted her hands until her fingertips were white. "I just want to be here with my son."

Jerry and Maria managed to get Katie to drink a glass of milk and take two bites of a cheese sandwich, which was the only one left in the vending machine. The cafeteria had closed for the evening.

"Sometimes when I look at him," Katie told them before they left, "I think he's just a feeding trough for this tumor."

Maria blinked hard several times and exchanged glances with Jerry. Her delicate eyebrows furrowed deeply.

"Try to keep your hopes up, Kate," Jerry offered gently. "I've seen children recover from far worse. Doug may need this time in a coma to heal. It's not uncommon."

"Yes." Katie smiled at him. "I'm sure that's what's happening."

"One of these mornings he'll open his eyes—" Maria lowered her wide, dark eyes. "Oh, Katie . . . forgive me."

"He doesn't have eyes anymore. Didn't Alan tell you?"

Jerry nodded. "He told us."

Katie, her own tearless eyes red with fatigue, said quietly, "I don't think he will wake up. I'm so terribly afraid we're going to lose him."

Tuesday became Wednesday and then Thursday, and Friday was the second of August. Alan spent some time with Doug early that morning before the surgeries began. The dawn was very pale and pearly pink that morning. Alan looked out the window a long time and then back at Doug.

Out of habit Alan listened to his son's heart and lungs and studied the EEG pattern on the monitor. Long, slow theta waves rolled across the green screen showing that Doug was in a deep coma. Alan gave the boy's hand a light squeeze.

"You remember when we went to see that band, Doug? In the parade?" Alan hung on to the limp hand. "Try to remember that time. You were only six. And you saw a bagpipe band—and they were wearing those great big black hats. Do you remember that? And when we went home you took a paper bag and drew black crayon feathers on it and marched around the house. You said you wanted to be a piper when you grew up. Well, you have to wake up to do that, Dougy. You can't be a piper when you're asleep. I want you to try and open your eyes."

Alan watched for any spikes on the EEG. There weren't any. The boy's eyelids lay heavily closed. Alan watched for several minutes and then gently let go of Doug's hand. He looked at the pillow that propped one of Doug's shoulders up slightly. Alan slipped the pillow out from underneath the shoulder and held it in his hands.

It would be so easy. At six o'clock in the morning no one would notice. He'd shut off the cardiac alarm . . . put the pillow down on the face . . . wait . . .

Alan switched off the alarm. The regular beep of the monitor died. He clutched the pillow in his hands. His own heart pounded in his ears. He held his breath.

Quietly he lowered the pillow and replaced it under Doug's bare shoulder. He switched the monitor back on, and it sprang to life, piercing the silence of the room with its steady beeps slicing through the quiet of the room.

"You'll be okay," Alan whispered before he left. "Whatever happens, you'll be okay."

"I have to live my life!" he shouted at Katie. They were in the bedroom arguing. Kate wanted to go to the hospital that evening, and Alan insisted they remain home with Rob. Kate had been at Doug's bedside all day.

"I can't just sit there!" he said more quietly. "I don't think you should either. We have Rob to think about.

And the baby. You haven't eaten a decent meal in days."

"What do you expect me to do then?" she asked. She sat on the bed wearing a loose white maternity smock and pink shorts. Her hair was limp, and she had not put on her makeup at all that Saturday.

"I expect you to go on living. I expect you to take care of our other son. And yourself."

"I have to bc at the hospital."

Alan took hold of her shoulders, which seemed more frail and narrower than he'd noticed before. "You *don't* have to be there. Doug's being well cared for—"

She shook off his grasp. "*You* go live your life! *You* go ahead! Just leave me alone."

Alan stood up over her. "I'm going to do just that, Katie. Exactly that. Because it's the right thing to do. We can't stop living because of Doug."

"You don't know what it's like to carry a child in your body, and give it a life, and watch that life be taken away." Her voice was shrill and shattered with pain. "You don't have any idea of that." She reached across the bed and gathered up a thick pillow in her arms, hugging it tight to her body.

"No—I guess I don't. But I know what it is to be a father, Katie. And not just to Doug. And that's what I'm going to be. A father."

"So go ahead!" she screeched at him, her mouth quivering. "I'm not stopping you!"

"You missed an appointment with Dr. Robertz yesterday." Alan tried to keep his voice calm. "You can't do that. You're carrying my child, and I'm going to do everything possible to take care of both of you. I made another appointment for you on Monday. At eleven thirty."

"I don't want this baby." Katie inhaled sharply. "Not

if it means I have to give up Dougy. I won't make that kind of a trade-off." She curled herself around the pillow and turned away from Alan.

"No one's asking you to. But if you're not careful, you could lose both."

He closed the door to the bedroom behind him. Hopefully, she would sleep, and Amanda would cajole her into eating something later.

Amanda eyed him sympathetically when he came into the kitchen. Robbie was at the table lining up pretzels and then eating every other one.

"I have to go out," Alan said. "I'll be back late."

"Is Mom going, too?" Rob asked.

"No, your mom's tired. I think she'll stay here and rest."

"Are you going to the hospital?" Rob asked him.

"Yes." Alan picked up his suitcoat that he'd hung over the kitchen chair. "I'll see you in the morning."

He hadn't said which hospital. He hadn't really lied to the boy, he thought while waiting at the San Jose International Airport, where he bought a ticket to Los Angeles. He'd be there by ten P.M. and return on the six thirty A.M. flight. Just enough time, he considered.

The flight to Burbank was uneventful. At that time of the evening, the interior lights on the plane were low, with a few individuals reading in golden showers of light, their heads bent over paperback novels or caches of official-looking papers. Alan put his head back and closed his eyes.

At Burbank, a much smaller airport than LAX, he took a taxi to San Gregorio, a ride that took about twenty-five minutes. At ten twenty-five Alan stood outside the gray concrete structure, which looked more ominous in the dark, despite spotlights on strategic shrubs and trees.

Ever since he'd found out Terry Cox was still alive, he'd thought about coming here. It was against everything he believed in, everything he worked for, but here he was. He had to finish something he'd started. Correct a mistake he'd made a long time ago.

The wide glass doors at the entrance to the Institute were locked, but there was a buzzer. Alan pressed it and waited.

"Hello?" a voice said. "Can I help you?"

"Hi—I'd like to speak to Dr. Michael Senter?"

"It's eleven o'clock at night! He's not here."

"I've tried to reach him at home—"

"Come back in the morning."

"I can't—I've got a plane to catch. If you'll let me in, I have some information for Dr. Senter."

"What's your name?"

"Dr. Campbell. Dr. Alan Campbell."

The door buzzed and Alan pushed on the door. It opened, and he found himself standing once more in the elegant entrance to the Institute. A man walked toward him.

"Dr. Campbell?" He extended his hand. "I'm Captain Thomas Shore, United States Army. Can I help you?"

Alan shook hands with the Captain. "Well, actually, I came here to talk to Dr. Senter. He called me several times, and I've been unable to reach him. I happened to be in L.A.—and his messages seemed urgent."

"Dr. Senter is on extended leave from San Gregorio," Shore said. "I'm quite surprised you have been in contact with him."

"He left two messages with my answering service. I haven't talked to him directly. Can you tell me where he is?"

"No, I'm afraid I can't."

"Well, if you'll tell him I was here—when he does return." Alan knew he'd blown every plan he'd made. He'd given his name, for one thing. "I would like to check on an old patient of mine—as long as I'm here. Terry Cox."

Captain Shore looked up slowly. His gray-blue eyes studied Alan for a few critical seconds. "Terry Cox died nearly ten days ago."

"He did?" Alan tried to keep his breathing slow and regular. "I'm sorry—I didn't know."

"An unusual case . . ." Shore mused. "You were the attending surgeon, as I recall."

"Yes, I was. At the time we didn't think he would live more than a few days." Alan took a deep breath. "It's almost a relief. Who would have thought he'd survive ten years."

"Is it a relief, Doctor?"

"Yes, of course it is. I've had some reservations about whether the initial surgery was—warranted. To preserve a life that is hopelessly flawed—"

Shore was staring at him. "I should inform you, Doctor, that Terry Cox was murdered. He had a potassium level of 11.6. A nurse, Emma Reese, has been charged with administering potassium chloride IV."

"It's over then . . ." Alan said quietly.

"Not for the nurse, unfortunately."

"In her place, I would have done exactly the same thing," Alan admitted. "That—little boy had sufffered long enough. No jury in its right mind will convict her."

"Possibly . . . possibly not."

"I don't suppose you'd care to tell me what your interest is in these cases, Captain Shore? Or why Lieutenant Colonel Stephen Reynolds is at my hospital in Los Altos studying all the patients' records?"

"Stephen's at Los Altos . . ." Shore said. "I wondered where he'd been assigned. No, Doctor, I can't give you the details, I'm afraid."

"And Michael Senter is somewhere on the old base at Fort Ord," Alan told the Captain. "That much I know. My only conclusion is that he is either being held against his will, or he is helping with some project."

"I assure you, it is the latter." Shore took Alan by the arm and led him to a row of comfortable chairs. "I want your word that you won't pass on that information."

Alan glared at him. "You know, under normal circumstances I might do that." He leaned close to Shore. "But my own son is lying in a hospital room at Lorimar Medical Center. He had surgery for a teratoblastoma. If you know *anything*—anything at all—I want you to tell me what is going on. And I want to speak to Michael Senter. I want to talk to him tonight." All the small moments of the last week, all the pain he'd concealed and the fear for Doug, crashed down on him. His chest heaved. Anger, or terror, burned his eyes. Finally, he felt the sting of his own tears.

Captain Shore stood abruptly. "I can't do that. It is against regulations, Doctor. But I'll tell you what I can do—I can give you the address of Terry Cox's father. I suggest you talk to him."

"I know that address," Alan said. He'd memorized it from Terry's chart.

Alan gave the taxi driver the address. It was a bar in Los Angeles, on Grand Street, a dimly lit area of run-down apartments and battered cars parked along the curbs. The bar was called "Paul's Place," the name emblazoned on a corner building in red and pink neon.

Unsteady, shadowed figures crept along the cracked sidewalks at that time of the night, and cats kept their vigils at doorways and wrought-iron railings. The bar seemed to be the only open business on the street. A laundry and deli across the street were boarded up for the night.

Alan got out, and asked the taxi to wait. He said he'd only be a minute.

"My time's your time," the driver told him. "Jus' don't be too long, buddy. This ain't my territory. You know what I mean?"

Alan pulled open the rough wooden door of the bar and stepped into a haze of smoke and the slightly sour smell of beer and unwashed men. He located the bartender and asked if he could speak to Paul Cox.

"As it happens," the man said, "I'm Paul Cox. What can I do for you?" He was spare and balding. Only his eyes seemed animated. The rest of his face seemed frozen.

Alan glanced around at the few men sitting at the bar. "I'd like to speak to you—in private, if I may."

"Anything you got to say to me you can say right here," Cox said. He poured another beer.

"It's about your son."

Paul Cox turned to Alan and frowned deeply. "My son? My son's dead, mister. He died ten days ago."

"I know that. I was the surgeon—when he was an infant. I want to ask you a few questions."

"You were the one—yes, I remember now. I remember you. What kind of questions you got in mind? What d'you want to know?"

"I wondered if anything unusual happened to your wife during that pregnancy . . . anything at all."

Cox snorted loudly. "Unusual! You mean all those experiments she was involved in! You can call that unusual if you want to. I call it criminal."

"What experiments?" Alan asked. The men at the bar seemed preoccupied with their beer.

"You didn't know she was supposedly sterilized when she was in the Army? In the service of her country and they shot her full of radiation . . . said it was an experiment." Paul Cox leaned against the well-worn oak bar. "You shoulda seen her belly—red and blistered for weeks. She had such pain she cried all night. And threw up for two weeks."

"You didn't want children? Is that why she was sterilized?"

"*She* didn't want children. *She* didn't want to give up her career—whatever that was. When she found out she was pregnant she wanted an abortion, but she couldn't get one in the Army. You know the rest of the story . . . how she killed herself."

"She called me," Alan said, his voice cracking. He cleared his throat several times. "She was hysterical— and then I heard a gunshot."

Paul Cox nodded. "She couldn't take it. She didn't want that baby to live—not like it was. Not all turned inside out like that. You don't know what that does to a woman. My son was a monster. He should never have been born. But I blame the Army. You know? I blame them for all of it."

Alan looked puzzled. "Because of the sterilization?"

"Because she was pregnant at the time. She just didn't know it."

"So the baby was exposed to radiation—"

"Microwave radiation. I found out later they used two of them—didn't look like microwave ovens, of course. Just two magnetrons—put one on each side." His eyes narrowed. "Like a double dose."

Alan's heart quickened. He could feel the vein in his

neck pulse. Microwaves . . . he was thinking. Microwaves.

"Far as I'm concerned, the whole damn Army should have showed up for her funeral. They wouldn't give her an abortion. I think they wanted to see how that baby would turn out—just for interest!" Paul Cox said. "You know how many was at my son's funeral? Two of us. A chaplain and me. That's all."

"But the military paid your son's medical bills."

"Guilt money."

One of the men at the bar waved his hand drunkenly at Paul Cox. "Aww, you tellin' that ol' story again? We're sick a'that story. Tell another one."

"An' git me another Bud," another one called.

Alan slid off the stool. "Thank you," he said. "If it's any consolation, I'm terribly sorry about your son. If I had it to do over again, I would never have operated on him."

"Not your fault, Doc," Cox said. "And it's too late anyway. Isn't it?"

"Maybe for our sons . . ."

"The thing is, you know, I told everybody I could think of about that radiation experiment and what it had done. Do you think anybody'd listen? Nope. Nobody was interested. They figured I'd made it all up. The problem these days is that nobody listens."

The taxi had waited. Alan was so glad to see him still parked in front of the bar, he vowed to tip him generously. He went to the airport and waited for the flight home. He dozed a little in the chair, but mainly he thought about what Paul Cox had said. Microwaves. They were certainly known to be mutagenic. He considered all the microwave communication dishes in the valley. But more than likely, it was the microwave oven. A leaking microwave oven. That would account for the clustering of cases in high-income areas.

He could not even close his eyes on the flight back to San Jose, and drove home like a madman. There was very little traffic that early on a Sunday morning. He was in the driveway within twenty minutes. Amanda was up and had the coffee brewing on the stove. Alan brushed past her without a word. He unplugged the Liberty 5000 microwave oven, carried it out through the garage to the concrete slab beside the house. He spread out a plastic drop cloth. He dropped the oven on the concrete. There was a loud crunch of metal and plastic. Alan picked up the mangled appliance and crashed it down again.

Katie came to the side garage door. "Alan? What's going on?" She stared at the trashed microwave.

"This—" Alan puffed. "This—is a—killer! This thing *leaks*! Or something! Doug—was exposed to microwaves, Katie. From a goddamned oven!"

Kate backed slowly into the garage. Amanda's eyes were wide and frightened when Kate went back into the kitchen. "It's all right," she said, clutching her bathrobe around her as if she were chilled. "Really. He's just upset."

Alan came in through the door. The two women watched him carefully. "Don't you see?" he shouted. "It was the microwave. All along we thought it was something unusual—something fantastic—and all the time, it sat on our kitchen counter. Kicking out those waves. Shooting them into people. Don't you see? We can stop this cancer—we know what's causing it now."

Katie clutched the back of the kitchen chair. "But what about Doug, Alan? What about this baby? And Rob?"

He ran his fingers through his hair. "I don't know. I

don't know . . . All I know is that I'm going to get the son of a bitch who produced this thing."

"How can you prove it leaks?" Katie asked. "You just destroyed the evidence."

Alan turned and looked at the garage door. He'd left the bits and pieces of the smashed Liberty 5000 wrapped in the plastic drop cloth. "There are hundreds —thousands more—just like it. We'll get them tested."

Robbie, drowsy and tousled, wandered into the kitchen. "What's going on?" he asked. "Is Doug okay?"

Katie hurried to him and put her arms around him, holding him close to her for a moment. "Doug's okay, sweetie. You're not to worry."

"Can I go see him today?"

"Not today. Wait until he's feeling better."

"Okay—tomorrow then."

Katie looked at his small, upturned face. Had he been exposed to radiation, too? Surely the price would not be two of her children? Surely not Rob, too.

Alan had two hours of sleep. Barefooted and wrapped up in a loose blue cotton robe, he located the two phone numbers Dr. Michael Senter had left with the answering service. He called the first number. It rang nearly fifteen times until a voice answered in a very tentative voice.

"Hello?"

"Hello . . . This is Dr. Alan Campbell. I'd like to speak to Dr. Michael Senter."

"Uh—" the voice said. "You've called a pay phone. There's nobody here but me."

"Thanks, anyway," Alan said. "Oh—can you tell me where the pay phone is?"

"Monterey, California."

"Thanks." Alan hung up and called the second number.

It was answered quickly. "Security. Sergeant Mains . . ."

"Sergeant Mains, my name is Dr. Alan Campbell. I want to get a message to Dr. Michael Senter—don't tell me he's not there. I know he is. Just tell him to check out the Dettler Liberty 5000 microwave. Tell him I think the son of a bitch is leaking radiation."

"There's no one here by that name . . ."

"I'm sure there isn't. Give him the message anyway." Alan hung up.

He made two more calls. One was to Lt. Col. Stephen Reynolds at Lorimar Medical Center, and the other was to the *San Jose Mercury News.* He told both of them about the possibility of radiation from the microwave oven.

"*All* microwave ovens?" Sue Tracey, a reporter in the newsroom of the *Mercury,* asked. "You mean *my* microwave that's sitting in my kitchen at this very moment leaks radiation?"

"It doesn't leak, necessarily," Alan explained as patiently as possible. "It may produce a different kind of radiation wave, far above the normal wavelength. A very dangerous wavelength."

"Good Lord, Dr. Campbell," Sue Tracey said, "you'd better have some proof! A lot of people made a cup of tea in their microwave this morning, and if it's not safe the whole damn world needs to know about it."

"It may not be *every* microwave oven. I just don't know yet."

Sue Tracey was breathing directly into the phone. "Will you let me know when you have more information?"

"Of course," Alan assured her.

"This is really important."

"I know."

The white Lincoln town car didn't look especially suspicious when Perry Moss checked it Sunday morning. Perry lived in the apartment building across the street from the DeLite Bakery on 42nd Street. Inside the car was the body of a man sprawled in the driver's seat. He'd been shot several times.

Perry Moss backed away from the car. "Better call the cops," he said primarily to himself. "There's a dead guy in there."

The police took their time coming, and a small crowd had gathered to peer inside the car.

"Lookit his shirt," someone commented. "Looks like he done tried to write something on that ol' shirt."

Officer Lindeman pushed the onlookers aside and studied the gruesome scene. "Seems like he popped himself off right here—how long's this car been here?"

"Jus' saw it this morning," Perry Moss volunteered.

"Still got wheels," a man said. "Cain't have been here too long if'n it still got wheels."

"Anybody hear anything this morning—or last night? Anybody see anything?"

No one had, naturally. They were all deaf mutes when it came to evidence, Lindeman thought to himself. He noticed the marks on the man's shirt, and the gun in his right hand.

"What's wrong with this picture?" he asked his partner, young Jimmy Watts.

Watts cocked his head. "The guy couldn't spell. Is that it?"

Across the white shirt of the victim there were three letters traced in blood. *Det,* it read.

"Wasn't he trying to spell debt? Like he owed a lot of money so he shot himself?" Watts prattled on.

"Look again, Jimmy, boy. He's holding a gun in his right hand, but he used his left hand to write those letters. See the blood on his finger?"

"Oh, yeah, sure, I see it now."

"We got ourselves a murder. Just what we needed on a Sunday morning," Lindeman grumbled. He searched the pockets of the clothing. No ID, only two gum wrappers. "Well, get on the radio, Watts. Trace this car through the rental agency. See if we can come up with a name. Meantime, I'll get an ambulance."

Lindeman turned to the group of people hovering around the car. "Get out of here!" he bellowed. "Show's over. Unless you have some information for me, I don't want to see nobody within ten feet of this vehicle. You hear me?"

Everyone heard him. They went back to reading the comics in the Sunday paper and having a second cup of coffee. The kids stayed to watch Watts radio in for information. Then they got back on their bicycles and sped away.

"Hey—yeah—Lindeman?" Watts called. "I got a name. Rented the car yesterday. Name's Fred Amans."

21

 Kate had gone to the hospital early that Sunday morning. It was like being thirsty, this need to see her son, to touch him. To see his chest rise and fall.

She discovered, to her surprise, that she was praying with every breath. It was like a chant. He's only ten years old, she said when she inhaled. Don't take him away from me, she cried to heaven each time she exhaled.

Pediatrics was quiet on that hot August Sunday morning. Penny Ortiz, the lead nurse during the day in Peds, was at the desk. She smiled at Katie.

"How is he?" Katie asked her.

"He had three seizures last night," the nurse told him. "He's on anticonvulsants. I think they're working."

"Convulsions," Katie said softly. "What does that mean?"

"It's not uncommon. His brain suffered a major insult with the surgery. It's not necessarily a bad sign, Mrs. Campbell."

The door to Doug's room was open. He lay quietly, breathing on his own. His cheeks were flushed.

She bent and kissed him on the cheek. His skin was warm and moist. "How's it going, Dougy?" She pulled up the chair again to begin the day's long vigil.

Alan came about eleven o'clock and found Katie dozing lightly. "How is he?"

"He had seizures last night—did you check his chart? But he seems okay now." Katie blinked hard several times. "I was singing to him a while ago. And I thought his hand moved. Just a little." She took a deep breath. "I asked him to move it again, but he didn't."

Alan nodded and checked the monitors. "Hello, sport," he said to Doug. "His heart and kidneys are functioning well," he told Katie.

"But that's not what counts at the moment, is it?" She hugged herself and rocked back and forth several times. "The only thing that counts now is having him wake up."

Monday morning Alan called Tim Barnette, head of Silicon Valley Techtronics, in Palo Alto.

"Can you test microwave ovens for leakage?" he asked when Barnette finally got on the line.

Tim Barnette laughed softly. "Well, I guess I could— but I never have. On the other hand, nobody's ever asked me. Most of them are tested before they're sold, as I understand it."

"I have reason to believe that some models of microwave ovens are leaking. I don't know how this is happening, but I'll tell you it's serious, if it's true."

Barnette thought a minute. "Well, bring it in. I'll see what I can do."

* * *

Alan drove to Amans Appliance, where he'd bought the Liberty 5000 nearly a year before. The entire store was in an uproar because of the death of the owner, Fred Amans.

"He was found dead in Los Angeles," a breathless young clerk named Sheila told him.

"I'm sorry." Alan tried to sound sympathetic. "But I just wanted to buy a Liberty 5000 microwave oven. I need it today."

"Oh, we've had our summer sale. I'm not sure we have any more of them. If you'd like to wait I'll check the inventory."

Alan paced, tried to look interested in dishwashers and an odd contraption, an electric food dehydrator.

Finally, Sheila returned. "No, I'm sorry. We're out of stock on that item. But I can show you some of our other models."

"No, it has to be the Liberty. You're sure you don't have one?"

"Well, only the one in the break room—for employees."

"Good—I'll take that one."

"It's used! I can't sell you that one."

"Yes, you can. I'll pay full price for it. No problem."

Sheila checked with Mr. Tate, who shrugged and said to sell it, if the guy wanted it that badly. Ten minutes later Alan walked out of the appliance store with the greasy Liberty 5000. He loaded it in the trunk of the station wagon and drove to Silicon Valley Techtronics. The hair on the back of his neck felt prickly with that microwave oven sitting at his back like a large dog.

Tim Barnette was a slightly pudgy man with a pleasant, ruddy face. He looked over the Liberty 5000, which sat on his counter like an overweight dog on the vet's table. "Hey, I've got one of these. They're terrific. What makes you think it leaks?"

"Just a hunch."

"If you want to wait, Dr. Campbell, I can tell you in about ten minutes if the oven is leaking radiation or not. You want to come back and watch?"

"I'd love to." Alan followed him through the assembly area of the company into a laboratory testing section. They slid the oven behind lead shields and checked the monitors.

"We're working on irradiators at the moment," Barnette told Alan. "It'll revolutionize the food industry."

"I'll bet," Alan commented. He shivered.

"Okay, turn it on—high," a technician instructed another man, who reached inside the shielding and set the timer for ten minutes on high.

"There has to be something in it," the man said. "You aren't supposed to run a microwave empty."

They located a ham sandwich and an apple, and set them into the oven. Alan tried to ignore the snickers and the silly smiles.

"These things don't usually leak," the technician said to Alan.

"I think this one does," Alan replied. "Let's just test it and find out."

The oven hummed away, and the food inside it was not visible because of the shielding.

"Nothing yet," the technician called. He sat behind an additional shield. It had been three and a half minutes.

"Microwaves are at a frequency around twenty-four hundred and fifty megahertz. You can watch the monitor on the wall." Barnette pointed to a white digital readout. "That's a semiconductor detector. The advantage is that it can distinguish between radiation particles that are close in energy."

Alan watched the monitor.

"We've been working with much higher wavelengths than microwaves," Barnette explained. "In fact, we have the capability of reading gamma rays, should we ever come across them. You're familiar with gamma rays, I imagine, in the treatment of cancer."

Alan nodded. The numbers on the monitor read a thousand eighty-nine.

"That's just normal wave frequencies—radio waves, mainly. I don't expect we'll see anything above that." Tim Barnette was looking slightly bored. "Five milliwatts of microwave leakage per square centimeter is allowed by the U.S. Bureau of Radiological Health."

"I forgot most of the physics I learned," Alan confessed, unsure of exactly what five milliwatts of power was.

Six minutes had elapsed.

"Nothing," called the technician.

Suddenly the digits shot upward so fast they were unreadable. The white flashes of light were so fast the monitor looked like a white blur.

"What the—" Barnette yelped, blanching. He joined the technician at the readout. "Was that a malfunction?"

"I don't think so—that was pretty close to gamma radiation. But that's not possible. Not in a microwave oven."

Alan heard the nervous strain in the technician's voice.

"Shut it down," Barnette barked at another technician, who was scrambling away from the microwave as fast as possible. The monitor had settled back into the thousand range, so any danger had passed. The technician crept back and gingerly reached into the shields and shut off the microwave oven.

Tim Barnette was studying the printed readout. "They're not gamma rays. It was a burst of radiation approximately eighty-seven hundred and seventy megahertz. Sweet Jesus!" He whistled softly. "That thing should have been glowing."

His hand was shaking slightly. "That's *extremely* close to gamma-ray radiation. Evidently the particles collide from the two magnetrons, both emitting at twenty-four hundred and fifty megahertz. But when they hit each other—bingo! You get a periodic burst of near gamma-ray radiation." He turned to Alan and frowned. "What made you suspect the oven?"

"We've seen a tremendous rise in the rates of certain kinds of tumors in this valley—and in the state." Alan could hardly believe he could tell it so casually. "We knew there was something mutagenic people were being exposed to—we just didn't know what."

"Don't they test these microwave ovens?" the technician asked of no one in particular. "I thought they tested this kind of thing."

"Unless they had the equipment to read gamma rays, they wouldn't pick it up," Barnette explained. "Most product safety labs wouldn't have the monitors."

"Now what do we do?" Alan asked.

"No problem," Barnette told him. "I'll have this thing recalled by noon! Leave it to me."

"I know a reporter at the *Mercury News*. We can let people know to unplug these if they have them in their homes," Alan said.

"Unfortunately, there will have to be more tests with a lot more sophisticated instruments than we have in this lab before the real story will be told to the public," Barnette said. "They'll recall it for testing for radiation leaks. They will never admit that a double magnetron can produce gamma rays. Think about it—what if that kind of information got into the wrong hands? Some banana republic dictator with the ability to produce gamma rays could wipe out another country easily. No, I'd bet that the real facts won't come out—until much later."

"But what about all the people who are going to use it *today*?" Alan asked.

Barnette looked helpless. "Let's just hope they don't."

"You're sure you can get it recalled?"

"That's no problem. I'll get on the phone to the State Department of Health and Safety this minute. At least we'll get it out of the public's hands soon," Barnette said.

"Yeah—if anybody listens to those recalls," the technician offered. "How many people bring in their cars when there's a recall? Or the bottles of baby food that somebody tampers with? Most people think it couldn't possibly apply to them."

"They'll listen," Alan said. "They'll have to listen. I'll call the newspaper. Maybe they can get a warning into the afternoon edition."

"The first call I'm making," Barnette said, "is to my wife. I want her to unplug our microwave oven." He shivered. "Ugh! It gives me the willies just thinking about it."

"You're practically a hero," the technician told Alan when Barnette hurried off to his office.

"Not me," Alan said. He just wanted to get back to the hospital to Doug.

John Lacey was unable to attend to the autopsies that Tuesday morning. He managed to hobble into his office and sat there for an hour thinking about what he had to do. Walking was difficult. That probably meant the cancer was spreading down into the pelvic area. He'd made a decision that weekend. He would not take any more of the Crist substrate for himself. Someone else needed it more.

He opened each drawer of his desk and fingered the contents, stowed in such orderly fashion. He got to the last drawer, which was locked. It took more effort than normal to unlock that drawer. He took out the small picture of Kate. He should never have kept it. He slid it into one of the pockets of his briefcase, open on his desk. He didn't want anyone to find that picture there. When he didn't return to his office.

In that drawer was also a long brown envelope. He laid it at the side of his briefcase. It contained a resignation and an explanation of the reasons for his resignation. There'd been enough secrecy, he'd decided.

Deena Crist knocked on his open door and came in when John looked around.

"Oh, hi, Deena—I was just getting a few things together."

Deena sat down beside the desk. "Something really weird is going on, Dr. Lacey. I've had Dr. Greer in the lab for about an hour and a half talking about the research. He wanted to know about the Crist substrate—and I didn't see any reason not to tell him. I mean, it's not a secret or anything."

"He already knows about Crist," John confessed. "He's been pumping me for information for a couple of weeks."

"What's his interest in it? I can't figure it out."

"Greer's the kind of guy who has to have his finger in every pie. There's some suspicion that he's been altering patient files here at Lorimar to distort the statistics about these teratomas. Philip Morrisey has some pretty convincing facts."

"Isn't that a criminal offense?" Deena asked.

"You bet it is. If he did it."

"He wanted to see the—" Deena looked up quickly at the door. "Oh, hello, Dr. Greer." She stood up hastily. "I'll be getting back to work."

"Don't let me interrupt anything," Greer said in his lazy monotone. "I just wanted to chew the fat with John."

"Haven't you got anything better to do?" John Lacey did not hide his distaste for Greer.

"Nope. It's Tuesday. I just wanted to ask you about the contract with Seneca Biological. They're funding the research with this new drug, aren't they?"

"Which new drug? We are working with two of them in the lab."

"The new one—the Crist substrate." He winked at Deena. "Must be quite an honor to have a new drug named after you."

"Excuse me," Deena said pointedly, and left the office, careful not to get too close to Greer.

"So, John—how about it? What's the scoop with Seneca?" Greer settled into Deena's chair.

"There's no scoop—look, I'm busy. Come back tomorrow. I should have more time then."

"Sure, tomorrow—except tomorrow might be too late." Greer stared openly at John Lacey. "Rumor has it that you're not well, old boy. In fact, rumor has it you've been spending weekends at San Gregorio, in the company of guys who deal with tumors . . ."

John felt his gut tighten anxiously. He relaxed those muscles. "That's correct."

"Well?" Greer's voice was demanding. "What gives?"

John laughed softly. "I have cancer. The first tumor was a small teratoma. Unfortunately, it spread."

"Sorry to hear that. You're sure it's a teratoma?" Greer shifted in the chair.

"Yes. No one altered the records at San Gregorio." He kept his voice low and nonthreatening.

"So you've heard those ridiculous accusations—you'd think it was illegal around here to study patient charts. I just want you to know I had nothing to do with any changes in any charts. I want you to know that." He met John Lacey's gaze with a level, innocent look.

"I hope not. For your sake. But what I'm certain of is that we are seeing an epidemic of teratomas that is being covered up. I had a post the other day—a woman who died of heart failure. She had a teratoma the size of an orange developing near her kidneys. It didn't kill her. But it would have."

"I think everyone's gone a little bananas over this so-called epidemic. We're seeing teratomas where simple adenomas exist. I mean, if one embryonic cell is spotted, everyone jumps on the bandwagon and calls it a teratoma."

John Lacey casually unbuttoned his white shirt. "This is not a case of bananas, I assure you." The series of large tumors was clearly visible along his rib cage.

"Funny they should follow the ribs," Greer observed coolly. "Never seen anything like that. So, John, how about that info on Seneca?"

"Get out of my office," Lacey growled. "I'm not giving you anything."

Dr. Greer stood up slowly. "I'm really sorry to hear that. But I guess there are other ways to skin the cat—so to speak."

"If you mean Deena, you're mistaken."

Greer smiled thinly. "Deena. Or Kate Campbell."

"You stay away from Kate."

"Oh, hey, buddy, I didn't mean to interfere with your little tryst—"

John stood up and winced. "Get out."

"Sure, I'm going. But I'm not finished. I'm not somebody you can push around anymore." He glanced out through the glass windows into the Pathology office. "I've got friends everywhere, John." He waved pointedly at several of the secretaries.

John's blood stood still. His heart thumped loud and hard, and the pain in his ribs forced him to sit down again. All he had to do now was talk to Katie. That's all. Then he'd fly to Los Angeles and check in to San Gregorio and see if there was anything else they could do. And after that? He wouldn't think about that.

Both Alan and Katie were with Doug that afternoon when John Lacey limped into the room on Pediatrics. Katie had been bathing Doug's face and arms with a cool cloth. It was hot in the room, despite the air conditioning. When she saw John she gasped.

He smiled benignly. "It's all right," he said, leaning on a chair to steady himself. "It's all out in the open now."

Alan looked perplexed and suddenly alarmed. "What's out in the open?" His blue eyes riveted on Katie.

"I have malignant teratocarcinoma, Alan. I've had it for four months." John steadied himself. "The first surgery was in April, but it has spread."

Alan inhaled sharply, and then shook his head, as if he couldn't believe what he was hearing.

Katie had suspected as much. "You've been injecting yourself with PreVent, haven't you . . ." She said it gently.

John nodded. "I was desperate. The chemotherapy and the new cholinesterase drug weren't working. I took the PreVent. And then I took Crist."

Katie looked up quickly. "You injected the Crist substrate? Does Deena know?"

"I haven't told her in so many words. I thought if it worked, I'd tell her. And it did work, Katie. That was the amazing part. It did work."

Katie let go of Doug's limp hand. "Crist substrate works? Are you sure?"

John nodded. "I've stopped taking it, however. I'm going into San Gregorio tomorrow evening—after I clear up things here. There's only enough left for one more person. Deena produces it a drop at a time. I think we should use what's left for Doug."

Katie's eyes widened. "You think we should give Doug Crist substrate? It hasn't been approved—"

"I can't tell you what to do. I'm only telling you what I did. And that it worked. You'll have to decide for your son whether the risks outweigh the possible benefits."

"He's dying," Katie cried. "There's not much more they can do for him."

"There's Vincristin," Alan reminded her. "And this Crist—it hasn't been approved by the FDA. I could be barred from medical practice in this state."

"If you decide to give him Crist, I'll administer it myself. They can take away my medical license if they want." He laughed a low, ironic laugh. "They can rip it off my headstone."

"I won't have any part of this," Alan said. "I forbid you to give Doug this drug." He glared at Katie. "I forbid it. You have our baby to think about. It's damn difficult to raise a child in prison." He stormed out of the room.

Katie and John stood in uncomfortable silence.

"I didn't mean to make things worse," John said. "It's just that I think this is Doug's best chance." He limped to the row of monitors over the child's head. The EEG remained in a steady theta rhythm.

"Is there enough for more than one dose?" Kate asked.

"For a child Doug's size, there should be two and a half doses. And Deena is in full production."

"Won't Deena refuse to let us take it?"

"I don't ask Deena. I admit I've replaced the Crist with frozen egg albumin. It'll distort her experiments—until she knows what's happened. And I'll tell her—before I—"

"Okay, John, get the Crist. I'm willing to take the chance."

Lt. Col. Stephen Reynolds located Alan in his office. "I've had a message from Dr. Michael Senter for you. He said they have tested that microwave oven, and it does emit a near gamma-ray radiation at varying cycles. That explains why we were only seeing this in certain populations."

"It does," Alan agreed, "but it doesn't help my son. And it doesn't help a lot of other people who've already been exposed."

"But think of the ones you've saved," Reynolds told him. "Think how long it would have taken to figure this out if you hadn't taken that oven in to be tested."

A long article had appeared in the *San Jose Mercury News* along with the recall notices. The article said nothing about gamma radiation. Recalls would be mailed to all those people who had purchased the Liberty 5000 microwave oven. Hopefully, they would see the notices in the media and unplug the devices.

"If it isn't a microwave oven, Lieutenant Colonel

Reynolds, it'll be something else—cellular phones, wristwatches, beepers, who knows . . ." Alan started out.

"I don't think so."

"No?" Alan turned back. "Well, sir, I thought it was perfectly safe for my son to cook a hot dog in that damnable machine. I never gave it a thought. And now my wife is pregnant. Don't tell me about everyone I've saved!" He tore the map off the wall. The small red pins scattered on the floor. They looked like drops of blood to Alan.

Sherman Dettler was sweating. He had to have his makeup reapplied three times before the news conference that was being televised by NBC. He ripped the white napkins away from his neck and shoulders and threw them on the floor. "Let's get this over with," he roared. "I haven't got all day. I'm a busy man, I'll have you know."

The woman patiently dabbing powder on his nose and forehead swore softly. "I'm going as fast as I can, sir." Clearly, she did not relish this task this morning.

"Five minutes . . ." Dettler was warned.

"Shit!" He stood up, forgoing the final touches of makeup.

He was shown his chair on a small set. There would be five newsmen and himself. He didn't like the odds. Maybe he should have told them he wouldn't do the news conference. That's what Tony Horbit advised.

"Tell them to get lost," Horbit had said.

But Sherman Dettler decided that if he didn't answer the questions he would look guilty. He straightened his tie. He had nothing to hide.

"Mr. Dettler," a reporter from the *Los Angeles Times* began, "I am curious about the testing of the Liberty

5000 microwave oven. Were any of these gamma rays evident during the testing for safety? Or was the oven tested?"

Dettler bristled. "Of course it was thoroughly tested. We had no indication of radiation leaks. And the waves that are being detected are not gamma rays, sir. They are below the frequency of gamma rays."

The reporter nodded. "But they are close, Mr. Dettler. Very close."

"How many of these devices have been sold to the American public?" a local anchorman on KVTV asked.

Sherman Dettler frowned. "I don't have the exact figures—"

"Can we say three thousand?"

"I suspect it's more like five or ten thousand." Dettler fussed with the few sheets of notes he'd brought along.

"Five or ten thousand people have been exposed to gamma-ray radiation in this country?" a young woman asked, incredulous.

Sherman Dettler had not wanted to appear unsympathetic to the American public. He had planned to maintain an air of disclosure and heartfelt concern about the problem.

"I repeat," he snapped at her, "the radiation is not gamma. I believe they have labeled it omega. And the verdict is still out about the effects of omega radiation."

"You contend that this epidemic of tumors throughout California and the West is *not* due to radiation?" That question was posed by Ned Adler of the *San Francisco Chronicle*.

"Mr. Adler, unless you have data with which I am not familiar, my understanding is that radiation and tumors have not been positively related."

"It's *pure coincidence* that many of the reported cases

of teratoma in the last year have been owners of this Liberty 5000?"

"I have no idea," Dettler fielded the question. "The Liberty 5000 has been very popular. I'm sure those same people also drank water and drove cars and who knows what else—no one's looking at that." His chest was feeling tight. He tried to relax. It wasn't something he was good at. He sipped water from the plastic glass in front of him when he was sure the camera wasn't aimed at him.

"What do you propose doing with the Liberty 5000?" the woman asked him.

"We have discontinued production, of course. Testing continues on the microwave oven, and we have issued a recall. We will make any necessary modifications, should we find a radiation leakage."

"In other words, you have not detected the omega waves in your testing labs?"

"That is correct."

"Are you capable of detecting gamma radiation in your lab?"

"I—" Dettler wasn't certain. "I believe so, sir."

"And what about the series of complaints you received about the faint glow in the microwave oven? Did you follow up on those?"

Dettler smiled thinly. "I wouldn't call ten letters a 'series' of complaints. Not compared to the thousands of letters testifying to the efficiency and convenience of the Liberty 5000."

The moderator, a senior editor with the *Santa Barbara Daily,* said, "Do you own a Liberty 5000 personally? Is there one in your own kitchen?"

"There certainly is," Dettler lied coolly. "I have no plans to unplug it until the questions about this radiation are answered."

"In how many states was the Liberty 5000 marketed?" Adler asked.

"Only in the western U.S.—California, Oregon, Washington, Arizona . . . and a small sampling in New York." Dettler waited for the last question. "And I want to mention that this is the first time one of Dettler Industries' products has been questioned."

"Mr. Dettler," the *L.A. Times* reporter addressed him. "What other new products do you have on the market? What else do we need to be careful of?"

The camera cut away sharply to Sherman Dettler. "That's an unfair question! Who the hell do you think you are?"

The producer, Hal Portsmouth, was waving one arm over his head and making frantic slicing motions with his finger across his throat.

"I don't give a shit if this is national TV. He doesn't have the right to say that! I want that deleted on the air!"

Ned Adler broke in. "By all estimates, your defective microwave oven has caused over a thousand known cases of cancer. I believe the public has the right to know the full facts of this outrage."

"Go to hell!" Dettler growled.

After the news conference, Tony Horbit consoled Sherman Dettler. "They crucified you. Didn't they tell you it was live?"

The Crist substrate was thawed, and John Lacey, after swallowing four Vicodins for the pain, measured out the dosage he'd calculated for Doug's weight. He was in the clean room, garbed in the white hood and jumpsuit. Deena had left, and things were quiet.

He filled the syringe and laid it on a metal tray, covering it with a sterile towel. After the initial dose there was one full dose left. He would give that in three hours. And the partial dose he would save until midnight.

In the air lock he stripped off the isolation clothing slowly and stepped out into the main room of the research lab. The mice clambered noisily in their cages, and the air conditioner hummed. He put on his suit coat and placed the syringe, wrapped in the towel, in his pocket. Not exactly good sterile technique, he thought, but the best he could do.

He hobbled to the elevator, and rested there a minute. He could feel the painkiller taking effect. He pressed the up button and didn't have to wait long. The elevator was empty at that time of the night. It was reserved for staff. John Lacey pushed the number three button, and the elevator rose.

If he was lucky, Kate and Alan would not be in Doug's room. He would close the door. That meant an examination was in progress and a nurse would not disturb him. Kate said Rob and Amanda were joining them at the hospital for a little cafeteria food. It would only take a minute to inject the Crist into the IV line.

The room was not empty. Alan sat in a chair facing the door. "I've been waiting for you," he said. "I've decided that I will give the drug myself."

John withdrew the syringe from his pocket. "This is the first dose—but think about it, Alan."

"I have . . ." He reached for the syringe, uncapped the needle, and plunged it into the IV. He injected the substrate and withdrew the needle. "This is my son. I will take responsibility for him."

"You'll forgive me if I tell you that I wish he had been *my* son," John said.

Alan disposed of the syringe and needle without looking at John Lacey.

"But I want you to know that having Katie return as

my research assistant was purely business. There were no ulterior motives."

Alan nodded. "I understand."

"I just didn't want there to ever be any doubt in your mind about Kate."

Alan looked up. The anger and jealousy he had felt for months melted at the sight of John Lacey standing there leaning heavily against Doug's bed. "Thanks, John. And if there's anything we can do for you . . ."

"No—the only thing we have to do now is watch and see if we get any alpha waves on Doug's EEG."

"How soon?" Alan asked. He checked Doug's monitors. His heart rate was stable. The EEG flowed in huge theta waves.

"I don't know . . . hours . . . days . . . I'll get the next dose ready at eight." And he worked his way, painfully, to the door.

The pain medication was wearing off. "I'll be in the research lab, if you need me—" He turned back to Alan. "You know, if this works, we have an enormous discovery—a drug that reverts cancerous cells to a normal growth pattern. The reversion rate in lab rats is very impressive.

"Until he wakes up, of course, it's difficult to assess the extent of the damage," Lacey said gently.

"Shuck took only a minimum of cerebral tissue, but that meant he had to leave part of the tumor. The plan is to start chemotherapy as soon as Doug is stable. The teratoblastomas are fairly responsive to chemo. And the Crist might give him some time for that chemo. It's why I decided it was worth the risk." Alan leaned against the pediatric bed. His shoulders drooped and his chin sank down wearily on his chest. "Even if there is minimal brain dysfunction, I've been trying to figure out what to say to Doug when he wakes up and figures out he'll never see again. Shuck had to take the eyes."

"He can live without his eyes, Alan. Lots of people have learned to live with blindness." John Lacey was pale, and his eyes had narrowed perceptibly with the pain. "He *can't* live with these tumors growing in his brain."

Alan nodded. "Is there enough of this Crist substrate to revert the growth of the teratoma that remains?" he asked Lacey.

"I don't know. I don't know if it will take one dose or a hundred. And we don't have a hundred doses. We have two and a half, calculated from the dosage used in the rat studies." John Lacey sagged against the door.

"Are you all right?" Alan asked, suddenly aware of the doctor's distress.

"No," John said, "but there's nothing to do about it." He sighed deeply. "The worst of it is that Deena and I are getting a paper ready on Crist for the journals. Deena will have to finish it, I'm afraid."

John Lacey went back to his office first. He took four more Vicodins. He only had to last until he got on that plane to Los Angeles, he told himself for the fiftieth time that day. Just today. He shuffled down the hall from his office to the research lab. He opened the door and went in. He did not see the man seated at Deena's desk.

Katie and Alan watched the monitor. There was no change. After dinner in the cafeteria with Rob and Amanda, Kate had brought Rob up to the pediatric visiting area, which was a windowed hallway that fronted on the patients' rooms. It gave children visual access to brothers and sisters who were ill.

"Gosh, he doesn't move," Rob said, standing beside Katie. He studied his brother through the wide window.

"He's very ill," she told him.

"Is he going to get better?"

"We hope so. Everyone's doing everything they can for him."

Rob was silent for a moment. "Can he hear me?"

"If you press this little red button, you can talk to him."

The boy reached up and pressed the button with his thumb. "Doug? This is Rob. I hope you're okay."

Alan turned to look out through the windows. He gave Rob a thumbs-up.

"Doug? I want you to come home real soon. I really miss you and we'll play *anything* you want—I won't care."

Alan leapt to the monitors. "There's an alpha spike! Keep talking, Rob."

Rob looked up at his mother, who nodded sharply. "Okay, I'll keep talking, but I wish you'd talk back to me. I miss you a whole lot. And so does Mark, and Tammy, and Joe, and even old Sydney the Snake wants to know when you're coming home. And you know how weird Sydney is . . ." Rob looked at his mother again. "Shall I keep going?"

"You did just fine, Rob. I'm sure Doug heard you."

Amanda and Rob decided to wait for a while in the main lobby of the hospital before going home. "If he wakes up I want to see him," Rob insisted.

Eight o'clock came and went, and John Lacey did not return with the second dose of Crist. Katie watched the clock and the EEG. Doug's brain waves had reverted to thetas after that short burst of alpha. But it was a good sign. It might not be related to the Crist, Katie considered. At eight thirty she told Alan she was going to the research lab.

She took the elevator and tried to shake off her irritation with John. After all, the man was sick. And dying. She checked his office. His briefcase lay on his desk. A large brown envelope was beside it. But John wasn't there.

Katie opened the door of the research lab and looked in. The lights were on. "John?"

No one answered. The door closed behind her. She noticed the air lock to the clean area of the lab was open. It should never be left open! John must have forgotten. She hurried to the lock to close it, climbed into the isolation garb, and entered the clean area. Her notebooks, so carefully arranged and filed, lay in disarray on the workbench. Trays of cultures stood open. They were totally ruined. Weeks of work. And the red light was flashing on the freezer.

"Oh, my God." Her knees jelled. The red light meant someone was inside. Why hadn't the alarm sounded?

She heard the air lock open and turned. Dr. Greer stood in it. He was wearing street clothes.

"I've come to get something," he said. "Your Dr. Lacey wouldn't give it to me."

Katie backed away. "I don't know what you're talking about."

"I want this new drug."

"What drug?"

"Don't play stupid. This Crist substrate."

"I don't have it—I have to open the freezer! The red light's on! Someone's in there."

"No one's in there." He walked slowly toward her. "Not anymore."

Katie's breath came in ragged gasps. She was shaking. "But unless you tell me where the drug is—" He stopped. "You see, I have one of those microwave ovens. Used it all the time."

Katie gulped. "My son—"

"I know all about your son. Teratoblastoma—or was it a papillary adenoma? I forget. Well, it doesn't matter. Not as long as I get the drug."

"You don't understand—" she panted, reaching for the lock on the freezer.

"Don't!" Greer warned.

Katie pulled it open. Inside, the body of John Lacey lay doubled up on the narrow floor. She knew if she went inside Greer would close the door. "See, it doesn't matter to me anymore—you understand? It doesn't matter what I have to do to get that drug. No money makes any difference now. Old Dettler thought he could buy me off—get me to do all the dirty work for him, and all the time he was pushing this microwave—he even gave them away to his friends. Isn't that funny? I think that's really funny! How come you're not laughing, Mrs. Campbell?"

Katie glanced at John Lacey. "He may still be alive—"

Greer laughed. "Alive? After an hour and a half at minus seventy degrees? I doubt it. He suffocated before he froze. Now, you just get in there like a good girl and get the drug for me."

"I'm not going in there. I don't know where Deena keeps it."

"Deena—yes, she wouldn't tell me much about it either. Must be a big secret, this Crist substrate . . ."

He pushed her roughly into the small freezer room. Kate clung to the edge of the doorway. Her hand hurt from the cold. The clean room itself was getting frigid. Frantically, she searched the wire boxes for the Crist. Deena usually froze it in ten-milliliter labeled tubes.

Where was it? In desperation she grabbed four tubes of frozen tissue cultures. They were unlabeled.

"Here it is." She clutched the tubes and hung on to the doorway. Her heart was racing. He must not close the door on her. He must not.

Greer grabbed the tubes from her right hand and slammed the door. She removed her left hand just in time or he would have crushed it in the door. Bone-cold darkness exploded around her, filling her lungs, piercing her eyes. She reached up and pressed the red alarm button. Her nostrils clung together almost immediately.

Why hadn't they heard the freezer alarm in the security office? Unless Greer had pulled the wires . . . Don't let me die, she prayed silently, please don't let me die. Not like this.

Deena Crist had a Big Mac in one hand and a diet Coke in the other. She had trouble opening the door to the research lab. It was eight forty-five and she had work to do. And something else. Usually she didn't bring food into the lab, but she'd decided to eat at her desk, far enough away from the animal cages and the tissue cultures. Besides, no one was around at night.

She went to her desk and put the food down. How odd. All her manuals were opened. She looked around cautiously. Damn, she swore silently when she saw the open air lock to the clean room. Had she left it open? She didn't think so. And through the glass panel she saw the madly blinking red light.

Deena plunged through the air lock and opened the freezer. Kate fell out into her arms. She sucked air greedily and stumbled toward a chair. She was dizzy.

"Greer," was all she could say.

Deena saw the other body lying on the floor of the freezer. She took Kate through the air lock and sat her down. Then she went back and examined John Lacey's body. His skin was a mottled gray-blue, and she could not find a heartbeat. She picked up the phone and dialed the Emergency Room.

"I've got two people in the research lab who I just pulled out of the freezer! Get somebody down here quick."

She was able to pull John's body out of the freezer and close the door. Two orderlies from the ER burst into the room.

"How long were you in there?" Deena quizzed Kate, who sat hugging herself and shivering until Deena was afraid she'd fall off the chair. One orderly swathed her in heated blankets while the other one examined John Lacey.

"He's got a big syringe of something in his pocket," the orderly called out. "But I'm afraid he's gone."

"Greer—" Katie's teeth were chattering. "Tried to kill me for—Crist."

Deena picked up the phone and called security. "See if you can find Dr. Lawrence Greer," she said. "If you do, call the police."

Deena rubbed Katie's arms and legs to get the circulation going. She went with her to the Emergency Room to make sure the baby was all right. Her color had gone from gray to pale pink.

"Deena," Katie said, "that syringe—in John's pocket —he's been injecting Crist. And PreVent."

Deena nodded solemnly. "I know. I've known for a couple of days. I couldn't figure out what was happening to my supply—but I knew John was sick. He was always getting phone calls from San Gregorio and flying off to Los Angeles. So I knew something was up. I just never thought he'd inject himself—not with an experimental drug."

"He gave it to Doug."

Deena stared at her. "He injected Doug, too?"

Katie nodded and felt tears sting her eyes. "We're desperate, Deena. You don't know what it's like to watch your child die."

"But the Crist," Deena sputtered, "in the concentrations I have available are for rats—very small rats. You'd have to multiply the dosage by a thousand to get enough for a human adult!"

Katie blinked at her. "You mean—"

"I mean, while it probably wouldn't hurt, it won't help either."

Kate struggled out of the warm blankets. "I have to get back to Pediatrics, Deena. Doug's EEG showed some alpha activity tonight. If it wasn't the drug—maybe he's waking up."

22

 "I have to get out of here," she told the physician on duty in the Emergency Room. "I'll come back—I have to see my son."

"You'll have to sign yourself out AMA—against medical advice," he grumbled. "I don't care if you are Dr. Campbell's wife. You'll have to sign the form."

"I'll sign anything you want," she shouted at him, pulling the warm blanket around her tightly. "But I'll do it later."

"You can't leave—"

"We're outta here!" Deena elbowed her way past the howling doctor.

Katie followed. She was feeling much warmer, and the need to get back to Alan and Doug felt like a magnetic pull. She could feel it in her marrow. They met Alan in the hallway outside the Emergency Room. He was very pale, and his hair was disheveled.

"Oh, my God, Katie!" He grabbed her and hugged her, rocking her back and forth as if she were a child. "I

went to the lab—they said they'd taken you to the ER—
and when I saw John Lacey's body—"

"I'm okay," she said softly, allowing him to hold her
and rock her. "I'm really okay."

"I was so scared—you'll never know how scared I
was—"

"I know, I know . . ."

Deena interrupted, "We have to get the police. Dr.
Greer murdered John Lacey—and he almost murdered
Kate."

"Greer?" Alan said slowly. "You're sure it was Lawrence Greer?"

"He shut me in the freezer, Alan. And he admitted
that he closed John in there, too. For hours . . . He
didn't have a chance. Greer must have disabled the au-
dio part of the alarm."

Alan grimaced. "John froze to death?"

"No, he suffocated," Deena said. "Long before his
body temperature dropped. He was in a very weakened
condition. He'd been taking a lot of pain medication
lately. And he'd had chemotherapy . . . I doubt he
lived more than five or six minutes."

Katie closed her eyes. The panic and the terror he
must have known in those five or six minutes, she shared
with him in a small way. And yet, she remembered, she
hadn't been so much afraid as furious. In that brittle
darkness there had come an odd sense of helplessness.
Maybe helplessness wasn't the right word for the sense
of resignation to the course of life itself, whatever it was,
whatever it would be, for however long she could hold
on to it. She would have this baby. Whatever happened
to Doug, she would do everything to ensure the health
and safety of the child she carried.

"We have to get back upstairs," Alan finally said, hugging Katie close to him.

"Have there been any more alpha waves?" Kate asked hopefully.

Alan shook his head. "No. And his heart has slowed. I think he's leaving us, Katie."

"No—he can't—" Katie had hold of Alan's shirt. She couldn't cry. "You can't let him, Alan. You have to do something."

"Dr. Shuck is with him right now. They're doing all they can." Alan steered her toward the elevators.

Deena followed and took Kate's other arm when the elevator doors opened. "I told Katie," she said weakly, "that the dosage of Crist John gave Doug was almost certainly insufficient. We don't know yet what the dosage is sufficient for a human yet—or if it will have any effects on human cancer cells."

Alan listened quietly, supporting Katie. He nodded slightly. "If there's ever any question, I administered that dose. Neither Katie nor John Lacey touched the syringe."

Katie felt dizzy again. She shivered in Alan's arms. The elevator stopped, and they walked the familiar corridor as if in a bad dream. The door was still closed to Doug's room. A nurse rushed past them pulling a crash cart behind her.

Kate and Alan followed her into Doug's room. Shuck had the child laid out on the bed and was giving him CPR. The nurse took over ventilating the boy.

"We can open the chest—" Shuck panted.

A young resident turned to Alan and Katie. "You have to leave—get them out of here!" he yelled at the nurse.

"Don't—" Katie cried. "Don't—"

"Don't open the chest?" Shuck asked, turning to look at her. "You don't want me to try and save him?"

"Save him for what?" she said.

Shuck slowed the CPR. After three or four more quick pushes on the child's narrow chest, he stopped and looked at the cardiac monitor. The heart beat several times, paused, and then beat again.

Katie and Alan slid in beside the surgeon. Katie took her child's limp shoulders and head in her arms. She would have liked to gather him up and cradle him against her as she did when he was very young.

"Dougy, you'll be okay," she whispered. "We love you. We will always love you. Nothing else is important."

Alan put his hands around Doug's head, caressing the bandages.

Then the green line on the cardiac monitor went flat. Doug's heart did not beat again. Shuck switched it off, and silence filled up the room. He reached out and touched Alan's shoulder. "I'm sorry."

There wasn't one moment of death. The child's life drained from him. He seemed to melt away. The only thing Katie knew was a final sense that her son was not there any longer. She stood up, her back aching. And then she wept.

Lawrence Greer injected the four tubes of culture media and collapsed afterward. The seizure was probably due to the dye contained in the media, the admitting doctor in the Emergency Room at Lorimar thought. And a seizure was a minor problem for Lawrence Greer, considering the cranial mass that had spread down one side of his neck and was occluding the carotid artery. If he was acting strange, it was probably because insufficient blood was reaching his brain.

After surgery to remove the mass and relieve the pressure, he freely admitted to altering patient records for a man named Sherman Dettler. Dettler had hired

Greer, and many others just like Greer, to delete information to make the epidemic of teratomas appear much less dramatic. Sherman Dettler was that afraid of lawsuits.

"He had a network of people working in the state," Greer said. "In almost every hospital. And he paid well. I guess he knew it wouldn't work for long."

"We'll probably never know just how high the percentages are," Dr. Philip Morrisey told a newspaper reporter on the phone. "It's impossible to tell exactly which patient files he altered. Luckily, many of our physicians thought something strange was happening and preserved original copies of their patients' medical records."

"Why would a man like Mr. Dettler do something like this, would you say?" the reporter asked. "What do you suspect is the motive?"

"He was clearly trying to protect his product."

"Was there any suspicion that a microwave oven was this dangerous to the public?"

"None. We had no idea that it could produce the kind of aberrant radiation that it does."

"Will there be an investigation of other commercial products?"

"I don't know. I'm a physician. Any further investigations will be made by the federal government and the state departments of health and safety."

"Does that mean that there are other things out there that may be equally dangerous?"

"Your guess is as good as mine," Morrisey responded, hoping his guess was inaccurate. "But if this happened once, it will probably happen again."

* * *

Sherman Dettler was not responding to phone calls. He didn't want to talk to anyone, not even old friends of his father who called him from Washington, D.C. After all, he complained to Tony Horbit, was *he* responsible for the laws of physics?

The two men had isolated themselves on the top floor of the large villa where Sherman Dettler lived. They sat in a lovely room filled with exotic plants. A wide expanse of glass gave them a view of the patio area below and a putting green beyond. The chairs were buttery leather, gray and mauve colored. The drapes were handwoven in muted multicolors.

"It'll blow over," Dettler said. He'd opened the bourbon and poured two glasses. "There'll be some lawsuits. I know that. But in a year or two everyone will forget they ever heard of the Liberty 5000." He sipped his drink. "You wait and see. Another catastrophe will come down the line. And then we'll be sitting pretty."

"In the meantime, boss," Horbit said slowly, "I think I'm going to make me and my family scarce. South America, somewhere."

"Good idea," Sherman Dettler agreed. He polished off the bourbon. "Get out of this pollution." He motioned to the gray-brown haze of car exhaust and other pollutants that blanketed the L.A. area.

"General Estivo Mulan is very anxious to get his hands on the information about the omega radiation. I understand he's practically drooling for it. As a weapon it will be invaluable. You can't put up lead shielding around a whole country. Just think of that—the ability to genetically alter a whole population."

"The Soviets tried something like that." Tony Horbit had not touched his drink. "They bombarded the American Embassy with microwaves."

"Child's play. Like throwing sand at tanks . . . No,

Tony, my friend, this is a giant step beyond microwaves. This is a revolution in international arms." Sherman Dettler raised his glass in a generally southern direction. "And all we have to do is be quiet. And find a good lawyer. And look damn sorry about the whole mess."

"I plan to look damn sorry in Argentina." Tony Horbit picked up the crystal glass. He studied the bourbon for a moment and then drank it.

Sherman Dettler smiled at him.

They had a service for Douglas Campbell in the backyard of the home of Jerry and Maria Greathouse. At first, Katie and Alan thought a memorial service would be too difficult for Rob, but it was clear after several days that a funeral left many things unsaid, many feelings unfinished. Many memories of a beautiful little boy unshared.

So the Greathouses set up benches and chairs, and about thirty people gathered on a Sunday evening. Katie had pictures of Doug in happier days on a long table, and the guests brought their own reminders of the life of Doug. Several of his teachers came with pictures he'd drawn at school. There were bundles of flowers, even some dandelions, that classmates clutched and laid on the table. Alan found the old paper bag with the feathers Doug had drawn on it. Robbie had the worn teddy bear that was Doug's. Mrs. Amandola, a neighbor of the Campbells', brought chocolate chip cookies—a mountain of them. There was a softball, a collection of butterflies . . . Katie sat and watched the display of memories grow on the table.

Phyllis Latimer came, along with several other women from MANA. Phyllis was looking much better. "I needed new glasses," she said, clearly embarrassed. "I thought I had—well, something a lot worse, with all those headaches. But it wasn't." She hugged Katie. "I'm so sorry about Dougy. I wish it had been me instead of him."

Kate didn't cry. She'd cried so much for those first few days she thought she didn't have any more tears left inside her. Her mother stayed very close to her, watching over her, and even Karl, her mother's husband, was some comfort.

A lot of people stood up and talked about Doug, or told a story about him. The sun faded, tracing long leafy patterns on the grass.

Jerry Greathouse talked about Doug getting his Indian name, Red Dawn. "When Black Bear was created, he had no eyes . . ." he began in his soft chant, mesmerizing the group of children and adults. ". . . and White Rabbit jumped. And soared," Jerry ended. "That's what Doug has done. Death is the jump. Now he soars."

Just as the coolness of the evening crept over the yard, a man stepped from the back door of the house. He was clad in full Scottish Highland regalia. Under his arm he had a bagpipe, and he stepped smartly to the front of the gathering. With a mighty breath he started the lonesome skirl of the pipes. They fell into tune. At first he played slow, the high primitive sound of a lament for the loss. But then the tune changed. Into something proud and noble.

"Doug wanted to be a piper," Katie told Deena Crist, who had come that evening.

And afterward they ate cookies and chocolate cupcakes that Rob and the Greathouse children had concocted. And they drank gallons of coffee and cherry Kool-Aid, which was Doug's favorite. And when it was dark, Jerry and Sean built a fire in the stone fire pit. They sat around talking and watching the fire lick at the pile of logs. Lazy smoke rose into the darkness. People drifted away, going quietly. At last, it was time to go home.

"It's not all right," Katie told her mother late that night. "It's just over."

Kate carried eleven-month-old Amanda Katherine Campbell across the snowy street in Marshall, Minnesota. It was ten days before Christmas, the second Christmas without Doug. Katie kept track of her life in the widening elapse of time since her son's death. Two Christmases, two birthdays, one Easter, one Fourth of July . . . one baby sister.

Alan and Rob, who had grown about a foot, followed close behind Kate and the baby. The street was dazzling with colored lights and garlands of greenery in every window framing the brightest, most tantalizing displays of toys, books, clothing, or perfume. Whatever the heart desired most that season, the frenzied retailers promised to supply. Shoppers, loaded with bags and boxes, traversed the ice and snow. Their laughter echoed sharply in the cold air.

Katie stopped in front of the appliance store. There sat all the newest, shiniest gadgets designed for the kitchen. "Safe, Reliable, Convenient," the lettered advertisement read. Katie shivered.

"A food irradiator," she said to Alan. "Do you believe that?"

She didn't know if they were safer in a small midwestern town. It felt safer. They were happy at times. Alan's nightmares had faded. He was admonished by the Medical Ethics Board, and suspended from the practice of medicine for sixty days for administering an untested drug to a patient. Dr. Viktor Straub testified that Dr.

Campbell was under enormous stress. He declined to divulge what the stress might be. It would have breached confidentiality, he told the Ethics Board. Now Alan had a small medical practice and surgical privileges in two area hospitals.

The lawsuit against Dettler Industries would take years to settle. In the meantime, it was Christmas.

They passed a jewelers, displaying the fashionable "atomic" watches with a lifetime battery inside.

"They're really cool," Rob said, studying the watches.

Alan pulled him away gently. "We'll get you a watch," he said, grinning at the boy's bright blue eyes. "It'll have a lot of little springs and gears and you'll have to wind it every day."

"Aw, Dad, they don't make that kind of watch anymore."

Alan pulled him close to his side. "Your mother will find you one. Believe me. If there's one left on the planet your mom will hunt it down."

Amanda Campbell clapped her mittened hands together happily, seeing her father and brother laughing and talking. Kate looked into the face of her daughter with her red cheeks and her wide, gray-blue eyes. Amanda Campbell was fine. So far.

SCIENCE FICTION/FANTASY